A SPATE OF GOBLINS

The goblin leader gave a gap-toothed grin of joyous malice. "Anybody we catch is hereby impressed into the goblin army!" He grabbed a faun by the arm. The faun was substantially larger than the goblin, but seemed unable to defend himself, paralyzed by fear.

The nymphs screamed and dived for water, trees, and mountains. So did the fauns. Dor saw that there were only eight goblins, and a hundred or more fauns and nymphs. Why didn't they fight?

Dor's hand went for his sword. "Wait, friend," Jumper chittered, waving several of his legs agitatedly. "This is not our affair."

"That's five," the goblin sergeant said. "One more good one we need." His eyes fell on Dor and Jumper. "Kill the bug; take the man."

Dor reached once more for his sword and said grimly, "I think it has just become our affair."

Also by Piers Anthony
Published by Ballantine Books:

A SPELL FOR CHAMELEON

THE SOURCE OF MAGIC

CASTLE ROOGNA

Piers Anthony

A Del Rey Book

BALLANTINE BOOKS • NEW YORK

A Del Rey Book
Published by Ballantine Books

Copyright © 1979 by Piers Anthony Jacob

All rights reserved under International and Pan-American Copyright Conventions. Published in the United States by Ballantine Books, a division of Random House, Inc., New York, and simultaneously in Canada by Random House of Canada, Limited, Toronto, Canada.

Library of Congress Catalog Card Number: 79-50375

ISBN 0-345-28937-4

Manufactured in the United States of America

First Edition: July 1979
Second Printing: December 1979

First Canadian Printing: August 1979

Cover art by Darrell Sweet

Contents

1. Ogre — 1
2. Tapestry — 20
3. Jumper — 58
4. Monsters — 90
5. Castle — 128
6. Zombie Master — 147
7. Siege — 169
8. Commitment — 191
9. Journey — 211
10. Battle — 242
11. Disaster — 273
12. Return — 306

Chapter 1. Ogre

Millie the ghost was beautiful. Of course, she wasn't a ghost any more, so she was Millie the nurse. She was not especially bright, and she was hardly young. She was twenty-nine years old as she reckoned it, and about eight hundred and twenty-nine as others reckoned it: the oldest creature currently associated with Castle Roogna. She had been ensorceled as a maid of seventeen, eight centuries ago, when Castle Roogna was young, and restored to life at the time of Dor's birth. In the interim she had been a ghost, and the label had never quite worn off. And why should it? By all accounts she had been a most attractive ghost.

Indeed, she had the loveliest glowing hair, flowing like poppycorn silk to the dimpled backs of her . . . knees. The terrain those tresses covered in passing was—was—how was it that Dor had never noticed it before? Millie had been his nurse all these years, taking care of him while his parents were busy, and they tended to be busy a great deal of the time.

Oh, he understood that well enough. He told others that the King trusted his parents Bink and Chameleon, and anyone the King trusted was bound to be very busy, because the King's missions were too important to leave to nobodies. All that was true enough. But Dor knew his folks didn't have to accept all those important missions that took them all over the Land of Xanth and beyond. They simply liked to travel, to be away from home. Right now they were far away, in Mundania, and nobody went to Mundania for pleasure. It was because of him, because of his talent.

Dor remembered years ago when he had talked to

the double bed Bink and Chameleon used, and asked it what had happened overnight, just from idle curiosity, and it had said—well, it had been quite interesting, especially since Chameleon had been in her beauty stage, prettier and stupider than Millie the ghost, which was going some. But his mother had overheard some of that dialogue, and told his father, and after that Dor wasn't allowed in the bedroom any more. It wasn't that his parents didn't love him, Bink had carefully explained; it was that they felt nervous about what they called "invasion of privacy." So they tended to do their most interesting things away from the house, and Dor had learned not to pry. Not when and where anyone in authority could overhear, at any rate.

Millie took care of him; she had no privacy secrets. True, she didn't like him talking to the toilet, though it was just a pot that got emptied every day into the back garden where dung beetles magicked the stuff into sweet-smelling roses. Dor couldn't talk to roses, because they were alive. He could talk to a dead rose—but then it remembered only what had happened since it was cut, and that wasn't very much. And Millie didn't like him making fun of Jonathan. Apart from that she was quite reasonable, and he liked her. But he had never really noticed her shape before.

Millie was very like a nymph, with all sorts of feminine projections and softnesses and things, and her skin was as clear as the surface of a milkweed pod just before it got milked. She usually wore a light gauzy dress that lent her an ethereal quality strongly reminiscent of her ghosthood, yet failed to conceal excitingly gentle contours beneath. Her voice was as soft as the call of a wraith. Yet she had more wit than a nymph, and more substance than a wraith. She had—

"Oh, what the fudge am I trying to figure out?" Dor demanded aloud.

"How should I know?" the kitchen table responded irritably. It had been fashioned from gnarled acorn wood, and it had a crooked temper.

Millie turned, smiling automatically. She had been washing plates at the sink; she claimed it was easier to do them by hand than to locate the proper cleaning spell, and probably for her it was. The spell was in powder form, and it came in a box the spell-caster made up at the palace, and the powder was forever running out. Few things were more annoying than chasing all over the yard after running powder. So Millie didn't take a powder; she scrubbed the dishes herself. "Are you still hungry, Dor?"

"No," he said, embarrassed. He was hungry, but not for food. If hunger was the proper term.

There was a hesitant, somewhat sodden knock on the door. Millie glanced across at it, her hair rippling down its luxuriant length. "That will be Jonathan," she said brightly.

Jonathan the zombie. Dor scowled. It wasn't that he had anything special against zombies, but he didn't like them around the house. They tended to drop putrid chunks of themselves as they walked, and they were not pretty to look at. "Oh, what do you see in that bag of bones?" Dor demanded, hunching his body and pulling his lips in around his teeth to mimic the zombie mode.

"Why, Dor, that isn't nice! Jonathan is an old friend. I've known him for centuries." No exaggeration! The zombies had haunted the environs of Castle Roogna as long as the ghosts had. Naturally the two types of freaks had gotten to know each other.

But Millie was a woman now, alive and whole and firm. Extremely firm, Dor thought as he watched her move trippingly across the kitchen to the back door. Jonathan was, in contrast, a horribly animated dead man. A living corpse. How could she pay attention to him?

"Beauty and the beast," he muttered savagely. Frustrated and angry, Dor stalked out of the kitchen and into the main room of the cottage. The floor was smooth, hard rind, polished until it had become reflective, and the walls were yellow-white. He banged his fist into one. "Hey, stop that!" the wall protested. "You'll fracture me. I'm only cheese, you know!"

Dor knew. The house was a large, hollowed-out cottage cheese, long since hardened into rigidity. When it had grown, it had been alive; but as a house it was dead, and therefore he could talk to it. Not that it had anything worth saying.

Dor stormed on out the front door. "Don't you dare slam me!" it warned, but he slammed it anyway, and heard its shaken groan behind him. That door always had been more ham than cheese.

The day outside was gloomy. He should have known; Jonathan preferred gloomy days to come calling, because they kept his chronically rotting flesh from drying up so quickly. In fact, it was about to rain. The clouds were kneading themselves into darker convolutions, getting set to clean out their systems.

"Don't you water on me!" Dor yelled into the sky in much the tone the door had used on him. The nearest cloud chuckled evilly, with a sound like thunder.

"Dor! Wait!" a little voice called. It was Grundy the golem, actually no golem any more, not that it made much difference. He was Dor's outdoor companion, and was always alert for Dor's treks into the forest. Dor's folks had really fixed it up so he would always be supervised—by people like Millie, who had no embarrassing secrets, or like Grundy, who didn't care if they did. In fact Grundy would be downright proud to have an embarrassment.

That started Dor on another chain of thought. Actually it wasn't just Bink and Chameleon; nobody in Castle Roogna cared to associate too closely with Dor. Because all sorts of things went on that the furniture saw and heard, and Dor could talk to the furniture. For him, the walls had ears and the floors had eyes. What was wrong with people? Were they ashamed of everything they did? Only King Trent seemed completely at ease with him. But the King could hardly spend all his time entertaining a mere boy.

Grundy caught up. "This is a bad day for exploring, Dor!" he warned. "That storm means business."

Dor looked dourly up at the cloud. "Go soak your empty head!" he yelled at it. "You're no thunderhead, you're a dunderhead!"

He was answered by a spate of yellow hailstones, and had to hunch over like a zombie and shield his face with his arms until they passed.

"Be halfway sensible, Dor!" Grundy urged. "Don't mess with that mean storm! It'll wash us out!"

Dor reluctantly yielded to common sense. "We'll seek cover. But not at home; the zombie's there."

"I wonder what Millie sees in him," Grundy said.

"That's what I asked." The rain was commencing. They hurried to an umbrella tree, whose great thin canopy was just spreading to meet the droplets. Umbrella trees preferred dry soil, so they shielded it against rain. When the sun shone, they folded up, so as not to obstruct the rays. There were also parasol trees, which reacted oppositely, spreading for the sun and folding for the rain. When the two happened to seed together, there was a real wilderness problem.

Two larger boys, the sons of palace guards, had already taken shelter under the same tree. "Well," one cried. "If it isn't the dope who talks to chairs!"

"Go find your own tree, twerp," the other boy ordered. He had sloping shoulders and a projecting chin.

"Look, Horsejaw!" Grundy snapped. "This tree doesn't belong to you! Everyone shares umbrellas in a storm."

"Not with chair-talkers, midget."

"He's a Magician!" Grundy said indignantly. "He talks to the inanimate. No one else can do that; no one else ever could do that in the whole history of Xanth, or ever will again!"

"Let it be, Grundy," Dor murmured. The golem had a sharp tongue that could get them both into trouble. "We'll find another tree."

"See?" Horsejaw demanded triumphantly. "Little stinker don't stand up to his betters." And he laughed.

Suddenly there was a detonation of sound right behind them. Both Dor and Grundy jumped in alarm, before remembering that this was Horsejaw's talent: projecting booms. Both older boys laughed uproariously.

Dor stepped out from under the umbrella—and his foot came down on a snake. He recoiled—but immediately the snake faded into a wisp of smoke. That was the other boy's talent: the conjuration of small, harmless reptiles. The two continued to laugh with such enthusiasm that they were collapsing against the umbrella trunk.

Dor and Grundy went to another tree, prodded by

another sonic boom. Dor concealed his anger. He didn't like being treated this way, but against the superior physical power of the older boys he was helpless. His father Bink was a muscular man, well able to fight when the occasion required, but Dor took after his mother more: small and slender. How he wished he were like his father!

The rain was pelting down now, soaking Dor and Grundy. "Why do you tolerate it?" Grundy demanded. "You are a Magician!"

"A Magician of communication," Dor retorted. "That doesn't count for much, among boys."

"It counts for plenty!" Grundy cried, his little legs splashing through the forming puddles. Absentmindedly Dor reached down to pick him up; the onetime golem was only a few inches tall. "You could talk to their clothes, find out all their secrets, blackmail them—"

"No!"

"You're too damned ethical, Dor," Grundy complained. "Power goes to the unscrupulous. If your father, Bink, had been properly unscrupulous, he'd have been King."

"He didn't want to be King!"

"That's beside the point. Kingship isn't a matter of want, it's a matter of talent. Only a full male Magician can be King."

"Which King Trent is. And he's a good King. My father says the Land of Xanth has really improved since Magician Trent took over. It used to be all chaos and anarchy and bad magic except for right near the villages."

"Your father sees the best in everyone. He is entirely too nice. You take after him."

Dor smiled. "Why thank you, Grundy."

"That wasn't a compliment!"

"I know it wasn't—to you."

Grundy paused. "Sometimes I get the sinister feeling you're not as naive as you seem. Who knows, maybe little normal worms of anger and jealousy gnaw in your heart, as they do in other hearts."

"They do. Today when the zombie called on Millie—" He broke off.

"Oh, you notice Millie now! You're growing up!"

Dor whirled on him—and of course, since the golem was in his hand, Grundy whirled too. "What do you mean by that?"

"Merely that men notice things about women that boys don't. Don't you know what Millie's talent is?"

"No. What is it?"

"Sex appeal."

"I thought that was something all women had."

"Something all women *wish* they had. Millie's is magical; any man near her gets ideas."

That didn't make sense to Dor. "My father doesn't."

"Your father stays well away from her. Did you think that was coincidence?"

Dor had thought it was his own talent that kept Bink away from home so much. It was tempting to think he was mistaken. "What about the King?"

"He has iron control. But you can bet those ideas are percolating in his brain, out of sight. Ever notice how closely the Queen watches him, when Millie's around?"

Dor had always thought it was *him* the Queen was watching disapprovingly, when as a child Millie had taken him to the palace. Now he was uncertain, so he didn't argue further. The golem was always full of gossipy news that adults found hilarious even when the news was suspect. Adults could be sort of stupid at times.

They came up to a pavilion in the Castle Roogna orchard. It had a drying stone set up for just such occasions as this. As they approached it, warm radiation came out, which started the pleasant drying of their clothes. Few things felt as good as a drying stone after a chill soaking! "I really appreciate your service, drier," Dor told it.

"All part of the job," the stone replied. "My cousin, the sharpening stone, really has his work cut out for him. All those knives to hone, you know. Ha ha!"

"Ha ha," Dor agreed mildly, patting it. The trouble with talking with inanimate objects was that they weren't very bright—but thought they were.

Another figure emerged from the orchard, clasping a cluster of chocolate cherries in one hand. "Oh, no!" she exclaimed, recognizing Dor. "If it isn't dodo Dor, the lifeless snooper."

"Look who's talking," Grundy retorted. "Irate Irene, palace brat."

"Princess Irene, to you," the girl snapped. "My father is King, remember?"

"Well, you'll never be King," Grundy said.

" 'Cause women can't assume the throne, golem! But if I were a man—"

"If you were a man, you still wouldn't be King, because you don't have Magician-caliber magic."

"I do too!" she flared.

"Stinkfinger?" Grundy inquired derisively.

"That's green thumb!" she yelled, furious. "I can make any plant grow. Fast. Big. Healthy."

Dor had stayed out of the argument, but fairness required his interjection. "That's creditable magic."

"Stay out of this, dodo!" she snapped. "What do you know about it?"

Dor spread his hands. How did he get into arguments he was trying to avoid? "Nothing. I can't grow a thing."

"You will when you're a man," Grundy muttered.

Irene remained angry. "So how come they call you a Magician, while I am only—"

"A spoiled brat," Grundy finished for her.

Irene burst into tears. She was a rather pretty child, with green eyes and a greenish tinge to her hair to match her talent, but her thumbs were normal flesh color. She was a girl, and a year younger than Dor, so she could cry if she wanted to. But it bothered him. He wanted to get along with her, and somehow had never been able to. "I hate you!" she screeched at him.

Genuinely baffled, Dor could only inquire: "Why?"

"Because you're going to be K-King! And if I want to be Q-Queen, I'll have to—to—"

"To marry him," Grundy said. "You really should learn to finish your own sentences."

"Ugh!" she cried, and it sounded as if she really were about to throw up. She looked wildly about, and spotted a tiny plant at the fringe of the pavilion. "Grow!" she yelled at it, pointing.

The plant, responsive to her talent, grew. It was a

shadowboxer, with little boxing gloves mounted on springy tendrils. The gloves clenched and struck at the shadows formed by distant lightning. Soon the boxer was several feet high, and the gloves were the size of human fists. They struck at the vague shadows of the pavilion's interior. Dor backed away, knowing the blows had force.

Attracted by his motion, and by the sharper shadow his body made, the plant leaned toward him. The gloves were now larger than human fists, and mounted on vines as thick as human wrists. There were a dozen of them, several striking while several more recoiled for the next strike, keeping the plant as a whole in balance. Irene watched, a small gloat playing about her mouth.

"How did I get into this?" Dor asked, disgruntled. He didn't want to flee the pavilion; the storm had intensified and yellow rain was cascading off the roof. The booming of its fusillade was unnerving; there were too many hailstones mixed in, and it looked suspiciously like a suitable habitat for tornado wraiths.

"Well, I don't know for sure," the pavilion answered. "But once I overheard the Queen talking with a ghost, as they took shelter from a small shower, and she said Bink always had been an annoyance to her, and now Bink's son was an annoyance to her daughter. She said she'd do something about it, if it weren't for the King."

"But I never did anything to them!" Dor protested.

"Yes you did," Grundy said. "You were born a full Magician. They can't stand that."

Now the boxing gloves had him boxed in, backed to the very edge of the pavilion. "How do I get out of this?"

"Make a light," the pavilion said. "Shadowboxers can't stand light."

"I don't have a light!" One glove grazed his chest, but as he nudged away from it, water streamed down his back. This was a yellow rain; did it leave a yellow streak?

"Then you'd better run," the pavilion said.

"Yeah, dodo!" Irene agreed. The plant was not bothering her, since she had enchanted it. "Go bash your head into a giant hailstone. Some ice would be good for your brain."

Three more boxing gloves struck at him. Dor plunged into the rain. He was instantly soaked again, but fortunately the hailstones were small and light and somewhat mushy. Irene's mocking laughter pursued him.

Gusts of wind buffeted him savagely and lightning played about the sky. Dor knew he had no business being out in this storm, but he refused to return home. He ran into the jungle.

"Turn about!" Grundy yelled into his ear. The golem was clinging to his shoulder. "Get under cover!" It was excellent advice; lightning bolts could do a lot of harm if they struck too near. After they had lain for a few hours on the ground and cooled off so that they were not so bright, they could be gathered and used for bolting together walls and things. But a fresh one could spear right through a man.

Nevertheless, Dor kept running. The general frustration and confusion he felt inside exceeded that outside.

He was not so confused as to blunder into the obvious hazards of the wilderness. The immediate Castle Roogna environs were spelled to be safe for people and their friends, but the deep jungle could not be rendered safe short of annihilation. No spell would tame a tangle tree for long, or subdue a dragon. Instead, certain paths were protected, and the wise person remained on these paths.

A lightning bolt cracked past him and buried its point in the trunk of a massive acorn tree, the brilliant length of the bolt quivering. It was a small one, but it had three good sharp jags and could have wiped Dor out if it had hit him. The tree trunk was blistering with the heat of it.

That was too close a miss. Dor ran across to the nearest charmed path, one bearing south. No bolts would strike him here. He knew the path's ultimate destination was the Magic Dust village, governed by trolls, but he had never gone that far. This time—well, he kept running, though his breath was rasping past his teeth. At least the exertion kept him warm.

"Good thing I'm along," Grundy said in his ear. "That way there's at least one rational mind in the region."

Dor had to laugh, and his mood lightened. "Half a mind, anyway," he said. The storm was lightening too, as if in tandem with his mood. The way he interacted with the inanimate, that was entirely possible. He slowed to a walk, breathing hard, but continued south. How he wished he had a big, strong, muscular body that could run without panting or knock the gloves right off shadowboxers, instead of this rather small, slight frame. Of course, he didn't have his full growth yet, but he knew he would never be a giant.

"I remember a storm we suffered down this way, just before you were born," Grundy remarked. "Your daddy, Bink, and Chester Centaur, and Crombie the soldier in griffin guise—the King transformed him for the quest, you know—and the Good Magician—"

"Good Magician Humfrey?" Dor demanded. "You traveled with him? He never leaves his castle."

"It was your father's quest for the source of magic; naturally Humfrey came along. The old gnome was always keen on information. Good thing, too; he's the one who showed me how to become real. Good thing for him, too; he met the gorgon, and you should have seen the flip she did over him, the first man she could talk to who didn't turn to stone. Anyway, this storm was so bad it washed out some of the stars from the sky; they were floating in puddles."

"Stop, Grundy!" Dor cried, laughing. "I believe in magic, as any sensible person does, but I'm not a fool! Stars wouldn't float in water. They would fizzle out in seconds!"

"Maybe they did. I was riding a flying fish at the time, so I couldn't see them too well. But it was some storm!"

There was a shudder in the ground, not thunder. Dor halted, alarmed. "What is that?"

"Sounds like the tramp of a giant, to me," Grundy hazarded. His talent was translation, and he could interpret anything any creature said, but footfalls weren't language. "Or worse. It just might be—"

Suddenly it loomed from the gloom. "An ogre!" Dor

finished, terrified. "Right on the path! How could the enchantment have failed? We're supposed to be safe on these—"

The ogre tramped on toward them, a towering hulk more than twice Dor's height and broad in proportion. Its great gap-toothed mouth cracked open horrendously. An awful growl blasted out like the breath of a hungry dragon.

"What say, li'l man—will you give me a han'?" Grundy said.

"What?" Dor asked, startled almost out of his fright.

"That's what the ogre says; I was translating."

Oh. Of course. "No! I need my hands! He can't eat them." Though he was uncertain how the ogre could be stopped from eating anything he wanted. Ogres were great bone-crunchers.

The ogre growled again. "Me not eat whelp; me seek for help," Grundy said. Then the golem did a double take. "Crunch!" he cried. "The vegetarian ogre!"

"Then why does he want to eat my hand?" Dor demanded.

The monster smiled. The expression most resembled the opening of a volcanic fissure. Gassy breath hissed out. "You little loudmouthed twerp, hardly bigger than a burp."

"That's me!" Grundy agreed, answering his own translation. "Good to see you again, Crunch! How's the little lady, she with hair like nettles and skin like mush, whose face would make a zombie blush?"

"She lovely as ever; me forsake she never," the ogre replied. Dor was beginning to be able to make out the words directly; the thing was speaking his language, but with a foul accent that nearly obliterated meaning. "We have good bash, make little Smash."

Dor was by this time reassured that the spell of the path had not failed. This ogre was harmless—well, *no* ogre was harmless, but at least not ravening—and therefore able to mix with men. "A *little* smash?"

"Smash baby ogre, 'bout like you; now he gone and we too few."

"You smashed your baby?" Dor asked horrified.

Maybe there was something wrong with the path-spell after all.

"Dodo! Smash is the name of their baby," Grundy explained. "All the ogres have descriptive names."

"Then why is Smash gone?" Dor demanded nervously. "Troll wives eat their husbands, so maybe ogres eat—"

"Smash wandered away in drizzle; now we search for he fizzle."

This recent storm was a mere drizzle to the ogres? That made sense. No doubt Crunch used a lightning bolt for a toothpick. "We'll help you find your baby," Dor said, grasping this positive mission with enthusiasm. Nothing like a little quest to restore spirits! Crunch's search for his little one had fizzled, so he had asked for help, and few human beings ever had such a request from an ogre! "Grundy can ask living things, because he knows all their languages, and I'll ask the dead ones. We'll run him down in no time!"

Crunch heaved a grateful sigh that almost blew Dor down. Quickly they went to the spot where the tyke had last been seen. Smash had, Crunch explained, been innocently chewing up nails, getting his daily ration of iron, then must have wandered away.

"Did the little ogre pass this way?" Dor asked a nearby rock.

"Yes—and he went toward that tree," the rock replied.

"Why don't you just have the ground tell you warm or cold?" Grundy suggested.

"The ground is not an individual entity," Dor answered. "It's just part of the whole land of Xanth. I doubt I could get its specific attention. Anyway, much of it is alive—roots, bugs, germs, magic things. They mess up communication."

"There is a ridge of stone," Grundy pointed out. "You could use it."

Good idea. "Tell me warm or cold, as I walk," Dor told it, and started to walk toward the tree. Crunch followed as softly as he was able, so that the shuddering of the land did not quite drown out the rock's voice.

"Warm—warm—cool—warm," the ridge called, steering Dor on the correct course. Dor realized suddenly that he was in fact a Magician; no one else could accomplish such a search. Irene's plant-growing magic was a strong talent, a worthy one, but it lacked the versatility of this. Her green thumb could not be turned to nonbotanic uses. A King, to rule Xanth, had to be able to exert his power effectively, as Magician Trent did. Trent could transform any enemy into a toad, and everyone in Xanth knew that. But Magician Trent was also smart; he used his talent merely to back up his brains and will. What would a girl like Irene do, if she occupied the throne? Line the paths with shadowboxing plants? Dor's talent was far more effective; he could learn all the secrets anyone had except those never voiced or shown before an inanimate object. Knowledge was the root of power. Good Magician Humfrey knew that. He—

"That's a tangler!" Grundy hissed in his ear.

Dor's attention snapped back to the surface. Good thing the golem had stayed with him, instead of questioning creatures on his own; Dor had been mindlessly reacting to the ridge's directives, and now stood directly before a medium-sized tangle tree. Which was no doubt why Grundy had remained, knowing that Dor was prone to such carelessness. If little Smash had gone there—

"I could ask it," Grundy said. "But the tree would probably lie, if it didn't just ignore me. Plants don't talk much anyway."

Crunch stepped close. "Growrrh!" he roared, poking one clublike finger at the dangling tentacles. The message needed no translation.

The tangler gave a vegetable keen of fear and whipped its tentacles away.

Dor, amazed, stepped forward. "Warm," the ridge said. Dor stepped nervously into the circle normally commanded by the tangler. "Cool," the ridge said.

So the little ogre had steered just clear of the tree and gone on. A close call—for tyke and tree! But now the trail led toward the deep cleft of a nickelpede warren. Nickelpedes would gouge disks out of the flesh of anything, even an ogre. If—but then the trail veered away.

The ridge subsided, but there were a number of individual rocks in this vicinity, and they served as well. On and on the trail went, meandering past a routine assortment of Xanth horrors: a needle-cactus, the nest of a harpy, a poison spring, a man-eating violent flower —fortunately Smash had been no man, but an ogre, so the flower had turned purple in frustration—a patch of spear-grass with its speartips glinting evilly. Plus similar threats, with which the wilderness abounded. Smash had avoided stepping into any traps, until at last the tyke had come to the lair of a flying dragon.

Dor halted, dismayed. This time there was no doubt: no one passed this close to such a lair without paying the price. Dragons were the lords of the jungle, as a class; specific monsters might prevail against specific dragons; but overall, dragons governed the wilds much as Man governed the tames.

They could hear the dragon cubs entertaining themselves with some poor prey, happily scorching each potential route of escape. Dragon cubs needed practice to get their scorching up to par. A stationary target sufficed only up to a point; after that they needed live lures, to get their reflexes and aim properly tracked.

"Smash . . . is there?" Dor asked, dreading the answer.

"Hot," the nearest stone agreed warmly.

Crunch grimaced, and this time not even an ogress would have mistaken his ire. He stomped up to the scene of the crime. The ground danced under the impact of his footfalls, but the dragon's lair seemed secure.

The lair's entrance was a narrow cleft that only the narrow torso of a small dragon could pass through. Crunch put one hand at each side of it and sent a brutal surge of power galumphing through his massively gnarly muscles. The rock split asunder, and suddenly the entrance was ogre-sized. The dragons were exposed, in their conservative nest of diamonds and other heat-resistant jewels. The thing about fire-breathing dragons was that ordinary nest material tended to burn up or melt or scorch unpleasantly, so diamonds were a dragon's best friend.

A little ogre, no larger than Dor himself, stood at bay amid three winged dragonets while the dragon lady glared benignly on. The ogreling was stoutly structured and would probably have been a match for any single dragon his size, but the three were making things hot for him. There were scorch marks all about, though the little ogre seemed as yet unhurt. Dragons did like to play with their food before roasting it.

Crunch did not even growl. He just leaned over and looked at the dragoness—and the smoke issuing from her mouth sank like chill fog to the floor. For Crunch massed as much as she did, and it would be redundant to specify the power-to-mass ratio of ogres. She was not up to this snuff, not even with a belly full of fuel. She never moved a muscle, petrified as if she had locked gazes with a gorgon.

Now Smash advanced on one dragonet. "Me tweak you tail, you big ol' snail!" he cried gleefully. He hauled on the tail, swung the dragon around, and hurled it carelessly against the far wall.

The second little dragon opened its mouth and wafted out a small column of fire. Smash exhaled with such force that the flame rammed right back inside the dragon, who was immediately overcome by a heated fit of coughing.

The third dragonet, no coward, pounced on Smash with all four clawed feet extended. Smash raised one fist. The dragon landed squarely on it, its head and tail whipping around to smack into each other. It fell on the bed of diamonds, stunned.

Even the littlest ogre was tougher than its weight in dragons, when the odds were evened. Dor had not believed this, before; he had thought it was mere folklore.

"Now games are through, to home with you," Crunch said, reaching in to lift his son out of the lair by his tough scruff of the neck. With his other fist, Crunch struck the nest so hard that the diamonds bounced out in a cloud, scattering all over the landscape. The dragoness winced; she would have a tedious cleanup chore to do. Without a backward glance at her, they tramped away.

Except for Grundy, who couldn't resist putting in a

last word: "Good thing for you you didn't hurt the tyke," he called to the dragon lady. "If you had, Crunch might have gotten angry. You wouldn't like him when he's angry."

Fortunately, Crunch was now in a good mood. "Little man help we; how pay we fee?" the ogre inquired of Dor.

Abashed, Dor demurred. "We were glad to help," he said. "We have to get home now."

Crunch considered. This took some time; he was big but not smart. He addressed Grundy: "Golem tell true: what can me do?"

"Oh, Dor doesn't really need any help," Grundy said. "He's a Magician."

Crunch swelled up ominously. "Me get mad, when truth not had."

Daunted, Grundy responded quickly. "Well, the boys around Castle Roogna do tease Dor a little. He's not as big and strong as the big boys, but he has more magic, so they sort of—"

Crunch cut him off with an impatient gesture. The ogre picked Dor up gently in one huge hand—fortunately not by the scruff of the neck—and carried him north along the path. Such was the ogre's stride, they were very soon at the edge of the Castle Roogna orchard. He set Dor down and stood silently while boy and golem proceeded forward.

"Thanks for the lift," Dor said weakly. He was certainly glad this monster was a vegetarian.

Crunch did not respond. Frozen in his hunched-over posture, he most resembled the massive stump of a burned-out gnarlbole tree.

Awkwardly, Dor went on toward his home, passing near the umbrella tree. As luck would have it, the two bullies were still there. Both jumped up when they saw Dor, and eager for sport, ran out to bar his way. "The little snooper's back!" Horsejaw cried. "What's he doing on a path meant for people?"

"I wouldn't," Grundy said warningly.

For answer, a little snake landed on his head. A sonic boom went off behind Dor. The boys laughed coarsely.

Then the ground shuddered. The bullies looked around wildly, fearing an avalanche from nowhere. There was another shudder, jarring Dor's teeth. It was the ogre tramping forward under full steam.

Horsejaw's mouth fell open as he saw that monster bearing down on him. He was too startled to move. The other boy tried to run, but the ground shook so violently that he fell on his face and lay there. Several small snakes appeared, squiggled nervously, and vanished; no help there. If there were any more sonic booms, they were drowned out by the violence of the ogre's approach.

Crunch strode up until he loomed over the small party, his thick torso dwarfing the slender metal trunk of a nearby ironwood tree. "Dor me friend," he thundered distinctly, and the umbrella tree collapsed into shambles with the vibration. "Help he lend." Small cracks opened in the hard ground of the path, and somewhere a heavy branch crashed to the forest floor. "If laugh at lad, me might get mad." And he swung one clublike fist around in a great circle, barely over Horsejaw's head, so that the wind made the bully's hair stand on end. At least, Dor thought it was the wind that did it; the boy looked terrified.

The ogre's fist smashed into the trunk of the ironwood tree. There was a nearly deafening clang. A tubular section of iron sprang out, leaving the top of the tree momentarily suspended in air; then it dropped heavily and fell over with a crash that made the ground shake once more. Ironwood was solid stuff! An acrid wisp of smoke wafted up from the stump: the top of it was glowing red with a white fringe, and part of it where the ogre's fist had touched had melted.

Crunch selected a jagged splinter of iron, picked his teeth with it, and wheeled about. His monstrous horny toes gouged a furrow from the path in the process. He tramped thunderously back south, humming a merry tune of bloodshed. In a moment he was gone, but the vibration of the terrain took a long time to quiet. Away in the palace, there was the tinkling crash of a window shattering.

Horsejaw stood looking at the iron stump. His eyes

flickered momentarily to Dor, then back to the steaming metal. Then he fainted.

"I don't think the boys will tease you so much any more, Dor," Grundy remarked gravely.

Chapter 2. Tapestry

Dor was not teased much any more. No one wanted to upset his friend. But this hardly eased his unrest. The teasing had not bothered him as much as it had bothered Grundy; Dor had always known he could use his superior magic to bring others into line, if he really had to. It was his general isolation from others that weighed on him, and his new awareness of Millie the ghost. What a difference there was between a brat like Irene and a woman like Millie! Yet Irene was the one Dor was expected to get along with. It wasn't fair.

He needed to talk with someone. His parents were approachable, but Chameleon varied so much in appearance and intellect that he never could be certain how to approach her, and Bink might not be sympathetic to this particular problem. Besides which, both of them were away on a trip to Mundania, on business for the King. The Land of Xanth was busy establishing diplomatic relations with Mundania, and after the centuries of bad relations this was a touchy matter, requiring the utmost finesse. So Dor's parents were out. Grundy would chat with him anytime—but the former golem was apt to get too cute about other people's problems. Such as calling Irene's green-thumb talent "stinkfinger." Dor hardly blamed her for retaliating violently, inconvenient as it had been for him personally. Grundy cared, all right—that was how he had become a real, living person—but he didn't really understand. Anyhow, he knew Dor too well. Dor's grandfather Roland, whose talent was the stun—the ability to freeze people immobile—was a good man to talk to, but he was at his home in the North Village, a good two days' travel across the Gap.

There was only one person Dor could approach who was human, competent, mature, discreet, male, and an equivalent Magician. That was the King. He knew the King was a busy man; it seemed the trade arrangements with Mundania were constantly complex, and of course there were many local problems to be handled. But King Trent always made time for Dor. Perhaps that was one root of Irene's hostility, which had spread to the Queen and the palace personnel in insidious channels. Irene talked to her father less than Dor did. So Dor tried not to abuse his Magician's privilege. But this time he simply had to go.

He picked Grundy up and marched to the palace. The palace was actually Castle Roogna. For many years it had been a castle that was not a palace, deserted and forlorn, but King Trent had changed that. Now it was the seat of government of Xanth, as it had been in its youth.

Crombie the soldier stood guard at the drawbridge across the moat. This was mainly to remind visitors to stay clear of the water, because the moat-monsters were not tame. One would think that was evident, but every few months some fool wandered too close, or tried to swim in the murky water, or even attempted to feed some tidbit to a monster by hand. Such attempts were invariably successful; sometimes the monster got the whole person, sometimes only the hand.

Crombie was asleep on his feet. Grundy took advantage of this to generate some humor at the soldier's expense. "Hey, there, birdbeak; how's the stinking broad?"

One eye cracked open. Immediately Grundy rephrased his greeting. "Hello, handsome soldier; how's the sweet wife?"

Both eyes came open, rolling expressively. "Jewel is well and cute and smelling like a rose and too worn out to go to work today, I daresay. I had a weekend pass."

So that was why the soldier was so sleepy! Crombie's wife lived in underground caverns south of the Magic Dust village; it was a long way to travel on short notice. But that was not exactly what Crombie meant. He had the royal travel-conjurer zap him to the caverns, and back again when his pass expired. Crombie's fatigue was not from traveling.

"A soldier really knows how to make a pass," Grundy observed, with a smirk he thought Dor wouldn't understand. Dor understood, more or less; he just didn't see the humor in it.

"That's for sure!" Crombie agreed heartily. "Women—I can take 'em or leave 'em, but my wife's a Jewel of a nymph."

That had special meaning too. Nymphs were ideally shaped female creatures of little intellect, useful primarily for man's passing entertainment. It was strange that Crombie had married one. But he had been under an omen of marriage, and Jewel was said to be a very special nymph, with unusual wit for the breed, who had an important job. Dor had asked his father about Jewel once, since none of the local artifacts knew about her, but Bink had answered evasively. That was part of the reason Dor didn't want to ask his father about Millie. Millie was nymphlike at times, and evasions were disquieting. Had there been something between—? No, impossible. Anyway, this sort of information could not be elicited from inanimate objects; they did not understand living feelings at all. They were purely objective. Usually.

"Watch out for the moat-monsters," Crombie warned dutifully. "They're not tame." Slowly his eyelids sank. He was asleep again.

"I'd sure like to watch one of his passes in a magic mirror, Grundy said. "But it'd break the glass in the pattern of an X."

They went on into the palace. Suddenly a three-headed wolf stalked out before them, growling fiercely. Dor paused. "Is that real?" he murmured to the floor.

"No," the floor responded in an undertone.

Relieved, Dor walked right into the wolf—and through it. The monster was mere illusion, a construct of the Queen. She resented his presence here, and her illusions were so proficient that there was no direct way to tell them from reality except by touch—which could be dangerous if something happened *not* to be an illusion. But his magic had nullified hers, as it usually did; she could never fool him long. "Sorceresses shouldn't mess with Magicians," Grundy observed snidely, and the wolf growled in anger as it vanished.

It was replaced by an image of the Queen herself, regal in robe and crown. She always enhanced her appearance for company; she was sort of dumpy in real flesh. "My husband is occupied at the moment," she said with exaggerated formality. "Kindly wait in the upstairs drawing room." Then, under her breath, she added: "Better yet, wait in the moat."

The Queen did not conceal her dislike of him, but she would not dare misrepresent the position of the King. She would inform Dor when the King was free. "Thank you, Your Highness," Dor replied as formally as she had addressed him, and walked to the drawing room.

Actually, the drawing room did not contain any drawings, only one huge tapestry hung on the wall. This had once been a bedroom; Dor's father mentioned sleeping in it once, back before Castle Roogna was restored. In fact Dor himself had slept in it, earlier in life; he remembered being fascinated by the great tapestry. Now the bed had been replaced by a couch, but the tapestry remained as intriguing as ever.

It was embroidered with scenes from the ancient past of Castle Roogna and its environs, eight hundred years ago. In one section was the Castle, its battlements under construction by a herd of centaurs; in other sections were the deep wilderness of Xanth, the awful Gap dragon, villages protected by stockades—such defenses were no longer used—and other castles. In fact there were more castles than there were today.

The more Dor looked at it, the more he saw—for the figures in the tapestry moved when watched. Since everything was more or less in proportion, the representations of men were tiny; the tip of his little finger could cover one of them over. But every detail seemed authentic. The whole lives of these people were shown, if one cared to watch long enough. Of course, their lives proceeded at the same rate contemporary lives did, so Dor had never seen a whole life pass; he would be an old man before that happened. And of course the process had to have some reasonable cessation, because otherwise the tapestry would long since have passed beyond the Castle Roogna stage and gotten right up to the present. So there were aspects of this magic Dor had not yet fathomed; he just had to accept what he saw. Meanwhile, the tapestry figures worked and slept and fought and loved, in miniature.

Memories flooded Dor. What adventures he had seen, years ago, riveted to this moving picture. Swordsmen and dragons and fair ladies and magic of every type, going on and on! But all in baffling silence; without words, much of the action became meaningless. Why did this swordsman battle this dragon, yet leave that other dragon alone? Why did the chambermaid kiss this courtier, and not that one, though that one was handsomer? Who was responsible for this particular enchantment? And why was that centaur so angry after a liaison with his filly? There was so much of it going on at once that it was hard to fathom any overall pattern.

He had asked Millie about it, and she had gladly told him the valiant tales of her youth—for she had been young at the time of Castle Roogna's construction. But though her tales were more cohesive than those of the moving pictures of the tapestry, they were also more selective. Millie did not enjoy healthy bloodshed or deadly peril or violent love; she preferred episodes of simple joy and family accommodation. That sort of thing could get dull after a while.

Also, she never talked about herself, after she had left her native stockade. Nothing about her own life and loves, or how she became a ghost. And she wouldn't tell how she had come to know the zombie Jonathan, though this could have happened quite naturally in the course of eight centuries of lonely association in Castle Roogna. Dor wondered whether, if he should ever happen to be a ghost for eight hundred years, zombies might begin to look good to him. He doubted it. At any rate, his thirst for knowledge had been frustrated, and he had finally given it up.

Why hadn't he simply made the tapestry itself talk to him, answering his questions? Dor didn't remember, so he asked the tapestry: "Please explain the nature of your images."

"I cannot," the tapestry replied. "They are as varied and detailed as life itself, not subject to interpretation by the likes of me." There it was: when performing its given function, the tapestry was painstakingly apt; but when speaking as a piece of rug, it lacked the mind to fathom its own images. He could learn from it whether a fly had sat on it in the past hour, but not the motive of an eight-hundred-years-gone Magician.

Now, as Dor contemplated the images, his old interest in history resurged. What a world that had been, back during the celebrated Fourth Wave of human colonization of Xanth! Then adventure had reigned supreme. Not dullness, as in the present.

A giant frog appeared. "The King will see you now, Master Do-oo-or," it croaked. It was of course another illusion of Queen Iris'; she was forever showing off her versatility.

"Thanks, frogface," Grundy said. He always knew when he could slip in a healthy insult without paying for it. "Catch any good flies in that big mouth of yours recently?" The frog swelled up angrily, but could not protest lest it step—or hop—out of character. The Queen disliked compromising her illusions. "How's your mother, the toad?" the golem continued blithely, the malice hardly showing in his tone. "Did she ever clean up those purple warts on her—"

The frog exploded. "Well, you didn't have to blow up at me," Grundy reproved the vanishing smoke. "I was only being sociable, frogbrain." Dor, with superhuman effort, kept his face straight. The Queen could still be watching, in the guise of a no-see-'em gnat or something. There were times when Grundy's caustic wit got him into trouble, but it was worth it.

The King's library was also upstairs, just a few doors down. That was where the King was always to be found when not otherwise occupied—and sometimes even when he was. It was not supposed to be generally known, but Dor had pried the news out of the furniture: sometimes the Queen made an image of the King in the library, at the King's behest, so he could interview some minor functionary when he was busy with more important things elsewhere. The King never did that with Dor, however.

Dor proceeded directly to the library, noting a ghost flitting across the dusky hall farther down. Millie had been one of half a dozen ghosts, and the only one to be restored to life; the others still hovered about their haunts. Dor rather liked them; they were friendly but rather shy, and were easily spooked. He was sure each had its story, but like Millie they were diffident about themselves.

He knocked at the library door. "Come in, Dor," the King's voice answered immediately. He always seemed to know when Dor came calling, even when the Queen was not around to inform him.

Dor entered, suddenly shy. "I—uh—if you're not too busy—"

King Trent smiled. "I am busy, Dor. But your business is important."

Suddenly it hardly seemed so. The King was a solid, graying man old enough to be Dor's grandfather, yet still handsome. He wore a comfortable robe, somewhat faded and threadbare; he depended on the Queen to garb him in illusion befitting whatever occasion occurred, so needed no real clothes. At the moment he was highly relaxed and informal, and Dor knew this was intended to make Dor himself feel the same. "I, uh, I can come back another time—"

King Trent frowned. "And leave me to pore over the next dull treaty amendment? My eyes are tired enough already!" A stray bluebottle fly buzzed him, and absentmindedly the King transformed it into a small bluebottle tree growing from a crevice in the desk. "Come, Magician—let us chat for a while. How are things with you?"

"Well, we met a big frog—'" Grundy began, but silenced instantly when the King glanced his way.

"Uh, about the same," Dor said. The King was giving him an opening; why couldn't he speak his mind?

"Your cottage cheese still sound?"

"Oh, yes, the house is doing fine. Talks back quite a bit, though." Inanity!

"I understand you made friends with Crunch the ogre."

Did the King know *everything*? "Yes, I helped find his child, Smash."

"But my daughter Irene doesn't like you."

"Not much." Dor wished he had stayed at home. "But she—" Dor found himself at a loss for a polite compliment. Irene was a pretty girl; her father surely knew that already. She made plants grow—but she should have been more powerfully talented. "She—"

"She is young, yet. However, even mature women are not always explicable. They seem to change overnight into completely different creatures."

Grundy laughed. "That's for sure! Dor's sweet on Millie the ghost!"

"Shut up!" Dor cried in a fury of embarrassment.

"An exceptional woman," King Trent observed as if he had not heard Dor's outcry. "A ghost for eight centuries, abruptly restored to life in the present. Her talent makes her unsuitable for normal positions around the palace, so she has served admirably as a governess at your cottage. Now you are growing up, and must begin to train for adult responsibilities."

"Adult?" Dor asked, still bemused by his shame. It was not the Queen-frog who had the big mouth; it was Grundy!

"You are the heir apparent to the throne of Xanth. Do not be concerned about my daughter; she is not Magician level and cannot assume the office unless there is no Magician available, and then only on an interim basis until a Magician appears, preserving continuity of government. Should I be removed from the picture in the next decade, you will have to take over. It is better that you be prepared."

Suddenly the present seemed overwhelmingly real. "But I can't—I don't—"

"You have the necessary magic, Dor. You lack

the experience and fortitude to use it properly. I would be remiss if I did not arrange to provide you with that experience."

"But—"

"No Magician should require the services of an ogre to enforce his authority. You have not yet been hardened to the occasional ruthlessness required."

"Uh—" Dor knew his face was crimson. He had just received a potent rebuke, and knew it was justified. For a Magician to give way to the likes of Horsejaw—

"I believe you need a mission, Dor. A man's quest. One whose completion will demonstrate your competence for the office you are coming to."

This had taken an entirely different tack than Dor had anticipated. It was as if the King had made his decision and summoned Dor for this directive, rather than merely granting an audience. "I—maybe so." Maybe so? For certain so!

"You hold Millie in respect," the King said. "But you are aware that she is not of your generation, and has one great unmet need."

"Jonathan," Dor said. "She—she loves Jonathan the zombie!" He was almost indignant.

"Then I think the nicest thing anyone could do for her would be to discover a way to restore Jonathan to full life. Then, perhaps, the reason she loves him would become apparent."

"But—" Dor had to halt. He knew that Grundy's remarks were only the least of the ridicule that would be directed at him if he ever expressed any serious ideas of his own about Millie. She was an eight-hundred-year-old woman; he was just a boy. One way to stifle all speculation would be to give her what she most wanted: Jonathan, alive. "But how—?"

The King spread his hands. "I do not know the answer, Dor. But there may be one who does."

There was only one person in the Land of Xanth who knew all the answers: the Good Magician Humfrey. But he was a sour old man who charged a year's service for each Answer. Only a person of considerable determination and fortitude went to consult Good Magician Humfrey.

Suddenly Dor realized the nature of the challenge King Trent had laid down for him. First, he would have to leave these familiar environs and trek through the hazardous wilderness to the Good Magician's castle. Then he would have to force his way in to brace the Magician. Then serve his year for the Answer. Then use the Answer to restore Jonathan to life—knowing that in so doing, he was abolishing any chance that Millie would ever—

His mind balked. This was no quest; this was disaster!

"Ordinary citizens have only themselves to be concerned about," Trent said. "A ruler must be concerned for the welfare of others as much as for himself. He must be prepared to make sacrifices—sometimes very personal ones. He may even have to lose the woman he loves, and marry the one he doesn't love—for the good of the realm."

Give up Millie, marry Irene? Dor rebelled—then realized that the King had not been talking about Dor, but about himself. Trent had lost his wife and child in Mundania, and then married the Sorceress Iris, whom he never professed to love, and had a child by her—for the good of the realm. Trent asked nothing of any citizen he would not ask of himself.

"I will never be the man you are," Dor said humbly.

The King rose, clapping him on the back so that Grundy almost fell off his shoulder. Trent might be old, but he was still strong. *"I* was never the man I am," he said. "A man is only the man he seems to be. Inside, where no one sees, he may be a mass of gnawing worms of doubt and ire and grief." He paused reflectively as he showed Dor firmly to the doorway. "No challenge is easy. The measure of the challenge a man rises to at need is the measure of the man. I proffer you a challenge for a Magician and a King."

Dor found himself standing in the hall, still bemused. Even Grundy was silent.

Good Magician Humfrey's castle was east of Castle Roogna, not far as the dragon flew, but more than a day's journey through the treacherous wilderness for a boy on foot. There was no enchanted path to Humfrey's retreat, because the Magician abhorred company; all paths led away only. Dor could not be sent there instantly by spell, because this was his quest, his private personal challenge, to accomplish by himself.

Dor started in the morning, using his talent to solve part of the problem of travel. "Stones, give me a warning whistle whenever I approach anything dangerous to me, and let me know the best route to the Good Magician's castle."

"We can tell you what is dangerous," the rocks chorused. "There were no stony silences for him! "But we don't know where the Good Magician's castle is. He has strewn little forget-spells all over."

He should have known. "I've been there," Grundy offered. "It's not far south of the Gap. Bear north toward the Gap, then east, then south to his castle."

"And if I'm off, and miss it, where will I wind up?" Dor inquired sourly.

"In the belly of a dragon, most likely."

Dor bore north, heeding the whistles. Most citizens of Xanth did not know of the Gap's existence, because it had been enchanted into anonymity, but Dor had lived all his life in this neighborhood and visited the chasm several times. Warned by his talent, he steered clear of diversions such as dragon runs, tangle trees, ant-lion prides, choke nettles, saw grass, and other threats. Only his father Bink could traverse the wilderness alone with greater equanimity, and maybe King Trent himself. Still, Grundy was nervous. "If you don't live to be King, I'll be in big trouble," he remarked, not entirely humorously.

When they got hungry, the stones directed them to the nearest breadloaf trees, soda poppies, and jellybarrel trunks. Then on, as the day waned.

"Say!" Grundy exclaimed. "There are one-way paths from Humfrey's castle to the Gap. We're bound to cross one. The stones will know where such a path is, because they will have seen people walking along them. The forget spells are just about the location of the Magician's castle, not about stray people, so we can bypass them."

"Right!" Dor agreed. "Stones, have any of you seen such travel?"

There was a chorus of no's. But he kept checking as he progressed, and in due course found some stones that had indeed observed such travelers. After some experimentation, he managed to get aligned with the path, and took a step toward the chasm. There it was, suddenly: a clear path leading to a bridge that seemed to span the full width of the Gap. But when he faced the other way, there was only jungle. Fascinating magic, these paths!

"Maybe if you walked backward—" Grundy suggested.

"But then I'd stumble into all sorts of things!"

"Well, you walk forward, and I'll face backward and keep an eye on the path."

They tried that, and it worked. The stones gave general guidance, and Grundy warned him whenever he drifted to one side or another. They made good progress, for of course the path was charmed, with no serious hazards in its immediate vicinity. But it had taken some time to find it, and when dark closed in they were still in the wilderness. Fortunately they located a pillow bush and fashioned a bed of multicolored pillows, setting out sputtering bugbombs from a bugbomb weed to repel predatory insects. They didn't worry about rain; Dor called out to a passing cloud, and it assured him that the clouds were all resting tonight, saving up for a blowout two days hence.

In the morning they feasted on boysengirls berries, the seeds like tiny boys a bit strong, and the jelly girls a bit sweet, so that they had to be taken together for full enjoyment. They washed the berries down with the juice from punctured coffee beans and took up the march again. Dor felt somewhat stiff; he wasn't used to this amount of walking. "Funny, I feel fine," Grundy remarked. He, of course, had ridden Dor's shoulder most of the way.

Another friendly cloud advised them when the Magician's castle was in sight. Humfrey had not thought to put forget spells on the clouds, or perhaps had found it impractical, since clouds tended to drift constantly. As it was, Dor realized he was fortunate these were good-natured cumulus clouds, instead of the bad-tempered thunderheads. By midmorning they were there.

The castle was small but pretty, with round turrets stretching up beyond the battlements, and a cute blue moat. Within the moat swam a triton: a handsome man with a fish's tail, carrying a wicked triple-tipped spear. He glared at the intruders.

"I think our first hurdle is upon us," Grundy remarked. "That merman is not about to let us pass."

"How did you get past, when you came to ask a Question?" Dor asked.

"That was a dozen years ago! It's all been changed. I snuck by a carnivorous seaweed in the moat, and climbed a slippery glass wall, and outsmarted a sword swallower inside."

"A sword swallower? How could he hurt you?"

"He burped."

Dor thought about that, and smiled. But the golem was right: past experience was no aid to the present. Not while the Good Magician's defenses kept changing.

He put a foot forward to touch the surface of the water. Immediately the triton swam forward, head and arm raised, trident poised. "It is only fair to warn you, intruder, that I have five notches on my spear shaft."

Dor jerked back his foot. "How do we get past this monster?" he asked, staring into the moat.

"I'm not allowed to tell you that," the water replied apologetically. "The old gnome's got everything counterspelled."

"He would," Grundy grumbled. "You can't outgnome a gnome in his own home."

"But there is a way," Dor said. "We just have to figure it out. That's the challenge."

"While the Magician chortles inside, waiting to see if we'll make it or get speared. He's got a sense of humor like that of a tangle tree."

Dor made as if to dive into the moat. The triton raised his trident again. The merman's arm was muscular, and as he supported his body well out of the water the points of his weapon glinted in the sun. Dor backed off again.

"Maybe there's a tunnel under the moat," Grundy suggested.

They walked around the moat. At one point there was a metallic plaque inscribed with the words TRESPASSERS WILL BE PROSECUTED.

"I don't know what that means," Dor complained.

"I'll translate," Grundy said. "It means: keep out."

"I wonder if it means more?" Dor mused. "Why should Humfrey put a sign out here, when there's no obvious way in anyway? Why say it in language only a golem understands? That doesn't seem to make sense—which means it probably makes a lot of sense, if you interpret it correctly."

"I don't know why you're fulminating about a stupid sign, when you need to be figuring out how to cross the moat."

"Now, if there were a tunnel that the Magician could use without running afoul of his own hazards, he'd need a marked place for it to emerge," Dor continued. "Naturally he wouldn't want anyone else using it without his permission. So he might cover it over and put a stay-away spell on it. Like this."

"You know, I think you've got a brain after all," Grundy admitted. "But you'd have to have a counterspell to get it open, and it's not allowed to tell you that secret."

"But it's only a stone. Not too bright. We might be able to trick it."

"I get you. Let's try a dialogue, know what I mean?" They had played this game before.

Dor nodded, smiling. They stepped up close to the plaque. "Good morning, plaque," Dor greeted it.

"Not to you, it ain't," the plaque responded. "I ain't going to tell you nothing."

"That's because you don't know nothing," Grundy said loudly, with a fine sneer in his voice.

"I do not know nothing!"

"My friend claims you have no secrets to divulge," Dor told the plaque.

"Your friend's a duh."

"The plaque says you're a duh," Dor informed Grundy.

"Yeah? Well the plaque's a dumdum."

"Plaque, my friend says you're a—"

"I am not!" the plaque retorted angrily. "He's the dumdum." What feelings objects had tended to be superficial. "He doesn't have my secret."

"What secret, dodo?" Grundy demanded, his voice even more heavily freighted with sneer than before.

"My secret chamber, that's what! He doesn't have that, does he?"

"*Nobody* has that," Grundy cried, scowling. "You're just making that up so we won't think you're the granitehead you really are!"

"Is that so? Well look at that, duh!" And the face of the plaque swung open to reveal an interior chamber. Inside was a small box.

Dor reached in and snatched out the box before the plaque caught on to its mistake. "And what have we here?" he inquired gleefully.

"Gimme that back!" the plaque cried. "It's mine, all mine!"

Dor studied the box. On the top was a button marked with the words DON'T PUSH. He pushed it.

The lid sprang up. A snakelike thing leaped out, startling Dor, who dropped the box. "HA, HA, HA, HA, HA!" it bellowed.

The snake-thing landed on the ground, its energy spent. "Jack, at your service," it said. "Jack in the box. You sure look foolish."

"A golem," Grundy said. "I should have known. Golems are insufferable."

"You oughta know, pinhead," Jack retorted. He reached into a serpentine pocket and drew out a shiny disk. "Here is an achievement button to commemorate the occasion." He held it up.

Dor reached down and took the button. It had two faces. On one side it said TRESPASSER. On the other it said PERSECUTED.

Dor had to laugh, ruefully. "I guess I fell for it! That's what I get for seeking the easy way through."

He put the button against his shirt, where it stuck

magically, PERSECUTED side out. Then he picked up the Jack, put him back in the box, closed the lid, set the works back inside the plaque's chamber, and closed that. "Well played, plaque," he said.

"Yeah," the plaque agreed, mollified.

They returned their attention to the moat. "No substitute for my own ingenuity," Dor said. "But this diversion has given me a notion. If we can be tricked by a decoy—"

"I don't see what you're up to," Grundy said. "That triton knows his target."

"That triton *thinks* he knows his target. Watch this." And Dor squatted by the water and said to it: "I shall make a wager with you, water. I bet that you can't imitate my voice."

"Yeah?" the water replied, sounding just like Dor.

"Hey, that's pretty good, for a beginner. But you can't do it in more than one place at a time."

"That's what you think!" the water said in Dor's voice from two places.

"You're much better than I thought!" Dor confessed ruefully. "But the real challenge is to do it so well that a third party could not tell which is me and which is you. I'm sure you couldn't fool that triton, for example."

"That wetback?" the water demanded. "What do you want to bet, sucker?"

"That water's calling you a kind of fish," Grundy muttered.

Dor considered. "Well, I don't have anything you would value. Unless—that's it! You can't talk to other people, but you still need some way to show them your prowess. You could do that with this button." He brought up the TRESPASSER / PERSECUTED button, showing both sides. "See, it says what you do to intruders. You can flash it from your surface in sinister warning."

"You're on!" the water said eagerly. "You hide, and if old three-point follows my voice instead of you, I win the prize."

"Right," Dor agreed. "I really hate to risk an item of this value, but then I don't think I'm going to lose it. You distract him, and I'll hide under your surface.

If he can't find me before I drown, the button's yours."

"Hey, there's a flaw in that logic!" Grundy protested. "If you drown—"

"Hello, fishtail!" a voice cried from the far side of the moat. "I'm the creep from the jungle!"

The triton, who had been viewing the proceedings without interest, whirled. "Another one?"

Dor slipped into the water, took half a breath, and dived below the surface. He swam vigorously, feeling the cool flow across his skin. No trident struck him. As his lungs labored painfully against his locked throat, he found the inner wall of the moat and thrust his head up.

He gasped for breath, and so did Grundy, still clinging to his shoulder. The triton was still chasing here and there, following the shifting voices. "Over here, sharksnoot! No, here, mer-thing! Are you blind, fishface?"

Dor heaved himself out. "Safe!" he cried. "You win, moat; here's the prize. It hurts awfully to lose it, but you sure showed me up." And he flipped the button into the water.

"Anytime, sucker," the water replied smugly.

The significance of Grundy's prior comment sank in belatedly. A sucker was a kind of fish, prone to fasten to the legs of swimmers and—but he hoped there were none here.

The decoy voices subsided. The triton looked around, spotting him with surprise. "How did you do that? I chased you all over the moat!"

"You certainly did," Dor agreed. "I'm really breathless."

"You some sort of Magician or something?"

"That describes it."

"Oh." The triton swam away, affecting loss of interest.

The second challenge was now before them. There was a narrow ledge of stone between the moat and the castle wall. Dor found no obvious entry to the castle. "It's always this way," Grundy said wisely. "A blank wall. Inanimate obstacle. But the worst is always inside."

"Good to know," Dor said, feeling a chill that was

not entirely from his soaking clothing. He was beginning to appreciate the depth of the challenge King Trent had made for him. At each stage he was forced to question his ability and his motive: were the risk and effort worth the prize? He had never been exposed to a sustained challenge of this magnitude before, where even his talent could help him only deviously. With the counterspells against things' giving away information, he was forced to employ his magic very cleverly, as with the moat. Maybe this was the necessary course to manhood—but he would much prefer to have a safe route home. He was, after all, only a boy. He didn't have the mass and thews of a man, and certainly not the courage. Yet here he was—and he had better go forward, because the triton would hardly let him go back.

The mass and thews of a man. The notion appealed insidiously. If by some magic he could become bigger and stronger than his father, and be skilled with the sword, so that he didn't have to have an ogre backing him up—ah, then wouldn't his problems be over! No more weaseling about, using tricks to sneak by tritons, arguing with plaques . . .

But this was foolish wishful thinking. He would never be such a man, even when full grown. "Full groan," he muttered, appreciating the morbid pun. Maybe he would have made a good zombie!

They circled the castle again. At intervals there were alcoves with plants growing in them, decorating the blank wall. But they weren't approachable plants. Stinkweeds, skunk cabbages, poison ivy—the last flipped a drop of glistening poison at him, but he avoided it. The drop struck the stone ledge and etched a smoking hole in it. Another alcove held a needle-cactus, one of the worst plant menaces of all. Dor hastened on past that one, lest the ornery vegetable elect to fire a volley of needles at him.

"You climbed a wall of glass?" Dor inquired skeptically, contemplating the blank stone. He was not a good climber, and there were no handholds, steps, or other aids.

"I was a golem then—a construct of string and gunk. It didn't matter if I fell; I wasn't real. I existed only to do translations. Today I could not climb that glass wall, or even this stone wall; I have too much reality to lose."

Too much reality to lose. That made sense. Dor's own reality became more attractive as he pondered the possible losing of it. Why was he wishing for a hero's body and power? He was a Magician, probable heir to the throne. Strong men were common; Magicians were rare. Why throw that away—for a zombie?

Then he thought of lovely Millie. To do something nice for her, make her grateful. Ah, foolishness! But it seemed he was also that kind of a fool. Maybe it came with growing up. Her talent of sex appeal—

Dor tapped at the stone. It was distressingly solid. No hollow panels there. He felt for crevices. The interstices between stones were too small for his fingers, and he already knew there were no ledges for climbing. "Got to be in one of those alcoves," he said.

They checked the alcoves, carefully. There was nothing. The noxious plants grew from stone planters sitting on the rampart; there was no secret entrance through their dirt.

But the niche of the needle-cactus seemed deeper. In fact it curved into darkness beyond the cactus. A passage!

Now all he had to do was figure out how to pass one of the deadliest of the medium-sized plants of Xanth. Needle-cactuses tended to shoot first and consider afterward. Even a tangle tree would probably give way to a needler, if they grew side by side. Chester the centaur, a friend of Dor's father, still had puncture scars marring his handsome rump where a needler had chastened him.

Dor poked his head cautiously around the corner. "I don't suppose you feel like letting a traveler pass?" he inquired without much hope.

A needle shot directly at his face. He jerked violently back, and it hissed on out to land in the moat. There was an irate protest from the triton, who didn't like having his residence littered.

"The needler says no," Grundy translated gratuitously.

"I could have guessed." How was he going to pass this hurdle? He couldn't swim under this cactus, or reason with it, or avoid it. There was barely room to squeeze by it, in the confined alcove.

"Maybe loop it with a rope, and haul it out of the way," Grundy suggested dubiously.

"We don't have a rope," Dor pointed out. "And nothing to make one with."

"I know someone whose talent is making ropes from water," Grundy said.

"So *he* could pass this menace. We can't. And if we did have rope, we'd get needled the moment we hauled the cactus out into the open."

"Unless we yanked it right into the moat."

Dor chuckled at the thought. Then he got serious. "Could we fashion a shield?"

"Nothing to fashion it from. Same problem as the rope. This ledge is barren. Now if cacti don't like water at all, maybe we can scoop—"

"They can live without it, but they like it fine," Dor said. "They get rained on all the time. Just so long as it doesn't flood too much. Splashing won't do any good, unless—" He paused, considering. "If we could send a lot of water flowing through there, flood out the cactus, wash the dirt from its pot, expose the roots—"

"How?"

Dor sighed. "No way, without a bucket. We just aren't set up to handle this cactus."

"Yeah. A firedrake could handle it. Those plants don't like fire; it burns off their needles. Then they can't fight until they grow new ones, and that takes time. But we don't have any fire." He shook a few drops from his body. "Sometimes I wish you had more physical magic, Dor. If you could point your finger and paralyze or stun or burn—"

"Then the Good Magician would have had other defenses for his castle, that those talents would be useless against. Magic is not enough; you have to use your brain."

"How can a brain stop a needler from needling?" Grundy demanded. "The thing isn't smart; you can't make a deal with it."

"The cactus isn't smart," Dor repeated, an idea forming. "So it might not grasp what would be obvious to us."

"Whatever you're talking about is not obvious to me, either," the golem said.

"Your talent is translation. Can you talk cactus language too?"

"Of course. But what has that to do with—"

"Suppose we told it we were dangerous to it? That we were salamanders, burning hot, about to burn it down?"

"Wouldn't work. It might be scared—but all it would do would be to fire off a volley of needles, to kill the salamander before the creature could get close."

"Hm, yes. But what about something that wasn't threatening, but was still sort of dangerous? A fireman, maybe, just passing through with flame on low."

Grundy considered. "That just might work. But if it failed—"

"Doom," Dor finished. "We'd be pincushions."

Both looked back at the moat. The triton was watching them alertly. "Pincushions either way," Grundy said. "I sure wish we were heroes, instead of golems and boys. We're not cut out for this sort of thing."

"The longer we stand here, the more scared I get," Dor agreed. "So let's get on with it before I start crying," he added, and wished he hadn't phrased it quite that way.

Grundy looked at the needle-cactus again. "When I was really a golem, a little thing like a needler couldn't hurt me. I wasn't real. I felt no pain. But now—I'm too scared to know what to say."

"I'll say it. It's my quest, after all; you don't have to participate. I don't know why you're risking yourself here anyway."

"Because I care, you twit!"

Which had to be true. "Okay. You just translate what I say into cactus talk." Dor nerved himself again and walked slowly toward the vegetable monster.

"Say something! Say something!" Grundy cried, as

the needles oriented on them visibly, ready to fly off their handles.

"I am a fireman," Dor said uncertainly. "I—I am made of fire. Anything that touches me gets burned to a crisp. This is my firedog, Grundy the growler. I am just taking my hot dog for a walk, just passing through, chewing idly on a firecracker. I love crackers!"

Grundy made a running series of scrapes and whistles, as of wind blowing through erect cactus needles. The needler seemed to be listening; there was an alert quiver about its needles now. Could this possibly work?

"We are merely passing through," Dor continued. "We aren't looking for trouble. We don't like to burn off needles unless we really have to, because they scorch and pop and smell real bad." He saw some needles wilt as Grundy translated. The message was getting through! "We have nothing against cactuses, so long as they keep their place. Some cactuses are very nice. Some of Grundy's best friends are cactuses; he likes to—" Dor paused. What would a firedog do with a compatible cactus? Water it down, of course—with a stream of fire. That wouldn't go over very well, here. "Uh, he likes to sniff their flowers as he dogtrots by. We only get upset if any needles happen to get in our way. When we get upset, we get very hot. Very very hot. In fact we just get all burned up." He decided not to overdo it, lest he lose credibility. "But we aren't too hot right now because we know no nice cactus would try to stick us. So we won't have to burn off any inconvenient needles."

The cactus seemed to withdraw into itself, giving them room to pass without touching. His ploy was working! "My, these firecrackers are good. Would you like a cracker, cactus?" He held out one hand.

The cactus gave a little keen of apprehension, much as the tangler had when Crunch the ogre growled at it. The needles shied away. Then Dor was past it, penetrating into the alcove passage. But he was still within range of the needler, so he kept talking. After all, if the thing caught on to his ruse, it would be a very angry cactus.

"Sure was nice meeting you, cactus. You're a real sharp creature. Not like the one I encountered the other day, who tried to put a needle in my back. I fear I lost my temper. Tempering takes a lot of heat. I fired up like a wounded salamander, and I went back and hugged that poor cactus until all its needles burst into flame. The scorch marks are still on it, but I'm happy to say that it will probably survive. Lucky it was a wet day, raining in fact, so my heat only cooked its outer layers some instead of setting the whole thing on fire. I'm sorry I did that; I really think that needle in the back was an accident. Something that just slipped out. I just can't help myself when I get hot."

He rounded the curve in the passage, so that he was no longer in view of the needler. Then he leaned against the wall, feeling faint.

Grundy's translation came to an end. "You're the best liar I've ever seen," he said admiringly.

"I'm the scaredest liar you've ever seen!"

"Well, I guess it takes practice. But you did well; I could hardly keep up with those whoppers! But I knew if I cracked a smile, I'd really get needled."

Dor pondered the implications. He had indeed achieved his victory by lying. Was that the way it should be? He doubted it. He made a mental resolution: no more lying. Not unless absolutely necessary. If a thing could not be accomplished honestly, probably it wasn't worth accomplishing at all.

"I never realized what a coward I was," Dor said, changing the subject slightly. "I'll never grow up."

"I'm a coward too," Grundy said consolingly. "I've never been so scared since I turned real."

"One more challenge to handle—the worst one. I wish I were man-sized and man-couraged!"

"Me too," the golem agreed.

The passage terminated in a conventional door with a conventional door latch. "Here we come, ready or not," Dor muttered.

"You're not ready," the door replied.

Dor ignored it. He worked the latch and opened the door.

There was a small room paneled in bird-of-paradise

feathers. A woman of extraordinary perfection stood facing them. She wore a low-cut gown, jeweled sandals, a comprehensive kerchief, and an imported pair of Mundane dark glasses. "Welcome, guests," she breathed, in such a way that Dor's gaze was attracted to the site of breathing, right where the gown was cut lowest yet fullest.

"Uh, thanks," Dor said, nonplused. This was the worst hazard of all? He needed no adult-male vision to see that it was a hazard few men would balk at.

"There's something about her—I don't like this," Grundy whispered in his ear. "I know her from somewhere—"

"Here, let me have a look at you," the woman said, lifting her hand to her glasses. Dor's glance was drawn away from her torso to her face. Her hair began to move under her kerchief, as if separately alive.

Grundy stiffened. "Close your eyes!" he cried. "I recognize her now. Those serpent locks—that's the gorgon!"

Dor's eyes snapped closed. He barged ahead, trying to get out of the room before any accident caused him to take an involuntary look. He knew what the gorgon was; her glance turned men to stone. If they met that glance with their own.

His blindly moving feet tripped over a step, and Dor fell headlong. He threw his arms up to shield his face, but did not open his eyes. He landed jarringly and lay there, eyelids still tightly screwed down.

There was the swish of long skirts coming near. "Get up, young man," the gorgon said. Her voice was deceptively soft.

"No!" Dor cried. "I don't want to turn to stone!"

"You won't turn to stone. The hurdles are over; you have won your way into the castle of the Good Magician Humfrey. No one will harm you here."

"Go away!" he said. "I won't look at you!"

She sighed, very femininely. "Golem, you look at me. Then you can reassure your friend."

"I don't want to be stone either!" Grundy protested. "I had too much trouble getting real to throw it away now. I saw what happened to all those men your sister the siren lured to your island."

"And you also saw how the Good Magician nullified me. There is no threat now."

"That's right! He—but how do I know the spell's still on? It's been a long time since—"

"Take this mirror and look at me through the reflection first," she said. "Then you will know."

"I can't handle a big mirror! I'm only inches tall, only a—oh, what's the use! Dor, I'm going to look at her. If I turn to stone, you'll know she can't be trusted."

"Grundy, don't—"

"I already have," the golem said, relieved. "It's all right, Dor, you can look."

Grundy had never deceived him. Dor clenched his teeth and cracked open an eye, seeing the lighted room and the gorgon's nearest foot. It was a very pretty foot, with fluorescently tinted toenails, topped by a shapely ankle. Funny how he had never noticed ankles before! He got to his hands and knees, his eyes traveling cautiously up her marvelously molded legs until the view was cut off by the hem of her gown. It was a shapely gown, too, slightly translucent so that the suggestion of her legs continued on up to—but enough of this stalling. He forced his reluctant eyes to travel all the way up past her contours until they approached her head.

Her hair, now unbound, consisted of a mass of writhing little snakes. They were appealingly horrible. But the face—was nothing. Just a vacuum, as if the head were a hollow ball with the front panel removed.

"But—but I saw your face before, all except the eyes—"

"You saw this mask of my face," she said, holding it up. "And the dark glasses. There was never any chance for you to look into my true face."

So it seemed. "Then why—?"

"To scare you off—if you lacked the courage to do what is necessary in order to reach the Good Magician."

"I just closed my eyes and ran," Dor said.

"But you ran forward, not back."

So he had. Even in his terror, he had not given up

his quest. Or had he merely run whichever way he happened to be facing? Dor wasn't sure.

He considered the gorgon again. Once he got used to the anomaly of her missing face, he found her quite attractive. "But you—what is a gorgon doing here?"

"I am serving my year's fee, awaiting my Answer."

Dor shook his head, trying to get this straight. "You —if I may ask—what was your Question?"

"I asked the Good Magician if he would marry me."

Dor choked. "He—he made you—serve a fee, for that?"

"Oh, yes. He always charges a year's service, or the equivalent. That's why he has so much magic around the castle. He's been in this business for a century or so."

"I know all that! But yours was a different kind of—"

She seemed to smile, behind her invisibility. "No exceptions, except maybe on direct order from the King. I don't mind. I knew what to expect when I came here. Soon my year will be finished, and I will have my Answer."

Grundy shook his little head. "I thought the old gnome was nuts. But this—he's crazy!"

"By no means," the gorgon said. "I could make him a pretty good wife, once I learn the ropes. He may be old, but he's not dead, and he needs—"

"I meant, to make you work a year—why doesn't he just marry you, and have your service for life?"

"You want me to ask him a second Question, and serve another year for the Answer?" she demanded.

"Uh, no. I was just curious. I don't really understand the Good Magician."

"You and everyone else!" she agreed wryly, and Dor began to feel an affinity for this shapely, faceless female. "But slowly I'm learning his ways. It is a good question you raise; I shall have to think about it, and maybe I can figure out that answer for myself. If he wants my service, why would he settle for a year of it when he could readily have it all? If he doesn't want my service, why not send me out to guard the moat or something where he won't have to see me every day? There has got to be a reason." She scratched her head, causing several snakes to hiss warningly.

"Why do you even want to marry him?" Grundy asked. "He's such a gnomy old gnome, he's no prize for a woman, especially a pretty one."

"Who said I wanted to marry him?"

Grundy did a rare double take. "You distinctly—your Question—"

"That is for information, golem. Once I know whether he will marry me, I'll be able to decide whether I should do it. It's a difficult decision."

"Agreed," Grundy said. "King Trent must have labored similarly before marrying Queen Iris."

"Do you love him?" Dor inquired.

"Well, I think I do. You see, he's the first man who ever associated with me without . . . you know." She nodded her head toward the corner. There was the statue of a man, carved beautifully in marble.

"That's—?" Dor asked, alarmed.

"No, I really am a statue," the stone answered him. "A fine original work of sculpture."

Humfrey won't let me do any real conversions," the gorgon said. "Not even for old times' sake. I'm just here to identify the foolish or to scare off the fainthearted. The Magician won't answer cowards."

"Then he won't answer me," Dor said sadly. "I was so scared—"

"No, that's not cowardice. Being terrified but going ahead and doing what must be done—that's courage. The one who feels no fear is a fool, and the one who lets fear rule him is a coward. You are neither. Same for you, golem. You never deserted your friend, and were willing to risk your precious flesh body to help him. I think the Magician will answer."

Dor considered that. "I sure don't feel very brave," he said at last. "All I did was hide my face."

"I admit it would have been more impressive had you closed your eyes and fenced with me blind," she said. "Or snatched up a mirror to use. We keep several handy, for those who have the wit to take that option. But you're only a boy. The standards are not as strict."

"Uh, yes," Dor agreed, still not pleased.

"You should have seen me when I came here," she said warmly. "I was so frightened, I hid my face—just as you did."

"If you didn't hide your face, you'd turn everyone to stone," Grundy pointed out.

"That too," she agreed.

"Say," Grundy demanded. "It was twleve years ago when you met the Good Gnome. I was there, remember? How come you're just now asking your Question?"

"I left my island at the Time of No Magic," she said frankly. "Suddenly no magic worked at all in the whole Land of Xanth, and the magic things were dying or turning mundane, and all the old spells were undone. I don't know why that was—"

"I know," Grundy said. "But I can't tell, except to say it won't happen again."

"All my former conquests reverted to life. There were some pretty rowdy men there, you know—trolls and things. So I got all flustered and fled. I was afraid they would hurt me."

"That was a sensible fear," Grundy said. "When they didn't catch you, they went back to the Magic Dust village where most of them had come from, and I guess they're still there. Lot of very eager women in that village, after all that time with all their men gone."

"But when the magic came back, the Magician's spell on my face was gone. It was one of the one-shot variety, that carried only until interrupted. A lot of spells are like that, mine included. So I had my face again, and I—you know."

Dor knew. She had started making statues again.

"By then, I knew what was happening," she continued. "I had been pretty naïve, there on my isolated island, but I was learning. I really didn't want to be that way. So I remembered what Humfrey had said about Mundania, where magic doesn't ever work—that certainly must be a potent counterspell laid on that land!—and I went there. And he was right. I was a normal girl. I had thought I could never stand to leave Xanth, but the Time of No Magic showed me that maybe I could stand it after all. And when I tried, I could.

It was sort of strange and fun, not nearly as bad as I had feared. People accepted me, and men—do you know I'd never kissed a man in Xanth?"

Dor was ashamed to comment. He had never kissed a woman other than his mother, who of course didn't count. He thought fleetingly of Millie. If—

"But after a while I began to miss Xanth," the gorgon continued. "The magic, the special creatures—do you know I even got to miss the tangle trees? When you're born to magic you can't just set it aside; it is part of your being. So I had to come back. But that meant—you know, more statues. So I went to Humfrey's castle. By that time I knew he was the Good Magician—he never told me that when we met! —and that he wasn't all that approachable, and I got girlishly nervous. I knew that if I wanted to be with a man in Xanth, I mean man-to-woman, it would have to be one like him. Who had the power to neutralize my talent. The more I thought about it—well, here I am."

"Didn't you have trouble getting into the castle?"

"Oh, yes! It was awful. There was this foghorn guarding the moat, and I found this little boat there, but every time I tried to cross that horn blasted out such columns of fog that I couldn't see or hear anything, and the boat always turned around and came back to shore. It was a magic boat, you see; you had to steer it or it went right back to its dock. I got all covered in fog, and my hair was hissing something awful; it doesn't like that sort of thing."

Her hair, of course, consisted of myriad tiny snakes or eels. They were rather cute, now that he was getting used to the style. "How did you get across the moat, then?"

"I finally got smart. I steered the boat directly toward the foghorn, no matter how bad the fog got. It was like swimming through a waterfall! When I reached the horn—I was across. Because it was inside, not outside."

"Oops—the gnome cometh," Grundy said.

"Oh, I must get back to work!" the gorgon said, hastily tripping out of the room. "I was in the middle of the laundry when you arrived; he uses more socks!" She was gone.

"Gnomes do have big dirty feet," Grundy remarked. "Sort of like goblins, in that respect."

The Good Magician Humfrey walked in. He was, indeed, gnomelike, old and gnarled and small. His feet were big and bare and, yes, dirty. "There's not a clean pair of socks in the whole castle!" he grumped. "Girl, haven't you done that laundry yet? I asked for it an hour ago!"

"Uh, Good Magician—" Dor said, moving toward him.

"It isn't as if socks are that complicated to wash," Humfrey continued irritably. "I've shown her the cleaning spell." He looked around. "Where is that girl? Does she think the whole Land of Xanth is made of stone, merely waiting on her convenience?"

"Uh, Good Magician Humfrey," Dor said, trying again. "I have come to ask—"

"I can't stand another minute without my socks!" Humfrey said, sitting down on the step. "I'm no barefoot boy any more, and even when I was, I always wore shoes. I spilled an itching-powder formula here once, and it gets between my toes. If that fool girl doesn't—"

"Hey, old gnome!" Grundy bawled deafeningly.

Humfrey glanced at him in an offhand way. "Oh, hello, Grundy. What are you doing here? Didn't I tell you how to become real?"

"I *am* real, gnome," Grundy said. "I'm just speaking your language, as is my talent. I'm here with my friend Dor, showing him how to get a Magician's attention."

"Dor doesn't need a Magician's attention. He's a Magician himself. He needs a quest. He ought to go find the secret of making zombies human, so he can please Millie the ghost. Besides, I'm not dressed for company. My socks—"

"To hell with your socks!" Grundy exclaimed. "The boy's come all the way here to ask you how to get that secret, and you have to give him an Answer."

"To hell with my socks? Not before they're clean! I wouldn't be caught dead in dirty socks."

"All right, gnome, I'll fetch your socks," Grundy said. "You stay right here on this step and talk to Dor, okay?" He jumped down and scurried from the room.

"Uh, I'm sorry—" Dor began hesitantly.

"It did take Grundy some time to get the message, but the cranial capacity of golems is very small. Now that he has left us alone, I can convey private reflections."

"Oh, I don't mind Grundy—"

"The fact is, Dor, you are slated to be the next King of Xanth. Now I suppose I could charge you the usual fee for my Answer, but that might be impolitic if you were to become King before I died. My references suggest that will be the case. One can never be absolutely sure about the future, of course; the future-history texts misrepresent it almost as much as the past history texts do the past. But why gamble foolishly? You are a full Magician in your own right, with power as great as mine, and of a similar genre. Given time, you will know as much as I. It becomes expedient to deal with fellow Magicians on an equal basis. Besides which, a year out of your life at this stage might in some devious way pose a threat to the welfare of your father, Bink, who cares greatly for you, and that would be an unconscionable mischief. I remember when I was attempting to fathom his talent, and the invisible giant came marching by with a tread worse than an ogre's and almost shook down the castle. But that's another matter. In this case I can not provide your full Answer anyway, because there is an ambiguity in the record. It seems it is a trade secret kept by another Magician. Are you willing to make a deal?"

"I, uh—" Dor said, not overwhelmed, but verging on it. Future history? Kingship in the foreseeable future? His father's mysterious talent? Another Magician?

"Very good. What you want is the Elixir of Restoration. What I want is historical information about a critically vague but important Wave of Xanth. The elixir is similar to the Healing Elixir that is common enough today, but is of a distinct variant formula adapted to zombies. Only the Zombie Master of the

Fourth Wave knows the formula. If I enable you to interview him, will you render me a complete accounting of your adventures in that realm?"

"The—the Fourth Wave? But—"

"Then it's agreed!" Humfrey said. "Sign your name to this release form, here, so I can tie my history text into the spell." He shoved a quill into Dor's flaccid hand and a printed parchment under it, and Dor almost automatically signed. "So good to do business with a reasonable Magician. Ah, here are my socks at last. High time!" For the golem had reappeared, staggering under the huge burden.

Humfrey leaned forward and began squeezing his big feet into the socks. It was no wonder, Dor thought, that they got dirty so rapidly! The Magician wasn't bothering to wash his feet before donning the socks. "The problem with the Fourth Wave of human colonization of Xanth is that it occurred circa eight centuries ago. I trust you are familiar with Xanth history? The centaur pedagogue gave you the scoop? Good. So I don't need to remind you how the people came in brutal Waves of conquest, killing and stealing and ravaging until they wasted it all, then had nothing better to do than settle down and watch their children turn magic, whereupon some new Wave of no-magic barbarians would invade and victimize them. So a Wave could be several generations in duration. The boldest of these, for reasons we won't go into now, was the Fourth Wave. The greatest of the ancient Magicians lived then: King Roogna, who built Castle Roogna; his archenemy and dinner companion, Magician Murphy; and the Zombie Master, whom you will interview. Plus lesser talents like the neo-Sorceress Vadne. How you will elicit the formula from the Zombie Master I don't know; he was something of a recluse, not sociable the way I am."

Grundy snorted derisively.

"Thank you," Humfrey said. He seemed to thrive on insult. "Sit down, Dor—right there will do." Dor, too disoriented to protest, sat down on the decorated carpet he had been standing on, Grundy beside him. The texture of it was luxuriant; he was comfortable. "But the main problem is the time frame. The Zombie Master can not come to you, so you must go to him. The only presently feasible way to do that is via the tapestry."

"The tapestry?" Dor asked, surprised by this familiar item. "The Castle Roogna tapestry?"

"The same. I shall give you a spell to enable you to enter it. You will not do so physically, of course; your body is much too big to be in scale. The spell will accommodate a reasonably close match, but you are hundreds of times too massive. So you will animate the body of one of the players already depicted there. We shall have to make an arrangement for your present body—ah, I know! The Brain Coral! I owe it a favor, or it owes me one—no difference. The Coral has always wanted to taste mortality. It can animate your body during your absence, so no one will know. The golem will have to help cover for you, of course."

"I've been doing that all along," Grundy said complacently.

"Now the carpet will take you to the Coral, then to the tapestry. Don't worry; I have preprogrammed it. Here, better take something to eat along the way. Gorgon!"

The gorgon hurried in with three vials. "You didn't wash your feet!" she cried to the Magician, appalled.

Humfrey took a white vial from her hand. "I had her fix this earlier, so if it turns your stomach to stone, blame her, not me." He almost chuckled as he handed the stoppered container to Dor. "Grundy, you better hang on to the spell. Remember, it's in two parts: the yellow puts him into the tapestry, the green puts the Coral into his body. Don't confuse them!" He gave the golem two tiny colored packets. "Or is it the other way around? Well, on with you. I don't have all day." He clapped his hands together with a sharp report— and the carpet on which Dor sat took off.

Too surprised to protest, Dor grabbed for the edges and hung on. "You *don't* have clean feet either," he heard the gorgon saying indignantly to Humfrey as the carpet looped the room, getting its bearings. "But I brought two dry-cleaning spells, one for each foot, so—"

Dor missed the rest. The carpet sailed out of the

room, through several other chambers, banked around a corner, angled up an interminably coiling stair, and shot out of a high turret window whose sides almost scraped skin off Dor's tight knuckles. Suddenly the ground was far below, and getting farther; already the Magician's castle seemed small.

"Hey—I think I'm scared of heights!" Dor cried, his vision recoiling.

"Nonsense," Grundy retorted. "You made it up here okay, didn't you? What are you going to do, jump?"

"Noooo!" Dor cried, horrified. "But I might quietly fall."

"What you need is a good meal to settle your stomach during the boring flight," Grundy said. "Let's just get this white bottle open—"

"I'm not hungry! I think I'm heightsick!"

The golem hauled at the cork, and it popped out. Fine smoke issued, swirled, and coalesced into two fine sandwiches, a brimming glass of milk, and a sprig of parsley. Dor had to grab at everything before the wind whipped it away.

"We're really traveling in style!" Grundy said, crunching his little teeth on the parsley. "Drink your milk, Dor."

"You sound just like Millie." But Dor gulped his milk. It was very good, obviously fresh from the pod, and the milkweed must have been grown in chocolate soil.

"I hear that in Mundania they squeeze milk out of animals," Grundy observed. That made Dor's stomach do another roil. They really were barbarians in Mundania.

Then he started in on a sandwich, as he had either to eat it or continue holding it, and he wanted his hands free to clutch the carpet again. It was a doorjam and turnip sandwich, his favorite; obviously the Good Magician had researched his tastes and prepared for this occasion before Dor ever arrived at the castle. The second one was a red potato soup sandwich, somewhat squishy but with excellent taste. The gorgon had a very nice touch.

Dor thought about the anomaly of so formidable a

creature as the gorgon reduced to being a common maid at the Magician's castle while she waited to learn whether Humfrey would marry her. Yet wasn't this the lot of the average woman? Maybe the Magician was merely showing her what she could expect if she married. That could be more important than his actual Answer. Or was that part of the Answer? The Good Magician had his peculiarities, but also a devious comprehension of the real situation. He had obviously known all about Dor himself, yet allowed him to struggle through the rigors of entry into the castle. Odd competence!

The carpet angled forward, causing Dor to suffer another spasm of vertigo. Yet his seat seemed secure. The material of the carpet seemed to hold him firmly yet comfortably, so that he did not slide off even when it tilted. Wonderful magic!

Now the carpet banked, circling for a landing—but it didn't land. It plunged at frightening speed directly toward a deep crevasse in the ground. "Where are we going?" Dor cried, alarmed.

"Into the teeth of a tangler!" Grundy replied. "A big one!" He pointed ahead, and for once he seemed less than cocksure.

"Right!" the rug agreed, still accelerating.

It was indeed a big tangle tree—one not even an ogre could cow. Its massive trunk grew from the base of the chasm, while its upper tentacles overlapped the rim. What a menace that must be to travelers seeking to cross the cleft!

The carpet banked again, accelerated again, and buzzed the crest of the tree. The tentacles reached up hungrily. "Has this rug gone crazy?" Dor demanded. "Nobody tangles with a full-sized tangler!"

"Oh, a big sphinx might get away with it," Grundy suggested. "Or the old invisible giant. Or a cockatrice."

The carpet banked yet again, sending Dor's hair flying to the side, and looped around for another nervy pass at the top of the tree. This time the tentacles were ready; they rose up in a green mass to intercept it. "Doom!" Grundy cried, covering his eyes. "Why did I ever turn real?"

But the carpet plunged directly below the tentacles, zooming right past the bared and scowling trunk of the tangler and into the ground at its base. Except that the ground opened into a small crevice transfixed by a root—and the carpet dropped into this hole.

Down, down—the horror of the heights had been abruptly replaced by the horror of the depths! Dor cowered, expecting to smash momentarily into a wall. But the carpet seemed to know its harrowing route; it never touched a wall.

There began to be a little light—a sustained glow from the walls. But this only showed how convoluted this region was. Chamber after chamber opened and closed, and passages branched at all angles. Yet the carpet sped unerringly along its programmed route, down into the very bowels of Xanth.

Bowels. Dor wished his thought hadn't phrased it that way. He still felt nervously sick. This harebrained ride—

The carpet halted abruptly beside a somber subterranean lake. In this faint illumination the water itself assumed a glow, revealing murky depths suggestive of mind-boggling secrets. The carpet settled to the cavern floor and became limp. "This must be our station," Grundy observed.

"But there's nothing here!" Nothing living, he meant.

I am here, something thought in his mind. *I am the Brain Coral—here beyond your sight beneath the lake. You bear the stigma of the Good Magician and are accompanied by his golem. Have you come to abate his debt to me?*

"I am my own golem!" Grundy protested. "And I'm not a golem any more. I'm real!"

"He said it was your debt to him," Dor answered the Brain Coral nervously. This was an uncomfortable place, and there was disquieting power in the mental voice, and an alien quality. This was a creature of Magician-class magic, but not at all human. "I think."

Same thing, the voice thought. Perhaps it was the thought voicing. *What is the offer?*

"You—if you would care to animate my body while

my spirit is away—I know it's not much of a body, just a juvenile—"

Done! the Coral replied. *Go work your spells; I will be there.*

"Uh, thank you. I—"

Thank you. I have existed a thousand years, storing mortals in my preservative lake, without ever enjoying the sensations of mortality myself. Now at last I shall experience them, however fleetingly.

"Uh, yes, I guess. You do understand that I will want my body back, when—"

Naturally. Such spells are always self-limiting; there will be no more than a fortnight before it reverts. Time enough.

Self-limiting? Dor hadn't known that. What a good thing the Good Magician had set it up. Had Dor tried to work such a spell by himself, he could have been stuck forever in the tapestry. The best spells were fail-safe.

The carpet took off without warning. "Farewell, Coral!" Dor cried, but there was no answer. Either the Brain Coral's communications range was short, or it had ceased to pay attention. Or it objected to inane courtesies.

The return trip was similar to the descent, with its interminable convolutions, but now Dor felt more secure, and his stomach stayed pretty much in place. He had new confidence in the Good Magician's planning and in the carpet's competence. He hardly winced as they shot up out of the crack into the bosom of the tangle tree, though he did have a qualm as the tentacles convulsed. The carpet merely dodged the embrace, allowing the tangler to catch nothing but the qualm, and zoomed along the base of the crevasse. When well clear of the tree, it rose smoothly out of the chasm and powered into the sky. The afternoon was blindingly bright, after the gloom of the caverns.

Now they flew north. Dor looked down, trying to spot the Magic Dust village, but all he saw was jungle. One area was dark, as if burned out, but no village. Then, all too soon, Castle Roogna hove in view. The carpet circled it once, getting its bearings as was its wont, then slanted down and into a window, through a hall, and into the tapestry room.

"Here's the first spell," Grundy said, lifting the yellow package.

"No, wait!" Dor cried, abruptly afraid of the magnitude of what he contemplated. He had supposed he would only have to search out some hidden spring in the contemporary world, and now faced a far more significant undertaking. To actually enter a picture— "I need time to uncramp my legs, to—" To decide whether he was really up to this challenge. Maybe—

But Grundy had already torn open the wrapping. Yellow mist spread out, diffusing into the air, forming a little cloud.

"I don't even know what body in the tapestry to—"

Then the expanding mist encompassed him. Dor felt himself swaying, falling without falling. For a moment he saw his body standing there stupidly, tousle-haired and slack-jawed. Then the great tapestry was coming at him, expanding hugely. There was a bug on it, then this too fuzzed out. He glimpsed a section of woven jungle, with a muscular young man standing with a huge sword, at bay against—

Chapter 3. Jumper

Dor stood at bay, his trusty blade unmasked. The goblins in front of him faded back, afraid, before he could get a close look at them. He hadn't seen goblins in the flesh before. They were small, twisted, ugly creatures with disproportionately large heads and hands and feet.

Goblins? Of course he hadn't seen them before! There had been few goblins in the surface of Xanth in daylight for centuries! They hid in the caverns beneath the surface, afraid of light.

Oh—this was no longer the present! This was the tapestry, depicting the world of eight hundred years ago. So there could be goblins here—bold ones, uncowed by light.

But he, himself—what of him? What body—oh, yes, the huge-thewed, giant young man. Dor had never before experienced such ready power; the massive sword felt light in his hands, though he knew that in his real body he would barely have been able to swing it two-handed. This was the kind of body he had daydreamed about!

Something stung him on the head. Dor clapped his hand there, knocking himself momentarily dizzy, but whatever it was was gone. It had felt, however, like a louse or flea. He had no antifleas spell with him. Already the penalties of the primitive life were manifesting.

The jungle was close. Great-leaved branches formed a seemingly solid wall of green. There were fewer magic plants than he was used to; these more closely resembled Mundane trees. Which, again, made sense; the Land of Xanth was closer to Mundania in nature than it would be in Dor's day. Evolution—the pedagogue centaur had taught him about that, how magic things evolved into more magical things, to compete and survive better.

Something entered the periphery of his vision as he looked around. Dor whirled—and discovered that it had not been his sword that made the goblins retreat.

Behind him stood a spider—the height of a man.

Dor forgot all about the lurking goblins. He lifted the great sword, feeling the facility with which his body handled it. This was a trained warrior whose muscles had been augmented by experience and skill —which was fortunate, because Dor himself was no swordsman. He could have sliced himself up, if this body hadn't possessed good reflexes.

The spider reacted similarly. It carried no sword, but hardly needed to. It had eight hairy legs and two huge green eyes—no, four eyes, two large and two small—no, there were at least six, scattered about its head. Two sharp fangs projected inward from the mouth parts, and two mouth-legs fitted outside. Overall, the creature was as horrible as Dor could imagine. Now it was preparing to pounce on him.

On top of that, the thing was chittering at him, making a series of clicking sounds that could only be some sort of threat. Grundy the golem could have translated instantly—but Grundy was eight hundred years or so away, now. The spider's two larger forelegs were raised; though they had neither fingers nor claws, they looked formidable. And those mandibles behind them, and those eyes—

Dor made a feint with his sword, surprising himself; his body was bringing its own expertise into play. The monster drew back, clicking angrily. "What's that thing trying to say?" Dor asked himself nervously, not at all sure he could fend the monster off despite his own greatly enhanced size and strength.

The sword he held thought he had spoken to it. "I know battle language. The monster says he doesn't really want to fight, but he's never seen a horror like you before. He wonders whether you are good to eat."

"A horror like me!" Dor exclaimed incredulously. "Is the monster crazy?"

"I can't be the judge of that," the sword said. "I only understand battle competence. This creature seems disoriented but competent enough to me. For all I know, you could be the crazy one."

"I'm a twelve-year-old boy from eight hundred years in the future—or from outside this tapestry, whichever makes more sense."

"Now my doubt has been allayed. You are indubitably crazy."

"Hell, you're in my hand now," Dor said, nettled. "You'll do as I direct."

"By all means. Swords have ever been the best servants of crazy men."

The monster spider had not actually attacked. Its attention seemed to be diverted. It was hard to tell what was the object of its diversion, because its eyes aimed in so many directions at once. Maybe it was only trying to understand his dialogue with the sword. Dor tried to spot what it was looking at—and saw the goblins returning.

One thing about goblins: they were enemies. No one knew exactly what had happened to them, but it had been conjectured that they had been driven underground after centuries of warfare, because of their implacable hatred of man. Once, legend claimed, the goblins had gotten along with man; indeed, they were distantly related to men. But something had changed—

"This is no good," Dor said. "If I fight the monster, the goblins will attack me from behind. But if I turn my back on the spider, it will eat me. Or something."

"So slay the monster, then fight the goblins," the sword said. "Die in honorable combat. It is the warrior's way."

"I'm no warrior!" Dor cried, thoroughly frightened. It had not occurred to him that the world of the tapestry would pose an immediate threat to him. But now he was in it, this world seemed thoroughly real, and he didn't want to find out whether he could die here. Maybe his death would merely catapult him back prematurely, terminating the spell, dumping him into his own body, mission unaccomplished. Maybe it would be more final.

"You were a warrior until a few minutes ago," the sword said. "A very stupid one, to be sure, to have gotten yourself trapped by this motley band of goblins, but nevertheless a warrior. Brains never were a requirement for war anyway; in fact they tend to be a liability. Now all of a sudden you're timid as hell, and you're also talking to me. You never did that before."

"It's my talent. Talking to inanimate objects."

"That sounds like an insult," the sword said, glinting ominously.

"No, not at all," Dor said hastily. He certainly didn't need to have his own sword mad at him now! "I am the only person privileged to talk to swords. All other people must talk to other people."

"Oh," it said, mollified. "That *is* an unusual honor. How come you never did it before?"

Dor shrugged. He didn't want to go into the insanity bit again. "Maybe I just didn't feel worthy."

"Must be," the sword agreed. "Now let's slay that monster."

"No. If it hasn't attacked by this time, I believe it when it says it doesn't want to fight. My father always says it's best to be friends if you can. He even made friends with a dragon once."

"You forget I was your father's sword before you inherited me. He never said anything of the kind. He said, 'Gorge, guzzle, and wench, for tomorrow we get gutted.' Then a wench's husband caught up with him while he was gorged and guzzled, and he got gutted."

Mundanes were brutes; Dor had already known that. So this news about the family of this body was not all that shocking. Still, it was a lot more immediate than it had been. "About making friends with a dragon—the word dragon may be taken as slang for an aggressive woman."

The sword laughed. "Oh, cle-*ver!* And absolutely crazy. You're right; your old man could have said it. Friends with a dragon!"

Dor decided to gamble. Though the sword could translate some of what the monster said into human language, it could not translate what Dor said into monster-spider language, for that was not the sword's talent. It was one-way. But communication should be possible, if he tried hard enough. "I'm going to make a peace overture by gesture," he told the sword.

"A peace overture! Your father would roll over in his booze-sodden grave!"

"You just translate what the spider says to me."

"I only understand combat language, not that sissy peace stuff," the sword said with warlike dignity. "If the monster doesn't fight, I have no interest."

"Then I shall put you away." Dor looked for the scabbard. He touched his hip, but found no sheath there. "Uh, where do you go?"

"The sword said something unintelligible.

"Where?" Dor repeated, frowning.

"Into my scabbard, idiot!" the sword said cuttingly.

"Where the hell is the scabbard? I can't find it."

"Don't you remember *anything*? It's across your big stupid back where it belongs!"

Dor felt his back with his left hand. There was a harness, with the scabbard angled from his right buttock to his left shoulder. He lifted the sword and maneuvered the point into the end of the sheath. Obviously there was an art to this, and he lacked that art. Had he allowed his body to do it automatically, there would have been no problem; but now he was opposing the nature of his body, putting away a sword in the face of battle. "Bro-*ther!*" the sword muttered with disgust.

But when Dor relaxed, distracted by his own chain of thought, his body took over, and the sword slid into its scabbard and was fastened into place at last.

"Then you, scabbard," Dor said. "You must understand peace, or at least truce."

"Yes," the scabbard replied. "I comprehend the language of negotiation-from-strength, of peace-with-honor."

Dor spread his arms wide before the monster spider, who had remained frozen in position all this time, while the goblins inched forward, suspecting a trap. Dor was trying to suggest peace. The monster spread its own front legs wide and chittered. Behind it the face of another goblin appeared, watching with suspicion. It seemed the goblins were not allied to the spider, and didn't understand it any better than Dor himself did.

"It says it was wondering when you would attack," the scabbard said. "It thought for a moment you intended peace, but now you are making ready to grasp it with your pincers so you can bite or crush or sting it to death."

Hastily Dor closed his arms.

The spider chittered. "Aha," the scabbard said. "Now it knows it has outbluffed you. You are huddled in terror. It can consume you without resistance."

Dor's embarrassment turned to anger. "Now look here, monster!" he snapped, shaking his left fist in the creature's hairy green face. "I don't want to have to fight you, but if you force me—"

Another chitter. "At last!" the scabbard said. "You have elected to meet it on equal terms, it says, neither threatening nor cowering. It is a stranger here, and is willing to declare a truce."

"Amazed and gratified, Dor held his pose. The spider brought its left foreleg forward. Still Dor did not move, afraid that any change might be misinterpreted. Slowly the segmented leg came up until the mittonlike tip touched Dor's fist. "Truce," the scabbard said.

"Truce," Dor agreed, relieved. The monster no longer looked so horrible; in fact its green fur was handsome in its fashion, and the eyes gleamed like flawless jewels. The top of its abdomen was variegated, so that seen from above it might resemble a smiling human face: two round black fur eyes, a white fur mouth, a broad black fur mustache, and delicate green complexion. Maybe the face-image was meant to frighten away predators, though what might predate on a spider this size Dor hesitated to conjecture. The eight legs were gray, tied neatly in to the base of the thorax. The two fangs were orange-brown, and long tufts of hair sprouted around some of the eyes. Really, quite a pretty creature, though formidable.

Suddenly the lurking goblins attacked in a swarm. Dor's body acted before he knew what it was doing. It whirled, drawing the sword from its sheath, and swung at the nearest enemy. "I thirst for your black blood, spawn of darkness!" the sword cried in a happy singsong. "Come let me taste your foul flesh!"

The goblins were hardly daunted. Two charged right at Dor. They were half Dor's height, and the outsized extremities made them look like cruel caricatures of the Good Magician Humfrey. But where the Magician was grumpy, these were evil; there was incredible malignance in their misshapen faces. Their bodies were thin, like the stalks of weeds, and bumpy. They carried crude weapons: chips of stone, splinters of wood, and small thorny branches.

"Stand back!" Dor cried, brandishing the hungry, thirsty sword. "I don't want to hurt you!" But emotionally he *did* want to hurt them; antipathy flooded through him, for no good reason he could fathom. He merely hated goblins. Maybe it was inherent in being a man, this revulsion by the caricatures of Man. Something completely alien could be tolerated, like the huge spider, but something that looked like a distorted man—

Then he jumped. A third goblin had sneaked in from the side and bitten him on the thigh. It hurt horribly. Dor punched him on the head with his left fist—and it hurt worse. The goblin's head was like a rock! Dor tried to grab an arm and haul the creature off, but it clung tenaciously, overbalancing him, still gnawing. Meanwhile, the other two were advancing, watching the gleaming blade with their beady eyes, trying to get safely around it. More goblins were crowding in behind.

Then a hairy leg swung in. It inserted itself between the goblin and Dor's leg and thrust out. The goblin was ripped away, screaming with rage.

Dor turned—and stared into the nearest eye of the monster spider. He saw his own reflection in the green depth: a large, flat, bearded man's face, wholly unlike his real face. Even after allowing for the distortion of the lens. "Uh, thanks," he said.

Then both goblins at the front dived for him. Their little gnarly legs propelled them with surprising power, perhaps because their bodies were so small and light. They sailed right at his head.

The body's mighty arm flexed. The sword swistled

joyfully across in an arc, pointing outward. There was an awful double jerk, as of a stick banging through weeds—and the two goblins fell in four pieces.

Had he done that? Dor stared at the dark-red blood, seeing it turn black as it spilled out over the ground. Those goblins were thoroughly dead, and he was a killer. He felt nauseated.

The spider chittered. Dor looked—and saw four goblins clinging to four of its legs, while others tried to reach its body. The spider was stretching its legs out, lifting its roughly globular body high to keep out of their reach, but was being inevitably borne down by their weight. The underside was unprotected; even small sharp stones could puncture it quickly.

Dor took his sword, pointed it at the nearest goblin, and thrust it violently forward. The sharp point transfixed the scrawny body and plunged into the earth beside the spider's foot. Not that the spider had any foot in the usual sense; the final segment of its leg bulged slightly and rounded off toelessly.

"Don't do that!" the sword cried. "Dirt dulls my edge!"

Dor jerked it out. The transfixed goblin came up with it. "Ghaaah!" it cried, its eyes bulging, arms and legs kicking wildly. The little monster couldn't even die cleanly, but had to make it as grisly and awful as possible.

Dor lifted one of his boots—he had not realized he was wearing them, before—braced it against the goblin's contorted face, and shoved the creature off his sword. Blood squirted across the blade as the thing collapsed in a messy heap.

Then Dor transfixed a second goblin, more carefully so as not to dull the edge of the blade, removing the remains more efficiently. Something in the back of his mind was throwing up, vomiting, puking out its guts, but Dor walled that off while he methodically did his job.

The spider reached behind him with a long foreleg. A goblin screamed; it had almost reached Dor's back. Dor hardly reacted; he stabbed and cleared the third goblin, then the fourth. He was getting pretty good at this.

Abruptly the goblins were gone. A dozen of them lay dead on the ground; the rest had fled. Dor had killed six, so the spider must have matched him kill for kill. They were a good fighting team!

Now, in the aftermath, Dor suffered realization of what he had done. The back of his mind burst its retaining dam and washed forward with grisly abandon. Dor looked upon the carnage, and spewed out the potato soup sandwich he had recently consumed, eight hundred years from now. At least it looked like potato soup, more than like goblin guts. He hardly cared. To kill humanoid creatures—

The spider chittered. Dor needed no translation. "I'm not used to bloodshed," he said, suppressing another heave. "If only they hadn't attacked—I didn't want to do this!" He felt tears sting his eyes. He had heard of girls being upset about losing their virginity; now he had an inkling what it felt like. He had defended himself, he had had to do that, but in the process had lost something he knew he could never recover. He had shed humanoid blood. How could he ever get the taint from his soul?

The spider seemed to understand. It moved to a dead goblin, held it with its palps, and sank its fangs into the body. But immediately it raised its head and spat out the goblin's blood. Again, Dor needed no translation: the goblin tasted awful!

There was no way to undo what had been done, no way to reclaim his lost innocence. His body had fought in the manner it was accustomed to. As his revulsion abated, Dor realized that both he and the monster spider had had a narrow escape. Had they not been together, and made their truce, and fought together, both would have fallen prey to the savage goblins.

Why had the goblins attacked? Dor could find no reason except that he and the spider had been present and had seemed vulnerable. If goblins thought they could prevail, they attacked; it seemed to be that simple. Maybe they had been hungry, and Dor and the spider had appeared to be easier prey than whatever else offered. At any rate, it had been the goblins who started it, so Dor told himself he should not feel complete guilt. He had only done to the goblins what the goblins had tried to do to him.

Still, there remained a grim pocket of negation in him, or horror at himself, at the capacity he had discovered in himself for slaughter. His new, powerful body had been the mechanism, but the will had been his own; he could not blame that on anything else.

If this was part of growing up, he didn't like it.

He turned his attention to the spider. Was this creature native to this jungle? This seemed unlikely. The scabbard had said the spider was a stranger here, and it surely would not have fallen prey to goblins on the ground if it were familiar with this region. It would have been safe in its web, high in some tree. Dor had not seen any giant spiders illustrated in the tapestry. So yes, this could be a stranger, as he himself was. In any event, a useful ally. If he could only talk to it.

Well, he could talk with it, if he worked out a system. If he could find some object that understood spiders, not just war talk or negotiation-from-strength talk. Some pebble on the ground where spiders foraged, perhaps, or—

"That's it!" he cried.

"What's it?" his sword replied, startled. "Are you going to clean me off now, so I won't rust?"

"Uh, of course," Dor said, abashed. Swords in his own day all had antirust spells, but now he was amid primitive times. He wiped the blade carefully on the freshest grass he could find, and sheathed it. Then he walked to the nearest tree and inspected its bark carefully.

Meanwhile the monster spider was cleaning its body, wiping the blood off its legs with its mouth parts, making itself look glossy-clean again. One of its eyes—it turned out to have eight of them, not six—watched Dor. Since the eyes faced in each direction, it did not have to move its body at all to watch everything around it, but Dor was sure one of those eyes was assigned to him.

"Aha!" Dor exclaimed. He had found a cobweb.

"Are you addressing me?" the cob inquired.

"I am indeed! You're from a spider, aren't you? You understand the language of spiders?"

"I certainly do. I was fashioned by a lovely Banded Garden Spider, the prettiest arachnid you never did see, all black-and-orange-striped, with the longest legs! You should have seen her snare a mosquito! But a mean old gnat-catcher bird got her. I don't know why, it certainly wasn't out of gnats—"

"Yes, very sad," Dor agreed. "Now I'm going to take you with me—may I put you on my shoulder? I want you to translate some spider talk for me."

"Well, my schedule is—"

Dor poked a finger at it warningly. "—really quite flexible," the web concluded hastily. "In fact I'm not doing anything at the moment. Do try not to mess up my pattern when you move me. My mistress put so much effort into it—"

Dor moved it carefully to his shoulder and fixed the pattern there, only messing up a few strands. Then he returned to the monster spider. "My, he's a big one!" the web remarked. "I never realized that species grew quite so large."

"Say something to me," Dor said to the spider. "I'll signal yes or no, some way you can understand."

The spider chittered. "I wish I knew what you wanted, alien thing," the web translated. This was almost like having Grundy the golem with him! But Grundy could translate both ways. Well, on with it; he was a human being, albeit a young and inexperienced one, and he should be able to work this out.

Dor raised his fist in the spider's greeting-among-equals mode. Maybe he could let this indicate agreement, and the wide-open-arms gesture the opposite.

"You desire to renew the truce?" the spider inquired. "It doesn't really need renewal—but of course you are an alien creature, so you wouldn't know—"

Dor spread his arms. The spider drew back, alarmed. "You wish to terminate the truce? This isn't—"

Confused, Dor dropped his arms. This wasn't working! How could he hold a dialogue if the spider interpreted everything strictly on its own terms?

"I wonder if something is wrong with you," the spider chittered. "You fought well, but now you seem to be at a loss. You don't seem to be wounded. I saw you regurgitate the refuse from your last meal; are you hungry again? How long has it been since you've eaten a really juicy fly?"

Dor spread his arms in negation, causing the spider to react again. "It is almost as if you are in some fashion responding to what I am saying—"

Gladly, Dor raised his fist.

Startled, the spider surveyed him with its biggest, greenest eyes. "You *do* understand?"

Dor raised his fist again.

"Let's verify this," the spider chittered, excited. "It hadn't occurred to me that you might be sapient. Too much to expect, really, especially in a non-arachnid monster. Yet you did honor the covenant. Very well: if you comprehend what I am saying, raise your forelegs."

Dor's hands shot up over his head.

"Fascinating!" the spider chittered. "I just may have discovered non-arachnid intelligence! Now lower one appendage."

Dor dropped his left arm. It was working; the spider was establishing communication with a non-arachnid sapience!

They proceeded from there. In the course of the next hour, Dor taught the spider—or the spider evoked from his subject, depending on viewpoint—the human words for *yes-good, no-bad, danger, food,* and *rest.* And Dor learned—or the spider taught—this:

He was an adult middle-aged male of his kind. His name was Phidippus Variegatus, "Jumper" for short. He was a jumping spider of the family Salticidae, the most handsome and sophisticated of the spider clans, though not the largest or most populous. Other clans no doubt had other opinions about appearance and sophistication, it had to be conceded. His kind neither lazed in webs, waiting for prey to fly in, nor lay in ambush hoping to trap prey. His kind went out boldly by day—though he could see excellently by night too, be it understood—stalking insects and capturing them with bold jumps. That was, after all, the most ethical mode.

Jumper had been stalking a particularly luscious-looking fly perched on the tapestry wall, when something strange had happened and he had found himself —here. He had been too disoriented to jump, what with the presence of this—pardon the description, but candor becomes necessary—grotesque creature of four limbs, and the onslaught of the goblin-bugs. But now Jumper was back in possession of his faculties—and seemed to have nowhere to go. This land was strange to him; the trees had shrunk, the creatures were horribly strange, and there seemed to be no others of his kind. How could he return home?

Dor was able, now, to fathom what had happened, but lacked the means to convey it. The little spider had been walking on the tapestry when Good Magician Humfrey's yellow spell took hold, and the spell had carried him into the tapestry world along with Dor. Since the spider was peripheral, his transformation had been only partial; instead of becoming small in scale with the figures of the tapestry, and occupying the body of a tapestry spider, he had kept his original body, becoming only somewhat smaller than before. Thus, here in the tapestry, Jumper seemed like a man-sized giant. Dor, had he entered similarly, would have been the size of several mountains.

The only way Jumper could return to his own world was by being with Dor when he returned. At least, so Dor conjectured. It might be that the spell would revert everything it had put into the tapestry, when the time came. But that would be a gamble. So it was safest to stay together, returning more or less as a unit: Dor to his body and size, Jumper to the contemporary world. Dor could not make the details clear, since he hardly had them clear in his own mind, but the spider was no fool. Jumper agreed: they would stay together.

Now both of them were hungry. The black flesh of the goblins was inedible, and Dor saw none of the familiar plants of his own time. No jellybarrel trees, flying fruits, water chestnuts, or pie fungi, and certainly no giant insects for Jumper to feed on. What were they to do?

Then Dor had an idea. "Are there any buglike forms around here?" he asked the web. "You know—

the big six-legged creatures, segmented, with feelers and pincers and things?"

"There are crabapple trees an hour's birdflight from here," the web said. "I have heard the birds squawking about getting pinched there."

An hour's birdflight would mean perhaps six hours' travel by land; it depended on the bird and on the terrain. "Anything closer?"

"I've seen some tree-dwelling lobsters right around here. But they have mean tempers."

"That should be just the thing; I'd feel guilty about fingering sweet-tempered ones." Dor faced Jumper. "Food," he said, pointing to the nearest tree.

Jumper brightened. It was not that his eyes glowed, but merely a heightening of posture. "I shall verify." He moved with surprising rapidity to the nearest trunk.

"Uh, is it safe?" Dor asked the web.

"Of course not. There are all manner of bug-eating birds up there, and maybe some bird-eating bugs."

Oh. Birds were deadly to spider-sized spiders. Jumper was something else. Still, best not to take chances. "Danger," Dor said.

Jumper clicked his tusks together. "All life is a danger. Hunger is a danger too. I am at home at the heights." And he continued climbing the tree with his marvelous facility, straight up the trunk. His eight legs really helped. Dor had assumed that two or four legs were best, but already he was having second or fourth thoughts. *He* could not mount a tree like that!

In a moment Jumper's worried chitter percolated down through the foliage. "Unless there are praying mantises up here?"

"What's a preying whatsit?" Dor asked the web quietly.

"That's p-r-a-y, not p-r-e-y. The mantis prays for prey."

"All *right*. What is it?"

"A bug-eating bug. Big. Bigger than almost any spider."

Just so. "None your size," Dor called up, hoping Jumper understood. Then he waited at the base, nervously. No mantises, surely—but wouldn't a steam dragon be as bad? His acquaintance with the big spider was recent, but he felt a certain responsibility for Jumper. It was Dor's fault Jumper was in this predicament, after all. And yet, if Jumper hadn't been brought along in the eddy-current of the spell, what would have happened to Dor himself, thrown innocent into the pack of goblins? The two of them together had overcome the menace, while Dor alone would have— He shudderd to think of it. He owed Jumper a considerable debt already, and his adventure in the tapestry had just begun!

Something loomed at his face. Dor ducked, alarmed, fingers scrambling at his hip for his sword—and of course not finding it there. Then he saw that the looming thing was a tree-lobster, descending on a thread. Except that lobsters didn't use threads! No, this one was tightly bound, helpless, its leaf-green claws tied close to its bark-brown body, swinging head down. A captive of the big spider!

Almost, Dor felt sympathy for the lobster, for it was still alive and struggling vainly against its webbands. But he remembered the time he had climbed a butternut tree to fetch some butter, and a lobster had nipped him. He had been nervous about them ever since; they were ornery creatures. This one's red antennae radiated malevolence at him.

Another bound lobster was lowered to hang a few feet above the ground, and then a third. Then Jumper himself floated down. "I ate the rest," he chittered. "Less juicy than flies, but nonetheless excellent. These ones I shall save for future repasts. My gratitude to you for your timely information, Dor-man."

"Yes," Dor said, using the best word he had to indicate a positive response directly. He was glad that he had been able to help, but it was not enough. His responsibility would not be through until he had returned Jumper to his own world.

Now it was Dor's turn to look for food. He asked the web, but it had seen mainly things that moved, while Dor preferred sedentary food. So he inquired of stones he saw, and sticks of wood, and soon located a hominy tree with a few ripe grits on it. This wasn't much, but it would hold him for a while. The magic vegetation did exist; it was merely sparser, more secretive than in his own day, forcing him to search it out more carefully.

By this time it was late afternoon. It would not be safe to spend the night on the ground; more goblins could come, or other threats could manifest. If this were Dor's own world, there would have been half a dozen bad threats already, as well as several nuisances and a couple of annoyances. But maybe the goblin band had cleaned out the local monsters, not liking the competition. "Rest," Dor said, pointing to the declining sun.

Jumper understood. "I can see very well in the dark, but it may be unsafe for Dor-man. The trees are not safe either; there are other things than birds up there, that I perceived a moment ago. One resembled a bird, but had a man-face and a bad odor—"

"A harpy!" Dor cried. "Face and bosom of a woman, body of a bird. They're awful!" Of course he knew Jumper couldn't follow all that, but he would pick up the tone of agreement.

"Therefore we should sleep in the air," Jumper concluded. "I will string you from a branch and you will swing safe for the night."

Dor was not sanguine about this notion either, but could neither express his objection adequately nor offer a better alternative. To be trussed up like one of those living lobsters—

With misgivings that he trusted were not evident to the spider Dor suffered himself to be looped by several strands of line. Jumper drew the material from his spinnerets, which were organs in his posterior. He cheerfully explained it in more detail than Dor cared to know, as he proceeded: "My silk is a liquid that hardens into a strong thread as it is drawn out. With my six spinnerets I shape it into strands of whatever texture, strength, and quality I happen to require. In this case I'm using single threads for the hammock and a multistrand cable for the main line. Now you wait here a moment while I make the connection."

There wasn't much else Dor could do at this stage except wait as requested. That silk was strong stuff!

Jumper climbed up through the air. Noting Dor's

startled reaction, he chittered down the explanation: "My dragline. I left it in place when I finished catching the lobsters. We spiders could not survive without our draglines. They keep us from falling, ever. Sometimes my hatchmates and I would have drag races, when I was young, jumping from high places to see who could bounce closest to the ground without touching . . ." He climbed on out of sight.

"Hatchmates?" Dor inquired, mainly to keep the spider chittering so he would know where he was.

"My siblings who hatched from the egg sac," Jumper responded from above. "Several hundred of us, shedding our first skins and emerging into the great outer world to disperse and fend for ourselves. Is this not the case with your kind too?"

"No," Dor admitted. "I am the only one in my family."

"My consolations! Did some monster consume all the rest before they could escape?"

"Uh, not exactly. My parents take good care of me, when they are home."

"Your sire and siress remain together? I fear I misunderstand your expression."

"Uh, well—"

"Intriguing notion, maintaining a relationship with one's mate and offspring after procreation. Perhaps I should check with my mate, when I return, just to see how she's managing with the egg sac. Wouldn't want my spiderlings to hatch prematurely." Then, abruptly, Dor was hoisted off the ground. Jumper was hauling him into the air like a lobster!

Yet it was oddly comfortable. Jumper had not bound him, but had placed his strands competently so that Dor was well supported without being confined. Most of the lines were invisible, unless he knew exactly where to look. The spider was really expert at this sort of thing!

It was easy to relax in this hammock, to rest—and he did feel safe. In a moment Jumper glided down to hang beside him. They dangled together as the serenity of the night closed in above them, secure from the threats of ground and tree.

Dor jumped. He scratched his head. Something scuttled away through his hair. It was that flea again, proably the same one who had bitten him when he first arrived. He thought of mentioning it to the spider, who should certainly know how to catch a flea, but then worried that he might lose an ear in the process. Those tusks of Jumper's were fierce! This was one problem he preferred to handle himself. Next time the critter bit him...

Dor woke as the light filtered in through the branches. He felt some discomfort, for he was not used to sleeping in a vertical position, but he knew he was better off than he might have been. His leg was sore where the goblin had bitten it, and his right arm was stiff from swinging the heavy sword, and his stomach rumbled with borderline dissatisfaction. But this was a well-conditioned body; the sensations were mere annoyances.

Jumper stirred. He dropped to the ground to make sure it was safe, then climbed back up to lower Dor. As Dor's foot touched the forest floor, the big spider moved his legs dexterously around him, and the net of web fell away. Dor was free.

Now, suddenly, he felt an urgent call of nature. He retreated to a bush to take care of it. Floating in air was nice, but was limiting in certain ways! He wondered whether real heroes were ever embarrassed by such problems; certainly the subject never came up in the heroic tales of this period.

Jumper chittered as Dor returned. Dor listened, but could make no sense of it. What had happened to his translator?

After a moment he found out: the big spider had removed it when he cut away the net-web. It was a natural error. Dor found a strand of Jumper's own left over silk and put that on his shoulder. "Translate," he ordered it.

"... mission, while mine is merely to return to my normal world," Jumper was saying. "So it behooves me to help you complete your mission, so that we can both return."

"Yes," Dor agreed.

"Obviously magic is involved. Some spell has

carried me to your world—except that you do not seem overly familiar with it yourself. So it must be a strange aspect of your world. You are here to accomplish something, after which you will be released from your enchantment. So if we stay together—"

"Yes!" Dor agreed. Jumper was one smart arachnid. He must have thought things out during the night, recognizing the seeming change in his size and Dor's ignorance of these surroundings as linked things.

"So the best thing to do is get your job done as fast as possible," Jumper concluded. "If you will indicate where you need to travel—"

"To the Zombie Master," Dor said. But of course that wasn't clear. Also, he had no idea where to find the Zombie Master. This led to a somewhat confused discussion. Finally Dor asked some of the local artifacts; they knew nothing of the Zombie Master, but had heard of King Roogna. It seemed a detachment of the King's army had passed this way.

"King Roogna! Of course!" Dor exclaimed. "He would know! He would know everything! I should talk with him first, and he will tell me how to find the Zombie Master."

Thus it was decided. Dor got general directions from the landscape, and they began their trek toward Castle Roogna. In one part of his mind Dor remained bemused by the fact that this was the tapestry world, and the entire tapestry was inside Castle Roogna. Yet they evidently faced a journey of many days to reach the Castle. It did make sense, somehow, he was sure. As much sense as magic ever did.

He was getting used to this new jungle. Rather, this old jungle. Many of the trees were giant, with voluminously proliferating foliage, but had very little magic. It was as if it took longer for magic to infuse the vegetation than the animals. Sweat gnats were present, and bluebottle flies, their bottle bodies refracting the beams of sunlight they buzzed through. But even these minor insects did not approach Jumper too closely. This was one advantage of traveling with a spider.

"No!" Dor cried suddenly. "Danger!" He pointed. "You're walking into a tangle tree!"

Jumper paused. "I gather there is some threat? All I see is the collection of vines."

In the spider's normal, small world there would be no tangle trees, Dor realized. Tanglers were there, to be sure, but they would hardly bother anything as small as a spider. Also, Jumper might have lived all his life in the tapestry room of Castle Roogna, so never encountered any of the jungle threats, regardless of relative sizes. Yet he seemed familiar with trees in general, so he must have spent some time outside.

"I'll show you," Dor said. He picked up a large stick and heaved it at the tree. The tangler's tentacles snatched it out of the air and tore it to splinters.

"I see what you mean," Jumper said appreciatively. "I believe I walked on the foliage of such a tree once in my youth, but it paid me no attenion. Now that I am on its scale, it is another condition. I am glad I am keeping your company, weird though your form is."

Which was a decent compliment. Dor inspected the tangler from a safe distance. He had identified it almost too late, because it was of a different subspecies from the ones he had known. It was cruder, more like a mundane tree, with light bark on the tentacles, and it lacked the pleasant greensward and sweet perfume beneath. Tanglers had grown more sophisticated over the centuries as their prey became more wary. For a person attuned to the end product, the cruder ancestral version was hard to identify. He would have to be more careful; there was less magic in the jungle, but what there was was just as dangerous to him and Jumper.

They resumed their journey. The Land of Xanth was a peninsula connected to Mundania by a narrow, mountainous isthmus at the northwest extremity. Dor's body appeared to be that of a Mundane who had recently crossed the isthmus; maybe that was why he had been easy for the goblins to trap. It took time to appreciate all the hazards of Xanth, and even a lifetime did not suffice for some people. A Mundane would have all the wrong reflexes, and perish quickly. Which perhaps was why the Mundanes invaded in Waves; there was security in great numbers.

Now they were proceeding toward the center of Xanth, Castle Roogna, in a southerly direction. How they would cross the Gap that cut Xanth in two Dor wasn't certain. In his day the northern wilderness was not as dangerous as the southern wilderness, and since there was less magic now—or rather, less-developed magic—Dor did not anticipate too much trouble this side of the Gap. But the Land of Xanth had a way of fooling people, so he remained on guard.

Castle Roogna. He wondered whether there was a tapestry on its wall, depicting—what? The events another eight hundred years past? Or the present, including himself coming toward the Castle? Intriguing thought!

Jumper paused, raising his two frontmost forelegs, which seemed to be the most sensitive to new things. Dor had noted no ears on the spider; was it possible he heard with his legs? "Something strange," Jumper chittered.

The spider had grown accustomed to the routine strangenesses of this land, so this must be something special. Dor looked. Before them stood a creature vaguely like a small dragon, yet obviously not a dragon. Yet with dragon affinities. It had an irregularly sinuous body, small wings that did not seem functional, claws, tail, and a lizard head, but lacked the formidable teeth and fire of a true dragon. In fact, it did not look very formidable.

"I think it will be safe to circle around it," Dor said. There was a swampy region to the west with malodorous bubbles, and a thicket of glistening brambles to the east, so it was necessary to pass through this creature's territory. "We're not looking for trouble, and maybe it isn't either." Knowing Jumper could hardly understand all that discussion, he set the example by detouring right, to circle the monster at a safe distance without going too near the bubbly swamp.

But the creature extended one leg enormously, so that it stretched way out to block Dor's progress. "You may not pass," it rasped. "This is my domain, my precinct, my territory. I govern."

At least it talked! "We do not seek any quarrel with

you," Dor said, remembering adult protocol for such things. "If you let us pass, we will not bother you."

"If you pass, you prevail," the monster said. "I am Gerrymander; I prevail by whatever devious configuration."

Dor knew of no such creature in his own time. This must have been an evolutionary dead end. Gerrymander—who prevailed by changing its shape to block the passage of others? A strange definition of success!

"I do not wish to damage you, Gerrymander," Dor said, placing his hand on the hilt of his sword. He feared it looked as if he were scratching his shoulder, and wished this body had a more conventional harness for the sword, but that couldn't be helped. "But we must pass."

Gerrymander's shape settled grotesquely. It contracted along its extremity and stood in its original form before Dor. "You shall not. I hold this office eternally, regardless of the need or merit of others."

The thing was meeting his challenge squarely. Dor was daunted. He was using the body of a powerful grown man, but he remained a boy at heart, and he never had been much for combat. Those goblins, the horrible way they had died—no, not that again! "Then I'll just have to go around another way." He backed off.

"You shall not!" Gerrymander repeated. "No one supersedes me by fair means!" Its neck extended in a series of odd jumps until its head came to rest behind Dor. Now he was half encircled.

Sudden fear prompted him to do what determination had not. Dor drew his sword with the practiced speed of his warrior-body and pointed it directly at the creature's heart region. "Get out of my way!"

For answer, the thing's left wing began extending with the same chunky jerks, forming a misshapen barrier around Dor's other side. "I am surrounding you, isolating your influence," Gerrymander said. "You have no power, your grass roots are shriveling, your aspirations fading away. Your strength will be mine."

And Dor did feel a sinister weakening, as if his body were being drained of some vital imperative.

Terrified by this strange threat, he reacted savagely. He struck with all his power at the thing's neck. The great sword cut cleanly through Gerrymander's substance as if it were mere cocoa from a nut, cleaving the monster in twain.

But no blood flowed. "I don't have to be contiguous," Gerrymander cried, its severed head forming little legs as its ears elongated. The ears were now limbs. "I don't have to be reasonable; I have the power of accommodation. I can be any shape and any number, anytime. I am master of form and number. I cover whatever territory I need, regardless of my actual base, to hold power."

Dor struck again, separating a section of body, but the thing did not die or yield. Dor cut it into half a dozen bloodless segments, yet they maintained their formation about him. An arm coalesced into a torso, the fingers of its hands stretching into separate arms and legs; a leg sprouted legs and a tail; the original tail grew a head. "I convolute, I divide, I conquer!" the original head cried, as the segments closed in.

"Help! Jumper!" Dor cried, entirely unnerved.

"I am here, friend," the spider chittered. "Sheathe your blade, lest you injure me, and I will aid you."

Dor obeyed. His body was shaking with fear and humiliation. Whatever had given him the notion that all he needed to be a hero was a hero's body?

Jumper bounded phenomenally, passing right over Gerrymander and landing beside Dor. "I will tie this creature," the spider chittered. "I will bind it together so that it cannot move."

Jumper rapidly drew yards of silk from his versatile spinnerets. He looped his line about Gerrymander's tail section, anchoring it in several places with sticky lumps. Then he looped another segment and drew the two together, making a package. Working rapidly with his eight legs and with marvelous dexterity, he looped more segments and drew them in tight. He was forcing Gerrymander to collect back into its original volume.

As the segments came together, they merged, forming one creature. The superfluous arms, legs, heads, and tails flowed back into the main mass. Gerrymander was being put back together. But this wasn't enough.

"I surround, I select, I conquer!" the monster cried, its tail re-expanding to fill the space it had occupied as a separate segment. Jumper's strands could not prevent this; they remained in place, anchoring the creature, but could not stop its projection from growing around and between them. All the spider had accomplished was the undoing of Dor's slicing; the monster's basic talent was not affected.

"I fear that I, like you, am being overcome," Jumper chittered. "Come, friend, let us retreat and reconsider." He flung a loop around Dor, then leaped straight up thirty feet to cling to the overhanging branch of a mundane tree. Then he hauled on his line, and drew Dor slowly up after him.

Gerrymander gave a shriek of pure anguish. "Ah, they escape me!" It tried to catch Dor's rising legs.

Dor yanked his feet out of the thing's grasp. The creature extended itself, rising high to pace him, and grabbed again. Dor drew his sword and slashed at the grotesquely reaching hand-limb. Gerrymander's catching claw was cut off, and it fell to the ground, where it quickly merged with the rest of the body. The thing might not be hurt by having chunks of itself cut off, but it was unable to lift such pieces very far into the air without support. "Aaahh!" it cried despairingly. "I have been outmaneuvered!"

"We had only to jump over it!" Dor cried with realization. "Just as it blocked us, knowing no laws of motion, we could pass it without such laws. The moment we pass it, we win. *That's* how you fight Gerrymander!"

Indeed, the defeated monster was rapidly dwindling into its smaller original form. Its power existed only so long as it was matching its challenge. According to its definition.

"Strange are the ways of this world," Jumper chittered.

Dor only shook his head, agreeing.

Jumper lowered Dor down beyond Gerrymander, and the two resumed their trek. Now Dor knew how the spider got his name! He had never before seen such jumping ability. He had thought all spiders made webs, but Jumper didn't, though he certainly had facility with silk. It was, Dor realized, not safe to categorize creatures too blithely; there were enormous variations.

They were becoming wise to the ways of this region, and traveled rapidly. Most wild creatures were wary of Jumper, who looked more ferocious than he was, and seemed quite alien to this world—which he was not. He was merely large for his type.

By nightfall they had traversed most of northern Xanth, Dor judged. They might have traveled faster, but had had to stop to forage for food every so often. He remembered that there was supposed to be a grove of peace trees in this vicinity; not a good place to sleep, for the sleeper might never find the initiative to wake again. So at his behest they camped just shy of the main forest, suspended from a solitary crabapple tree in a field. A stream nearby provided water for Dor, and the crabs from the tree were a minor feast for Jumper.

Next morning they passed hastily through the peace grove, never stopping to rest. Dor felt lethargy overwhelming him, but these trees, too, had not developed their magic to its potency of later centuries, and he was able to fight it off. Jumper, unused to this effect, became sluggish, but Dor goaded him on until they were out of the grove.

At last they stood at the brink of the Gap. A thousand paces across, here, and just as deep, it was Xanth's most scenic and devastating landmark. "It doesn't appear on any maps of my day," Dor said, "because there is some kind of forget spell associated with it. But most of us at Castle Roogna have become more or less immune to the effect, so we can remember. I don't know how we can get across except by climbing down this wall and up the other. You could do that readily, I'm sure, but I'm not nearly as good a climber as you, and I get nervous about heights."

They had conversed during their trek, and Jumper was already picking up a small versatile vocabulary of Dor's words. He could now make out the general gist of Dor's speech. "I believe we can cross this, if we must," he chittered. "There is however, a certain element of risk."

"Yes, the Gap dragon," Dor said, remembering.

"Danger?"

"Big danger, at the bottom of the chasm. Dragon —like Gerrymander, only worse. Teeth."

"We can jump over it?"

"The dragon would—the teeth—it's just not safe," Dor said, frustrated. He could not remember whether the Gap dragon was a fire-breather or a steamer, but didn't want to risk it either way. Nobody in his right mind, and not too many in their wrong minds, messed with a full-sized dragon!

"However, we do not need to descend," Jumper chittered. "I contemplate ballooning."

"Ballooning?"

"Floating across the chasm on an airborne line. There is updraft here; I believe conditions are favorable, in the height of the day when the warm air rises. But there remain risks."

"Risks," Dor repeated, stunned by the whole notion. "Flying on silk?"

"If the air current should change, or a storm arise—"

The more Dor thought about it, the less he liked it. Yet his other options did not seem better. He did not want to go down into the Gap, or to try to walk all the way around it. He had a couple of weeks here in the tapestry to complete his mission, and had used two days already; going the way around the Gap could use all the rest. He needed to get to Castle Roogna as rapidly as possible. "I guess we'd better balloon," he said reluctantly.

Jumper stood at the edge of the Gap and drew out some silk. Instead of attaching it to anything, he let the wind take it. Soon it was unreeling rapidly, the end of the silk being drawn upward like a magic kite. Dor could see only a few feet of it; beyond that the silk became invisible in the distance no matter how carefully he traced it. He did not see how this could carry anything across the chasm.

"It is almost ready," Jumper chittered. "Let me fasten it to you, friend, before it hauls me away." Indeed, the huge spider was now clinging to the ground.

There was evidently quite a strong pull from that invisible thread. "Please approach."

Dor stepped close, and with deft motions of his forelegs the spider fashioned a hammock to support him. Then an extra gust of wind came, and Dor was hauled into the air and out over the Gap.

Too startled to move or scream, Dor stared down into the awesome depths. He swung down on the end of his tether as his kite achieved its special orientation. He thought he would sink right down into the chasm, but then the updraft caught hold strongly and carried him upward.

The walls of the chasm angled down on either side to form a wedgelike base. The sunlight angled down from the east, making stark shadows in the irregularities of the cliff. Even so, the depths remained gloomy. No, he didn't want to go down there!

As he rose back above the rim of the canyon the wind eased. It lifted him slowly, but also carried him westward along the chasm. He was not really getting across. Jumper remained on the rim, spinning a balloon line for himself—but this took time, and the distance between them was extending alarmingly. Suppose they got completely separated?

Dor had known Jumper only two days, but he had come to depend on the big spider. It was not merely that Jumper was company, or that he fought well, or that he had so many useful tricks with his silk—such as ballooning!—it was that Jumper was adult. Dor had the body of a man, but fell far short of the judgement or certainty of a man. He got frightened when alone, and insecure, not always for sufficient reason.

Jumper, in contrast, coolly assessed every situation and reacted with level-minded precision. He could make mistakes, but they didn't throw him. He was a stabilizing influence, and Dor needed that. He hadn't realized it until this moment—which was part of his problem. He was not good at analyzing his own motives ahead of a crisis. He needed the company of someone who understood him, someone who could prepare for Dor's mistakes without making an embarrassing issue of it. Someone like Jumper.

There was a pain in his scalp. Dor swatted at it. Damn that flea!

The wind was, if anything, picking up now. Dor sailed faster and higher. His apprehension mounted. It hardly seemed he was going to come down anywhere, certainly not the far side of the Gap. He might be blown all the way out to sea and drown or be consumed by sea monsters. Or he might float higher and higher until he starved. Worst of all, he might even land in Mundania. Why hadn't Jumper anticipated this?

The answer was, he had. The spider had warned of the risk. And Dor had decided to take that risk. Now he was paying the price of that decision.

A speck appeared among the clouds. A bug, no a bird, no a harpy, no a dragon—no, it loomed larger still. A roc—it must be a roc-bird, largest of all winged creatures. But as it came closer yet, and he gained perspective on it, he knew that it was after all to small to be a roc, though it certainly was large. It was a bird with bright but tasteless plumage; patches of red, blue, and yellow on the wings, a brown tail speckled with white, and a body streaked in shades of green. The head was black with a white patch about one eye and two purple feathers near the gray beak. In short, a hodgepodge.

The bird loomed close, cocking one eye at Dor. This was another danger he hadn't thought of: attack by a flying creature. He grabbed for his sword, but restrained himself, afraid he would cut through his silken line and plummet into the chasm. He had been lucky he didn't sever his line when he was escaping from Gerrymander—but that had been a far lesser height than this. Yet if he didn't defend himself, the bird might eat him. It did not look like a predator; the beak was wrong. More like a scavenger. But the way it peered at him—

"Hoo-rah!" the bird cried. It dived forward, extended its big handlike feet, and snatched Dor out of the air. "Hoo-rah! Hoo-rah!" and it stroked powerfully south, carrying Dor along.

This was the direction he had wanted to go, but not the manner. Prey for a monstrous, loud-beaked bird! Now he was glad Jumper wasn't with him, for the spider could not have helped him against so large a creature, and would only have fallen prey too. A big bird would be the worst possible menace to a big spider!

Now that his fate was upon him, Dor found himself much less afraid than he had thought he ought to be. Here he was going to be cruelly consumed, but most of what he felt was relief that his friend had escaped that destiny. Was this a sign he was growing up? Too bad he would never have the chance to complete the process!

Of course Jumper would be stuck in the tapestry world, without Dor's spell to release him from it, unless the spell automatically reverted whatever didn't belong here. Such as one live spider, and the digested refuse of—still, it wasn't his own body getting eaten. Maybe a compromise: his spirit halfway dead, so he would return as a zombie. He could wander about the dismal countryside swapping ghoul stories with Jonathan. Yuck!

"Hoo-rah!" the bird cried again, descending toward a hugely spreading mundane-type tree. In a moment it landed on a tremendous nest, depositing Dor in its center.

The nest was incredible. It had been fashioned from every imaginable and some unimaginable substance: string, leaves, bark, snakeskins, seaweed, human clothing, feathers, silver wire—Dor's father had mentioned a silver oak somewhere in the jungle; the bird must have found that tree—dragon's scales, a petrified peanut-butter sandwich, strands of hair from a harpy's tail—harpies had hairy feathers, or feathery hairs—a tangle-tree tentacle, pieces of broken glass, seashells strung together, an amulet fashioned from centaur mane, several dried worms, and a mishmash of less identifiable things.

But what filled the nest was even more remarkable. There were eggs, of course—but not this bird's own eggs, for they were of all colors, sizes, and shapes. Round eggs, oblong eggs, hourglass eggs; green ones, purple ones, polka-dotted ones; an egg the size of Dor's head, and another the size of his littlest fingernail. At least one was an alabaster darning egg. There were also assorted nuts and berries and screws. There were dead fish and live wires and golden keys and brass-bound books, and pine and ice-cream cones. There was a marble statue of a winged horse, and marbles carved from unicorn horn. There was an hourglass with a quarter hour on it, and three linked rings made of ice. A soiled sunbeam and a polished werewolf dropping. Five goofballs. And Dor.

"Hoo-rah!" the bird cried exultantly, flapping its wings so that papers, leaves, and feathers flew about in a miniature windstorm within the nest. Then it took off.

It seemed this bird liked to collect things. Dor had become part of the collection. Was he the first man so collected, since he saw no other here? Or had the others been eaten? No, he saw no human bones. Not that that proved anything; the bird could digest the bones along with the flesh. Probably he had become collect-worthy because he had seemed to be a flying man: an unusual species.

Dor made his way past the bric-a-brac to the nearest rim of the nest so that he could peer over. But all he could see were layers of leaves. He was sure he was far up in the tree, however; it would be suicidal to jump. Could he climb down? The limb of the tree on which the nest perched was round, smooth-barked, and moist; only the fact that it branched at the base of the nest made it possible for anything to remain on top of it. Dor was almost certain he would fall off. He simply was not a good climber.

He knew he should make a decision soon, and take action before the Hoorah bird returned, but he found himself paralyzed with objections to any positive course. To jump was to fall and die; to climb was to fall and die; to remain here was—to be eaten? "I don't know what to do!" he cried, near tears.

"That's easy," the unicorn statue said. "Make a rope from fragments of the Hoorah's nest, and let yourself down to the ground."

"Not from *my* substance!" the nest protested.

Dor took hold of a piece of cord and yanked it out of the nest. It snapped readily. He drew on some long straw with similar result. He tried for some cloth; it, too, lacked cohesion. He took hold of the silver wire, but it was so fine it cut into his hands. "You're right, nest," he said. "Not from your substance." He looked about, however, taking some faint heart. "Any other notion, things?"

"I am a magic ring," a golden circlet said. "Put me on and make a wish, any wish, any wish at all. I am all-powerful."

Then how had it ended up here? But he couldn't afford to be too choosy. Dor put it on his little finger. "I wish I were safe on the ground."

Nothing happened. "The ring is a liar," the werewolf dropping growled.

"I am not!" the ring cried. "It just takes a little time. A little patience. Have faith in me. I'm out of practice, that's all."

Its statement was greeted by a rumble of derisive laughter from many other artifacts of the Hoorah's nest. Dor cleared junk from one area and lay down, trying to think of something. But his mind would not perform.

Then a hairy leg came up over the rim of the nest, followed by another, and a pair of huge green eyes plus a collection of smaller black eyes. "Jumper!" Dor cried, delighted. "How did you find me?"

"I never needed to search for you," the spider chittered, hauling his pretty abdomen over the brim. That variegated fur-face had never looked so good! "As a matter of routine I attached a dragline to you. When the Hoorah took you, I was carried along behind, though at a fair distance. I daresay I was virtually invisible. I did get hung up on the tree, but once I climbed the line to its end I found you."

"That's great! I was afraid I'd never see you again!"

"You forget I need your magic to escape this world." Actually their dialogue was not nearly this concise, because Jumper still did not know many human words, but it seemed like normal conversation in retrospect. "Now shall we depart?"

"Yes."

Jumper attached a new line to Dor and made ready to lower him down through the foliage. But just then they heard the beat of huge wings. The Hoorah was returning!

Jumper sprang out of the nest and disappeared below. Dor, alarmed, remembered almost immediately that no spider ever fell; his dragline protected him. Dor might have jumped similarly, but wasn't sure his own dragline was properly anchored. The Hoorah's approach had become audible just when Jumper was seeing to it, interrupting the process.

Or maybe, Dor reminded himself savagely, he was simply too scared to do what he had to, in time.

The Hoorah's mishmash plumage appeared. It covered the nest. Something dropped. "Hoo-rah!" Then the bird was off again on its insatiable mission of collection.

The thing most recently deposited stirred. It flung limbs about, and a curtain of hair. It righted itself and sat up.

Dor stared.

It was a woman. A young, pretty, girl-type maiden.

Chapter 4. Monsters

As the big bird disappeared, Jumper climbed back over the side of the nest. The girl spied him and screamed. She flung her hair about. She kicked her feet. She was a healthy young thing with a penetrating scream, marvelous blond tresses, and extremely well-formed legs.

"It's all right!" Dor cried, not certain whether he was thinking more of the situation, which was hardly all right, or of her exposed legs, which were more than all right. This body really noticed such things! "He's a friend! Don't bring back the Hoorah!"

The maiden's head snapped about to face him. She seemed almost as alarmed by Dor as by the huge spider. "Who are you? How do you know?"

"I'm Dor," he said simply. Maybe one year he would learn how to introduce himself to a lady with flair! "The spider is my companion."

Distrustfully, she watched Jumper. "Ooo, ugly! I've never seen a monster like that before. I think I'd rather be eaten by the bird. At least it's familiar."

"Jumper's not ugly! He doesn't eat people. They don't taste good."

She whirled to face him again, and once more her golden hair flung out in a spiral swirl. She looked suddenly familiar. But he was sure he had not seen her here before; he had encountered no girls here in the past. "How does he know?"

"We were attacked by a band of goblins. He tasted one."

"Goblins! They aren't real people! Of course they taste bad!"

"How do you know?" Dor countered, using her own query.

"It just stands to reason that a sweet maid like me tastes better than any old messy goblin!"

Dor found it hard to refute that logic. Certainly he would rather kiss her than a goblin.

Now what had put that thought in his mind?

"I am unable to follow your full dialogue," Jumper said. "But I gather the female of your species does not trust me."

"Right on target, monster!" she agreed.

"Uh, you do take some getting used to," Dor said. "You, uh, appear as strange to her as she does to you."

Jumper was startled. "It could not be that extreme!"

"Well, maybe I exaggerated." Diplomacy or truth?

"The thing actually talks!" the girl exclaimed. "Only it throws its voice to your shoulder."

"Well, that's hard to explain—"

"Nevertheless," Jumper cut in, "we had better vacate this nest quickly."

"Why does its voice come from your shoulder?" the girl insisted. Evidently she had a lively curiosity.

"I made a translation web," Dor explained. "Jumper's voice is the chitter. You should at least say hello to him."

"Oh." She leaned forward, giving Dor his first conscious peek down into a buxom bodice. Stunned, he stood stock-still. "Hello, Jumper-monster," she said to the web.

"Wow!" said the web. "Get a load of that—"

"You don't have to speak to the web," Dor said quickly, though he was sorry to undeceive her. Now she wouldn't be leaning at him any more. A background region of his mind wondered why a spiderweb would care to remark on the particular view offered, as it was surely not of interest to spiders.

". . . yellow silk," the web finished, even as Dor's guilty thought progressed. Oh—of course. Spiders were interested in silk, and colored silk would be a novelty.

"That's hair, not silk," he murmured. Then, more loudly to the girl: "Jumper understands you without the web."

"About vacating the nest—" Jumper chittered.

"Yes! Can you make another dragline for her?"

"Immediately." Jumper moved toward the girl.

"Eeeeek!" she screamed, flinging her silk about. "The hairy monster's going to eat me!"

"Be quiet!" Dor snapped, losing patience despite the impression her attributes had made on him. Either this body had singular appetites, or he had been missing a whole dimension of experience all his prior life! "You'll bring back the Hoorah."

She quietened reluctantly. "I won't let that thing near me."

She would talk to the spider, but not cooperate with him. She seemed almost as juvenile as Dor himself. "I can't carry you down," he told her. "I'm only—" He broke off. He was no longer a twelve-year-old boy in body, but a powerful man. "Well, maybe I can. Jumper, will the line hold two of us?"

"Indubitably. I have only to make a stronger cable," the spider chittered, his spinnerets already at work. In moments he had made a new harness for Dor, with a stronger cable.

Meanwhile the girl, with her irrepressible feminine curiosity, was exploring the nest. "Oh, jewels!" she exclaimed, clapping her cute little hands together excitedly.

"What kind?" Dor asked, wondering whether they would be useful for buying food or shelter later on. Jewels were not nearly as valuable in Xanth as in Mundania, but many people liked them.

"We are cultured pearls," several voices chorused. "Most refined and well mannered, with our lineage dating back to the emperor of all oysters. We are aristocrats among jewels."

"Oh, I'll take you!" the girl cried, seeming unsurprised at their speech. She scooped them up and filled her apron pockets.

Now they heard the Hoorah returning. Dor put his left arm around the girl's slender and supple waist and lifted her easily off her feet; what power this body had! Maybe it wasn't his muscles so much as her lack of mass; she was featherlike though firmly fleshed. There must be a special magic about girls like this, he thought, to make them full yet light.

He leaped over the edge of the nest, trusting Jumper's dragline to preserve them from a fall. The girl screamed, kicked her feet, and flung her hair in his face. "Quiet," he said around a mouthful of golden strands, holding her close so she wouldn't wriggle loose. He was feeling very heroistic at the moment.

The line went taut. It was springy, like a big rubber band from a rubber tree. They bounced back up almost to the base of the nest. The girl jiggled against him, all soft and intriguing in a fashion he would have liked to understand better. But he had no chance to explore that matter at the moment.

As they steadied, Jumper came down to join them. He did not jerk and bounce; he glided to a controlled halt beside them, for he was paying out his dragline as he went. "I have set up a pulley," he chittered. "My weight will counterbalance yours—but the two of you weigh more than I do, so I'm depending on friction to keep it slow."

Dor did not follow all of that. But if the magic called friction could safely lower them, good. They were all three descending at a fair but not frightening rate, and that was satisfactory. The branches of the huge tree were passing interminably, its layers of leaves concealing them from the nest.

A shadow fell across them. It was the Hoorah bird, circling down to spy out its lost artifacts. In a moment it would spot them, for they were in a slanting sunbeam.

Dor tried to draw his sword with his right hand, but this was difficult while he was supporting the girl with his left arm. Light she was, but she seemed to be getting heavier. Again, he worried about severing his own lifeline as the blade emerged from its scabbard.

"Hang still!" Jumper chittered. "A still target is very hard to locate."

Dor gave up on the sword. But they couldn't hang still. Dor and the girl weighed too much; they kept dropping, while the spider rose, hauled by the magic of the pulley. Jumper grabbed on to a branch with several legs, did something, and scurried along the branch toward the trunk of the tree. Dor and the girl did not fall; Dor realized that Jumper had fastened his line to the branch, halting the pulley action.

That left Dor and the terrified girl dangling like bait for the Hoorah. She was squirming, twitching her silk, and kicking her feet uselessly. His left arm, despite its mighty thews, was tiring. Pretty soon he'd be down to one thew, then none. Girls certainly were a nuisance at times.

The Hoorah spied the motion. "Hoo-rah!" it cried, and angled down.

Suddenly a green and gray-brown shape hurtled at them from the side. It seemed to have a mustached face on it. The girl screamed piercingly and flung out her arms, banging Dor's nose with her cute elbow. He almost dropped her. But the shape was now in contact with them, its momentum shoving them all to the side, swinging on the line until they came up against a leafy branch. The hurtling Hoorah missed, swerving barely in time to avoid smacking its beak into the main tree trunk.

"I will attempt to distract it," Jumper chittered—for of course he was the one who had rescued them. It was the variegated abdomen face-pattern Dor had noted. "I have tied you to this branch; the bird may not see you if you remain motionless and silent."

Fat chance! The girl inhaled and opened her pretty mouth to scream again. Dor put his big ugly right hand across it. "Quiet!"

"Mmmph mmmph, you mmmph!" she mmmphed, one eye above his hand filling with anger while the other eye retained its terror. He hoped she wasn't saying the unmaidlike thing he feared she was saying; it would be detrimental to her image.

"Well, if you'd only accepted a dragline for yourself, we wouldn't be in this picklement." Dor whispered back. But he knew that was unfair. The Hoorah had returned too soon, regardless.

"Come and get me, featherbrain," Jumper chittered from another branch. Of course the translation came from Dor's shoulder. But the spider also waved his forelegs, and that attracted the bird's attention. The Hoorah zoomed toward that branch—and the spider sprang twenty feet to another, chittering vehemently. Dor knew the big bird could not understand Jumper's actual words, but the tone was unmistakable.

Then again, why shouldn't birds comprehend spider language? The two species interacted often enough. Which illustrated the supreme courage Jumper was displaying, for the thing he most feared was birds. To save his friend and a stranger, the spider was baiting his personal nightmare menace.

"You can do better than that, squawkhead!" Jumper chittered. And jumped again, as the bird wheeled in the air. The Hoorah was remarkably agile for its size.

After several futile passes, the bird realized that Jumper was too quick for it to catch. Just as well, as the translations of the spider's insults were turning the girl's ears a delicate shell-pink. The Hoorah looked around, casting about for the other prey. Fortunately all they had to do was remain still and silent.

Dor, trying to make his fatigued left arm more comfortable, shifted his hold slightly. The girl slipped down a bit, her bosom getting squeezed. She screamed, almost without taking a breath, catching him off guard.

Oh, no! Dor, needing his right hand to help hold on to the branch, had uncovered her mouth. Foolish mistake!

The Hoorah oriented immediately on the sound. It zoomed directly toward them. Jumper was behind it, unable to distract it this time. The Hoorah knew easy prey when it found it.

With the inspiration of desperation, Dor grabbed with his right hand at the girl's clothing, questing for her pockets. Though she wore a showy dress that was cut high at the knees and low at the bodice, her apron covered much of that, and was utilitarian.

She screamed as if attacked—not unreasonably, in this case—but he continued until he found what he was looking for: the cultured pearls she had picked up from the nest. "What is your pet peeve?" he demanded as he flipped the first pearl into the air.

"I don't make pets of peeves!" the pearl retorted. "But I hate people who drop me off branches!" It dropped out of sight—and the Hoorah, tracing the sound of its voice, followed it down.

Jumper half-bounded, half-swung across to them.

"Marvelous ploy!" he chittered. "Throw the next to the side, and I will lower you quietly to the ground."

"Right!" Dor agreed. He faced the girl. "And don't scream," he warned.

She inhaled to scream.

"Or I'll tickle you!" he threatened.

That got her. Meekly she let herself deflate. She even handed him a pearl from her apron breast pocket, so he wouldn't have to dig it out himself. That was almost more cooperative than he liked.

"And what is your peeve?" he inquired of the pearl, and hurled it to the side.

"I hate uncultured people who can't appreciate cultured pearls!" it cried.

They heard a "Hoo-rah!" in the distance as the bird went after it. The bird certainly appreciated cultured pearls!

By the time they reached the ground, they were out of pearls—but also out of peril. They had lost the bird. Dor picked up a few sticks of wood for emergency use in case the Hoorah came near again, and the three of them hurried away.

"You see!" the ring on Dor's finger cried. "I granted your wish! You are safe on the ground!"

"I guess I can't argue with that," Dor agreed. But he maintained a healthy private reservation.

Dor judged they were now fairly close to Castle Roogna, since the Hoorah bird had carried them in the right direction, but the day was waning and he didn't want to hurry lest they fall into another trap. So they foraged for supper, locating a few marshmallow bushes and an apple pine and some iced-tea leaves. Jumper tried a bit of pine apple, but declared he preferred crustaceans. The girl had finally come to accept the big spider as a companion, and even allowed Jumper to string her up for the night. She was, she confessed daintily, afraid of bugs and things on the ground, and at the moment was none too keen on birds in trees either.

Thus the three of them hung comfortably from silken threads, safe from the predators above and below. There were advantages to the arachnid mode, Dor decided.

Jumper fell silent, no doubt already asleep and recuperating from his formidable exertions of the day. But Dor and the girl talked for a while, in low tones so as not to attract unwanted and/or hazardous attention.

"Where do you come from?" she inquired. "Where do you go?"

Dor answered as briefly as he could, omitting the details about his age and the relation of his world to hers. He told her he was from a strange land, like this one but far removed, and he had come here looking for the Zombie Master, who might help him obtain an elixir to help a friend. He made clear that Jumper was from that same land, and was his trusted friend. "After all, without Jumper, we would never have escaped from the Hoorah's nest."

Her story was as simple. "I am a maid of just barely maybe seventeen, from the West Stockade by the lovely seashore where the gaze-gourds grow, traveling to the new capital to seek my fortune. But when I crossed a high ridge—to stay away from the tiger lilies, you know, because they have a special taste for sweet young things, those lilies of the valley—the Hoorah bird spotted me, and though I screamed and flung my hair about and kicked my feet exactly as a maid is supposed to—well, you know the rest."

"We can help you get to Castle Roogna, since we're going there too," Dor said. It probably was not much of a coincidence, since the Castle was the social and magical center of Xanth; no doubt everyone who was anyone went to Castle Roogna.

She clapped her hands in that girlishly cute way she had, and jiggled in her harness with that womanly provocation she also had. "Oh, *would* you? That's wonderful!"

Dor was pleased too. She was delightful company! "But what will you do at Castle Roogna?" he inquired.

"I hope to find employment as a chambermaid, there to encounter completely by surprise some handsome courtier who will love me madly and take me away from it all, and I shall live happily ever after in his rich house when all I ever expected was a life of chambermaiding."

Dor, even in his youth, knew this to be a simplistic ambition. Why should a courtier elect to marry a common chambermaid? But he had sense enough not to disparage her ambition. Instead he remembered a question he had overlooked before, perhaps because he had been looking at other aspects of her nature. Those aspects she kicked and bounced and flung about so freely. "What is your name?"

"Oh." She laughed muscically, making a token kick and bounce and fling. "Didn't I tell you? I am Millie the maid."

Dor hung there, stunned. Of course! He should have recognized her. Twelve years younger—eight hundred twelve years younger!—herself as she was before he ever had known her, young and inexperienced and hopeful, and above all innocent. Stripped of the grim experience of eight centuries of ghosthood, a naïve cute girl hardly older than himself.

Hardly older? Five years older—and they were monstrous years. She was every resilient inch a woman, while he was but a boy of— "I wish I were a man!" he murmured.

"Done!" the ring on his finger cried. "I now pronouce you man."

"What?" Millie inquired gently.

Of course she didn't recognize him. Not only was he not in his own body, he wouldn't even exist for eight hundred years. "Uh, I was just wishing—"

"Yes?" the ring said eagerly.

Dor bopped his head. "That I could get rid of this infernal flea that keeps biting me, and get some sleep," he said.

"Now wait," the ring protested. "I can do anything, but you're asking for two things at once!"

"I'll settle for the sleep," Dor said.

Before long, the sleep came to pass. He dreamed of standing near a huge brightly bedecked gumball bush, wanting a gumball awful bad, especially a golden one close by, but restrained by the magic curse that might be protecting the fruits. It was not merely that he wasn't certain how to pluck a gumball without invoking the curse, it was that the bush was in the yard of another house, so that he really was not sure he had the right to pluck from it. It was a tall bush, with its luscious fruits dangling out of his normal reach. But he was up on magic stilts, very long and strong, so that now he stood tall enough to reach the delightful golden globe easily. If only he dared. If only he should.

More than that, he had never as a child liked gumballs that well. He had seen others liking them, but he had not understood why. Now he wanted one so badly—and was suspicious of this change in himself.

Dor woke in turmoil. Jumper was hanging near him, several eyes watching him with concern. "Are you well, friend Dor-man?" the spider chittered.

"I—just a nightmare," Dor said uncertainly.

"This is an illness?"

"There are magic horses, half illusion, who chase people at night, scaring them," Dor explained. "So when a person experiences something frightening at night, he calls it a night-stallion or a night-mare."

"Ah, figurative," Jumper agreed once he understood. "You dreamed of such a horse. A mare—a female."

"Yes. A—a horse of another color. I—I wanted to ride that mare very much, but wasn't sure I could stay on that golden mount—oh, I don't know what I'm trying to say!"

Jumper considered. "Please do not be offended, friend. I do not as yet comprehend your language well, or your nature. Are you by chance a juvenile? A young entity?"

"Yes," Dor replied tightly. The spider seemed to understand him well enough.

"One beneath the normal breeding age of your species?"

"Yes."

"And this sleeping female of your kind, her with the golden silk—she is mature?"

"I—yes."

"I believe your problem is natural. You have merely to wait until you mature, then you will suffer no further confusion."

"But suppose she—she belongs to another—?"

"There is no ownership in this sort of thing," Jumper assured him. "She will indicate whether she finds you suitable."

"Suitable for what?"

Jumper made a chitter-chuckle. "That will become apparent at the appropriate occasion."

"You sound like King Trent!" Dor said accusingly.

"Who I presume is a mature male of your species—perhaps of middle age."

On target. Despite his confusion and frustration, Dor was glad to have such a person with him. The outer form hardly mattered.

Millie stirred, and Dor suffered a sudden eagerness to halt this conversation. It was dawn, anyway; time to eat and resume the trek to Castle Roogna.

Dor got bearings from the local sticks and stones, and they set off for the Castle. But this time they encountered a large river. Dor didn't remember this from his own time—but of course the channel could have shifted in eight hundred years, and with the charmed paths he might not have noticed a river anyway. The water was quite specific in answer to Dor's question: the Castle lay beyond the far side, and there was no convenient way across the water.

"I wish I had a good way to pass this river," Dor said.

"I'll see to it," the ring on his finger said. "Just give me a little time. I got you to sleep last night, didn't I? You have to have patience, you know."

"I know," Dor said with half a smile.

"Gnome wasn't built in a day, after all."

"I could balloon us across," Jumper offered.

"Last time we ballooned, the Hoorah nabbed us," Dor pointed out. "And if it hadn't, we would probably have been blown right out of Xanth anyway. I don't want to risk that again."

"Ballooning is somewhat at the mercy of the winds," the spider agreed. "I had intended to fasten an anchor to the ground, before, so that we could not be blown too far and could always return to our starting point if necessary, but I admit I reckoned without the big bird. I had somehow thought no other creatures had been expanded in size the way I have been—in retrospect, a foolish assumption. I agree: ballooning is best saved for an emergency."

"In my stockade, we use boats to cross water," Millie offered. "With spells to ward off water monsters."

"Do you know how to make a boat?" Jumper chittered. The question was directed at Millie, but the web on Dor's shoulder translated it anyway. Inanimate objects tended to become more accommodating when they associated with him for prolonged periods.

"No," she said. "I am a maid."

And maids did not do anything useful? Maybe she simply meant she was not involved in masculine pursuits. "Do you know the anti-water-monster spells?" Dor asked her.

"No, only our stockade monster-speller can do those. That's his talent."

Dor exchanged glances with several of Jumper's eyes. The girl was nice, but she wasn't much help.

"I believe your sword would proffer some discouragement to water predators," Jumper chittered. "I could loop their extremities with silk, and render them vulnerable to your sharp edge."

Dor did not relish the prospect of battling water monsters, but recognized the feasibility of the spider's proposal. "Except the boat. We still need that," he pointed out, almost with relief.

"I think I might fashion a craft from silk," Jumper chittered. "In fact I can walk on water sometimes, when the surface is calm. I might tow the boat across."

"Why not just go across and string up one of your lines?" Millie inquired. "Then you could draw us across, as you drew us up into the tree last night."

"Excellent notion!" the spider agreed. "If I could get across without attracting attention—"

"Maybe we could set up a distraction," Dor suggested. "So they wouldn't notice you."

They discussed details, then proceeded. They gathered a number of sticks and stones for Dor to talk to, which could serve as one type of distraction, and located a few stink bugs, which they hoped would be another type of distraction. Stink bugs smelled mild enough when handled gently, but exploded with stench when abused. Jumper fashioned several stout ropes of silk, attaching one to an overhanging tree and leaving the others for the people to use as lariats.

When all was ready, Jumper set off across the water. His eight feet made dents in the surface but did not break through; actually he was quite fleet, almost skating across.

But all too soon there was a ripple behind him. A great ugly snout broke the surface: a serpentine river monster. All they could see was part of the head, but it was huge. No small boat would have been safe—and neither was Jumper. This was the type of monster much in demand for moat service.

"Hey, snoutnose!" Dor called. He saw an ear twitch on the monster's head, but its glassy eye remained fixed on the spider. More distraction was needed, and quickly!

Dor took a stick of wood, as large as he thought he could throw that distance. "Stick, I'll bet you can't insult that monster enough to make it chase you." Insults seemed to be a prime tool for making creatures react.

"Oh yeah?" the stick retorted. "Just try me, dirtface!"

Dor glanced into the surface of the water. Sure enough, he had dirt smeared across his face. But that would have to wait. "Go to it!" he said, and hurled the stick far out toward the monster.

The stick splashed just behind the great head: an almost perfect throw. Dor could never have done that in his own body! The monster whirled around, thinking it was an attack from behind. "Look at that snotty snoot!" the stick cried as it bobbled amidst its ripples. Water monsters, it was said, were quite vain about their ferocious faces. "If I had a mug like that, I'd bury it in green mud!"

The monster lifted its head high. "Honk!" it exclaimed angrily. It could not talk the human language, but evidently understood it well enough. Most monsters who hoped for moat employment made it a point to develop some acquaintance with the employers' mode of communication.

"Better blow out that tube before you choke," the stick said, warming up to its task. "I haven't heard a noise like that since a bull croak smacked into my tree and brained out its brainless brains."

The monster made a strike at the stick. The diversion was working! But already Dor saw other ripples following, the pattern of them orienting on Jumper. The spider was moving rapidly, but not fast enough to escape these creatures. Time for the next ploy.

Dor grabbed the rope strung to the tree, hauled himself up, and swung out over the water. "Hoorah!" he cried.

Heads popped out of the water, now orienting on him. Toothy, glared-eyed excrescences on sinuous necks. "You can't catch me, deadpans!" he cried. Deadpans were creatures who lurked around cooking fires, associating with slinky copperheads and similar ilk, and had the ugliest faces found in nature.

Several of the monsters were quite willing to try. White wakes appeared as the heads coursed forward.

Dor hastily swung back and jumped to shore. "How many monster *are* there?" he demanded, amazed at the number.

"Always one more than you can handle," the water replied. "That's standard operating procedure."

That made magical sense. Too bad he hadn't realized it before Jumper exposed himself on the water. But how, then, could he distract them all?

He had to try, lest Jumper be caught. It was not as if he were a garden-variety traveler; he was a Magician.

Dor picked up a stink bug, rolled it into a ball, and threw it as hard as he could toward the skating spider. Jumper was now over halfway across the river, and making good time. The bug, angered by this treatment, bounced on the water behind the spider and burst into stench. Dor could not smell it from this distance, but he heard the monsters in that vicinity choking and retreating. Dor threw three more bugs, just to be sure; then Jumper was out of range.

Millie was doing her part. She was capering beside

the water and waving her hands and calling out to the monsters. Her flesh bounced in what had to be, to a monster, the tastiest manner. Even Dor felt like taking a bite. Or something. The trouble was, the monsters were responding too well. "Get back, Millie!" Dor cried. "They have long necks!"

Indeed they did. One monster shot its head forward, jaws gaping. Slaver sprayed out past the projecting tiers of teeth. Glints shot from the cruel eyes.

Millie, abruptly aware of her peril, stood frozen. What, no kicks and screams? Dor asked himself. Maybe it was because she had been kicking and screaming, in a manner, before, so that would have represented no contrast.

Dor's fingers scrambled over his shoulder for his sword as he leaped to intercept the monster. He jerked at the hilt—and it snagged, wrenching out of his hand as the sword cleared the scabbard. The blade tumbled to the ground. "Oh, no!" the sword moaned. Dor found himself striking a dramatic pose before the monster, sword hand upraised—and empty.

The monster did a double take. Then it started to chuckle. Dor somewhat sheepishly bent to retrieve his weapon—and of course the toothed snout dived down to chomp him.

Dor leaped up, legs spreading to vault the descending head, and boxed the monster on one ear with his left fist. Then he landed, whirled, and brought his sword to bear. He did not strike; he had the gleaming blade poised before one of the monster's eyeballs. The gleam of the blade bounced the eye's glints away harmlessly.

"Now I spare you, where you did not spare me," he said. "Do you take that as a signal of weakness?"

The eye stared into the swordpoint. The monster's head quivered in negation as it slid back. Dor strode forward, keeping his point near the eye. In a moment the head disappeared beneath the surface of the river.

The other monsters, noting this, did not advance. They assumed Dor had some powerful magic. And he realized this truth, which his body had known: deal with the leader, and you have dealt with the followers.

"Why, that's the bravest thing I ever saw!" Millie

exclaimed, clapping her hands again. She did that often now, and it sent most interesting ripples through her torso—yet Dor had never seen her do it in his own world. What had changed?

Eight hundred years of half-life: That was what had changed her. Most of her maidenly bounce had been pressed out of her by that tragedy.

But more immediately: what had changed in him? He should never have had the nerve to face up to a full-fledged river monster, let alone cow it into retreat. Yet he had done so unthinkingly, when Millie was threatened. Maybe it was his body taking over again, reacting in a conditioned way, even to the extent of facing down a monster in such a way as to abate the whole fleet of monsters at once.

What kind of a man had this body been, before Dor arrived? Where had he gone? Would he return when Dor went back to his own world? He had thought this body was stupid, but now there seemed to be considerable compensations. Maybe the body had never needed to worry too much about danger ahead, because of its competence in handling that danger when it faced it. This body, without Dor present to mess it up, could have handled that whole goblin band alone.

The flea bit him just over the right ear. Dor almost sliced his own head off, trying to swat it with his sword hand. Here he could face down a monster, but could not get rid of a single pesky flea! One of these days he was going to find a flea-repellent plant.

"Look—the spider has made it across!" Millie cried.

So he had. Their distractions had been sufficient after all. Maybe there had been one more monster than Dor could handle—but he had not been alone.

Relieved, Dor went to the tree where the crossing cable had been anchored. Already it was tightening, lifting out of the water, as Jumper labored at the other end to draw it taut. The spider could exert a lot of force on a line, achieving special leverage with his eight legs. Soon the cable stretched from tree to tree, sagging only slightly in the middle of the river, as nearly as Dor could see. It was an extremely stout line, compared to Jumper's usual, but still it tended to disappear in the distance.

"Now we can hand-walk it across," Dor said. And asked himself: *We can?*

"Maybe you can," Millie said. "You're a big brave strong rugged man. But I am a little diffident weak soft maid. I could never—"

If only she knew Dor's true state! "Very well; I'll carry you." Dor picked her up, set her in the tree at the end of the line, then hauled himself up with a convulsive heave of his thews. He placed his boots on the cable, found his balance, and picked Millie up in his arms.

"What are you doing?" she cried, alarmed. She kicked her feet. Dor noticed again how dainty her feet were, and how cutely they kicked. There was an art to foot-kicking, and she had it; the legs had to flex at the knees, and the feet had to swing just so, not so fast that the legs could not be seen clearly. "You can't possibly keep your balance."

"That so?" he inquired. "Then I suppose we will fall into the river and have to swim after all." He walked forward, balancing.

"Are you crazy?" she demanded, horrified. And he echoed to himself: *Am I crazy?* He knew such a feat of balancing was impossible without magical assistance —yet here was this body, doing it.

What superb equilibrium this barbarian body had! No wonder Mundane Waves had conquered Xanth over and over, despite all the power of magic brought to bear against them.

Millie stopped kicking, afraid she would make him lose his balance. Dor marveled as he went; had he realized the potentialities of this body before, he would have been much less afraid of heights. He realized now that his concern about certain things, such as taking a fall, was not inherent, but more a product of his frailty of physique. When he had confidence in his abilities, fear faded. So, to that extent, the body of a man did make him more of a man in spirit too.

Then more trouble came. Big, ugly shapes flitted out of the forest to hover above the river. They were too solid for birds; their heads were man-sized.

The grotesque flock milled for a moment, then spied

the figures on the cable. "Heee!" one cried, and they all wheeled and bore on Dor.

"Harpies!" Millie cried. "Oh, we are undone!"

Dor wanted to reach for his sword, but couldn't; both arms were taken with the girl. The river monsters were lurking at a discreet distance; they were cautious about approaching this formidable man while he kept his feet, but might have second thoughts if he were floundering in the water—as he soon would be if he grabbed for his sword, dropped Millie, and lost his balance. He was helpless.

The harpies closed on them, their dirty wings wafting a foul odor down. Dirty birds indeed! They were greasy avians with the heads and breasts of women. Not pretty faces and breasts like Millie's; their visages were witchlike and their dugs grotesque. Their voices were raucous. Their birdy legs had great ugly chipped talons.

"What a find, sisters!" the leader harpy screeched. "Take them, take them!"

The flock plunged down, screaming with glee. Claws closed as half a dozen foul creatures clutched at Millie, who screamed and kicked and flung her tresses about to no avail, as usual. She was torn from Dor's grasp and lifted into the sky.

Then about ten more harpies converged on Dor himself. Their talons closed on his forearms, his biceps, his calves, thighs, hair, and belt. The claws were rounded, without cutting edges, so did not hurt him so long as the points were clear; they merely clamped onto his appendages like manacles. The grimy wings beat powerfully, and he was borne upward in their putrid midst.

They carried him across the water and into the forest at treetop level, so that his sagging posterior almost brushed the highest fronds. They hoisted him on through the forest until they reached a great cleft in the ground, where they glided down. This was not the Gap; it was far smaller, more on a par with the crevasse he had entered on the magic carpet. Could it be the same one? No; the location was wrong, and the configuration different. Dug into the clifflike sides of this one were grubby holes: caves made by the harpies for their nests. They bore him down into the largest cave and dumped him unceremoniously on the filthy floor.

Dor got up, brushing dirt off his body. Millie was not here; they must have taken her to another cave. Unless there were connecting passages—which seemed unlikely, since these creatures flew better than they walked—he would be unable to reach her by foot. He retained his sword, but could not hope to slay all the harpies in this degenerate harpy city; they would overwhelm him. Either they knew this and so had contempt for his blade, or they simply hadn't recognized it in its mundane sheath across his back. The latter seemed more likely. At last he was beginning to appreciate that location! So it would be foolish to betray his possession of the weapon by making a premature move. He would have to wait and see what they wanted from him, just in case it wasn't a quick meal of his flesh, and fight only as a last resort.

One thing about being a hero: the threats were larger than life, and the glooms gloomier. In his real life he would never have gotten into a situation like this!

The harpies scuttled back, leaving one especially hideous crone before him. "My, aren't you the husky one!" she cackled, her ropy hair flying about wildly as she pecked her head forward, chickenlike. Maybe those were feathers on her pate; it was hard to tell under the muck. "Good teeth, good muscle tone, handsome—yes, you'll do just fine!"

"Just fine for what?" Dor demanded with more belligerence than he felt. He was scared.

"Just fine for my chick," the old hen clucked. "Heavenly Helen, Harpy Queen. We need a man on alternate generations, a vulture the other times."

"What have you done with—the girl?" Dor decided not to name her, lest the polluted monsters assume he was closer to her, or she to him, than he/she was and try to coerce him by torturing her. He knew monsters would do this sort of thing. That was the nature of monsters, after all.

He was quite right. "She will be cooked upon a fire of dung for supper," the canny old bird screeched gleefully. "She's such a delectable morsel! Unless you do as we demand."

"But you haven't told me what you demand."

"Haven't we now?" The dirty bird cocked her head at him cannily. "Are you trying to feign innocence? That will get you nowhere, my pretty man-type male buck! Into the nest with you!" And she partly spread her awful wings and advanced, her stink smiting him anew. Dor backed off—and stumbled into an offshoot cave.

So there were interconnecting passages. This one was not large enough for him to stand in; it was more suitable for scuttling. So he scuttled around a bend, and the tunnel opened into a fair-sized chamber whose domed ceiling did permit him to climb back to his feet.

Another harpy faced him there—but what a difference there was! This was a young bird, with metallic sheen on her feathers, shiny brass claws, the face and breasts of a lovely maiden—and she was clean. Her hair was neatly brushed, each tress luxuriant; if there were any feathers in it, they were silken ones. She was the prettiest harpy Dor had ever seen or imagined.

"So you are the man Momma found for me," Helen Harpy murmured. Her voice was sultry, no screech.

Dor looked around. The chamber was bare except for the large nest in the center, formed of fluffy down feathers so that it sprang up like a magic bubble bath. The room opened out on the canyon—a sheer drop of a couple hundred feet. Even if he were able to navigate that, how could he rescue Millie? One could hardly climb a sheer rock face while screaming and kicking one's feet.

"I think I'm going to enjoy this," Helen murmured. "I had my doubts when Momma said she'd find me a man, but I did not know how fine a man she intended. I'm so glad I wasn't in the vulture generation, the way Momma was."

"Vulture?" Dor asked, casting about for some other exit. If he could sneak through a tunnel, find Millie—

"We're half-human, half-vulture," she explained. "Since there are no males of our species, we have to alternate."

Dor had not realized there were no male harpies.

Somehow he had supposed there were, in his day. But he had never looked into the matter. All he had ever actually seen were females; any males there were kept pretty much to themselves, making the females do the foraging. At any rate, this was not his present concern.

He had a bright idea. "Nest, what's the best way out of here?"

"Oblige the harpy," the nest replied, its down feathers wafting softly as it spoke. They were of pastel hues, pretty. "They hardly ever kill breeders, unless they're really hungry."

"I don't even know what the harpy wants!" Dor protested.

"Come here," the fair harpy murmured. "I'll show you what I want, you delightful hunk of man."

"I wish I were out of here," Dor muttered.

"I'm still working on the river crossing," the ring on his finger complained.

"What's that?" Helen asked, spreading her pretty wings a little. Her down feathers were as white as her breasts, and probably as soft.

"A magic ring. It grants wishes," Dor said, hoping this was not too great an exaggeration. Actually, he hadn't caught the ring failing; he just was never sure that its successes were by any agency of its own magic.

"Oh? I've always wanted one of those."

Dor pulled it off his finger. "You might as well have it; I just want to rescue Millie." Oops—he had said her name.

Helen snatched the proffered ring. Harpies were very good at snatching. "You're not a goblin spy, are you? We're at war with the goblins."

Dor hadn't known that. "I—we killed a number of goblins. A band of them attacked us."

"Good. The goblins are our mortal enemies."

Dor's curiosity was aroused. "Why? You're both monsters; I should think you'd get along together."

"We did, once, long ago. But the goblins did us the foulest of turns, so now we are at war with them."

Dor sat down on the edge of the nest. It was as soft and fluffy as it looked. "That's funny. I thought only my own kind waged wars."

"We're half your kind, you know," she said. She

seemed fairly nice as he got to know her. She smelled faintly of roses. Apparently it was only the old harpies who were so awful. "A lot of creatures are, like the centaurs, mer-folk, fauns, werewolves, sphinxes, and all—and they all inherited man's warlike propensities. The worst are the pseudo-men, like the trolls, ogres, elves, giants, and goblins. They all have armies and go on rampages of destruction periodically. How much better it would be if we half-humans had inherited your intelligence, curiosity, and artistry without your barbarity."

She was making increasing sense. "Maybe if you had inherited our other halves, so you had the heads of vultures and the hindquarters of people—"

She laughed musically. "It would have made breeding easier! But I'd rather have the intelligence, despite its flaws."

"What did the goblins do to the harpies?"

She sighed, breathing deeply. She had a most impressive human portion, that way, and Dor was glad it was the upper section she had inherited. "That's a long story, handsome man. Come, rest your head against my wing, and I'll preen the dirt from your face while I tell you."

That seemed harmless. He leaned back against her wing, and found it firm and smooth and slightly resilient, with a fresh feather smell.

"Way back when Xanth was new," she said in a dulcet narrative style, "and the creatures were experiencing the first great radiation of forms, becoming all the magical combinations we know today, we half-people felt an affinity for each other." She licked his cheek delicately with her tongue; about to protest, Dor realized that this was what she meant by preening. Well, he had agreed to it, and actually the sensation was not bad at all.

"The full-men from Mundania came in savage Waves, killing and destroying," she continued, giving his ear a little nip. "We half-people had to cooperate merely to survive. The goblins lived adjacent to we harpies—or is that us harpies? I never can remember —sometimes even sharing the same caves. They slept by day and foraged by night, while we foraged by day.

So our two species were able to use the same sleeping areas. But as our populations grew there was not enough room for us all." Her preening, fitted between words, had progressed to his mouth; her lips were remarkably soft and sweet as they traversed his own. If he hadn't known better, he might have thought this was a kiss.

"Some of our hens had to move out and build nests in trees," she continued, reaching the other side of his face. "They got to like that better, and still do perch in trees. But the goblins became covetous of our space, and reasoned that if there were fewer of us there would be room for more of them. So they conspired against our innocence. Their females, some of whom in those days were very comely, lured away our males, corrupting them with—with—" She paused, and her wing shuddered. This was evidently difficult for her. It was none too easy for Dor, either, because now her breast was against his cheek, as she strained to reach the far side of his neck. Somehow he found it difficult to concentrate on her words.

"With their arms and—and legs," Helen got out at last. "We had not been so long diverged from human beings that our males did not remember and lust after what they called real girls, though most human and humanoid women would not have anything to do with vulture tails. When the lady goblins became approachable—I would term them other than ladies, but I'm not supposed to know that sort of language—when these creatures beckoned our cocks—oh, males are such foolish things!"

"Right," Dor agreed, feeling pretty foolish himself, half-smothered between her neck and bosom. He knew better than to argue with the *really* foolish sex.

"And so we lost our cock-harpies, and our hens became soured. That's why we have a certain exaggerated reputation for being impolite to people. What's the use of trying, when there are no cocks to please?"

"But that was only one generation," Dor protested. "More cocks should have hatched in the next generation."

"No. There were no more eggs—no fertile ones. There had never been a great number of cocks—our kind hatched about five females for every male—and now there were none. Our hens were becoming old and bitter, unfulfilled. There's nothing so bitter as an old harpy with an empty nest."

"Yes, of course." She seemed finally to have completed the preening; he had no doubt his face was shiningly clean now. "But why didn't all the harpies die out, then?"

"We hens had to seek males of other species. We abhor the necessity—but our alternative is extinction. Since we derived originally from a cross between human and vulture—I understand that was quite a scene, there at the love spring—we have had to return to these sources to maintain our nature. There are some problems, however. The human and vulture males aren't inclined generally to mate with harpies, and we can't always get them to the love spring to make it happen—and when they do, the result is always a female chick. It seems only a harpy cock can generate males of our species. So we have become a flock of old hens."

That was some history! Dor had heard about the nefarious love springs, where diverse creatures innocently drank, then plunged into love with the next creature of the opposite sex they met. Much of the population of Xanth was the fault of such springs, producing the remarkable crossbreeds that thereafter bred true. Fortunately the love-water had to be fresh, or it lost its potency; otherwise people would be endlessly slipping it into the cups of their friends as practical jokes. But he could see how this would create a problem for the harpies, who could not always carry a potential mate to the spring, or make him drink from it.

Now Helen's whole body shook with rage, and her voice took on a little of the tone of the older hens. "And this is what the cursed goblins did to us, and why we hate them and war against them. We want to kill off all *their* males, as they did ours. We shall fight until we have our vengeance for the horrible wrong they did us. Already we are massing our armies and gathering our allies among the winged kinds, and we shall wreak a fittingly horrible vengeance by scratching the goblin nation from the fair face of Xanth!"

By this time Dor had fairly well grasped the purpose for which he had been brought here. "I, uh, I sympathize with your predicament. But I can't really help you. I'm too young; I'm not a man yet."

She drew back and twisted her head to look at him, her large eyes larger yet. "You certainly look like a man."

"I got big quite suddenly. I'm really twelve years old. That's not much for my kind. I just want to help my friend Millie."

She considered momentarily. "Twelve years old. That just might be statutory seduction. Very well. I'll accept the ring you offered, in lieu of—of the other. Maybe it can wish me a fertile egg."

"I can! I can!" the ring exclaimed eagerly.

"I didn't really want to do this anyhow," Helen said as she screwed the ring onto her largest claw. She had merely held it, up till now. "Momma insisted, that's all. You can have the girl, though at your age I really don't know what you'll do with her. She's four caves to the right."

"Uh, thank you," Dor said. "Won't your mother object— I mean, if I just walk out?"

"Not if I don't squawk. And I won't squawk if the ring works okay."

"But that ring takes time to operate, even if—"

"Oh, go ahead. Can't you see I'm trying to give you a break?"

Dor went ahead. He wasn't sure how long she would have patience with the ring, or whether she would simply change her mind. Of course it was always possible that the ring really could produce. How nice for the harpies if it could give them a male chick! But meanwhile, he didn't want to waste time.

The old harridan eyed him suspiciously, but did not challenge him. He counted four subcaves to the right and went in. Sure enough, there was Millie, disheveled but intact. "Oh, Dor!" she cried. "I knew you'd rescue me!"

"I haven't rescued you yet," he warned her. "I traded my wishing ring to get to you."

"Then we'd better get out of here in a hurry! That ring couldn't wish itself out of a dream."

Why would it want to? he wondered. He checked the cave exit. Like the other, it opened onto a formidable drop. "I don't think we can just walk out. I don't think there are any exits that don't require flying. That's why the harpies aren't worried about us escaping."

"They—they were threatening to cook me for supper. I'd rather jump, than—"

"That was just to get me to cooperate," Dor said. Yet he had the grisly fear that it had been no bluff. Why should they have told *her* the threat, when he wasn't there to hear? The harpies were not nice creatures.

"To cooperate? What did they want from you?"

"A service I couldn't perform." Though this body of his had masculine capabilities and probably could— no, that wasn't the point.

Millie looked at his face. "It's clean!" she exclaimed.

"I, uh, had it washed."

Her eyes narrowed. "About that service—are you *sure*—?"

Damn that female intuition! Dor kneeled by the exit hole, feeling around it with his fingers. "Maybe there are handholds or something."

There weren't. The face of the cliff was as hard and smooth as glass, and the drop looked horrendous. He saw harpies flitting from other caves, coming and going, always flying. No hope there!

Even if there had been handholds, they would have required both of his hands. He would have been unable to hold on to Millie with one, and she would have screamed and kicked her feet and flung her hair about and fallen to her death the moment she attempted to make such a climb by herself. She was a delectable female, but just not much use at man-business.

Not that he could make any such claim himself, after that session with Heavenly Helen Harpy.

Helen had said that the harpies had once shared quarters with the goblins. The goblins did not fly, and he doubted they could climb well enough to handle this sheer cliff. If they had shared these caves, there had to be footpaths to them, somewhere. Maybe these had been cemented over, after the goblins had been driven out. "Walls, do any of you conceal goblin tunnels?" he asked.

"Not me!" the walls chorused.

"You mean the goblins never used these caves?" Dor demanded, disappointed. Had Helen lied to him —or had she been referring to other caves, before the harpies moved here?

"Untrue," the walls said. "Goblins originally hollowed out these caves, hollowed and hallowed, before the war started."

"Then how did the goblins get in and out?"

"Through the ceilings, of course."

Dor clapped the heel of his hand to his forehead. Of course! One problem with questioning the inanimate was that the inanimate didn't have much imagination and tended to answer literally. He had really meant to question all the artifacts in and of this chamber, but he had only actually named the walls, so only they had responded. "Ceiling, do you conceal a goblin passage?"

"I do," the ceiling replied. "You could have saved a lot of trouble if you'd asked me first, instead of talking with those stupid walls."

"Why isn't it visible?"

"The harpies sealed it over with mud plaster and droppings. Everyone knows that."

"That's why the stink!" Millie cried. "They use their dung for building."

Dor drew his sword. "Tell me where to strike to free the passage," he said.

"Right here," the ceiling said at one side.

Dor dug his swordpoint in and twisted. A chunk of brown plaster dropped to the floor. He dug harder and gouged more out. Soon the passage opened. A draft of foul air washed down from the hole.

"What's that fresh smell?" a harpy voice screeched from the cavern hall.

"Fresh smell!" Dor exclaimed, almost choking on the stench. He and Millie had become more or less acclimatized to the odor pervading the caves, but now that the air was moving, his nostrils could not so readily filter it out. Yet perhaps this breeze was offensive to the harpies.

The old hen appeared in the entrance. "They're trying to sneak out the old goblin hole!" she screeched. "Stop them!"

Dor strode across to block her advance, sword held before him. Afoot, unable to spread her wings, the harpy was at a disadvantage, and had to retreat. "Climb up into the hole!" Dor cried to Millie. "Use the goblin passage to escape!"

Millie stared up into the blackness of the hole. "I'm afraid!" she cried. "There might be nickelpedes!"

That struck him. Nickelpedes were vicious insects five times as ferocious as centipedes, with pincers made of nickel. They attacked anything that moved in darkness.

Now more harpies were pressing close. They respected Dor's bared blade, but did not retreat farther than they had to. He could not swing freely in the passage, and didn't really want to shed their blood; after all, they were half-human, and it wasn't nice to kill females.

What was he going to do? With the harpies in front, and Millie balking, and an open cliff outside—in this situation he couldn't fool anyone by making the walls talk. He was stuck. He might hold off the dirty birds indefinitely, but he couldn't escape. Actually, if they started flying in from the cliffside, he would have trouble, because he couldn't very well cover both entrances, and Millie would not be much help. And in due course he and Millie would get tired, and hungry and thirsty, and would have to sleep. They would be captive again.

"Millie, you've got to get up that goblin passage!" he cried.

"No good, no good!" the harpies outside screeched. "We know where it goes, we're covering the exit. You can't escape!"

Then why were they telling him this? Easier to nab him at the goblin-tunnel exit. So they must be bluffing.

Then Millie screamed. Dor looked—and spied a huge hairy shape dropping out of the hole. Green eyes looked back at him. "Jumper!" How glad he was to see the big spider again!

"I could not place my lines," the spider chittered. "The lady-man-birds would have spied me on the face of the cliff. So I had to come in this way."

"But the harpies are watching the exit—"

"They are. But they did not follow me inside, because of the nickelpedes."

"But you—"

"Nickelpedes are pinching bugs. I was hungry anyway. They were delicious."

Naturally a spider would be able to handle big bugs! But the harpies were more formidable. "If we can't use the goblin tunnel—" Dor began.

Jumper fastened a line to Millie, and another to Dor. "I am generating sufficient lines to lower you to the bottom, but you will have to let yourselves down. I suggest you swing and slide so the birds will not be able to catch you readily."

"I can't do that!" Millie protested. "I don't have big arm muscles and things!"

Dor glanced at her. She was half right; she did lack big arm muscles, but she certainly had things. "I'll carry you again." He flicked his swordpoint, warning back the encroaching harpies.

"You'll need both arms to lower yourself," Jumper pointed out. "I will jump across and string a guideline. That way you can swing from the center of the cleft, not banging the walls. But you will be caught in mid-air."

"Can't be helped. You'll have to relax the guideline, so we can drop slowly lower. Just be sure that line is tight when we start."

"Yes, that is possible, though difficult. Your two weights will make a great deal of tension."

Dor poked at the witchly face of another harpy. "Millie can watch you, and tell me when it's ready. You wave to her from the far side."

"Correct." Jumper ran to the cliff opening and disappeared. There was an outcry from the harpies outside; they had never seen a jumping spider this size before, and were amazed and frightened.

"He's waving!" Millie cried.

That had been quick! Dor made a last poke at the harpies, whirled, grabbed her with his left arm, and flung himself out over the cliff. Then he remembered: he still had the sword in his right hand. He had forgotten to hang on to the line.

They plummeted toward the bottom of the chasm. Millie screamed and kicked her feet, and her hair smacked Dor's face.

Then, with a wrench, the line drew taut. He didn't need to hold on; Jumper had attached the cable to him, and tied the other end to the center of the trans-chasm cable. Once more the spider's mature foresight had saved him. Now Dor surmised when the attachment had been made; he had been distracted by the encroaching harpies, and had not noticed.

They were swinging down and across the chasm, bouncing slightly. The harpies were milling about, screaming, but not doing anything effective. They saw his waving sword.

Across they swung, grandly, almost colliding with the far wall. Jumper had kept the line short so they would not crash, but it was so close that Dor had to put his feet out and brake against the cliff, momentarily. Then they were swinging back. And forth again, in lessening arcs. As they came to rest, they were suspended about halfway down the depth of the chasm.

The harpies were beginning to organize, trying to catch Dor and Millie in their claws, as they had before.

But Dor had his sword out this time, and that made the difference. He waved it threateningly, and the harpies stayed just clear, screaming imprecations and losing feathers to the flashing tip of his weapon. It was hard for the dirty birds to match velocities with him, because of the swinging and bouncing. They were not, however, about to give up the pursuit.

Jumper, on the far side of the chasm, levered the line in the manner only he could do, and Dor and Millie descended. The rage of the harpies increased as the range increased. "Don't let them get to the bottom!" one cried. "The enemy is there!"

That hardly reassured Dor. What good would it be,

escaping one menace only to fall into the clutches of another? Well, he would have to worry about that in due course. At least the harpies hadn't thought to cut the trans-chasm cable. Or if they had thought, they had rejected the notion. They didn't want to kill Dor, for then he would certainly be useless to them. And Millie might not taste as good scraped up from the floor of the—but enough of such thoughts!

Now the base of the chasm was close. It was rocky and narrow and curvy, with holes and ridges. There seemed to be no way out, though this was uncertain since it twined out of sight in either direction.

As they swung lower, their orientation shifted, thanks to Jumper's maneuvering of the lines, so that now they were traveling along the cleft rather than across it. The harpies became more desperate. "Keep them away from ground!" the oldest and ugliest crone screeched. "Grab them! Snatch them! Lift them up. Drop the girl if you have to, we don't really need her, but save that buck!"

Dor swung his sword in increasingly desperate arcs, keeping them at bay, trying not to sever his own line. A talon lanced into his shoulder from behind, and great foul wings beat about his head. Millie screamed loudly and kicked her feet harder, and her hair formed a golden splay in a passing sunbeam. None of that helped. Dor aimed his sword up and thrust violently over his own head and down behind it. The point jammed into something. There was an ear-shattering scream that momentarily drowned out Millie's racket, and the talon released his shoulder. When he yanked the sword forward there was blood on the tip. He slashed in another circle, slicing feathers off the harpies in front. This violence sickened him, as it had when he fought the goblin band, but he kept on.

Suddenly the line dropped. Millie emitted a truly classic *Eeeeek!* as they fell—but the drop was very short. The mighty muscles and sinews of Dor's legs flexed expertly, breaking his fall, preserving his balance. He still had Millie; now he set her down gently. Her skirt and bodice had separated; Dor stared briefly, not realizing that they were different pieces, and she tucked them together self-consciously. At least she had stopped screaming.

A greenish shape dropped down beside them. "Sorry about that drop," Jumper chittered. "The harpies attacked me, and I had to move."

"Quite all right," Dor said. "You got us out of the harpy caves."

The harpies were still milling in the chasm, but no longer attacking. Jumper had plunged through them by surprise, using his dragline to brake at the last moment so he hadn't been hurt. What a marvelous thing that dragline was!

"Why are the harpies staying clear?" Millie asked.

It was a stupid question that like so many of its kind was not so stupid after all. The harpies were raucous, ugly, and evil-smelling—except for Helen—but not notably cowardly. Why were they afraid of this rocky path?

"One of them said something about the enemy down here," Dor said, remembering.

Millie screamed and pointed. Charging along the crevice-path was a contingent of goblins. No sooner feared than realized!

"I can hold them off," Dor said, striding forward with his sword leading. He didn't know whether this was his body's impulse or his own, but it was a fact that heroism was greatly facilitated by this powerful and well-coordinated physique. He *knew* it could devastate the little goblins, so he could afford to be bold. In his own twelve-year-old-sized body he would have been justifiably hesitant—and been thought a coward.

"I will lead the way out," Jumper chittered. "Perhaps there will be a slope I can enable you to climb, anchored by my lines. You can serve as rearguard."

They moved east, Dor walking backward so as to face the goblins without getting separated from his party. Obviously there would be no escape toward the goblin caves.

"It's just a small band," a harpy screeched. "We can handle them! Wipe them out, hens!"

Suddenly the harpies were plummeting toward the goblins. There was an instant melee punctuated by cries, screeches, groans, and rages. A cloud of feathers formed. Dor craned to see what was happening, but the dust stirred up to obscure it. They seemed to be fighting claw-to-nail, and it was not at all gentle.

"Trouble ahead!" Jumper chittered, and Millie screamed.

Dor glanced there—and saw more goblins charging from the west: a larger band. The spider stood to fight, though he could easily have jumped clear and clung to the cliff wall, saving himself. Except that he would not desert his friends. To no avail; the horde quickly overran him. Millie's piercing screams did not help her; a dozen goblin hands grasped her flailing arms and kicking feet and swirling tresses.

Dor whirled to help, but was already too late. Goblins grabbed him everywhere and bore him to the ground. He tried to kick his feet, but they were weighted by sheer mass of goblin. Just like that, they had been captured by the enemy.

All three of them were borne rapidly eastward, helpless. Suddenly a cave opened in the chasm wall, and the goblin band charged inside. It was dark here, and cool; Dor had the impression of descent, but couldn't be sure.

In due course they were brought to a room lit by guttering torches. This amazed Dor, for in his day goblins were desperately afraid of fire. But in his day goblins did not go abroad by day, either; in fact there were very few on the surface of Xanth at all. So this was another thing that had changed in eight centuries.

At one end of the chamber was a throne fashioned from a massive complex of stalagmites. It looked as if stone had run like hot wax, making layers and colored trails over itself until the whole had melded into this single twisted yet beautiful mass. An especially fierce-looking goblin bestrode it, his gnarled black legs almost merging with the stone.

"Well, trespassers!" the goblin chief cried angrily. "What made you suppose you could intrude on these our demesnes with impunity?"

Millie was quietly screaming and still trying to kick her feet; she didn't like the goblins' mottled hands on her legs. The goblins, however, seemed more interested than antipathetic. Jumper was chittering, but Dor knew the goblins could not comprehend that. So he stepped forward, breaking free of those who restrained him. "We did not mean to intrude, sir," he said. "We were only trying to escape the harpies." He had little hope of mercy from these monsters, but had to try.

The goblin's dusky brows lifted in astonishment. "You, a Man, call a goblin sir?"

"Well, if you'll tell me your proper title, I'll use it," Dor said nervously, though he tried to keep up a moderately bold front. Somewhere along the way his sword had been wrenched from his hand, and he felt naked without it.

"I am Subchief Craven, of the Chasm Clan of Goblins," the chief said. "However, sir will do nicely for an address."

Several goblin guards snickered. It was Craven, not Dor, who reacted to that derisive mirth. "You find the notion of sir humorous?" he demanded of them furiously.

"This is obviously no hero-man, but an impostor who knows naught of honor or combat," another goblin retorted. "His sir is so worthless as to be an insult."

"Oh yeah?" Craven cried. "We'll verify that, Crool. Will you meet him in honor challenge?"

Crool examined Dor, somewhat taken aback. But now the laughter of the clan was turning on him. "A single goblin does not meet a single human, even an impostor. The normal ratio is four or five to one."

"Then bring on your henchmen!" Craven cried. He turned to the guards at the other side of the hall. "Return to this man-warrior his sword. We shall discover whether his sir is valid."

What a devious and wonderful thing was pride, Dor thought. Now the subchief was rooting for the captive to prevail against the goblin kind.

Two goblins dashed up, carrying Dor's sword and lifting the hilt for him to take. He was glad to have it back, but did not like the prospective combat. He had not been at all pleased about the goblin-killing he had done before, and that misgiving grew as he observed how similar to his own kind these creatures were. They looked different, but their pride was similar.

The goblins gave him no choice. They cleared a disk in the center of the cavern, and the five goblins of Crool's clan came at him. They were armed with small clubs and sharp fragments of stone, and looked determined. They obviously intended to do him in if they got the chance.

Dor's body took over. He strode toward the band, his blade swinging. The goblins threw themselves to the sides. Dor turned to his right, kicking one goblin so hard the creature scooted across the smooth rock to fetch up against a wall, his stone knife fragmenting. Dor whirled on the others, swinging his blade, and they scattered again. One further foray, to clear the goblin sneaking in behind him; Dor caught the moving club on his blade and punched underneath it with his left fist. He scored on the goblin's head, the thing hard as a rock, driving the creature back, shaken.

Suddenly Dor stood alone in the circle. He had vanquished the band, thanks to the power and expertise of his body—and he hadn't killed a single goblin. That made him feel better. It could not make up for the four he had killed before, but it eased his guilt somewhat.

Craven smiled grotesquely. "Now is that a suitable sir or is it not?" he demanded rhetorically. "Keep your sword, Man; you have established your status. Come— you and your party are my guests."

Jumper chittered. "It seems goblins set great store by status," the web translated. "You were very clever to utter that mark of respect."

Dor was abashed. "I just thought that was what you said to a chief."

"It seems you were correct."

The captivity had, by this miracle of courtesy, become a visit. The goblin chief treated them to a sumptuous meal of candied cavelice, sugared slugs, and censored centipedes. Jumper pronounced it excellent. Dor and Millie weren't so sure.

"So you were fighting the horrendous harpies," Craven said, making conversation as he politely ripped several segments from a large centipede with his big yellow teeth and strained out the legs through the gap between teeth. He had seemed a bit wary of Jumper at first, but after appreciating the way the spider's chelicerae, which were the big nippers where another creature's jaws would be, crushed the food, Craven seemed quite satisfied. The crunching was even more vicious than that of the goblins, therefore better table manners. Then when the spider secreted digestive liquid that dissolved the delicacies into goo, and sucked that into his stomach, the goblins had to applaud. They had never been able to eat like that!

"Good thing we rescued you," the goblin chief said during a respite from his own attempt to emulate Jumper's mode of feasting. No matter how hard he tried, he was unable to dissolve his food with his saliva before swallowing it.

"Yes," Dor agreed. Actually, the slugs weren't bad, the flesh being spongy and juicy, and Millie was getting the hang of the lice. She chewed them and spat out the fibrous legs in approved goblin fashion, somehow making it seem dainty. The banquet table was littered with legs.

"Why were they after you?" Craven asked. "We came out because we heard the commotion, and brought you in because any enemy of the harpies may be a friend of ours."

"They wanted—" Dor was not sure how to express it. "They wanted me to do something for Heavenly Helen Harpy."

"Heavenly Helen?" Millie inquired, her brow furrowing suspiciously.

Craven laughed so hard he sprayed centipede legs on the cavern ceiling. The goblin courtiers applauded the marksmanship. "Heavenly Helen! So that's how they do it! Grabbing human men for studs! No wonder you fought them off! What a horrible fate!"

"Oh, I don't know—" Dor began, then caught Millie's look. He shifted the subject. "They said it was all because of you goblins. That you stole away their men."

"We were just getting even for what they did to us!" Craven cried. "Once we shared caves, but they were greedy for our space, so they wreaked a foul enchantment on us. They blighted the sight of our females so that they perceived the merits of our men in reverse. The boldest, bravest, handsomest, brightest goblins became anathema to them; they were drawn infallibly to the weakest, ugliest, stupidest cowards and thieves among us, and with those they mated. In this manner our whole species was inevitably degraded. We were once more handsome than the elves and smarter than the gnomes and stronger than the trolls and had more honor than the Men themselves—and now look at us, warped and gnarled and stupid and cowardly and given to treachery, so that five of us cannot threaten one of you. The harpies set that enchantment on us, and only they can lift it, and the vile birds refuse to do that. So we must seek whatever vengeance we can, while we yet retain some power in Xanth."

This was a side of the story the harpies hadn't told! Dor realized that peace was impossible, for there was now no way to undo the damage done to the harpies. Unless there could be an original mating between human and vulture to produce a male harpy—but he could hardly imagine any person or bird doing that! So the goblin-harpy war would continue, until—

"But we shall have the final chortle," Craven said with grim satisfaction. "Already the clans of the goblins are massing, augmented by our brothers of the deep caverns, numberless in number, and by our allies of similar species. We shall extirpate the harpies and their ilk from the face of Xanth!"

Dor remembered how the harpies were also massing their winged forces for the final battle. That would be some engagement!

The honored visitors were given a fine dark cave for the night, with healthy rats to fend off the nickelpedes, and a vent in the ceiling through which the dark air rose. They were guests—yet there was something about the firmness of their hosts that gave Dor disquieting pause. He recalled Craven's remarks about the nature of goblins, their propensity for treachery. Were they so eager to practice their low arts that, rather than kill prisoners outright, they preferred to pretend they were honored guests—who could then be betrayed? Did the goblins really intend to set them free, or were they merely fattening up fresh meat for their repasts? Craven, by his own statement, could hardly be trusted.

Dor exchanged glances with Jumper's largest eyes. No words were exchanged, for the goblins could be listening through holes in the walls, but it was evident the spider had similar misgivings.

"Make loud snoring sounds," Dor murmured to the floor where he lay in the dark. The floor obliged, and soon all other sounds were drowned out by the rasps, groans, and wheezes of supposed sleep. Under that cover, Dor held a whispered conference with his friends.

So at night—it was hard to tell the time of day down here, but Jumper had an excellent sense of time—they set about sneaking out. The goblins had not realized the potential of the giant spider, since Jumper had stood to fight instead of jumping clear. Thus Craven had not set guards in the ceiling aperture. Actually, the goblins really were rather stupid, as the subchief had said.

Jumper jumped to the ceiling, clung there, walked into the ventilator hole and explored where it led. Soon he was back to hoist Dor and Millie up. They wound their way through the darkness as silently as possible, while the raucous snores faded in the distance. At length—the length of a silken guideline—they emerged at the starlit surface.

It had been surprisingly simple. Dor knew it would have been impossibly difficult had Jumper not been with them. Jumper, with his superlative night vision, his silken lines, and his scaling ability. The spider made the impossible possible.

Chapter 5. Castle

They found a safe tree to hang from for the rest of the night, then resumed their trek in the morning. The local sticks and stones were as helpful as usual, and they located Castle Roogna without difficulty about noon. Dor was able to recognize the general lay of the land, but the vegetation was all different. There was no orchard; instead there were a number of predaceous plants. And—the Castle was only half complete.

Dor had seen Castle Roogna many times, but in this changed situation it stood out like a completely novel structure. It was large—the largest castle in all the Land of Xanth—and its outer ramparts were the tallest and most massive. It was roughly square, about a hundred feet on a side, and the walls rose thirty feet or more above the moat. It was braced by four great towers at the corners, their square outlines projecting halfway out from the main frame, enlarging it, and casting stark shadows against the recessed walls. In the center of each side of the castle was a smaller round tower, also projecting out by half its diameter, casting more subtle shadows. Solid battlements surmounted the top. There were no windows or other apertures. In Dor's day some had been cut, but this was a more adventurous period, and the defenses had to be as strong as possible. Overall, this was as powerful and impressive an edifice as Dor cared to imagine.

But the inner structure was virtually nonexistent; the beautiful palace portion had at this stage to be a mere courtyard. And the north wall lacked its upper courses; the huge stones stair-stepped down in the center, and the round support tower was incomplete.

A herd of centaurs was laboring on this section, using hoists and massive cables and sheer brute force to draw the blocks to the top. They worked with somewhat less efficiency and conviction than Dor would have expected, based on his knowledge of the centaurs of his own day. They looked rougher, too, as if the human and equine sections were imperfectly joined. Dor was reminded that not only had new species risen in eight hundred years, the old ones had suffered refinement.

Dor marched up to the centaur supervisor, who stood outside the moat, near a crude wooden scaffold supporting the next block to be hoisted. He was sweating as he trotted back and forth, calling out instructions to the pulley crew, trying to maneuver the stone up without cracking into the existing wall. Horseflies buzzed annoyingly about his hindquarters—not the big flying-horse variety, but the little horse-biting variety. They buzzed off quickly when Jumper came near, but the centaur didn't notice.

"Uh, where is King Roogna?" Dor inquired as the centaur paused to give him a harried glance.

"Go find him yourself!" the surly creature retorted brusquely. "Can't you see we're busy here?"

The centaurs of Dor's time were generally the soul of courtesy except when aroused. One notable exception was "Uncle Chester," sire of Dor's centaur playmate Chet. This centaur supervisor was reminiscent of Chester, and the other members of this herd resembled him too. Chester must have been a throwback to this original type: ugly of facial feature, handsome of posterior, powerfully constructed, surly of disposition, yet a creature of sterling qualities once his confidence was won.

Dor and his party retreated. This was obviously not the occasion to bug the centaurs. "Stone, where is King Roogna?" Dor inquired of a section of a block that had not yet been transported across the moat.

"He resides in a temporary hut south of here," the stone responded.

As Dor had suspected. There would have to be a lot more work on the Castle before it was habitable for a King, though in the event of war the inner court should be safe enough for camping. No one would choose to live there while the centaurs were hoisting massive rocks about.

They went south. Dor was tempted to make a detour to the spot where his cottage cheese existed in his own day, but resisted; there would be nothing there.

They came across a hut adapted from a large pumpkin, set in a small but neat yard. A solid, graying man in soiled shorts was contemplating a chocolate cherry tree while chewing on the fruit: evidently a gardener sampling the product. The man hailed them without waiting for an introduction: "Welcome, travelers! Come have a cherry while they are available."

The three stopped. Dor plucked a cherry and found it excellent: a delicious outer coating of sweet brown chocolate, a firm cherry interior with a liquid center. Millie liked the fruit too. "Better than candied cavelice," she opined. Jumper was too polite to demur, but evidently had another opinion.

"Pretend it is a swollen tick," Dor suggested in a low voice. The spider waved a foreleg, acquiescing.

"Well, let's try it again," the gardener said. "I'm having some difficulty with this one." He concentrated on the tree.

Nothing happened.

"Are you trying to do a spell?" Dor inquired, plucking another cherry. "To add fertilizer to it, or something?"

"Um, no. The centaurs provide plenty of fertilizer. As a matter of fact—" The man's eyes widened, startled. "Hold that cherry a moment, sir, if you please. Don't bite into it."

Dor paused, cherry near mouth. The first had been so good, he was a bit put out to have the gardener deny him the second so arbitrarily. He looked at the fruit. It lacked the chocolate covering, and its surface was bright red and hard. "I won't," he agreed. "This must be a bad one." He flipped it away."

"Don't—" the man cried, too late. "That's a—"

There was an explosion nearby. Millie screamed. The noise was deafening, and heat blasted at them.

130

All four of them stumbled to the side, away from the blast.

The concussion subsided. Dor looked around dazedly. There was a wisp of smoke rising from the vicinity of the explosion. "What was that?" Dor asked, shaken. He discovered he had his sword in hand, and put it away self-consciously.

"The cherry bomb you threw," the gardener said. "Lucky you did not bite into it."

"The cherry—that was a chocolate cherry, from this—" Dor looked at the tree. "Why, those *are* cherry bombs, now! How—?"

"This must be King Roogna," Millie offered. "We didn't recognize him."

Nonplused, Dor worked it out. He had pictured King Roogna as a man somewhat like King Trent, polished, intelligent, commanding of demeanor, a man nobody would care to take lightly. But of course the folklore of eight hundred years would clothe the Magician in larger-than-life grandeur. It was not a person's appearance that counted in Xanth, it was his magic talent. So this pudgy, informal, gardener-type man with the gentle manner and thinning, graying hair and sweaty armpits, unprepossessing—this could indeed be the King. "This tree—he changed it from chocolate cherry to cherry bomb—Magician King Roogna's talent was adapting magic to his purpose—"

"Was?" the King inquired, raising a dust-smeared eyebrow.

Dor had been thinking of the historical figure, who was of course contemporary in the tapestry world. "I, uh, *is*. Your Majesty. I—" He started to bow, changed his mind in midmotion, started to kneel, changed his mind again, and found himself dissolving in confusion.

The King set a firm, friendly hand on his shoulder. "Be at ease, warrior. Had I desired obeisance, I would have made it known at the outset. It is my talent that sets me apart, rather than my office. In fact, my office is insecure at the moment. My troops are all on furlough because we have no quarters yet for them, and difficulties plague the construction of my Castle. So pretension would ill befit me, were I inclined toward it."

"Uh, yes, Your Majesty," Dor mumbled.

The King contemplated him. "I gather you are from Mundania, though you seem to have had some garbled account of Xanth." He glanced at Millie. "And the young lady has the aspect of the West Stockade. They do raise some pretty fruits there." He looked at Jumper. "And this person—I don't believe I have encountered a jumping spider of your magnitude before, sir. Is it an enchantment?"

"He called me sir," Jumper chittered. "Is a King supposed to do that?"

"A King," Roogna said firmly, "can do just about anything he chooses. Preferably he chooses to rule well. I note your voice is translated by a web on the warrior's shoulder." His aspect hardened, and he began to suggest the manner Dor had expected in a King. "This interests me. There appears to be unusual magic here."

"Yes, Your Majesty," Dor said quickly. "There is considerable enchantment here, but it is hard to explain."

"All magic is hard to explain," Roogna said.

"He makes things talk," Millie said helpfully. "The sticks and stones don't break his bones. They talk to him. And walls and water and things. That's how we found our way here."

"A Mundane Magician?" Roogna asked. "This is a virtual contradiction in terms!"

"I, uh, said it was hard to explain, Your Majesty," Dor said awkwardly.

A figure approached: a compact squarish man of the King's generation, with a slightly crooked smile. "Do I smell something interesting, Roogna?" he inquired.

"You do indeed, Murphy," the King replied. "Here, let's introduce ourselves more adequately. I am Magician Roogna, pro-tem King. My talent is the adaptation of living magic to my purpose." He looked meaningfully at Dor.

"I, uh, I am Dor. Er, Magician Dor. My talent is communication with the inanimate." Then, in case that wasn't clear, he added: "I talk to things."

The King prompted Millie with another glance. "I

am Millie the maid, an innocent girl of the West Stockade village," she said. "My talent is—" She blushed delicately, and her talent manifested strongly. "Sex appeal."

On around the circle: "I am Phidippus Variegatus of the family of Salticidae: Jumper the spider for short," Jumper chittered. "My talent, like that of all my kind, is silk."

At last it came to the newcomer. "And I am Magician Murphy. My talent is making things go wrong. I am the chief obstacle to Roogna's power, and his rival for dominance in Xanth."

Dor's mouth dropped open. "You are the Enemy Magician? Right here with the King?"

King Roogna laughed. "What better place? It is true we oppose each other, but this is a matter of politics. Magicians, as a rule, do not practice their talents directly on each other. We prefer to manifest our powers more politely. Murphy and I are two of the three Magicians extant. The third has no interest in politics, so we two are the rivals for power in Xanth. We are trying our strength in this manner: if I can succeed in completing Castle Roogna before the year is out, Murphy will yield me uncontested title to the throne. If I fail, I will abdicate the throne, and since there is no other Magician suitable for the office, the anarchy that follows will likely foster Murphy as the dominant figure. Meanwhile we share the camaraderie of our status. It is an equitable arrangement."

"But—" Dor was appalled. "You treat the welfare of the whole Land of Xanth as if it were a game!"

The King shook his head gravely. "No game, Magician Dor. We are absolutely serious. But we also indulge ourselves in honor. If one of us can prevail in war, he can surely do it by humane rules of conduct. This is warfare of the civilized kind."

Jumper chittered. "There is warfare of the uncivilized kind approaching," the web translated. "The harpies and the goblins are massing their forces to exterminate each other."

Murphy smiled. "Ah, you betray my secret, spider!"

"If anything can go wrong, it will," Dor said. "You mean the war between monsters is your doing?"

"By no means, Magician," the Enemy demurred. "The war of monsters has roots going well back before our time, and no doubt will continue long after our time. My talent merely encourages the most violent outbreak at the least convenient time for Roogna."

"And we need hardly guess where the two armies will randomly meet," King Roogna exclaimed, his gaze turning northward toward the incomplete Castle.

"I had hoped it would be a surprise," Murphy admitted ruefully. "That would prevent you from calling back your troops in time to defend the Castle. But for the intrusion of these visitors, it might have been unforeshadowed."

"So your talent fouled *you* up, this time!" Millie said.

"Perhaps an eddy-current," Jumper chittered.

"My talent is not proof against the influence of other Magicians," Murphy said. "The ramifications of the talents of Magician caliber extend well beyond the apparent aspects. If another Magician were to oppose me, my talent would feel the impact, regardless of the specific nature of the opposing talent. And it seems another Magician has indeed entered the picture. It will take time to comprehend the significance of this new element."

That was an apt remark: Dor had entered the picture literally, for this was the tapestry, the picture-world.

Murphy studied Dor with a certain disquieting intensity. "I would like to get to know you better, sir. Would you care to accept my hospitality for the duration of your stay here, or until we all hie into the Castle to avoid the ravages of the monsters? We had thought there were no unknown Magicians in Xanth at this time."

"Sir?" Jumper chittered. He was still having a problem with this word, having seen its power.

"But you are the enemy!" Dor protested.

"Oh, go with him," Roogna said. "I lack proper facilities for three, at the moment, though soon the

Castle will be in order. The maid can stay with my wife, and the spider I daresay would be happiest hanging from a tree. I assure you Murphy will not hurt you, Dor. It is his prerogative, by the rules of our contest, to be given opportunity to fathom significant new elements, particularly if they add to the strength of my position. I have a similar privilege to inspect his allies. You may both rejoin me and your companions for the evening repast."

Somewhat bemused, Dor went with Murphy. "I don't understand this business, Magician. You act as if you and King Roogna are friends!"

"We are peers. That's not the same as friends, but it will do. We have no others except the Zombie Master, and he is not one to associate with on this basis. There is of course neo-Sorceress Vadne, who would have assisted me had I agreed to marry her, but I declined and so she joined the King. But she is not a dominant figure. So if we desire the companionship of our level, we must seek it in each other. And now, it seems, in you. I am extremely curious about you, Dor."

This was awkward. "I am from a far land."

"Obviously. I had not been aware that any Magicians resided in Mundania."

"Well, I'm not really from Mundania." But could he afford to tell the whole truth?

"Don't tell me, let me guess! Not from Mundania—so it must be somewhere in Xanth. North of the Gap?"

"You remember the Gap?"

"Shouldn't I?"

"Uh, I guess it's all right. I—my people have trouble remembering the Gap, sometimes."

"Strange. The Gap is most memorable. So you're south of it?"

"Not exactly. You see, I—"

"Let's see your talent. Can you make this jewel talk?" Murphy held up a glittering emerald.

"What is your nature?" Dor asked the stone. "What are you worth? What is your secret?"

"I am glass," the jewel responded. "A fake. I am worth almost nothing. The Magician has dozens like me to give to greedy fools for their support."

Murphy raised an expressive eyebrow. "But *you* are not fake, Dor! There must be few secrets hidden from you! A remarkable informational talent!"

"Yes."

"So the mystery expands! How could a full Magician have remained concealed so long? Roogna and I once harnessed a magic sniffer and surveyed this whole region. That was how the site for the Castle was selected. There is a high concentration of useful magic here, and overall the effect is very strong. If the source of all magic is not in this vicinity, it can not be far from it. So we found enchantment aplenty, but no Magicians. Yet in our experience, no really strong magic emerges from the hinterland. How could a man of Mundane aspect, with a warrior's reflexes, turn up suddenly with such a talent? It hardly seems possible."

Dor shrugged.

"In fact, I suspect it is impossible—or rather, it must be the result of magic beyond our present comprehension. Some special enchantment—" He broke off, lifting one finger expressively. "An anachronism! That would account for it! You are from the Land of Xanth—in another time!"

"Uh, yes," Dor said. Murphy was no fool!

"Not the past, surely, for there is no record of such a talent historically. Of course many of the ancient records have been lost, owing to Waves and such. Still, talents tend to grow more sophisticated with time, and yours is quite sophisticated. So it must be the future. How far?"

The truth could not be concealed from this clever man! "Eight hundred years," Dor admitted.

They had arrived at Murphy's tent. "Come in, have a drink of cider—a fine sweet-cider press just fruited in my yard—and tell me all about it."

"But I'm not on your side!" Dor blurted. "I want King Roogna to win!"

"Naturally you do. All right-thinking people do. Fortunately for me, there are as many wrong-thinking people as right-thinkers. But surely you must realize that ignorance serves my purpose, not his. Only the orderly categorization of facts can promote a stable kingdom."

"Then why do you want this information? Are you going to try to do something to me?" Dor's hand touched his sword.

"Magicians do not act against Magicians," Murphy reminded him. "Not directly. I mean you no personal mischief. Rather, I am trying to determine the impact and meaning of your presence here. The addition of another full Magician to the equation could change the outcome of our contest. If your force is sufficient to tip the balance in Roogna's favor, and I cannot reverse it, then I would have to concede the throne to him without further ado, and save us all much torment. Therefore it behooves both Roogna and me to ascertain your nature, early and accurately. Why do you think he sent you with me?"

"You two are the strangest enemies I ever saw! I can't follow the convolutions of your game."

"We merely abide by the rules. Without rules, there is no game." Murphy handed him a glass of cider. "Tell me the whole story, Dor, and we shall ascertain how your presence affects our situation. You will be welcome then to explain it to the King."

Dor seemed to have no choice. He wished Jumper were here to advise him, or Grundy the golem; he just didn't have confidence in his own judgment. Yet he always felt most at home with the truth. So he told the Enemy Magician as much of the story as he could organize: his quest to help restore a zombie, the inclusion of Jumper in the spell, the adventure within the tapestry.

"No problem about locating the Zombie Master," Murphy said. "The problem is, he won't help you."

"But only he knows the secret of restoring zombies! That's the whole purpose in my—"

"He may know," Murphy said. "But he won't tell. He does nothing for anyone. That is why he lives alone."

"I still have to ask him," Dor said stubbornly. "Meanwhile, what about you? Now that you know King Roogna did—I mean will—complete the Castle—"

"That is indeed a ponderous matter. Yet there are several considerations. One is that what you say may not be true."

Dor was stung. His body's hand, responsive in its fashion to his mood, reached over his shoulder for the sword.

Murphy held up a hand, unalarmed. "You sound so uncertain, yet your body reacts so aggressively! This corroborates your story, of course. Do not force me to use my magic against you. You would suffer mishap before ever you brought your weapon to bear. I did not call you a liar. I merely conjecture that you could be misinformed. History is notorious for misinformation. That castle you knew could have been built a century later and given the name of Roogna, to lend verisimilitude to the new order. How would you know?"

"Very what?" Dor asked, confused.

"Verisimilitude. Realism. To make it seem likely and true."

Dor was startled. A Castle built much later, called Roogna. He had never thought of that.

"But there are other approaches," Murphy continued. "Assume your version of history is accurate—as indeed it may be. Now you have returned. What can you do—except change your history? In which case your presence can at best be neutral, and at worst reverse the outcome of the present competition between Roogna and Murphy. So your excursion may be an auspicious omen for me. I hardly mean to interfere with you! I think it may be my talent that brought you here, to foul up Roogna."

Dor was startled again. Himself, an agent of the enemy? Yet it was suddenly all too plausible!

"But I rather suspect," Murphy continued, "that you will in fact prove unable to change history in any significant respect. I visualize it as a protean thing. Yielding to specific imperatives yet always reasserting itself when the pressure abates. I doubt anything you can do will have impact after you depart. It will be an interesting phenomenon to watch, however."

Dor was silent. This Magician had neutralized him thoroughly, expertly, without doing a thing except talk. The worst of it was, he was very much afraid that

Murphy was correct. The more Dor might try to interfere, here in the tapestry world, the more likely he was to hurt King Roogna's chances. So Dor would have to remain as neutral as possible, lest even his help prove disastrous.

They finished their cider and returned to King Roogna. "This man is indeed a Magician," Murphy announced. "But I deem him no threat to my designs, though he aligns himself with you. He will explain as he chooses."

The King glanced at Dor inquiringly. "It is true," Dor said. "He has shown me that any help I may try to render you . . . can have the opposite effect. We don't know that for sure, but it is a risk. So I must remain neutral, to my regret." Dor had surprised himself by making a very adult-sounding statement. Maybe it was Murphy's influence.

"Very well," the King said. "Murphy is many things, but his integrity is unimpeachable. Since you may not help me, may I help you?"

"Only by telling me where to find the Zombie Master."

"Oh, you can't get anything from him," the King assured Dor. "He helps no one."

"So Magician Murphy informed me. Yet it is vital that I see him, and after that I shall depart this land."

"Then wait a few days, until I complete the present phase of the Castle. Then I can spare you a guide and guard. I owe you this in deference to your Magician status. The Zombie Master lives east of here, in the heart of the wilderness; it is difficult to pass."

Dor chafed inwardly at the delay, but felt it best to accede. He and his friends had had too many narrow escapes already. A guide and guard would help.

They rejoined Millie and Jumper. "The King has given me a job!" Millie exclaimed immediately, bouncing and clapping her hands and swinging her hair in such a full circle that it lapped around her face, momentarily concealing it. "As soon as the Castle is complete."

"If we have time to wait," Jumper chittered, "I should like to recompense the King's hospitality by offering my service for the duration of our stay here."

"Uh—" Dor started to protest, realizing that what applied to himself should also apply to the spider.

"That is most courteous of you," the King said heartily. "I understand from the young lady that you are adept at hoisting and lowering objects. We have dire need of such ability at the moment. Rest tonight; tomorrow you will join my sturdy centaur crew."

Murphy glanced meaningfully at Dor. The Enemy Magician was satisfied to make this trial of the validity of his conjecture. And Dor—had to be satisfied too. Maybe Murphy was wrong, after all. They could not afford to assume he was right, if he were not. So Dor was silent, not wanting to alarm the King or Jumper unnecessarily. Silent, but not at ease.

The King served them royally enough with pies from a pie tree he had adapted for this purpose: pizza, shepherd's, mince, cheese, and pecan pies, washed down with excellent fruit punch from a punchfruit tree.

"In my land," Dor remarked, "the King is a transformer. He changes living things into other living things. He can change a man into a tree, or a dragon into a toad. How does this differ from your own talent, Your Majesty?"

"A transformer," King Roogna murmured. "That's a potent talent! I can not change a man into a tree! I only adapt forms of magic to other purposes—a sleep spell to a truth spell, a chocolate cherry to a cherry bomb. So I would say your King is a more powerful Magician than I am."

Dor was abashed. "I'm sorry, Your Majesty. I didn't mean to imply—"

"You didn't, Dor. I am not competing with your King for status. Nor am I competing with you. We Magicians have a certain camaraderie, as I mentioned; we respect each other's talents. I'd like to meet your King sometime. After I have completed the Castle."

"Which may be never," Murphy said.

"Now with *him* I am competing," the King said goodnaturedly, and bit into another piece of pie. Dor said nothing, still having trouble accepting this friendly-rivalry façade.

In the morning Jumper reported to the Castle construction crew. Dor went along to help translate, since no one else could understand the spider's chittering—and because he was privately concerned about Jumper's possible influence on history. Or lack of it. If anything Dor or Jumper did could affect King Roogna's success—

Dor shook his head uneasily. King Roogna was busy today, adapting new spells to preserve the roof of the Castle—once the construction reached that stage. The magic, it seemed, had to be built right into the Castle; otherwise it would not endure. This business of adapting spells, such as the one a water dragon used to prevent the water from dousing its flame—converting that to make an unleakable roof—well, that was certainly something a transformer couldn't do! So King Roogna had no reason to be modest. It was very difficult to compare the strength of talents. But if Jumper's offer of help were only to hurt—

They approached the same centaur supervisor who had brushed them off before. It seemed he had charge of the north wall, the one still under construction. The creature was pacing and fretting about the arrival of additional blocks of stone; it seemed the quarriers had fouled up a spell or two and were running behind schedule.

"King Roogna would like to have my friend help," Dor said. "He can lift stones into place with his silken lines, or climb sheer walls to—"

"A giant bug?" the centaur demanded, swishing his tail rapidly back and forth. "We don't want his kind among us!"

"But he's here to help!"

Now the other centaur workers were dismounting from the wall and crowding in close. They loomed uncomfortably large. A centaur standing the height of a man actually had about six times the mass of a man, and these stood somewhat taller than Dor—whose present body was a giant among men. "We don't associate with no bugs!" one cried. "Get that weirdo out of here!"

Nonplused, Dor turned to Jumper. "I—they don't—"

"I understand," Jumper chittered. "I am not their kind."

Dor eyed the massed centaurs, who seemed eager for

any pretext to take time off from their labors. *"I don't understand! You can do so much—"*

"We don't care if he can throw droppings at the big green moon!" one yelled. "Get him out of here before we fetch a fly swatter!"

Dor got angry. "You shouldn't talk to him like that! Jumper's not a fly; he *eats* flies! He can keep all the horseflies away—"

"Bug-lover!" the supervisor snapped. "You're as bad as he is! Now watch I don't pound you both into the ground!"

"Yeah! Yeah!" the other centaurs agreed, stomping their hooves.

Jumper chittered. "These creatures are hostile. We shall depart." He started off.

Dor followed him, but not with docility. With each step he took his anger grew. "They had no right to do that! The King needs help!" Yet at the same time he wondered whether this were not for the best. If Jumper were not allowed to participate, Murphy's curse couldn't operate, could it? They would not change history.

Soon they were back at the royal tent. The King was outdoors beside a pond, where a small water dragon was captive. The thing was snorting smoke angrily and lashing up a froth with its tail, but Roogna seemed not to be concerned. "Now climb up on this roofing material," he was telling the dragon. "Propinquity facilitates adaptation." Then he looked up and spied Dor and Jumper. "Some problem at the construction site?"

Dor tried to be civilized, but it burst out of him. "The centaurs won't let Jumper work! They say he's ... different!"

"So I am," Jumper chittered.

King Roogna had seemed like an even-tempered, harmless sort of man. Now that changed. He stood up straight and his jaw hardened. "I will not have this attitude in my kingdom!" He snapped his fingers, and in a moment a flying dragon arrived: a beautiful creature armored in stainless steel, with burnished talons and a long snout suitable for aiming a jet of fire accurately from a distance. "Dragon, it seems my work crew is getting balky. Fetch your contingent and—"

Jumper chittered violently. "No, Your Majesty!" the web translated, almost shredding itself in its effort to transmit the force of the spider's conviction. "Do not chastise your workers. They are no more ignorant than my own kind, and they are doing necessary work. I regret I caused disruption."

"Disruption? By offering to help?" The King's brow remained stormy. "At least I must chastise them with my magic. Centaurs do not have to have such pretty tails, so useful for swishing away flies. I can adapt them to lizards' tails, useful for slinking along between rocks. That will dampen their o'erweening arrogance!"

"No!" Jumper still protested. "Do not allow the curse to distort your judgment."

Roogna's eyes widened. "Murphy! You're right, of course! This is his doing! If alienophobia could interfere, it does interfere!"

Dor too was startled. That was it, certainly! Magician Murphy had laid a curse on the construction of the Castle, and Jumper's offer had triggered it. The centaurs were not really to blame.

"You are a sensible, generous creature," the King said to Jumper. "Since you plead the cause of those who wrong you, I must abate my action. I regret the necessity, and the wrong done you, but it seems I cannot take advantage of your kind offer of assistance." He dismissed the flying dragon with a kingly offhand gesture. "The centaurs are allies, not servants; they labor on the Castle because they are most proficient at this sort of construction. I have done return favors for them. I regret that I let my temper slip. Please feel free to use my facilities until I can arrange for your escort. Meanwhile, you are welcome to watch me operate here, though I hope you will not interrupt my concentration with foolish questions."

They settled down to watch the King. Dor was quite curious about the actual mechanism for adapting a spell. Did the King just command it, as Dor commanded objects to speak, or was it a silent effort of will? But hardly had Roogna gotten the balky water dragon placed before a messenger-imp ran up. "King, sir—there's been a foul-up at the construction site! The wrong spell was on the building blocks, and they're pushing each other apart instead of pulling themselves together."

"The wrong spell!" Roogna roared indignantly. "I adapted that spell myself only last week!" There followed a brief discussion. It turned out that a full course of blocks had been laid in the wrong place, causing their spells to conflict with those of the next course instead of meshing. Someone had fouled up, and the error had not been caught in time. They were large blocks, each weighing many hundreds of pounds.

Roogna tore out a few hairs from his rapidly graying head. "The curse of Murphy again! This will cost us another week! Do I have to lay every block with my own frail hands? Tell them to rip out that course and replace it with the correct one."

The imp scurried off, and the King returned to his task. But just as he was about to work his magic, another imp arrived. "Hey, King—a goblin army is marching from the south!"

Grimly the King asked: "What is its estimated time of arrival?"

"ETA zero minus ten days."

"That's one shoe," the King muttered, and returned to his work. Naturally the water dragon had wandered out of place, and had to be coaxed laboriously back. Murphy's curse operated in small ways, too.

The King was shortly interrupted by yet another imp. "Roog, old boy—a harpy flight is massing in the north!"

"ETA?"

"Ten days."

"The other shoe," Roogna said resignedly. "The two forces will converge on this spot, courtesy of Murphy, and by the time they have destroyed each other, the landscape will be in ruins and Castle Roogna in rubble. If we had only been able to complete the breastworks in time—but now that is hopeless. My enemy has done some remarkably apt scheming. I am forced to admire it."

"He's a smart man," Dor said. "There must be some way to divert those armies, if they're not really after the Castle. I mean, if the goblins and harpies don't care about the Castle at all, but only happen to be fighting here." He was disturbed. It didn't seem that his presence had caused this problem, but he wasn't quite sure. If his encounters with the harpies and goblins had set them both off—

"Any direct attempt at diversion would cause them both to attack us," Roogna said. "They are extremely intractable creatures. We lack the inclination and means to fend off either of those brute hordes. In your world, Man may be the dominant creature, but here that has not yet been established."

"If you recruited some more creatures to help you—"

"I would have to dissipate my magic repaying them for that service—instead of working on the Castle."

"Your human army—can't you call it back from furlough?"

"Murphy's curse is especially apt at interfering with organizational messages. I doubt we could summon the full complement back before the monsters arrived. And I'm sure those men need to protect their own homesteads from the advancing monsters. I think it better to defend the Castle with what we have on hand. That's a small chance, but as good as the alternative. I fear Murphy has really checked me, this time."

Maybe another Magician could help—" Dor interrupted himself with another thought. "The Zombie Master! Would his help make the difference?"

The King considered. "Yes, it probably would. Because he represents a primary focus of magic, with all its ramifications, and because he is relatively close, with no Gap to navigate in getting here, and because his zombies could man the battlements without number or upkeep: the ideal army in this kind of situation. Just feeding my own army during siege would be a terrific problem; we have supplies only for the crews working here now. But this is useless conjecture; the Zombie Master does not participate in politics."

"I have to go see him anyway," Dor exclaimed, excited. "I could talk to him, explain what is at stake—" To hell with caution! If the King was about to lose without Dor's help, why not take the risk? He really could do no harm. "Jumper could come along; he's better than I am at lots of things. The worst I could do is fail."

The King stroked his beard. "There is that. I regard it as a long shot, but since you are willing—tell the Zombie Master I would be willing to make some reasonable exchange for his assistance." He cocked a finger, and another imp appeared. Dor wondered where those imps hid when not in use; the King was evidently well attended, though he made little show of it. Like King Trent, he masked his power except when show was necessary. "Prepare an escort and guide for an excursion to the castle of the Zombie Master. Magician Dor will depart in the morning on a mission for me."

But in the morning there was one more: Millie the maid. "With the Castle delayed, and the household staff shipping out during the emergency, I have no job yet," she explained. "Maybe I can help."

In future centuries she would be a sad ghost, and come to know the zombie Jonathan, and seek to restore him. She knew nothing of this now, but Dor did. How could he deny her her chance to assist him in this mission—since it was ultimately for her? Maybe in some way she could help.

Why did he feel so glad for her company? He knew he could never—she was not—his body appreciated aspects of her that he himself had hardly glimpsed, but she could never be his in that way. So why should he fool himself with impossible notions?

Yet how glad he was to be with her, even this brief time!

Chapter 6. Zombie Master

The escort was a dragon horse, with the front part of a horse and the rear of a dragon. The guide was another imp. "Well, sport, let's get on with it," the imp exclaimed impatiently. He was a good deal larger than Grundy the golem, but smaller than a goblin, and reminded Dor somewhat of each.

There were three saddles spaced along the creature's back. Dor took one, Millie another, and Jumper clung to the third, unable to sit in it. The imp perched on the equine head, whispering into the expressive ears.

Abruptly they were moving. The horse forelegs struck the ground powerfully, while the reptilian hind legs dug their claws in and shoved back. The monster half-galloped, half-slithered forward in great lurches. Millie screamed, and Dor was almost catapulted out of the saddle. The imp chuckled impishly. He had known this would happen.

Jumper bounded over Dor's head, landing just behind the girl. With deft motions the spider trussed her to the saddle with silken threads so that she could not be dislodged. Then Jumper did the same for Dor. Suddenly there was no question of being shaken loose; they did not even have to hold on. "Ah, you take all the fun out of it!" the imp complained.

The dragon moved rapidly. The lurching smoothed as the creature got up speed, and became a more or less even rising and falling. Dor closed his eyes and imagined he was on a boat, sailing the waves. Up, down, sway; up, down, sway. He began to feel seasick, and had to open his eyes again.

The foliage was rushing past. This creature was

really moving! It threaded neatly through seemingly impassable tangles, avoiding tangle trees and monster warrens, hardly abating its pace even for fair-sized rifts. The imp was an obnoxious little man-thing, typical of his kind, spreading insults imp-partially—but he really knew his route and controlled the dragon expertly. Dor appreciated expertise wherever he found it.

Which was not to say the whole trip was smooth. There were hills and dales and curves. Once the dragon splashed through a boggy lake, swimming strongly but soaking their feet and lower legs in the process. Another time it ascended a steep bank, going almost vertically before crushing it. Once a griffin rose up challengingly before it, squawking; the dragon horse neighed warningly and feinted with its hooves, and the griffin decided to give way.

Soon they neared the demesnes of the Zombie Master—and Dor realized with a start that this was the same site as that of Good Magician Humfrey's castle, eight hundred years later. But maybe that was not strange; that place which seemed fit for one Magician might also appeal to another. If Dor were to build a castle someday for himself, he would look for an ideal site, and might be governed by considerations similar to those of some former Magician.

However, the Zombie Master had his own defenses, and these turned out to be as formidable in their fashion as those of Magician Humfrey. A pair of zombies rose up before the dragon horse—and the fearless creature sheered off, unwilling to suffer contact with this rotting flesh. Millie, seeing the zombies, screamed, and even the imp looked disgusted.

"This is as far as we go," the imp announced. "Nothing will bother you here—except zombies. How you get in to talk with their master I don't even care to know. Dismount and let us go home."

Dor shrugged. Zombies posed no special horror for him, since he had more or less associated with Jonathan all his life. He didn't like zombies, but he wasn't afraid of them. "Very well. Tell the King we are in conference with the Zombie Master, and will send news soon."

"Fat chance," the imp muttered. Dor pretended not to hear that.

The three dismounted. Immediately Dor felt cramps in his legs; that ride had really battered them! Millie stood bowlegged, unable even to kick her feet properly. Only Jumper was unkinked; he had perched atop his saddle throughout, being unable to sit at all.

The dragon horse neighed, wheeled on hoof and claw and tail, and shoved off. The three were showered with dirt and twigs thrown up by its feet. It was certainly glad to get away from here!

Dor worked the knots out of his legs as well as he could, and limped up to the guard-zombies. "We come on a mission from King Roogna. Take us to your Master."

The zombie opened its ponderous and marbled jaws. "Nooo nnn ffasssess!" it declared with fetid breath.

Dor concentrated, trying to make out the words. Was his talent operating here? These things were dead, yet fashioned from organic material. Wood was organic, and he could speak to it when it was dead. Did the spell that gave these monsters animation also give them sufficient pseudo-life to nullify his communication with inanimate things? Or was it partially operative? Probably the latter; he could converse, but with difficulty.

Jumper chittered. "I believe it said 'No one passes,'" the web on Dor's shoulder said.

Dor glanced at the spider, surprised. Had it come to the point where Jumper could understand Dor's language better than Dor himself could?

Jumper chittered again. "Do not be dismayed; all of your words are strange to me; this is merely another aspect of strangeness."

Dor smiled. "That makes sense! Very well; you can help me converse with the zombies." He returned his attention to the guards, who had remained as silent as the grave, as patient as time. They had no living urges to impel them. "Tell your Master he has visitors. He must see us."

"Nooo," the zombie insisted. "Nooo nnnn!"

"Then we shall just have to introduce ourselves." Dor made to pass.

The zombie raised a grisly arm to block his way. Shreds of rotten flesh festooned it, and the white bone showed through in places. Millie screamed. She certainly had no affection for any zombie at this stage of her life! But centuries of ghosthood could change a person's perspective, Dor concluded.

Dor reached for his sword, but Jumper was there before him, trussing up the zombie in silk. In a moment the other zombie was similarly incapacitated. Dor had to admit this was the better way; zombies were messy to slay, he understood, because they could not be killed. They had to be dismembered, and even the pieces fought on. Which was one reason they would make such a good army for King Roogna, if that could only be arranged. This way, they were efficiently neutralized, and in a manner that should not offend the Zombie Master.

But they had not gone far toward the castle that stood on a mound in the forest—in Dor's day both mound and forest were gone—before a zombie serpent challenged them. It hissed and rattled in a fashion only deviously reminiscent of a live serpent, but there was no doubt it sought to bar their progress. Jumper neutralized it as he had the others. Whatever would they have done without the big spider!

Then a zombie tangle tree menaced them. This was too much even for the spider; the tree stood four times the height of a man and had perhaps a hundred moldering tentacles. Even if it were feasible to truss it up, the thing would have the strength to snap the strands. Therefore Dor menaced it with his gleaming sword while the others sidled past; even a zombie tree had some care for its extremities.

In this manner they achieved the castle. It, too, was an animated ruin. Stones had fallen from its walls to reveal fossilized inner supporting timbers, and shreds of cloth hung in the window apertures. There had once been a moat, but it had long since filled in with debris; a stench rose from what thick liquid remained. There was—yes, a zombie bog-monster languishing in the mire. Its slime-coated orbs focused on the intruders with as much glare as their sunken condition permitted them to mount.

The party crossed the broken-down drawbridge and pounded on the sagging door. Splinters and fragments were dislodged, but of course there was no answer. So Dor completed the demolition of the door with a few strokes of his sword, and the three marched in. Not without a qualm or two.

"Hallooo!" Dor called, and his voice reverberated through the tomblike halls. "Zombie Master! We are on a mission for the King!"

A zombie ogre appeared. Millie screamed and did a little skip back, her hair swinging almost straight up; she must have kicked her feet, forgetting that she was standing on them. Jumper braced her with one leg to prevent her falling backward into the moat, where the moat-monster was trying vainly to slaver. "Noo. Goo," the ogre boomed hollowly, for its chest had been eviscerated by decay. Dor remembered Crunch the ogre, and retreated; a zombie ogre was still an ogre.

"We must see the Zombie Master," Millie said, though pale with fear. In her cute way, she too, had courage.

"Soo? Ooh." The ogre shuffled down a hall, and the party followed.

They entered a chamber like a crypt. Another zombie glanced up, resting its cadaverous hands on the table before it. "On what pretext do you intrude here?" it demanded coldly.

"We want to see the Zombie Master!" Dor exclaimed. "Now get out of the way, you bundle of bones, if you're not going to help."

The zombie stared somberly at him. It was an unusually well-preserved specimen, gaunt but not yet rotten. "You have no business with me. You are not yet dead."

"Of course we're not yet—" Dor paused. That "yet" distracted him.

Jumper chittered. "This man is alive. He must be—"

"The Zombie Master himself!" Millie finished, horrified.

Dor sighed. He had done it again. When would he grow up and learn to check things out before making assumptions? First King Roogna, whom he had thought to be a gardener; now the Zombie Master. He fumbled for an apology. "Uh—"

"Why do the living seek me?" the Zombie Master demanded.

"Uh, King Roogna needs your help," Dor blurted. "And I need the elixir to restore a zombie to life."

"I do not indulge in politics," the Zombie Master said. "And I have no interest in restoring zombies to life; that would undermine my own talent." He made a chill gesture of dismissal and returned to his business—which was the corpse of an ant lion that he was evidently about to animate.

"Now see here—" Dor began angrily. But the zombie ogre stepped forward menacingly, and Dor was cowed. His present body was big and strong and swift, but in no way could it match the least of ogres. One swing of that huge fist—

Jumper chittered. "I think our mission has failed."

Dor took another look at the ogre, remembering how Crunch had snapped an ironweed tree off at the base with one careless blow. This creature was not in good condition, being dead, but could probably snap an aluminumwood tree off. Mere human flesh would be no problem at all. So his second thought was much the same as his first: he could not prevail here.

Dor turned about. He knew that they could not coerce a Magician to help; it had to be voluntary. The Zombie Master, as the others had warned, was simply not approachable.

A hero would have found some way. But Dor was just a lad of twelve, accompanied by a giant spider and a girl who screamed constantly and who would become a ghost at an early age. No heroes here! And so he accepted the gall of defeat, for both his quests. The gall of growing up, of becoming disillusioned.

Dor half-expected one of the others to protest, as Grundy the golem always did. But Millie was only a helpless maid, possessing little initiative, and Jumper was not Dor's kind; the spider comprehended human imperatives only imperfectly.

They walked out, and the zombies did not bother them. They trekked down the hill. The dragon horse was gone, of course. They might have had it wait, but they had not expected to need it this soon. Dor's lack of foresight had penalized him again. Not that delay made much difference, at this stage. So they would simply have to march back themselves.

They untied the two zombie guards Jumper had trussed in silk. "Nothing personal," Dor explained to them. "Our business with your Master is finished."

They marched. Millie made a very pretty marcher, when she wasn't screaming or kicking her feet; her hair still flung about naturally. He was getting used to her as she was now, and found her rather intriguing. In fact, he wouldn't mind—but that wouldn't be right. He had to guard against the thoughts his Mundane body put into his head; Mundanes weren't very subtle.

Abruptly they happened on a campfire. This was strange, because fire was hardly used in the Land of Xanth. Few things needed cooking, and heat was more efficiently obtained by pouring a little firewater on whatever needed warming. But this was obviously an organized fire, with sticks formed into a circular pile. The flames licked merrily up through the center. Someone had been here recently; in fact the person must have departed moments before Dor and his party arrived.

"Stand where you are, stranger," a voice called from the shadow. "I've got you covered with a bow."

Millie screamed. Dor reached for his sword, then stopped; he couldn't draw before an arrow struck him. No sense in compounding his yet-again lack of foresight by getting himself unnecessarily killed. Jumper jumped straight up and disappeared into the foliage of a tree overhanging them.

The challenger stepped forth. He was a brutish man, Mundane by the look of him, and he had not been bluffing about the bow. The string was taut, and the arrow nocked and centered on Dor's midsection. Knowing the capabilities of his own Mundane body, Dor had little reason to doubt the competence of this challenger. It seemed as if all Mundanes were born warriors. Perhaps this was in compensation for their abysmal lack of magic. Or maybe the soft, gentle, peaceful Mundanes didn't go out invading other lands.

"Who the hell are you, poking around my campfire?" the brute demanded. "What happened to that creep with you, the hairy thing with the legs?"

"I am Dor, on mission for the King," Dor said. He spoke more boldly than was his wont, fresh from the pain of failure of his missions. "The others are my companions. Who are you, to challenge me thusly?"

"So you're a Xanthie!" the man exclaimed sneeringly. "You sure could've fooled me; you look just like a man. You try a spell on me and I'll drill you!"

So this really was a Mundane. Dor had never seen one in the flesh before. "You don't have a talent?"

"Don't get smart with me, creep!" Then the man looked at him more closely. "Say, you're even dressed like one of us! You sure you're not a deserter?"

"Would you like to see my talent?" Dor asked evenly.

The man considered. "Yeah, in a moment. But no tricks." He turned his head and yelled. "Hey, Joe! Come and set guard on a pair here!"

Joe arrived. He was another brutish man, unclean and malodorous. "What's all this noise about—"

He broke off. His lips pursed in a crude whistle. "Get a load of that babe!"

Oops, Dor thought. Millie's talent was operating.

Millie made a token scream and stepped back. Joe stepped forward aggressively. "Boy, I could really use a number like this!" His hand shot out, catching her slender arm. This time Millie's scream was in earnest.

Dor's body took over. His left hand grabbed at the first Mundane's bow while his right snapped over his shoulder to whip out the sword. Suddenly the two Mundanes were standing at bay. "Leave her be!" Dor cried.

Millie turned on him, surprised and gratified. "Why Dor—I didn't know you cared!"

"I didn't know either," he muttered. And knew it was a lie. He had resolved to stop lying, but it seemed to come naturally at times like these. Was that part of growing up too: learning to lie socially? He had always cared for Millie, but had never known how to express it. Only the immediate threat to her had prompted his action.

"You won't get away with this!" Joe said angrily.

"We've got troops all around here, looking for plunder."

Dor spoke to the club that dangled from the man's waist. "Is that true, club?"

"It's true," the club said. "This is the advance unit of the Mundane Fifth Wave. They marched down the coast past the Gap, then cut inland. They are completely immune to reason. All they want is wealth and women and easy living, in that order. Flee whilst you can."

The first Mundane's mouth dropped open. "Magic! He's really got magic!"

Dor backed away, Millie beside him. This was a tactical error, for the moment the two Mundanes were beyond sword-slash range they drew their own weapons. And set up a shout: "Enemy escaping! Cut him off!"

A shape dropped from above: Jumper. He landed almost on top of the two Mundanes and trussed them up before they knew what was happening. But the alarm had already been given, and there were sounds all around of men closing in.

"We had better use the upper reaches," Jumper chittered. "The Mundanes will not pursue us there."

"But they can shoot their arrows at us!" Dor protested.

"They may not see us." Jumper fastened safety lines to Dor and Millie, and they scrambled up the trunk of a tree.

The Mundanes were arriving. These alien men were worse than goblins! Dor was climbing rapidly, thanks to his body's huge muscles, but Millie was slow. She would surely be caught. "I will distract them!" Jumper chittered, and dropped low on his dragline.

Dor waited for Millie to catch up with him, then continued on up into the foliage. Just as they got to some reasonable cover, the Mundanes converged on the tree. Jumper chittered at them, swinging across to another tree.

"Get that bug!" a Mundane cried. He lunged for Jumper, but missed as the spider zipped a few feet up his line. Jumper could have escaped then, by going on up into the heights, or simply jumping over the Mundanes and running—but Dor was still struggling to haul Millie to safety. So the heroic spider dangled low, chittering in a manner that sounded challenging and insulting even without translation.

Another Mundane lunged—and missed. Mundanes just didn't think of an enemy rising suddenly up. But there were too many; now the spider had nowhere to go. One Mundane had the wit to chop at the dragline with a sword, severing the invisible silk. Jumper dropped to the ground. Instantly the men pounced on him, grabbing him one man to a leg, much as the goblins had, so that he was helpless.

Men and goblins: was there really much difference between them? The Mundanes were bigger, but . . .

Dor was about to turn back, to aid his friend, but one of Jumper's eight eyes spied him. "Don't waste my effort!" he chittered, knowing that no one besides Dor could understand him. "Return to the Zombie Master; it is the only place you can keep the girl safe."

Dor hadn't thought of that. The Zombie Master might not be friendly, but at least he was not too hostile. It was the best place to be until the Mundane horde passed.

He climbed up into the protective splay of leaves, urging Millie on. His last sight of Jumper was of the men bearing him to the ground, striking his soft body brutally with their fists. They weren't trying to kill, they were trying to hurt, to make their enemy suffer as long as possible before the end. Because Jumper had balked them from capturing the girl—and because Jumper was different. Dor winced, feeling the pain of the blows in his own gut. What would they do to his friend?

Jumper had left a network of silken lines strung through the upper foliage, guiding Dor and Millie and providing rapid transit from one great tree to another. It was amazing how much he had accomplished in the brief time he had been aloft, and with what foresight. Dor had never thought his friend was deserting him—but neither had he anticipated the sacrifice Jumper would make. He felt the unmanly tears stinging his eyes, was afraid Millie would notice them, then decided he didn't care. Jumper—to have Jumper trapped like this, perhaps badly hurt, because of Dor's own carelessness—

Suddenly there was a piercing terrible, great chittering from below. It translated into a sheer scream of agony, chilling in its implication.

"They are pulling off his legs!" Millie whispered in horror. "That's what Mundanes do to spiders. The wings off butterflies—"

Dor saw that her beautiful face was streaked with helpless tears. *She* was not ashamed to cry!

Then something congealed in Dor. "Come on!" he snapped, and swung forward at a faster pace.

"Don't you care, that—?" she demanded plaintively.

"Hurry!"

Reproachfully, she hurried. Dor felt like a heel from a No. 1 shoe-tree, knowing she thought concern for his own safety motivated him, but he wasted no effort trying to explain. Jumper had eight legs; it would take the Mundanes time to get them all, and he had to use that time well.

In moments they ran out of Jumper's lines and dropped to the ground. They were now at the base of the hill on which the Zombie Master's castle sat. A zombie rose up to challenge them, but Dor shoved it aside so roughly that it collapsed in a jumble of shredded meat and chipped bone. He dragged Millie on.

They never paused at the chopped-open castle door. Dor charged right in. The zombie ogre rose up; Dor parried it with his blade, ducked under its arm, and plunged on through the gloomy hall. At last he burst into the Zombie Master's chamber, where the zombie ant lion was now taking its first steps.

"Magician!" Dor cried. "You must save my friend the spider! The Mundanes are pulling out his legs!"

The Zombie Master shook his cadaverous head and waved with an emaciated hand. "I have no interest in—"

Dor menaced him with his sword. "If you do not help this instant, I will surely slay you!" Such was his hurt and desperation, he was not bluffing, though he feared the Magician could turn him into a zombie.

Now the Zombie Master showed some spirit. "So you, a mortal, dare to threaten a Magician?"

"I am a Magician too!" Dor cried. "But even if I weren't, I would do anything to save my friend, who sacrificed himself for me and Millie!"

Millie put a restraining hand on Dor's arm. "Please," she said. "You can not threaten a Magician. Let me handle it, Dor. I am not a Magician like you, but I do have my talent."

Dor paused, and Millie stepped close to the Zombie Master, smiling with difficulty. "Sir, I am not a forward maid, and no Sorceress, but I too would do anything to help the bold friend who preserved us. If you but knew Jumper the spider—please, now, if you have any compassion at all—"

The Magician looked at her closely for the first time. Dor remembered what her talent was, and knew how it softened men. He was just beginning to appreciate its impact on himself. The Zombie Master was after all a man, and he too had to feel the impact.

"You . . . will tarry with me?" he asked incredulously.

Dor did not like the sound of that word, *tarry*.

Millie spread her arms toward the Zombie Master. "Save my friend. What becomes of me is not important."

A kind of shudder ran through the Magician. "This becomes you not, maid," he said. "Yet—" He turned to his ogre. "Gather my forces, Egor; go with this man and do as he desires. Save the spider."

Dor took off, running through the gloomy halls and from the castle. The true horror was what lay ahead of him. The zombie ogre followed, crying out to the things of the castle: "Ssome ccome!"

Zombies erupted from the adjacent rooms, in their haste dripping stray clods, bones, and teeth. They closed in behind the ogre: men, wolves, bats, and other creatures too far gone to identify. In grisly procession they followed Dor down the hill.

His concern for his friend lent him swiftness, and somehow the zombies kept up. Yet even as he ran,

Dor wondered whether he had not left Millie to as bad a fate as the one he strove to rescue Jumper from. The spider had sacrificed himself to save the two of them; Millie had sacrificed herself to save the spider. The full nature of Millie's talent had never been apparent to him, though it was coming clearer; it included holding and kissing and—

His mind balked. Kissing the Zombie Master? He ran faster yet.

They burst upon the Mundanes. The first thing Dor saw was Jumper: the brutal men had hung him up by four legs, and yanked off the other four. The spider was alive, but in terrible pain after this torture.

Dor went mad. "Kill!" he screamed, and his sword was in his hand. Almost of its own volition, the blade chopped into the neck of the Mundane nearest Jumper —the one holding the spider leg that had been torn off most recently. Dor was reminded of the centipede legs spat out at the goblin banquet. But this was his friend! The keen edge sliced through the flesh with surprising ease. It passed right through the neck, and the man's head popped off. Dor stared, momentarily numb to the implication; then he looked again at the severed leg, and whirled on the next Mundane.

Meanwhile the zombies were attacking with a will. The Mundanes panicked, becoming aware of the horror that had fallen on them. Dor had heard that Mundanes were a superstitious lot; zombies should play on that propensity. The men scattered, and in a moment there was nothing in the glade except the victors, three bodies, and Jumper.

Dor couldn't let himself relax. "Carry the spider to the castle," he ordered the ogre. "Carefully!" He turned to the other zombies. "Collect the severed legs and bring them along." Would it be possible to convert them into usable zombie legs and put them back on the spider?

The ogre picked up the mutilated body. Other zombies found the missing legs, and dragged along the dead Mundanes. The strength of the zombies was surprising—or maybe it was just willpower. They brought their prizes grimly to the castle.

Millie met them at the entrance. She looked all

right. Her clothes were still on, and her hair was unmussed. Dor had trouble phrasing his question. "He —did he—?"

"The Zombie Master was a perfect gentleman," she said brightly. "We just talked. He's an educated man. I think he's lonely; no one ever visited with him before."

And no wonder! Dor's attention returned to Jumper. "He's alive, but in terrible pain. They—they pulled off four legs!"

"The brutes!" she exclaimed with feeling. She had seemed a rather innocent, helpless maid before, but now she was reacting to stress and horror with increasing personality. "How can we help him?"

Jumper revived enough to chitter weakly. "Only time will help me. Time to regrow my lost limbs. A month or so."

"But I must return to the King in mere days!" Dor cried. "And to my own land—"

"Return without me. Perhaps I can render some service to the Zombie Master in return for his hospitality."

"But I must take the Zombie Master with me, to help the King!" Yet that, too, was an impasse; the Magician had already refused to get involved in politics.

The Zombie Master was there; in his distraction Dor had not been aware of his arrival. "Why did the men torment the spider?"

"I am alien to this world," Jumper chittered. "I am a natural creature, but in my enchantment in this realm of men I become a thing of horror. Only these friends, who know me—" His chittering ceased abruptly; he was unconscious.

"A thing of horror, yet with sentience and courage," the Zombie Master murmured thoughtfully. He looked up. "I will care for this creature as long as he requires it. Egor, carry him to the guest chamber."

The ogre picked Jumper up again and tromped away.

"I wish there were some way to cure him faster," Dor said. "Some medicinal spell, like the healing elixir—" He snapped his fingers. "That's it! I know where there's a Healing Spring, within a day's journey of here!"

Now he had the Magician's attention. "I could use such elixir in my art," the Zombie Master exclaimed. "I will help you fetch it, if you will share the precious fluid with me."

"There's plenty," Dor agreed. "Only there's one catch. You can't act against the interest of the Healing Spring, or you forfeit its benefit."

"A fair stipulation." The Zombie Master showed the way to an inner courtyard. A monstrous zombie bird roosted there.

Dor stared. This was a roc! The largest of all birds, restored to pseudo-life by the talent of this Magician. The entire world of the dead was under the power of this man!

"Carry this man where he will," the Zombie Master directed the roc. "Return him safely with his burden to this spot."

"Uh, I'll need a jug or something—" Dor said.

The Magician produced two jugs: one for each of them. Dor climbed onto the stinking back of the roc, anchored himself by grasping the rotting stubs of two great feathers, and tied the jugs with a length of Jumper's silk left over from his last dragline.

The roc flapped its monstrous wings. The spread was so great, the tips touched the castle walls on either side of the courtyard. Grimy feathers flew wide, bits of meat sprayed off, and the bony substructure crackled alarmingly. But there was tremendous power remaining in this creature. A roc in its prime could carry an elephant—that was an imaginary creature the size of a small sphinx—and Dor weighed far less than that. So even this animated corpse could perform creditably enough.

They lumbered into the air, barely clearing the castle roof. There were so many holes in the great wings that Dor marveled that they did not fall apart, let alone have sufficient leverage to make flight possible. But the spell of the Zombie Master was a wondrous thing; no zombie ever quite disintegrated, though all of them seemed perpetually on the verge of doing so.

They looped above the castle. "Go east!" Dor cried.

He hoped he knew the terrain well enough by air to locate the spot. He tried to visualize the tapestry to orient himself—was he actually flying above it now? —but this world was too real for that.

Dor had only been to the Healing Spring once with his father Bink, who had needed elixir for some obscure adult purpose. On that trip Bink had reminisced about his adventures there: how he had met Dor's mother Chameleon, she being then in the guise of Dee, her normal phase, at such and such a spot, and how he had found the soldier Crombie at this other spot, wounded, and used the elixir to restore him to health. Dor and Bink had visited briefly with a dryad, a wood nymph associated with a particular tree, resembling a pretty girl of about Millie's present age. She had tousled Dor's hair and wished him well. Ah, yes, it had been a fine trip! But now, high in the air, Dor could not ask the objects of the ground where the Spring was, and there were no clouds close enough to hail—hail-call, that is, not hail-stone—and his memory seemed fallible.

Then he spied a channel of especially healthy jungle, obviously benefitting from the flowing water from the Spring. "Down there," he cried. "At the head of that stream."

The zombie roc dropped like a stone, righted itself, glided in for a landing, tilted a little, and clipped a tree with one far-reaching wing tip. Immediately the wing crumpled, and the roc's whole body swerved out of control. It was a crash landing that sent Dor tumbling from his perch.

He picked himself up, bruised but intact. The roc was a wreck. Both wings had been broken; there was no way the creature could fly now. How was he to get back in time to do Jumper much good? If he walked, it would take him a day in the best of conditions; carrying two heavy jugs it would be longer. Assuming he didn't get snapped up by a tangle tree, dragon, or other monster along the way.

He reconnoitered. They had missed the Spring, but there was a handsome tree nearby on the hillside. And—he recognized it. "Dryad!" he cried, running toward it. "Remember me, Dor?"

There was no response. Suddenly he realized: this was eight hundred years earlier! The dryad would not remember him—in fact there probably was no dryad here yet, and this was probably not the same tree. Even if the time had been correct, the nymph still would hardly have recognized him in his present body. He had been boyishly foolish. Yet again.

Disconsolately he trekked down the slope. Of course this was not the same tree! The real one had been some distance from the Spring, not right beside it. And an average tree of today would be an extraordinary tree by Dor's own time; even plants aged considerably in eight centuries. His hopes had really fouled up his thinking! He would have to find his own way out of this mess, without help from any dryad.

Well, not entirely without help. "What is the best route out of here?" he asked the nearest stone.

"Ride that roc bird out," the rock replied.

"But the roc's wings are broken!"

"So sprinkle it with some elixir, idiot!"

Dor stopped dead in his tracks. So obvious! "I *am* an idiot!" he exclaimed.

"That's what I said," the stone agreed smugly.

Dor ran up to the roc, got his jugs, and ran to the Spring. "Mind if I take some of your elixir?" he inquired rhetorically.

"Yes, I mind!" the Spring replied. "All you creatures come and steal my substance, that I labor so hard to enchant, and what recompense do I get for it?"

"What recompense!" Dor retorted. "You demand the stiffest price of all!"

"What are you talking about? I never made any demands!"

Something was wrong. Then Dor caught on. Again, that eight-hundred-year factor. The Spring had not yet developed its compensatory enchantment. Well, maybe Dor could do it a favor. "Look, Spring, I intend to pay you for your substance. Give me these two jugs full of elixir, and I will tell you how to get fair recompense from all other takers."

"Done!" the Spring cried.

Dor dipped the jugs full, noting how the bruises

vanished from his body as he touched the water. This was the Spring, all right! "All you need is a supplementary enchantment, requiring that anyone who benefits from your elixir cannot thereafter act against your interests. The more your water is used, the more your power will grow."

"But suppose someone calls my bluff?"

"It will be no bluff. You will take back your magic. It will be as if he never was healed by you."

"Say, yes—I could do that!" the Spring said excitedly. "It would take a while, maybe a few centuries, to build that extra spell, but since it's just a refinement of the original magic, a termination clause as it were—yes, it will work. Oh, thank you, thank you, stranger!"

"I told you I would repay you," Dor said, gratified. Then he thought of something else. "Uh—I'm only a visitor to this land, and what I do may fade out after I leave. So you'd better get right on that spell, so you don't lose it once I'm gone."

"How long do I have?"

Dor did a quick calculation. "Maybe ten days."

"I'll fix it in my mind," the Spring said. "I'll memorize it so hard that nothing can shake it loose."

"That's good," Dor said. "Farewell!"

"I'm not a well, I'm a spring!" But it was a good-natured correction.

"Maybe you're a wellspring," Dor suggested. "Because you make creatures well again."

" 'Bye," the Spring said, dismissing him.

Dor returned to the roc and sprinkled elixir from his jar on its wings. Immediately they healed; in fact, they were better than they had been. But they remained zombie wings, dead flesh. There were, after all, limits; the elixir could not restore the dead to life. Which was why he was on this quest. Only the Zombie Master could do what needed to be done. Meanwhile, he had to get back to Jumper soon, lest the spider also require restoration from the dead.

Dor boarded, tied the jugs, and hung on. "Home, roc!" he cried.

The roc taxied about to face the channel forged by its crash landing, worked its legs to accelerate, flapped its wings, and launched violently into the air. This takeoff was far more precipitous than the first one had been; it was all Dor could do to hang on. The elixir had given the wings new power. Fortunately there were a few droplets remaining on his hands, and these healed the feathers to which he clung. Now they were great long fluffy colorful puffs of plumage suitable for ladies' hats, easy to grasp.

The roc wheeled in the sky, then stroked powerfully for the Zombie Master's castle. The landscape fairly whizzed by below. They reached their destination in half the time it had taken to make the outbound trip. No wonder the Magician wanted the elixir; his zombies would be twice as good now!

But a new problem manifested. From above, Dor could see that the Mundanes had rallied, and now were laying siege to the castle. There were many of them; their whole advance army must have gathered for this effort. They evidently were not cowards; they had been panicked by the ferocity of the zombies' attack, but now they were angry at the three deaths and sought revenge. Also, they probably thought that any castle so well guarded must conceal enormous riches, so their greed had been invoked. In helping his friend Jumper, Dor had brought serious mischief to the Zombie Master. Dor was sure his father would have had more sense than that; it was yet another reminder of his own youth and inexperience and thoughtlessness. When, oh when, would he ever grow up and be adult?

The roc dived, hawklike, banked, and plopped into place in the courtyard. The landing was heavy, for the bird's feet had not been healed; the sound carried throughout the castle.

The Zombie Master and Millie rushed up. "You got it!" Millie cried, clapping her hands.

"I got it," Dor agreed. He handed one jug to the Magician, keeping the other for himself. "Take me to Jumper."

Millie guided him to the guest room. The big spider lay there, ichor leaking from his stumps. The variegated fur face on the back of his abdomen seemed to be making a grimace of distress. His eyes, always open, were filmed with pain. He was conscious again, but so weak he could chitter only faintly. "Good to see you again, friend! I fear the injuries have been too extensive. Legs can be regrown, but internal organs have been crushed too. I cannot—"

"Yes you can, friend!" Dor cried. "Take that!" And he poured a liberal dose of elixir over Jumper's shuddering body.

Like magic—unsurprisingly—the spider was whole again. As the liquid coursed over the fur-face, the green and white and black brightened until they shone. As it touched each stump, the legs sprouted out, long and hairy and strong. As it was absorbed, the internal organs were restored, and the body firmed out. In a moment there was no sign that Jumper had ever been injured.

"It is amazing!" he chittered. "I did not even need to have my original legs returned! I have not felt so good since I was hatched! What is this medicine?"

"Healing elixir," Dor explained. "I knew where there was a Spring of it—" He broke off, overcome by emotion. "Oh, Jumper! If you had died—" And he embraced the spider as well as he could, the tears once more overflowing his eyes. To hell with being adult!

"I think it was worth the torture," Jumper chittered, one mandible moving against Dor's ear. "Watch I don't nip your antenna off."

"Go ahead! I have plenty more healing elixir to use to grow a new ear!"

"Besides which," Millie added, "human flesh tastes awful. Maybe even worse than goblin meat."

The Zombie Master had followed them. "You are human, yet you hold this alien creature in such esteem you cry for him," he remarked.

"And what's wrong with that?" Millie demanded.

"Nothing," the Magician said wanly. "Absolutely nothing. No one ever cried for me."

Even in the height of his relief, Dor perceived the meaning of the Zombie Master's words. The man had been alienated from his own kind by the nature of his magic, rendered a pariah. He identified with Jumper, another alien. That was why he had agreed to take care of Jumper. More than anything else, the Magician must want people to care for him the way Dor and Millie cared for Jumper.

"Will you help King Roogna?" Dor asked, disengaging from his friend.

"I do not indulge in politics," the Zombie Master said, the coldness returning.

Because the King was no pariah. This Magician might assist those who showed him some human compassion, but King Roogna had not done that. "Would you at least come to meet the King, to talk with him? If you helped him, he would see that you received due honor—"

"Honor by fiat? Never!"

Dor found he could not argue with that. He would not have wanted that sort of honor either. If there were such a thing as dishonorable honor, that would be it. He had made another stupid error of approach, and squelched his chances—again. Some emissary he was proving to be!

But there was another problem. "You know the Mundanes of the Fifth Wave are getting ready to attack this castle?"

"I do know," the Zombie Master agreed. "My zombie eye-flies report there are hundreds of them. Too many to overcome with my present force. I have sent the roc out to round up more bodies, to shore up my defenses. To facilitate this, the roc will not even land here at the castle; it will drop the bodies in the courtyard and proceed immediately for more."

"The Mundanes are mad at us," Dor said, "because we killed three of them. Maybe if we leave—"

"My zombies helped you," the Zombie Master pointed out. "You can gain nothing other than your own demises by departing now. The Mundanes have this castle surrounded. To them, it is a repository of unguessable riches; no reasonable demurral will change their fixed minds."

"Maybe if they saw us leave," Dor said. "The roc could carry us out. Oh—the roc's away for the duration."

"It seems we must remain, at least for a time,"

Jumper chittered. "Perhaps we can assist in the defense of the castle."

"Uh, yes, we'd better," Dor agreed. "Since we seem to have brought this siege down upon it." Then, for no good reason, he found himself making another appeal: "Uh, Magician—will you reconsider the matter of the zombie restorative elixir? This is not a political matter, and—"

The Zombie Master glanced at him coldly. Before the Magician could speak, Millie put her sweet little hand on his lean arm. "Please," she breathed. She was excruciatingly attractive when she breathed that way. Yet she could not know that it was as a favor to herself, of eight hundred years later, that Dor was obtaining this precious substance.

The Zombie Master's coldness faded. "Since she asks, and you are a good and loyal man, I do reconsider. I will develop the agent you require." But it was evident that most of the responsibility for his change of heart was Millie's. And her breathing.

Dor knew victory of a sort—yet it was incomplete. He was succeeding in his private personal mission, while failing in his mission for the King. Was that right? He didn't know, but had to take what he could. "Thank you, Magician," he said humbly.

Chapter 7. Siege

The siege was serious. The Mundanes were reasonably apt at this sort of thing, since they were an army. Motivated by vengeance and greed and the knowledge that at least one measurelessly pretty girl was inside the castle, they knew no decent limits. They closed in about the castle and readied their assault.

At first the Mundanes simply marched across the rickety drawbridge and up to the blasted main gate. But the zombie ogre came charging out, much of his strength restored by the healing elixir, and tossed them into the moat, where the restored bog-monster chomped them. It did not actually eat them, because zombies had no appetite, but its chomping was effective. After that the Mundanes were more cautious.

"We have to clear the junk out of that moat," Dor said. "They can just about wade across, as it is now, and the monster can't get them all. If we do it now, while they're recovering from the shock of meeting Egor Ogre—"

"You have the makings of an excellent tactician," the Zombie Master said. "By all means handle it. I am working out your zombie restorative formula, which is devious in detail."

So Dor took a squad of zombies out. "I am mortal, so should not expose myself," he told them as he eyed the bog-monster. It had been trained not to attack other zombies, but that did not help him. "Arrows cannot kill you. So I will stand watch from the ramparts and call down directions. You will go down into the moat and start hauling armfuls of garbage out." He felt less than heroic in this role, but knew it was the expedient course. The Mundanes were surely excellent archers. He was here to get the job done, after all, not to make himself look good.

The zombies marched down. They milled about uncertainly. They did not have very good minds, their brains being mostly rotten. The healing elixir worked wonders with their bodies, but could not restore the life and intellect that had once made them men and animals. Dor found his original revulsion for their condition giving way to sadness. What zombie ever knew joy?

"You with the skullhead," Dor called. "Scoop up those water weeds and dump them on the shore." The zombies started in, laboriously. "You with the scarred legs—haul that log out and bring it to the front gate. We can use it to rebuild the door." It was almost pointless to explain such things to zombies, but he couldn't help himself. It was part of his process of self-justification.

If what he did had no permanence in this tapestry world, what of this present situation? But for him, the Mundanes would not have laid siege to the castle of the Zombie Master. If the Magician were killed, would he be restored after Dor departed the scene? Or was the siege inevitable, since the Fifth Wave had already been headed this way? It was a matter of history, but Dor could not recall the details, assuming he had ever learned them. There were aspects of history the centaur pedagogues did not teach their human pupils, and Dor had not been a terrifically attentive pupil anyway. He would remedy that when he got home again.

If he got home again...

A few arrows came from the forest to plunk into the zombie workers, but with no effect. That evidently gave the Mundanes pause for thought. Then a party of warriors advanced with swords drawn, intending to cut the zombies into pieces too small to operate. Dor used a bow he had picked up from the castle armory, ancient and worn but serviceable. He was no expert at this, but his body had evidently been trained to this weapon too; it was very much the compleat warrior. He fired an arrow at a Mundane but struck the one beside his intended target. "Good shot!" Millie exclaimed, and Dor was ashamed to admit the truth. No doubt if he had let the body do the whole thing itself, it would have scored properly, but he had tried to select his own target. He had better stick to swords in future.

But it sufficed to discourage the attack, since this was just an offhand Mundane gesture, not a real assault on the castle. Also, they didn't know that there was only a single archer on the wall. The Mundanes retreated, and the moat-clearing continued. Dor was pleased: he was accomplishing something useful. It would be ten times as hard to storm the castle with that moat deep and clear. Well, maybe eight times as hard.

Meanwhile, Jumper was climbing about the rafters and inner walls of the castle, routing out vermin— which he gobbled with glee—and shoring up weak spots. He lashed subsiding members with silk cords, and he patched small holes, using wood and chinks of stone fastened in place by sticky masses of silk. Then he strung alarm lines across the embrasures to alert him to any intrusions there. This was a small castle, somewhat haphazardly constructed, with a single peaked roof, so in a short time the spider was able to accomplish much.

Millie went over the living and cooking facilities. The Zombie Master, a bachelor, had a good store of provisions but evidently survived mainly on those that required least effort to prepare: cheese balls, fried eggs from the friers that nested on the rafters, hot dogs from the dogwood that grew just inside the moat, and shrimp from the shrimp plants in the courtyard. The courtyard was south of the roofed region, so that the sunlight could slant in over the south wall to reach the ground inside; a number of plants and animals existed there, since the zombies did not bother them.

Millie set about making more substantial meals. She found dried fruits in the cellar, and dehydrated vegetables, all neatly spelled to keep them from spoiling, and cooked up a genuine handmade mashed peach and potato cobblestone stew. It was amazing.

And the Zombie Master, after due experimentation

in his laboratory, produced for Dor a tiny vial of life-restorative elixir, brewed from the healing water by the art of his talent. "Do not mislay this, or use it incautiously," he cautioned. "The dosage suffices only for one."

"Thank you," Dor said, feeling inadequate. "This is the whole reason I came to this—this land. I can't tell you how important this vial is to me."

"Perhaps you could offer me a hint, however," the Magician said. "Since we are about to sustain a determined siege, from which we may not emerge—I admit a certain curiosity."

Delicately put! "I'm sorry about that," Dor said. "I know you prefer living alone, and if I'd known we'd cause all this trouble—"

"I did not say I objected to either the company or the trouble," the Zombie Master said. "I find I rather enjoy both. You three are comparatively simple people, not given to duplicity, and the mere presence of a challenge to survival evokes an appreciation for life that had been lacking."

"Uh, yes," Dor said, surprised. The Magician was becoming quite sociable! "You deserve to know." Dor was feeling generous now that he had this much of his mission accomplished, and the Zombie Master's candor was nice to receive. "I am from eight hundred years in your future. There is a zombie in my time I wish to restore to full life as a favor to—to a friend." Even in this moment of confidence, he could not quite confess his real interest in Millie. This vial would make her happy, and himself desolate, but the thing had to be done. "You are the only one who knows the formula for such restoration. So, by means of enchantment, I came to you."

"A most interesting origin; I am not certain I believe it. For whom are you doing this favor?"

"A—a lady." The thought of letting Millie learn of her eight-hundred-year fate appalled him, and he resolved not to utter her name. He had not had much luck in keeping such resolutions before, but he was learning how. What horror would this knowledge wreak on so innocent a maid, who screamed and flung her hair about and kicked her feet so fetchingly at the slightest alarm? Far better that she not know!

"And who is the zombie?" the Magician prodded gently. "I do not mean to pry into what does not concern me—but zombies do concern me, for surely every zombie existing in your day is a product of my magic. I have a certain consideration for their welfare."

Dor wanted to balk, but found that, ethically, he could not deny the Zombie Master this knowledge. "She—the lady calls him Jonathan. That's all I know."

The man stiffened. "Ah, the penalty of idle curiosity!" he breathed.

"You know this zombie?"

"I—may. It becomes a lesson in philanthropy. I never suspected I would be doing such a favor for this particular individual."

"Is he one of your zombies here at the castle?" Already Dor felt a tinge of jealousy.

"Not presently. I have no doubt you will encounter him anon."

"I don't *want* to—" No, he could not say that. What was to be, was to be. "I don't know whether it would be wise to tell him—I mean, eight hundred years is a long time to wait for restoration. He might want to take the medicine now, and then he wouldn't be there for the lady—" Which was itself a fiendishly tempting notion he had to suppress. The elimination of Jonathan from his own time would not only rid him of competition for Millie's favor—it would eliminate his whole reason for coming here. How could he restore a zombie who had already been restored eight centuries ago? But if he *didn't* do it—paradox, which could be fatal magic.

"A very long time," the Zombie Master agreed. "Have no concern; I will not betray your secret to any party." He dismissed the subject with a brusque nod. "Now we must see to the castle defenses. My observer-bugs inform me that the Mundanes are massing for a major effort."

The defenders girded to meet that effort. Jumper guarded the east wall and the roof, setting up a series of traplines and interferences for intruders. The Zombie Master took the south wall, which enclosed the courtyard. Dor took the west. All were augmented by contingents of zombies, and of course the ogre handled the north gate. Millie remained inside—to watch for hostile magic, conjurations and such, they told her. No one wanted to put her on the ramparts during the violence, where her cute reactions would serve as a magnet for Mundanes. She also had charge of the supply of healing elixir, so she could come to the aid of the wounded.

The zombie bugs must have made excellent use of their elixir-restored eyes, for the attack occurred right on schedule. A wave of Mundanes charged the side of the castle. Not the front gate, where Egor's reputation more than sufficed, but the weakest wall—which happened to be Dor's.

They threw down logs to form a makeshift bridge, stationed men with outsize shields on either side of it to block the moat-monster, and funneled about half their number across. They carried three scaling ladders, which they threw up against the wall. The castle had been constructed foolishly, with a ledge above the first two stories, ideal for ladders to hook to. The ledge terminated abruptly at the corner where the courtyard commenced, but led to a small door near the northern edge. Presumably this access was intended to facilitate cleaning of the gutter spouts—but it also ruined the integrity of the castle's defense. A blank wall, with no ledge and no door, would have been so much better!

Dor stationed himself before the door and waited, hoping he was ready. His stomach was restless; in fact at the moment he felt in urgent need of a toilet. But of course he couldn't leave. None of them could leave their posts until the attack was over; that had been agreed. There was no telling what tricks the Mundanes might try to draw the defenders out of position, making the castle vulnerable.

Men swarmed up the ladders. They were met at the top by zombie animals: a two-headed wolf with rotting jaws but excellently restored teeth; a serpent with gruesomely articulated coils; and a satyr with sharp horns and hooves.

The first men up were evidently braced for human

zombies; these animals unnerved them, causing them to be easy prey. Then Dor ducked in with a long crowbar—he had no idea what the crows used them for—and levered off the first ladder, pushing it away from the wall so that it fell with its burden into the moat. The splashing Mundanes screamed. Dor felt a shock of remorse; he would never be acclimatized to killing! Actually, he reminded himself, the fall was not far as these things went, and the watery landing was soft. But the men were in a certain amount of armor that hampered their swimming.

Dor moved to the next ladder, but this one was really hooked on tightly. The zombie serpent was having trouble holding off the onslaught. "What's holding you on?" Dor cried in exasperation as he labored to pry it up.

"I am an enchanted ladder," it replied. "The stupid Mundanes stole me from a stockade arsenal; they don't know my properties."

"What are your properties?" Dor inquired.

"I anchor irrevocably when emplaced—until someone utters the command 'weigh anchor.' Then I kick loose violently. This facilitates disengagement."

"Way anchor?"

"That doesn't sound quite right. It's weigh as in lifting, spoken with authority."

"Weigh anchor!" Dor cried with authority.

"Oooh, now you've done it!" the ladder cried, and kicked off violently, dumping its occupants into the moat.

Dor went on to the next. The delay at the second ladder had cost him vital time, however. The top warrior had gotten over his shock of encountering the satyr, and had hacked it to pieces. Now three warriors stood on the deck, with more crowding up. Fortunately there was not room for them to stand abreast; they were in a line, and until they moved, the fourth man could not dismount from the ladder.

The first Mundane gave a loud cry and brought his sword down on Dor as if chopping wood. Dor's body parried automatically blocking the descending sword with his crowbar so that it glanced off to the side. Simultaneously he dodged forward, coming inside the

Mundane's guard, striking into the man's gut with his left fist. The man doubled over, and Dor caught his leg and heaved him over the parapet into the moat. He rose to face the next Mundane in one fluid motion.

This man was smarter about his attack. He came at Dor carefully, sword extended like a spear, forcing him back. The Mundane knew he did not need to slay Dor yet; all that was required was that he widen the stretch of ledge held by his forces, so that others could get off the ladder.

Dor, on the other hand, had to keep the man penned until he could eliminate him and the next man and get at the ladder. So he met the Mundane's thrust with his own, pointing the bar, refusing to give way. In this restricted locale, the crowbar was an excellent weapon.

The Mundane's eyes widened in an expression of astonishment. "Mike!" he cried. "You survived! We thought you were lost in that damned magic jungle!"

He seemed to be addressing Dor. It might be a ruse. "Look to yourself, Mundane," Dor said, and forced the man's sword out of the way so he could shove him outward with his arm and shoulder.

The Mundane hardly tried to resist. "They told me there was a man looked like you, but I didn't believe it! I should've known the best infighter in the troop would make it okay! Hell, with your strength and balance—"

"Balance?" Dor asked, remembering how his body had walked Jumper's line across the river.

"Sure, you could've joined a circus! But you kept pushing your luck too far. What are you doing here, Mike? Last I saw you, we got separated by goblin bands. We had to cut out to the coast, thought you'd rejoin us—and here you are! Lost your memory or something?"

Then Dor's wedging prevailed, and the Mundane, surprised, toppled into the moat. Quickly Dor charged the third, jamming the dull point of his bar into the man's middle before he got his guard up, and this one also fell. Then Dor jammed his pole into the ladder hooks and wrenched so hard that a whole section of the stone parapet gave way and the ladder lost purchase. All the men on it fell screaming. The job was done.

Now, standing victorious on the edge, looking down, Dor suffered a multiple reaction. He had killed, again, this time not in ignorance or in the agony of reaction to his friend's mutilation, but to do his job defending the castle. Murder had become a job. Was that how he proposed to forward his career? The sheer facility with which he had done it—maybe that was partly the natural prowess of his body, but he had also used his talent to gain the ladder's secret. No, it was he himself who was responsible, and he felt a great and growing guilt—after the fact.

And the Mundane—that man had recognized Dor, or rather Dor's body, calling him Mike. That must mean this body *was* that of a Mundane, part of this army, a man separated from his companions in the jungle, trapped by goblins, and presumed dead. Dor had taken over that body, preventing its return to its army. What had happened to the personality of the real Mike?

Dor bashed his hand against his head. The flea had bitten him again. Infernal bug! Oops—others called Jumper a bug, and Dor didn't like that; maybe the flea didn't like being called a—oh, forget it!

Where had he been, as he pondered things and watched the Mundanes drown below? Oh, yes: the fate of the personality of the original Mike Mundane. Dor couldn't answer that. He presumed the real Mike would return when Dor left. What bothered him more was the fact that he had taken advantage of the Mundane's recognition of him, to hurl the man from the wall. The Mundane had paused, not wishing to strike a friend—and had paid for that understandable courtesy with his position, perhaps his life. How would Dor himself feel if he encountered Jumper, and welcomed him—and Jumper struck him down? That had been a cruel gesture!

Nevertheless, he had held his position. He hoped the others had held theirs. He didn't dare check directly; this was his position to defend, and another ladder crew could arrive the moment he deserted his post.

War was not nice. If Dor ever got to be King, he would see that problems were settled some other way if at all possible. No one would ever convince him that there was any glory in battle.

The sun sank slowly before him. The Mundanes scrambled out of the moat, dragging their wounded and dead. They took their ladders, too, though these were sadly broken.

At last Millie came. "You can come down, now, Dor," she said hesitantly. "The zombie bugs say the Mundanes are too busy with their wounded to mount another attack today, and they won't do it by night."

"Why not? A sneak attack—"

"Because they think this is a haunted castle, and they're afraid of the dark."

Dor burst out laughing. It was hardly that funny, but the tension in him forced itself out.

It drained from him quickly. With relief he followed her down the winding stairs to the main hall. He noted the pleasant sway of her hips as she walked. He was noticing more things like that, recently.

They organized a night-watch system. There had been no attack on the other sides; Dor had handled it all. "We would have come to your aid," Jumper chittered. "But we feared some ruse."

"Exactly," Dor agreed. "I would not have come to help you, either."

"If we don't have discipline, we have nothing," the Zombie Master said. "We living are too few."

"But tonight you rest," Millie told Dor. "You have labored hard, and have earned it."

Dor didn't argue. He was certainly tired, and somewhat sick at heart, too. That business with the Mundane who recognized him . . .

Jumper took the first watch, scrambling all about the walls and ceilings inside and out. The Zombie Master retired for half a night's sleep before relieving the spider. That left Millie—who insisted on keeping Dor company while he ate and rested.

"You fought so bravely, Dor," she said, urging a soupnut on him.

"I feel sick." Then, aware of her gentle hurt, he qualified it. "Not from your cooking, Millie. From the killing. Striking men with a weapon. Dumping them into the moat. One of them recognized me. I dumped him, too."

"Recognized you?"

How could he explain? "He thought he did. So he didn't strike me. It wasn't fair to strike him."

"But they were storming the castle! You had to fight. Or we would all have been—" She squiggled, trying to suggest something awful. It didn't come across; she was delectable.

"But I'm not a killer!" Dor protested vehemently. "I'm only a twelve-year-old—" He caught himself, but didn't know how to correct his slip.

"A twelve-year veteran of warfare!" she exclaimed. "Surely you have killed before!"

It was grossly misplaced, but her sympathy gratified him strongly. His tired body reacted; his left arm reached out to enclose her hips in its embrace, as she stood beside him. He squeezed her against his side. Oh, her posterior was resilient!

"Why, Dor!" she said, surprised and pleased. "You like me!"

Dor forced himself to drop his arm. What business did he have, touching her? Especially in the vicinity of her cushiony posterior! "More than I can say."

"I like you too, Dor." She sat down in his lap, her derrière twice as soft and bouncy as before. Again his body reacted, enfolding her in an arm. Dor had never before experienced such sensation. Suddenly he was aware that his body knew what to do, if only he let it. That she was willing. That it could be an experience like none he had imagined in his young life. He was twelve; his body was older. *It could do it.*

"Oh, Dor," she murmured, bending her head to kiss him on the mouth. Her lips were so sweet he—

The flea chomped him hard on the left ear. Dor bashed at it—and boxed his ear. The pain was brief but intense.

He stood up, dumping Millie roughly to her feet. "I have to get some rest," he said.

She made no further sound, but only stood there, eyes downcast. He knew he had hurt her terribly. She had committed the cardinal maidenly sin of being forward, and been rebuked. But what could he do? *He did not exist in her world.* He would soon depart, leaving her alone for eight hundred years, and when they rejoined he would be twelve years old again. He had no right!

But oh, what might have been, had he been more of a man.

There was no attack in the night, and none in the morning—but the siege had not been lifted. The Mundanes were preparing another onslaught, and the defendants simply had to wait for it. While precious time slipped by, and the situation worsened for King Roogna. Magician Murphy was surely smiling.

Dor found Millie and the Zombie Master having breakfast together. They were chatting merrily, but stopped as he joined them. Millie blushed and turned her face away.

The Zombie Master frowned. He was halfway handsome after one acclimatized to his gauntness. "Dor, our conversation was innocent. But it appears there is something amiss between you and the lady. Do you wish me to depart?"

"No!" Dor and Millie said together.

The Magician looked nonplused. "I have not had company in some time. Perhaps I have forgotten the social niceties. So I must inquire somewhat baldly: would you take exception, Dor, if I expressed an interest in the lady?"

A green icicle of jealousy stabbed into Dor. He fought it off. But he could not speak.

Now Millie turned her large eyes on Dor. There was a mute plea in them that he almost understood. "No!" he said. Millie's eyes dropped, hurt again. Twice he had rejected her.

The Zombie Master shrugged his bony shoulders. "I do not know what else I can say. Let us continue our meal."

Dor thought of asking him to help the King, but realized again that what the Magician might do at his behest was suspect—and had an inspiration. What Dor himself did might lack validity, and what Jumper did —but what Millie did should hold up. *She* was of this world. So if she persuaded the Zombie Master to help the King—

A zombie entered. "Ttaakk," it rattled. "Hhoourr."

"Thank you, Bruce," the Zombie Master said. He turned to the others. "The Mundanes are organizing for another attack in an hour. We had best repair to our stations."

This time the attack came on Jumper's side. The Mundanes had assembled a massive battering ram. Not a real ram; those animals did not seem to have evolved yet. A mock ram fashioned from a heavy trunk of ironwood, mounted on wheels. Dor heard the boom and shudder as it crashed over the bridge they laid down over the moat and collided with the old stone. He hoped the wall was holding, but could not go to see or help: his post was here, not to be deserted lest another ladder attack come without warning. The others had had the discipline to stay clear of his section, last time, for the same reason. This was a special kind of courage, this standing aloof and ignorant.

An arrow dropped to his ledge. It had slid over the roof of the castle and fallen, its impetus spent. "What's the news over there?" Dor asked it.

"We're trying to batter a hole in the wall," the arrow said. "But that damned huge bug keeps yanking out our moat-crossing planks with its sticky lines. We're trying to shoot that spider, but it dodges too fast. Thing runs right across a sheer brick wall! I thought I had it—" The arrow sighed. "But I didn't, quite."

"Too bad," Dor said, smiling.

"Don't patronize me!" the arrow cried sharply. "I am a first-class weapon!"

"Maybe you need a more accurate bowman."

"That's for sure. More good arrows are ruined by bad marksmanship—oh, what's the use! If arrows ruled the world, instead of stupid people—"

Life was tough all over, Dor thought. Even for the nonliving. He did not speak to the arrow again, so it could not answer. Objects had to be invoked each time, initially. Only when he gave them a continuing command, voiced or unvoiced, as with the spiderweb that translated Jumper's chittering, did they speak on their own. Or when, through constant association with him, they picked up some of his talent, as with the walls and doors of his cheese cottage, his home.

How far removed that home seemed, now!

After a while the furor subsided, and Dor knew Jumper had succeeded in balking the attack. He considered going to check, since the threat had now abated, but decided to stay at his post. His curiosity was urgent, but discipline was discipline, even when it became virtually pointless.

And, quietly, a ladder crew came to his side. They were trying to sneak in! Dor waited silently for them to work their way across the moat and lift and hook the ladder and mount it. They thought he was absent or asleep, or at least not paying attention. How close they had come to being correct!

Then, just as the first Mundane came over the parapet, Dor charged across with his lever, wedged the ladder up, and shoved it away from the wall. He hardly noticed the screams and splashes as the men landed in the moat. By his constancy he had stopped the sneak raid and helped save the castle! Had he yielded to temptation and left his post prematurely . . .

He felt somewhat more heroistic than he had before.

Finally the zombie eye-spy announced that the Mundanes had withdrawn their main attack force, and Dor rejoined the others within. It was midday. They ate, then whiled away the long afternoon working on a jigsaw puzzle that Millie had discovered while cleaning the drawing room.

It was a magic puzzle, of course, for the jigs and saws were magical creatures who delighted in their art. When assembled, it would be a beautiful picture; but now it was in myriad little pieces that had to be fitted together. No two pieces fit unless spelled by the proper plea, which was often devious, and the portions of the picture that showed kept changing. The principle seemed to be similar to that of the magic tapestry of Dor's own time, with the little figures moving as in life. In fact—

"This is it!" Dor exclaimed. "We are weaving the tapestry!"

The others looked up, except for Jumper, whose

eyes were always looking up, down, and across, without moving. "What tapestry?" Millie inquired somewhat coldly. She was still sweetly angry with him for his rejection of her.

"The—I, uh, I can't exactly explain," he said lamely.

Jumper caught on. "Friend, I believe I know the tapestry you mean," he chittered. "The King mentioned it. He is looking for a suitable picture to hang upon the wall of Castle Roogna, that will entertain viewers and be representative of what he is trying to accomplish. This one should do excellently, if the Zombie Master will yield it up."

"I yield it up to you," the Magician said. "Because I respect your nature. Take it with you when you return to Castle Roogna."

"This is generous of you," Jumper chittered, placing another piece. His excellent vision made him adept at this task; he could look at several places at once, superimposing them in his brain, checking the fit without ever touching the pieces. He paused to chitter at the piece he held, and it evidently understood the invocation, because it merged seamlessly into the main mass of the forming picture. "But unless we are able to assist the King, the Castle will never be complete."

The Zombie Master did not answer, but Millie looked up, startled. She caught Dor's eye, and he nodded. She had caught on!

But she frowned. Dor knew the problem: she was interested in him, Dor, and did not want to practice her charms on the Magician. She was in no position to understand why Dor eschewed her, or why he did not continue to plead the cause of Castle Roogna himself. So she was sullen, concentrating on the puzzle. The afternoon wore on.

The puzzle was fascinating, an excellent device for whiling away the tense time. They all seemed to share its compulsion, vying together against its challenge as if it were the Mundane army.

"I have always enjoyed puzzles," the Zombie Master remarked, and indeed he was the best of the human participants. His skeletal hands became quick and sure as they fetched pieces and jerked them across to likely slots, comparing, rejecting, comparing again and matching. Thin, gaunt, but basically healthy and alert, the Magician seemed more human with each hour that he passed in Millie's company. "The excitement of discovery, without threat. When I was a child, before my talent was known, I would smash blocks of stone with a hammer, then reassemble them into the original. Of course it lacked the cohesion—"

"Was that not an aspect of your talent?" Jumper chittered. "Now you reassemble creatures, but they lack the cohesion of life."

The Magician laughed, the first time they had heard him do that. He flung back his shaggy brown hair so that his eyebrow ridges and cheekbones stood out more prominently. "A significant insight! Yes, I suppose creating zombies is not so very different from restoring stones. Yet it becomes a lonely pursuit, because others—"

"I understand," Jumper chittered. "You are a normal creature, as I am, but this world does not see it that way. I have my own world to return to, but you have only this one."

"Would that I could go to your world," the Magician said, lightly but with a certain longing beneath. "To begin fresh, unprejudged. Even among spiders, I would feel more at home."

Millie did not speak, but her demeanor softened. They worked on the puzzle. It occurred to Dor that human relations were similar to such a puzzle, meshed by the conventions of language. If only he knew where the piece that was his whole life should be fitted!

"When I was young," the Zombie Master remarked after a bit, "I dreamed idly of marrying and settling down in the normal fashion, raising a family. I had no thought of being—as you see me now. I had better appetite, was more fully fleshed, was hardly distinguishable from normal boys. Then one day I found a dead flying frog, and was sorry for it, and tried to will it back to life, and—"

"The first zombie!" Millie exclaimed.

"True. I watched that frog fly away with amazement, thinking I had wakened the dead. But it was less than that; I could only half-waken the dead. Except, perhaps, in special cases." He glanced at Dor, obviously thinking of the restorative elixir. But that was more than the Zombie Master's magic; that incorporated the magic of the healing elixir too, so was a collaboration. "From that point, my career was set. Against my preference, I achieved far greater status and isolation than any other of my time. It seemed that many others desired what I could do for them—making zombie animals to guard their homes, or fight their battles, or do their work—but none cared to associate with me on a personal level. I became disgusted; I do not like being used without respect."

Millie's softening became something more. "You poor man!" she exclaimed.

"You three are the first who have associated with me without revulsion," the Zombie Master continued. "True, you came begging favors—"

"We didn't understand!" Millie cried. "These two are from another land, far away, and I am only an innocent maid—"

"Yes," the Magician agreed, looking at her with muted intensity. "Innocent, but with a talent that causes others to react."

"Except for the three of you," she said. "Every other man has wanted to grab me. Dor dumped me on the floor." She cast a dark look at him.

"Your friend restrains himself because he is not of your world and must soon depart, and cannot take you with him," the Zombie Master said. Dor was amazed and gratified at the man's comprehension. "He can thus make you no commitments, and is too much the gentleman to take advantage on a temporary basis."

"But I would go with him!" she cried naïvely.

Jumper interjected a chitter: "It is impossible, maid. There is magic involved."

Her chin thrust forward in cute rebellion.

"Yet if you cared to remain here at my castle, Millie, you could have a life of status—" the Magician began, then reined himself. "But also of isolation. That must be confessed."

"You really have a lot of company," Millie said. "The zombies aren't so bad when you get to know them. They have different personalities. They . . . can't help it if they're not quite alive."

"They are often better company than the living creatures," the Zombie Master agreed. "They do possess muted emotions and dim memories of their prior lives. It is ignorance that makes them suspect—the ignorance of the majority of normal people. All the zombies need are set jobs to do, and a comfortable gravesite to sleep in between tasks—and acceptance."

Dor listened, noting how Millie and the Magician were coming together, forcing himself to stay out of it. His direct involvement could invalidate anything that happened—if Murphy was right. Yet it bothered him increasingly, this attempt to use the Zombie Master, who was after all a decent man.

"I don't think I'd mind living among zombies," Millie said. "I met a girl zombie in the garden; I think in life she must have been almost as pretty as I am."

"Almost," the Zombie Master agreed with a smile. "She was slain by a pneumonia spell intended for another. But when I restored her, her family would not take her back, so she remains here. I regret that I cannot undo my magic, once it has been applied; she is doomed like the others to live half-alive forever."

"I screamed when I met the first zombie. But now—"

"I realize your primary interest is elsewhere," the Magician said, glancing obliquely at Dor. "But if, accepting the fact that you cannot be with him, you would consider remaining here with me—"

"I have to help the King," she said. "We promised to—"

The Zombie bowed to the inevitable. "For you, I would even indulge in politics. Ad hoc. Employ my zombies to—"

"No!" Dor cried, surprising himself. "This is wrong!"

The Zombie Master glanced at him expressionlessly. "You are after all asserting your interest in the lady?"

"No! I can't have her. I know that. But we stay here only because we are under siege, and the moment the siege lifts we'll go back to King Roogna. It is dishonorable to let her play upon your loneliness only to gain your help for the King. The end does not justify the mean." He had heard King Trent say that, in his own time, but had not appreciated its full meaning until now. End and mean—or was it ends and means? "You have been generous to me and Jumper, because you understood our needs and respected them. How could you respect Millie if—"

For the first time, they saw Millie angry. "I wasn't trying to use him! He's a nice man! It's just that I made a promise to the King, and I can't just go off and do something else and let the whole Kingdom fall!"

Dor was chagrined. He had not really understood her innocence. "I'm sorry, Millie. I thought—"

"You think too much!" she flared.

"Yet your thought does you credit," the Zombie Master said to Dor. "And your naïveté does you credit, too," he said to Millie. "I was aware of the ramifications. I am accustomed to trading for favors. This is not an evil, when the conditions of exchange are openly negotiated. I am simply prepared to compromise, in this circumstance. If it is necessary to save the Kingdom to make the lady happy, then I am prepared to save the Kingdom. Quid pro quo. I am pleased that the damsel keeps her word to the King so stringently; I can reasonably suppose that she would similarly keep her word to you, Dor. Or to me, were she to give it."

"I haven't given it!" Millie protested. "Not to anyone! Not that way." But she seemed subtly flattered.

"The matter may be academic," Jumper chittered. "We are under siege here, and lack the means to do more than defend ourselves within this castle, with the aid of the loyal zombies. We cannot help the King anyway."

"And even if there were no siege," the Magician said, "I have suffered attrition of zombies. They are immortal, but when physically destroyed, with the pieces lost, they become useless. I could only bring a token force to the aid of the King. Not enough to overwhelm the curse on Castle Roogna."

"You could make more zombies," Dor said. "If you had more dead bodies."

"Oh, yes, without limit. But I need intact bodies, and fresh ones are best."

"Could we but overcome the Mundanes," Jumper chittered, "we could use their bodies to fashion a mighty army."

"If we had a mighty army, we could use it to vanquish the Mundanes," Dor pointed out. "Closed circle."

"I do not wish to interfere with human concerns," Jumper chittered. "But I believe I see a course through the impasse. There is some risk entailed—"

"There is risk entailed in remaining under siege," the Zombie Master said. "Present your notion; we can consider its merit jointly." He placed another piece of puzzle, uttering the mergeance spell under his breath.

"It is an arrangement, a series of agreements utilizing all our efforts," Jumper chittered. "The Zombie Master and Millie must defend this castle for a time alone, while I convey Dor outside by night. I can swing him along a line to a near tree so that no one will notice. The Mundanes can not see as well as I can in darkness. Then Dor must use his talent to locate some of the real monsters of the wilderness—the dragons and such—and enlist their aid."

"Dragons will not help men!" Dor protested.

"They would not be helping men," Jumper chittered. "They would be fighting men."

"But—" Then Dor caught on. "Mundanes!"

"But we are people too," Millie said.

Jumper angled his head to cock eyes of three different sizes at her. He was obviously not human.

"Well, still—" she faltered.

"I will be with Dor," Jumper chittered. "They will know me for a monster, and him for a Magician. Inside the castle will be another Magician and a woman, and many zombie animals. No normal human men. We will convey this promise: any monsters who die in the battle to lift the siege will be restored as zombies. But mainly, they will have the thrill of killing men with impunity. The King will not condemn them for what they do, since it is to assist him."

"It just might work!" Dor exclaimed. "Let's go!"

"Not until dark," Jumper chittered.

"And not until you've eaten," Millie added. She bounced off to the kitchen.

Jumper placed a final puzzle-piece and retired to an upstairs rafter to rest. That left Dor and the Zombie Master with the puzzle, which was coming along nicely. They had largely completed the center, with the scene of Castle Roogna, and were working toward the Zombie Master's castle. Dor was increasingly curious to know how it would turn out. Would they be able to see themselves in it, under Mundane siege? How much of reality did these magic pictures reflect?

"Are you really going to help the King?" Dor asked. "I mean, if we break the siege here?"

"Yes. To please the lady. And to please you."

Still Dor was troubled. "There is something else I must tell you."

"You are about to risk your life in the defense of my castle. Speak without inhibition."

"The lady . . . is doomed to die young. I know this from history."

The Zombie Master's hand froze, with a translucent piece of puzzle held between gaunt fingers. The piece changed from warm red light to cold blue ice. "I know that you would not deliberately deceive me."

Maybe he had spoken too uninhibitedly! "I would be deceiving you if I failed to warn you. She—maybe death is not the right word. But she will be a ghost for centuries. So you will not be able to—" Dor found himself overcome by remorse at what he could not prevent. "I think someone will murder her, or try to. At age seventeen."

"What age is she now?"

"Seventeen."

The Magician rested his head against his hand. The puzzle-piece turned white. "I suppose I could make a zombie of her, and keep her with me. But it wouldn't be the same."

"She—if you're helping the King to please her—or to please any of us—we'll all be gone within the year. So it may not be worth it, to—"

"Your honesty becomes painful," the Zombie Master said. "Yet it seems that if I am to please any of you, I must do it promptly. There may not again in my lifetime be opportunity to please anyone worth pleasing."

Dor did not know what to say to this, so he simply put out his hand. The Magician set down the puzzle-piece, which had turned black, and shook Dor's hand gravely. They returned to the puzzle, speaking no more.

The puzzle, Dor wondered—for his mind had to get away from the grim prior subject. How could this puzzle be the tapestry, when they were all within the tapestry? Was it possible to enter this forming picture, by means of a suitable spell, and find another world within it? Or had the tapestry been merely a gateway, the entry point, not the world itself? Was it coincidence that he should be assembling this particular picture at this juncture? The Zombie Master was the key to this whole quest, the vital element—and he had the tapestry, the key to the entry to this world. Yet he had given it to Jumper. How did this relate?

Dor shook his head. Such mysteries were beyond his fathoming. All he could do was . . . what he could do.

Chapter 8. Commitment

That night Dor and Jumper departed the castle on the spider's line. It would have been possible to convey Millie out in the same manner, but they cared neither to subject her to the risk nor to desert the Zombie Master, even had circumstances been otherwise. There were Mundane sentries posted; Millie would have screamed, and that would have been disastrous. As it was, Dor trusted Jumper's night vision to thread them through the dark foliage, and they managed to pass without being detected. Soon they were deep in the jungle, beyond the Mundane ring of troops.

"We'd better start with the lord of the jungle," Dor said. "If he goes along with it, most of the rest will. That is the nature of jungles."

"And if the lord does not cooperate?"

"Then you will use your safety line to yank me out of his reach, in a hurry."

Jumper affixed a dragline to him, then carried the other end. In an emergency, the spider would be able to act quickly. Dor found himself wishing he had a silk-making gland; those lines were extremely handy.

The spider found him a rock in the dark. "Where is the local dragon king?" Dor demanded of it.

The stone directed him to a narrow hole in a rocky hillside. "This is it?" Dor inquired dubiously.

"You'd better believe it," the cave replied.

"Oh, I believe it!" Dor said, not wishing to antagonize the residence of the monster he hoped to bargain with.

"And if you care to depart uncooked, you'd better not wake the monarch," the cave said.

Jumper chittered. "That small cave has a large mouth."

"What?" the cave demanded.

Dor gulped. "I have to wake him." Then he put his hands to his mouth and called. "Dragon! I must parlay. I have news of interest to you."

There was a snort from deep within the cave. Then a plume of smoke wafted out, white in the blackness, followed by a rolling growl. The scent of scorch suffused the air.

"What does he say?" Dor asked the cave.

"He says that if you have news of interest, come into his parlor. Your life depends on the accuracy of your advance promotion."

"His parlor?" Jumper chittered. "That is an ominous phrasing. When a spider invites—"

Dor had not bargained on this. "In there? In the dragon's cave?"

"See any other caves, man-roast?" the cave demanded.

Jumper made another soft chitter. "Huge mouth!"

"I guess I'd better go down," Dor said.

"I have better night vision; let me go," Jumper chittered.

"No. You can't use objects to translate the dragon's speech, and I can't jump into trees and string a line to the castle wall. I must talk with the dragon. You must be ready to bear the news." He swallowed again. "In case my mission fails. You can communicate with Millie, now, by signals."

Jumper touched him with a foreleg, the pressure expressive. "Your logic prevails, friend Dor-man. I shall listen by this entrance, and return alone if necessary. I will draw you up by the dragline if you call, rapidly. Have courage, friend."

"I'm scared as hell." But Dor remembered what the gorgon had said about courage: that it was a matter of doing what needed to be done despite fear. He was bleakly reassured. Maybe technically he would be a dead hero, instead of a dead coward. "If—if something happens, try to salvage some piece of me, and keep it with you. I think the return spell will orient on it, and carry you home when the time is up. I wouldn't want you to be trapped in this world."

"It would not be doom," Jumper replied. "This world is a novel experience."

More of an experience than Dor had bargained for! He took a breath, then slid into the cave's big mouth. The interior was not large enough to permit him to stand, as the throat constricted, but that did not mean the dragon was small. Dragons tended to be long and sinuous.

The passage curved down and around, so black it was impossible to see. "Warn me of any drops, spikes, or other geographic hazards," Dor said.

"There are none, other than the dragon," the wall replied. "That's more than enough."

"I wish there were a little light," Dor muttered. "Too bad I gave away my wishing ring."

The dragon growled from below. "You want light?" the wall translated. "I'll give you light!" And tongues of bright flame snaked up the passage.

"Not that much!" Dor cried, cringing from the heat.

The flames subsided. It was evident that the dragon understood human speech, and was not blasting him indiscriminately. That was both reassuring and alarming. If there was anything more dangerous than a dragon, it was an intelligent dragon. Yet of course the smartest dragon would be most likely to rise to leadership in the complex hierarchy of the wilderness. Provided it also possessed sufficient ferocity.

Dor emerged at last in the stomach of the cave. This was the dragon's lair. The light waxed and waned, here, as the monster breathed and the flames washed out of his mouth. In the waxing the whole cave glittered, for of course the nest was made of diamonds. Not paltry ones like those of the small flying dragon Crunch the ogre had cowed; huge ones, befitting the status of the lord of the jungle. They refracted the light, reflected it, focused it, and broke it up into rainbow splays. Colors cascaded across the walls and ceiling, and bathed the dragon itself in re-reflected hues. Crunch the ogre would never beard *this* monster in his den!

And the dragon himself: his scales were mirror-polished, iridescent, and as supple and overlapping as the best warrior's mail. The great front claws were burnished brass tapering to needlepoints, and its snout was gold-plated. The eyes were like full moons, their veins reminiscent of the contours of the green cheese there, and as the light changed the cheese changed flavor.

"You're beautiful!" Dor exclaimed. "I've never seen such splendor!"

"You damn me with faint praise," the dragon grumped.

"Uh, yes, sir, I come to—"

"What?" the dragon demanded through a blaze of fire.

"Sir?"

"That was the word."

Dor had suspected it was. "Uh, sir, I—"

"All right already. Now what does a Man-Magician want with the likes of me, a mere monster monarch?"

"I come to, uh, make a deal. You know how it is not safe, uh, I mean expedient, for you to, uh, eat men, and—"

The dragon snorted a snort of flame uncomfortably close to Dor's boots. "I eat what I eat! I am lord of the jungle."

"Yes, sir, of course. But men are not of the jungle. When you eat too many of them, they start making, er, difficulties. They use special magic to—"

"I don't care to talk about it!" This time the snort was pungent smoke.

"Uh, yes. Sir. What I'm trying to say is that there are some men who need, er, eating. Mundane men from outside Xanth, who don't have magic. If you and your cohorts cared to, uh—"

"I begin to absorb your drift," the dragon said. "If we were to indulge in some, shall we say, sport, your Magicians would not object? Your King Whatshisname—?"

"King Roogna. No, I don't believe he would object. This time. Provided you ate only Mundanes."

"It is not always easy to tell at a glance whether a given man is native or Mundane. You all taste alike to us."

Good point. "Well—we'll wear green sashes," Dor said, thinking of some bedspreads he had seen in the Zombie Master's castle. They could be torn into sashes. "It would be only in this region; don't go near Castle Roogna."

"Castle Roogna is in the territory of my cousin, who can be touchy about infringements," the dragon said. "There is plenty to eat in this area. Those Mundanes are especially big and juicy. I understand. Is there a time limit?"

"Uh, would two days be enough?"

"More than enough. Shall we say it commences at dawn tomorrow?"

"That's fine."

"How can I be sure you speak for your King?"

"Well, I—" Dor paused, uncertain. "I suppose it would be best to verify it. Do you have a swift messenger?"

The dragon snapped his tail. It was out of sight, far down the bowels of the cave, but the report was authoritative. It was answered by a squawk, and in a moment a chickenlike bird fluttered into the main chamber. It was a woolly hen, with curly fleece instead of feathers. Dor knew little about this breed, except that it was shy, and could move quite rapidly.

"Uh, yes," he said. "Uh, have you anything to write with?" He had certainly come unprepared.

The dragon jetted smoke toward a wall. Dor looked. There was a niche. In the niche were several papershell pecans and an inkwood branch. "I have a secretary-bird," the dragon growled in explanation. "She likes to write to her cousin across the Gap. Then she carries the letter herself, because she trusts no one else to do it. Why she doesn't simply chatter out her gossip directly I don't know. But she's good at keeping track of things around here such as which monster needs a chomping and which a scorching, and when the next rainstorm is due, so I keep her on. She's across the Gap now; she'll set up an unholy squawk when she finds her stuff's been used, but go ahead and use it."

Dor unfolded a length of paper from a shell, took

a splinter of inkwood, and somewhat laboriously wrote:

> KING ROOGNA: PLEASE AUTHENTICATE PERMISSION FOR MONSTERS TO SLAY MUNDANES FOR TWO DAYS WITHOUT PENALTY. NECESSARY TO LIFT MUNDANE SIEGE OF CASTLE OF ZOMBIE MASTER, WHO WILL COME TO YOU THEREAFTER. ALL XANTH CITIZENS IN VICINITY TO WEAR GREEN SASHES TO DISTINGUISH THEM FROM MUNDANES. SIGNED, MAGICIAN DOR.

He folded the note and gave it to the woolly hen. "Take this to the King, and return immediately with his answer."

The bird took the note in her beak and took off. She was gone in a puff of wool dust, so quickly that he never saw her move.

"I must admit this prospect pleases me," the dragon king remarked, idly stirring up a mound of diamonds with one glistening claw. "If it should fall through, I might recall how you disturbed my sleep. Don't count on your spider friend to draw you out; my flame would burn up his line instantly."

The nature of the threat was absolutely clear to Dor. He felt like screaming and kicking his feet, certain that would relieve some tension; it always seemed to work for Millie. But he wore the guise of a man; he had to act like a man. "I was aware of the hazard when I committed myself to your lair."

"You do not attempt to beg, or to threaten me with vague retribution," the dragon said. "I like that. The fact is, it is impolitic to toast Magicians, and I especially do not want to aggravate the Zombie Master. That roc of his has been scouring the area for bodies. I would not care to tangle with that big bird for esthetic reasons. So I do not intend to toast you—unless you attempt to do me mischief."

"I thought that might be your attitude. Sir."

The woolly hen returned in another cloud of dust, bearing another note. Dor took it and read it aloud:

> PERMISSION AUTHENTICATED. GO TO IT. SIGNED, THE KING.

He showed it to the dragon.

"That would seem to be it," the dragon said, puffing out a satisfied torus of smoke. "Hen, go out to my subjects and summon them for a rampage. Tell them to get their tails swinging or I'll burn them off. I will instruct them in one hour." He angled his snout toward Dor. "It has been a pleasure doing business with you, sir."

But Dor was wary. He remembered Magician Murphy's curse on Castle Roogna: anything that could go wrong, would. This message had related to that project. Why hadn't the curse operated? This had been too easy.

"You had better depart before my cohorts arrive," the dragon said. "Until I instruct them, they will consider you and the spider fair game."

"Uh, I—" Then Dor had an idea. "Let me just check something, sir. A mere formality, but . . ." He addressed the paper he held. "Did you come from the King?"

"I did," the paper replied.

"And the message you bear really is his message?"

"It is."

"Your magic seems to endorse the message," the dragon said. "I am satisfied. Why question it?"

"I'm just . . . cautious. I fear something could have gone wrong."

The dragon considered. "Obviously you are not experienced with conspiracies and bureaucratic entanglements of the sort we encounter in the wilderness. Ask it which King."

"Which King?" Dor repeated blankly.

"The Goblin King," the paper answered.

Dor exchanged a dismayed glance with the dragon. "The Goblin King! Not King Roogna?"

"Not," the paper agreed.

"That idiotic bird!" the dragon exploded, almost singeing Dor with his fiery breath. "You sent it to the King, without specifying which King, and the Goblin King must have been closer. I should have realized the response came too fast!"

"And naturally the Goblin King sought to mess us

up," Dor concluded. "Murphy's curse *did* operate. A misunderstanding was possible, so—"

"Does this mean we have no deal?" the dragon inquired ominously through a ring of smoke.

"It means our deal has not been authenticated by King Roogna," Dor said. "I'm sure the King would agree to it, but if we can't get a message through—"

"Why would the Goblin King authenticate it? I have had some experience with goblins, and they are not nice creatures. They don't even taste good. Surely the goblins should be more pleased to foul up our deal than to facilitate it. The goblins have no love for men, and not much for dragons."

"That *is* strange," Dor agreed. "He should have sent a note saying 'deal denied,' so we couldn't cooperate. Or else just held it without answering, so we would be stuck waiting."

"Instead he gave exactly the response we wanted from the Human King, so we would not delay," the dragon said. He puffed some more smoke, thoughtfully. "What mischief would occur if beasts started slaying men in great numbers, without approval?"

Dor considered that. "A great deal of mischief," he decided. "It would become a matter of principle. The King can't allow unauthorized slaying; he is opposed to anarchy. Such an act could possibly lead to war between the monsters and all the King's men."

"Which could result in internecine slaughter, leaving the goblins dominant on land," the dragon concluded. "They already have considerable force. Those netherworld goblins are tough little brutes! I think your kind would have real trouble, were it not for the distraction the harpies pose to the goblins. The one thing those creatures do well is breed. There are now a great many of them."

"Well, one man can slay five goblins," Dor said.

"And one dragon can slay fifty. But there are more than that number per man or dragon."

"Um." Dor agreed pensively.

"Do you know, I would have been fooled by that note, if you had not questioned the paper," the dragon remarked. "I do not like being fooled." This time it was not smoke but a ring of fire that he puffed. The thing wafted up the tunnel entrance, rotating, glimmering like a malignant eye.

"Neither do I," Dor agreed, wishing he could puff fire.

"Would your King have any objection if a few goblins got incidentally chomped during the rampage?"

"I think not. But we'd better get another message to King Roogna."

"While we allow the goblins to think they have fooled us into an act of interspecies war."

Dor smiled grimly. "Have you another messenger—a more reliable one?"

"I have other messengers—but let us use your talent this time. We shall send a diamond from my nest to your King, along with the paper; he must return the diamond with his spoken reply. No lesser man would give up such a jewel, and no other but you could make it speak."

"Terrific!" Dor exclaimed. "It is hard to imagine any goblin faking *that* message! You are a genius!"

"You praise me with faint damns," the dragon growled.

It was almost dawn by the time Dor rejoined Jumper. Quickly they returned to the castle with their news.

Millie and the Zombie Master greeted them with joyed relief. "You must be the first to have *our* news," the Magician said. "Millie the maid has done me the honor of agreeing to become my wife."

"So the commitment has been made," Jumper chittered.

"Congratulations," Dor said, with highly mixed emotions. He was glad for the Zombie Master, who was a worthy Magician and a decent man. But what of himself?

Millie made green sashes for them all, including the spider, who settled for an envelope covering his abdomen. Then she fed them a breakfast of hominy from another plant she had discovered in the courtyard. The Zombie Master had worked all night making new zombies from the corpses the roc had found, so that the castle defenses were back to full strength.

The Zombie Master radiated a mood of restrained joy. He knew Millie would not live long, but at least he had snatched his meager share of paradise from what was available.

Millie seemed less elated, yet hardly upset. It was evident that she liked the Magician, and liked the life he offered her, and was being practical—yet there was the restraint born of Dor's presence, and of his rejection of her. They all understood the situation, except for a couple of elements. Millie did not know how soon she would perish; neither Dor nor the Zombie Master knew how she would die, for she had never spoken of that to Dor in his own world. Also, none of them were certain how the coming campaign would turn out; maybe the aid of the zombies would not be enough to bring victory to King Roogna. Yet overall, Dor felt this was the best contentment they could achieve with what they had. He tried not to look at Millie's delightful figure, because his body was too apt to respond.

I wish I were a man, he thought fiercely. As it was, how much difference was there between him and a zombie? His mind animated an otherwise largely defunct body. The Magician's magic animated the zombies. But of course zombies did not notice the figures of women. They had no interest in sex.

Then what about Jonathan Zombie, in his own time? Why did he cleave to Millie, instead of resting quietly in some nice grave? If Millie's sex appeal did not turn him on, what else motivated him? Did some zombies, after all, get lonely?

Well, if Dor got back to that world, and managed to restore Jonathan, he would inquire. There had to be something different about Jonathan, or Millie would have fled him centuries before, while she remained a ghost.

So many little mysteries, once he got on that tack! Maybe what Dor needed was not more answers, but fewer questions.

The Mundanes attacked again at dawn, this time rolling a huge wagon up to the moat. It had a projecting boom, tall enough to match the height of the outer wall and long enough to reach right across the moat. They could march their soldiers right across this to the castle! They must have worked all night, building it, and it was quite a threat.

Then the monsters struck. The lord of the jungle had really produced! He led the charge, galumphing from the deepest forest with a horrendous roar and a belch of flame that enveloped the wooden tower. Behind him came a griffin, a wyvern, a four-footed whale, several carnivorous rabbits, a pair of trolls, a thunderbird, a sliver cat, a hippogriff, a satyr, a winged horse, three hoopsnakes, a pantheon, a firedrake, a monoceros, a double-headed eagle, a cyclops, a flight of barnacle geese, a chimera, and a number of creatures of less ordinary aspect that Dor could not identify in the rush. This seemed to be the age of monsters; in Dor's own day, the dragons were more common and the others less so. Probably the fittest had survived the centuries better, and the dragons were the fittest of monsters, just as men were the fittest of humanoids and the tanglers were the fittest of predatory plants. Right now the Land of Xanth was still experimenting, producing many bizarre forms.

The Mundanes were no cowards, however, and they outnumbered the assorted monsters. They formed a new battle array to meet this onslaught, swordsmen to the fore, archers behind. Dor, Millie, Jumper, and the Zombie Master watched from the ramparts with gratified amazement as the battle swirled around the castle, leaving them out of it. Now and then a flying monster buzzed them, but sheered off when it spied their green sashes. The Dragon King seemed to have excellent discipline in his army! Dor was glad once more that he had been brought up to understand the importance of cooperation; the monsters were an invaluable asset.

Yet was this not the result of his own action, rather than Millie's? Would it turn out to be invalid in the end? Millie had persuaded the Zombie Master to help King Roogna, so that was valid—but if this help could only arrive in time through Dor's agency, did it become invalid? It was so hard to know!

Right now, however, all he could do was hope Murphy was mistaken, meanwhile enjoying the battle. The Dragon King completed his charge to the burning wooden wagon tower, and chomped the boom in half with a single rearing bite. There was nothing quite like a dragon in combat! The Mundane archers rained arrows upon the polished scales, but the missiles bounced away without visible effect. The swordsmen slashed at the armored hide, but only blunted their blades. The dragon swept his great glittering tail about, knocking men off their feet and piling them in a brutal tangle of arms and legs. He swung his snout around the other way, burning another swath. Dor was glad he was not out there himself, trying to fight that dragon. There were wild stories about single men slaying large dragons in fair combat, but that was folklore. The fact was no single man was a match for even a small dragon, and no twenty men could match a large one. Anyone who doubted this had just to watch an engagement like this one, where fifty armed men in battle formation could not even wound the King of Dragons.

Meanwhile the other monsters were busy. The winged horse was rearing and stomping; the rabbits were gnawing into legs; the double-headed eagle was plucking eyeballs neatly from their sockets and swallowing them whole, the satyr was— Dor stared for a moment in amazement, then forced his gaze away. He had never imagined killing men that way. The more formidable monsters were laying about them with similar glee, reveling in an orgy of slaughter. For centuries they had restrained themselves from attacking men too freely, for men could be extremely ornery about vengeance. Now the monsters had license. Now, and perhaps never again.

The Mundanes, however, were tough. They had no magic of their own, but compensated by being extremely disciplined in combat and skilled with their weapons. Quickly realizing that they could neither prevail nor escape on the open battlefield, they fell back to natural and artificial defenses. The burning wagon made a good barricade, and next to it the moat made another. Mounds of dirt and debris had been formed by the dragon's thrashing tail, and these made excellent cover. The archers, nestled behind such shelter, were scoring on the lesser monsters, bringing down the barnacle geese and rabbits and hurting the thunderbird and sliver cat. The swordsmen were mastering the trick of sliding their blades up under the scales of the armored creatures, penetrating to their vital organs. Perhaps a quarter of the Mundanes had perished in the initial clash, but now half the monsters were dead or injured, and the tide of battle was turning. Dor had never anticipated this. What phenomenal brutes men were!

"Now we must assist our allies," the Zombie Master said.

"Oh no you don't!" Millie protested protectively. "You'll get killed, and I haven't even married you yet."

"My life is complete, receiving such a caution from such as you," the Magician murmured.

"Don't make fun of me! I'm worried!"

"There was no fun intended," he said seriously. "All my life I have longed for attention like this. Nevertheless, there is an obligation to acquit."

"No!"

"Peace, my dear. Zombies cannot die."

"Oh." Her innocence became her yet.

Dor, hearing this brief dialogue, suffered again his bit of jealousy. Yet he recognized that Millie had found in the Magician as good a man as was available. The Zombie Master loved her, but loved honor too. He knew she was to die, yet was going to marry her. He had the kind of discipline Dor was striving to master. For the Zombie Master, there was no special conflict between love and honor; they merged.

The Magician sent out a zombie contingent, wearing green sashes. Both monsters and Mundanes were startled. But the monsters let the zombies pass without hindrance. The undead charged into the Mundane positions, picking up fallen weapons along the way and hacking with unsteady but gruesome conviction.

The Mundanes had come to fight zombies. Yet they were taken aback by this sally, and repulsed by the repulsiveness of the half-dead things. The living men overreacted, hacking violently at the things in their midst—and scoring on each other.

Then the monsters rallied and bore in again. The zombies had made the difference; the defensive positions of the Mundanes were overrun, and the carnage resumed.

But the monsters were tired now, and some were pausing to glut themselves on the bodies of slain Mundanes. The monsters had been great in ferocity, not number, and some were dead. The Mundanes still outnumbered them, and after their lapse with the zombies, their excellent fighting discipline reasserted itself. The tide of battle was turning again, despite the zombies' efforts. There were too few of them to last long.

Then some wickedly smart Mundane caught on to the significance of the green sashes. He ripped one from a dismembered zombie and put it around himself. And of course the monsters did not attack him.

"Disaster!" Dor exclaimed, remembering Murphy. "In a moment they'll all be wearing green!" He started for the front gate.

"I will swing us down," Jumper chittered. "It is faster."

"But—" Millie started, appalled. Dor experienced a flush of gratitude: she was solicitous of his welfare, too.

Jumper fastened a dragline to Dor's waist. Dor jumped over the parapet. Jumper played out the line, letting him drop swiftly but carefully into the moat.

Millie made a stifled scream, but Dor was all right. The water softened the impact, and the commotion outside was such that not even the moat-monster noticed him. He sloshed to land. Jumper bounded to ground, then skated on the surface of the water to make sure Dor was all right.

No one paid attention to them. They passed the griffin, who was busy disemboweling a Mundane; the creature glanced up, saw the sashes, and returned to its business. Dor and Jumper proceeded unmolested to the nearest green-sashed Mundane. The man was laying about him with vigor, slashing at the chimera, who was backing off uncertainly. The monster didn't know whether it was legitimate to crunch this green-clad foe, however obnoxious the man became.

Dor had no scruples. He charged up, sword bared.

The Mundane saw him. "Come, friend—let's get this dumb monster!" And Dor's blade ran him through. The Mundane's only reaction as he died was surprise.

"Okay, chimera—go to it!" Dor urged the monster. The chimera, its doubt resolved, returned to the attack against unsashed Mundanes.

Dor proceeded to the next green-sashed Mundane. Now a scruple caught up to him. He felt a twinge of guilt for what he was doing, until he reminded himself that it was the same thing the Mundanes were doing: masquerading as a friend. If they hadn't started impersonating monster-exempt humans, they would not have been fooled by the real green-sashes. Dor was merely restoring the validity of the designations. So the scruple paused, then reluctantly retreated. A battlefield was not a fit home for scruples.

Jumper was an anomaly: he resembled a monster, yet wore the sash. A wyvern glanced at him, startled, then returned to the fray. Jumper looped silk around a sashed Mundane, chomped him neatly on the head with his chelicerae nippers, and went on. The spider was enjoying this; after all, these Mundanes had tortured him by pulling out four of his legs.

Thanks to Dor and Jumper's activity, the monsters swung into a slow ascendency again. The Mundanes did not stem the tide this time; they fell back toward their base camp, taking losses, pressed by monsters, zombies, and Dor and Jumper. The battle was almost over.

Then another smart Mundane popped up. Smart Mundanes were a nuisance! He ducked under Dor's swing, came in close, and ripped Dor's sash from his body. "Now fight!" he screamed.

Dor's return thrust skewered him. But the damage was done. The sash was buried under the body, and the hippogriff was bearing down on him. There was now no way Dor could distinguish himself from the Mundanes.

The hippogriff had the forepart of a griffin and the hind part of a horse. That gave it excellent fighting ability, coupled with superior running ability. The eagle's beak and claws stabbed viciously forward. Dor danced aside, then cut at a wing with his sword. He didn't strike too hard, because he did not want to hurt or kill a creature on his own side, but he had to defend himself. It was the hippogriff's turn to take evasive action. But then it closed its wings and bore in again, and Dor knew he could not survive the onslaught long. The monster was too big, too fast, too strong; it was wary of Dor's sword, but able to dodge it. The hippogriff was tired, but so was Dor.

"Jumper!" Dor cried. But then he saw that Jumper was engaged with three unsashed Mundanes, and could not extricate himself, let alone come to Dor's rescue. The four-footed whale rose up between them, opening its huge cetacean maw to engulf-gulp a Mundane; it incidentally blocked off Dor's approach to Jumper. Now he had nowhere at all to go. Oh, this was terrible!

But the Zombie Master, high in the castle, was watching out for him. Millie's faint scream came, and there was a spark of sunlight from her swirl of hair; then the Magician's faint command: "Egor!" And the zombie ogre charged out of the castle, bearing a gargantuan club. He swept aside Mundanes and monsters alike, bearing down on Dor.

Until he encountered the land whale. This monster was simply too big to move, and it was not about to give way to an ogre, even a green-sashed zombie ogre. The whale did not attack; it just hulked. It had the head and tusks of a boar, and rows of spikes on its body, with powerful lion's legs: a slow but formidable creature. The ogre had to make a detour around it—and in that critical period of delay, the hippogriff spread its wings, fanned a cloud of battle dust into Dor's face so that he was momentarily blinded, and clawed swiftly at his sword, disarming him. Dor threw up his arms in a futile defensive gesture—

And found himself lifted high, unharmed. Startled, he blinked vision back into his watering eyes, getting the dust out, and discovered himself hooked on the long tip of the Dragon King's tail. Fifty feet away, the dragon's snout growled, emitting puffs of smoke.

"What's he saying?" Dor demanded of a stone as he was being carried past.

"Better be more careful of your sash, Magician!" the stone translated.

The Dragon King had recognized Dor, and saved him. In a moment Dor was dumped beside the moat, out of the fray. The tail snaked back, to emerge with Jumper. "With your concurrence," the Dragon roared, "I will personally slay a few sashed men. There are none here on your side, apart from the zombies, correct?"

"Correct!" Dor cried, thankful for the dragon's perspicacity. The regular monsters might not know the difference, but the Dragon King obviously did.

"No wonder he is King," Jumper chittered. The spider had lost a foot, but was otherwise intact. "We must get back inside the castle; the monsters will prevail."

"Right. Should we call back Egor?"

"He is having such a good time; let him rampage."

They re-entered the castle, where Millie was waiting with healing elixir. In a moment the spider's foot was whole, and Dor's many abrasions were gone.

Millie hugged Jumper briefly, turned to Dor, and refrained from making a similar gesture. After all, she was now betrothed to another man. They returned to the upper ledge to watch the conclusion of the battle.

In this installment, the monsters were mopping things up. The tough Mundanes became less tough as they perceived defeat looming, and finally they broke and fled. The monsters pursued, cutting them down without mercy. The vicinity of the castle was deserted, the ground strewn with the bodies of men and monsters, and with struggling pieces of zombies.

"Now I must work," the Zombie Master said. "Dor, if you will supervise the carrying of bodies to my laboratory, I will render them into loyal zombies. It will require a few minutes and some effort for each, so you need not hurry—but the faster we perform, the stronger the zombies will be. Also, we shall need to march within a day, to reach King Roogna's castle in time to be of service."

Dor nodded agreement. He saw how tired the Magician looked, and remembered that he had spent all the prior night making new zombies. The man needed a rest! But that would have to wait. After all, Dor himself had had no more rest.

They organized it and got to work. Millie spotted the best corpses of man and animal, now so accustomed to the gore that she worked without even token screams. Dor carried the bodies to a staging area. Jumper attached lines and hauled the objects across the moat to the castle. They concentrated first on Mundanes. When a number of these had been animated, the new zombies took over the labor of transporting corpses, and the pace accelerated. Soon there was a backlog of bodies awaiting the Magician's attention.

The Dragon King returned. He was spattered with blood, and several of his mirror-scales had been hacked off, but he was in fairly good condition. "That was some fun!" he growled. "There is not a man alive, here." There was no flame when he spoke; he had used it all up for the nonce.

"Oh, let me give you some elixir!" Millie exclaimed. She sprinkled some on him, and the dragon was instantly restored to full health. Then she went to the other monsters straggling back, and restored them similarly.

"One could almost get to like a creature like that, human though she be," the dragon said reflectively. "There is something about her—"

"The dead we shall reanimate as zombies, as promised," Dor said quickly.

"No need. The survivors will consume the dead, as is our custom. We do not care to become zombies."

"We have been taking the intact corpses. If you are satisfied to eat the dismembered ones—"

"They will do nicely." And the monsters fell to their repast, crunching up bodies. It was a strange and grisly scene: dragon and griffin and serpent, ripping into corpses, while zombies carried other corpses around them in sepulchral silence, and the pretty maid Millie wandered amid it all sprinkling healing elixir.

"Where is Egor?" Jumper chittered.

Good question! There was no sight of the zombie

ogre who had fought so valiantly to rescue them. They spread out, searching.

"You mean the ogre?" the Dragon King inquired, ripping the delicious guts out of a Mundane and smacking his long lips. "He got in a bit of trouble down by the Mundane camp, last I noted."

They ran down to the deserted camp. There, in pieces, was Egor Ogre. The last surviving Mundanes had hacked him to quivering pieces.

"Maybe we can still help," Dor said, his stomach roiling. He had become acclimatized to gore, but this was a friend! "Let's collect all we can find of him, put it together, and sprinkle some elixir."

They did this—and the ogre was restored, except for part of one hand and foot and some of his face they had not been able to locate. The zombie could no longer speak, and walked with a limp. But in his condition that was not too noticeable. They trekked back to the castle.

"Would you monsters care to join us at Castle Roogna?" Dor inquired. "I'm sure the King—the Man King—would welcome your help."

"Fighting whom?" the Dragon King inquired, slurping a tasty intestine.

"Goblins and harpies, mostly."

The dragon snorted a smoke helix. "Now I do have a gripe against the Goblin King, but let's not lose our perspective. Killing men is fun; killing other monsters is treason. We cannot join you there."

"Oh. Well, sir, we certainly thank you for—"

"Our pleasure, sir." The dragon dipped a tooth into the body and brought out a splendid liver. "I haven't eaten this well in fifty years. I'll catch my death of a stomachache." He slurped the liver down.

"Uh, yes," Dor agreed. Liver had never been his favorite food, and after this he doubted that taste would change.

"Since we monsters will not be participating, but do have a grievance against the goblins and no liking for harpies, I feel free to make a comment," the dragon said, fixing a bright eye on Dor. "This battle for the zombie castle has only been your rehearsal for the siege to come. The goblins are tougher than men.

Prepare well—better than you did this time, or you are doomed."

"Tougher than Mundanes? But goblins are so small—"

"Heed my warning. 'Bye." The Dragon King moved off in quest of another succulent corpse.

Dor shook his head, ill at ease. If the dragon thought the upcoming battle would be worse...

They returned to the castle, where the Zombie Master was still hard at work. A new zombie army was shaping. The others helped all they could, but this was the Zombie Master's labor, and his magic alone sufficed. He worked through the day and into the night, growing even more gaunt than usual—but the zombies continued to shuffle out of the laboratory and form ranks in the courtyard. There had been a great number of Mundanes!

They ate a restive supper of poached jumping beans and bubblejuice, with the beans jumping into the juice at odd moments. Millie forced some on the Magician, who continued working. Most of the bodies were gone from the surrounding landscape now; the monsters had gorged themselves and staggered off to their lairs with toothy smiles and a final fusillade of belches. A zombie detail was burying the uneaten, unusable fragments. The night settled into morbid silence.

Finally the last corpse was done. The Zombie Master sank into a sleep like a coma, and Millie hovered near him worriedly. Dor and Jumper slept too.

Chapter 9. Journey

In the morning, early but not bright, they set off for Castle Roogna. It would have been easiest to have the roc carry them singly to the Castle, but two things argued against this. First, there was an army of about two hundred and fifty zombies to transport, and for this number marching seemed to be the only way. Second, the skies were now being patrolled by aerial sentinels, harbingers of the harpies. The roc, huge as it was, would be torn apart in midair by the vicious creatures, if they decided it was an enemy. As perhaps it was.

The Zombie Master had lived as a recluse so long that he was only vaguely familiar with the terrain, and Dor had not viewed the scenery with an eye to zombie travel when he rode in. The zombies tended to shuffle, and their feet snagged on roots and vines, tripping them or even ripping off their feet. The majority were Mundane zombies, sounder of body than the older ones; but these were as yet inexperienced and prone to accidents. So it was necessary to scout ahead for a suitable route: one more or less level, avoiding dangerous magic, and reasonably direct.

Dor and Jumper did the scouting, with the man checking the lay of the ground and the spider reviewing the threats lurking in the trees. They worked together to flush out anything uncertain, to determine whether it should be ignored, eliminated, or avoided.

When they had determined a suitable portion of the route, they set magic markers along it for the zombie army to follow. All they had to do was stay well ahead, so that they had time to backtrack and change the route if necessary.

The wilderness of Xanth was not as sophisticated now as it would be in Dor's own time; the magic had not had as much time to achieve the devastating little refinements and variations that made unprotected paths so hazardous. But there was plenty of raw magic here, and no enchanted paths to follow. Overall, Dor judged the jungle to be as dangerous for him as anything he had known—if he allowed himself to get careless.

One of the first things they ran afoul of was dog fennel. The plants had evidently been taking a canine nap, noses tucked under tails, but woke ugly when Dor blundered into them. First they barked; then, gathering courage, they started nipping. Angered, Dor laid about him with his sword, clearing a circle. Then he suffered regret as the creatures yiped and whined, for they really were no threat to him. Each dog grew on a stem, rooted in the turf, and could not move beyond its tether. Its teeth were too small to do much harm.

Jumper had jumped right out of the pooch-patch, unnipped. The dogs were whimpering now, cowed by the sight of their dead packmates. It was a sad sight.

Dor strode out of the patch, bared blade held warningly before him, feeling low. Why did he always react first and think last?

"Yet an animal plant who bites strangers must suffer the consequence," Jumper chittered consolingly. "I fell among aphids once, and their ant-guardians attacked me and I was forced to kill a number of them before the rest gave over. Had they any wit, they would have realized that my presence was accidental. I had been fleeing a deadly wasp. Spiders prefer consuming flies, not aphids. Aphids are too sickly sweet."

"I guess ants aren't very bright," Dor said, comforted by the analogy.

"Correct. They have excellent inherent responses, and can function in societies far better than spiders can, but as individuals they tend to be rigid thinkers. What was good enough for their grand-ants remains sufficient for them."

Dor felt much better now. Somehow Jumper always

came through, rescuing him from physical or intellectual mishap. "You know, Jumper, when this quest is over, and we return to our own worlds—"

"It will be a sad parting," Jumper chittered. "Yet you have your life to pursue, and I have mine."

"Yes, of course. But if we could somehow stay in touch—"

Dor broke off, for they had suddenly come upon the biggest fennel of them all. It was as massive as Dor himself, with a stem like a tree trunk, reaching its horned head down to graze in the nearby grass.

"That more closely resembles a herbivorous animal," Jumper chittered. "See, its teeth are grazers, not flesh renders."

"Oh, a vegetable lamb," Dor said. "A historical creature, extinct in our day. It grows wool to make blankets from. In my time we cultivate blanket trees directly."

"But what happens when it grazes everything within its tether range?" Jumper inquired.

"I don't know." Dor saw that the grass had been mowed quite low in the disk the lamb could reach; little was left. "Maybe that's why they became extinct."

They went on. The terrain was fairly even here; the zombies would have no problems. Dor set his markers as they went, certain this route would be all right. They approached a wooded section, the trees bearing large multicolored blooms whose fragrance was pleasant but not overwhelming. "Be on guard against intoxicating fumes," Dor warned.

"I doubt the same chemicals would intoxicate me," the spider chittered.

But the scents were innocent. Bees buzzed around the flowers, harvesting their pollen. Dor passed under the trees without molestation, and Jumper scrambled through them. Beyond the trees was an attractive glade.

There was a shapely young woman, brushing her hair. "Oh, pardon me," Dor said.

She smiled. "You are a man!"

"Well—"

"Are you lonely?" She stepped forward. Jumper dropped down from the trees, a little to one side.

What Dor had first taken as clothing turned out on closer inspection to be overlapping green leaves, like the scales of a dragon. She was a soft, sweet-smelling creature, with a pretty face.

"I—uh—we're just on our way to—"

"I live for lonely men," she said, opening her arms to embrace him. Dor, uncertain what to do in this case, did nothing; therefore she succeeded in enfolding him. Her body was cool and firm, her lips sweet; they resembled the petals of roses. His body began to react, as it had with Millie; it wanted to—

"Friend," Jumper chittered, standing behind the green-leafed woman. "Is this customary?"

"I—don't know," Dor admitted, as her lips reached hungrily for his.

"I refer to the shape of the female," the spider chittered. "It is very strange."

Maybe it was, to a spider! "It—seems to be—" Dor paused, for her lips had caught up to his. Oh, she was intriguing! "To be a good shape," he concluded after a moment. Those breasts, that slim waist, those fleshy thighs—

"I hesitate to interrupt your ritual of greeting. But if you would examine her backside—"

"Uh, sure." Her frontside was fully interesting enough, but he did not object to seeing the rest. His body well knew that an attractive woman was interesting from any side. Dor drew back a bit and gently turned the woman around.

From behind, she was hollow. Like a plaster cast made of some object, or a pottery bowl shaped on a rock. She was a mere solidified shell. She had no functioning internal organs at all, no guts. Cracks of light showed through the apertures where her eyes, nostrils, and mouth were in the front.

"What are you?" Dor demanded, turning her about again. From the front she remained extremely womanly.

"I am a woodwife," she replied. "I thought you knew. I comfort lonely men."

A façade covering absolute vacuity! A man who made love to such a creature—

"I—uh, guess I don't need that kind of comfort," Dor said.

"Oh." She looked disappointed. Then she dissolved into vapor, and drifted away.

"Did I do that?" Dor asked, chagrined. "Did I make her into nothing? I didn't mean to!"

"I think she existed only for whatever man she might encounter," Jumper opined. "She will no doubt re-form for the next traveler."

"That will likely be a zombie." Saying that, Dor felt humor bubbling up inside him, until it burst out his mouth in a laugh. "A zombie lover!" Then he remembered Millie's lover of his own time, Jonathan, and sobered. It wasn't funny at all!

They went on. The glade opened into a rocky valley. The rocks were irregular, some of fair mass, with cuttingly sharp edges: a disaster for zombies. But down the center was a clear path, with only a little coronet supported on four hornlike twigs in the way. All they had to do was remove that object and its supports, and the path would be clear.

Dor moved toward it—then paused. This was suspicious. "Something wants us to touch that coronet," he said.

"Allow me." Jumper fastened a small stone to a line of silk, and tossed it at the coronet.

The ground erupted violently. A snake emerged, whose head bore the four horns; it had lain buried in the ground except for those points. The reptile struck at the stone as Jumper jerked it along on the string, making it seem alive. "Lucky we checked," Dor said, shaken. "Better you than us, stone."

The stone shuddered. "Oh, the poison!" it wailed, and fragmented into gravel.

"That must have been some poison!" Dor exclaimed.

"It was," the gravel agreed, and fractured into a mound of sand.

"What would poison do to a zombie?" Jumper inquired.

215

"Nothing, I think. How can you kill a thing that is already dead?"

"Then we can ignore the hornworm."

Startled, Dor had to agree. "Except we must post a warning for Millie and the Zombie Master, so they know to send a zombie ahead." He walked back and emplaced a magic marker of the WARNING type. When they saw that, they would send Egor Ogre ahead to spring the trap. If the hornworm was smart, it would scoot right out of there!

The valley spread into a field of grassy growth dotted with Mundanish trees. It was pretty scenery— but all of this country was lovely, and improving as they went. If only he had watched more carefully when he rode the dragon horse! One missed a lot by riding swiftly.

Then he recognized the vegetation. "Roats!" he exclaimed happily. "If there are any mature ones—"

"What are roats?" Jumper chittered.

"A cereal. Soak old roats in water or milkweed, and they transform into excellent porridge." He shook some stems, obtaining the flat kernels. "And those are primitive mixed-nut trees."

"Nuts grow on trees?" the spider inquired dubiously.

"With magic, all things are possible." Dor went to a tree and took hold of a cluster of nuts, drawing it down. They clung to the branch. "These are tough nuts!" he said. Then the cluster let go, and he staggered back. The branch snapped up, and a small hail of nuts fell about him. One shot by his nose, and he coughed. Others came, and he coughed again. "Oh, no—some of them are cough drops!" he said, retreating.

But he had his old roats and mixed nuts. "Now all I need is water."

The field dropped down to a river, its liquid crystalline but not, fortunately, crystal. Catfish swam in it, meowing hopefully as they spied Dor, then stalking away as well as their flukes permitted when they saw there was no red meat. A pack of sea dogs sniffed up, but soon spied the cats and went baying after them. Obviously this water was wholesome.

Dor dipped his double handful of substance into a pothole, and abruptly had a doughy mass of food. He offered some to Jumper, but the spider declined, preferring to fish the river for crabs. So Dor ate his potroats himself, enjoying it immensely.

However, this seemingly excellent route was cut off by the same river they had looked for. The stream was small but deep; no trouble for Jumper and Dor to cross, but disaster for the marching zombies, who would never emerge from it intact. Wading in the quiet moat had been one thing; swimming across the current was another.

It would be possible to fell some trees to form a crude bridge across the water, but this would take time and possibly alert hostile magic. So they followed the river down a way, looking for a better fording place. It was never possible to anticipate what lay ahead; there could be some natural bridge just out of sight.

There was not. There was a hill. The river flowed merrily up over it and down the other side. Dor and Jumper contemplated this, wondering what to do. A river that flowed up as well as down was unlikely to be tractable. "I could make a silk sling to swing them across one by one," Jumper chittered.

"That would wear you out and take forever," Dor objected. "And we would have to wait here until the zombies arrive, instead of scouting out the dangers ahead. We need a bridge or a ford."

They followed the river over the hill. "I wonder whether we could divert it temporarily," Jumper chittered.

"We'd still have to get the zombies across it *somewhere*," Dor pointed out. "Unless we could turn it back on itself—and that hardly seems reasonable."

At the top of the hill, a cockfish crowed. "Oh, shut up," Dor told it. But it was alive, so did not obey him.

At the foot of the other side of the hill was an orc: a huge fat water monster with teeth overflowing its mouth. The water flowed over and around it; no point in trying to cross the stream here!

They returned to the top of the hill. "I'd hate to backtrack all the way and try to scout a new route," Dor said. "This is an excellent route for the zombies —up until this point. We've got to figure out a way across!"

"What makes it flow uphill?" the spider inquired.

"Magic, of course. Something in the ground here that makes it seem to fall, when actually it is rising."

"I note a different texture of stone, here. Would that be it?"

"Could be. Enchanted stone. The magic can't be in the water itself, or it would be floating right up into the sky. I think." Now Dor wondered how water did get into the sky, to make it rain. Maybe there were streams that fell upward. So much of the magic of Xanth was unexplained! "But if we moved the stone, the river would merely change channels, and then that orc would get dry and come looking for us. The only thing madder than a wet hen is a dry orc. We need to cross the river, not move it."

"Still, we might experiment." Jumper poked a leg into the water, shifting stones. The water responded by rising higher, forming a little arc in air, then dropping back into its channel.

"Say—if we could make it jump high enough, we could pass right under it!" Dor exclaimed. He plunged in, helping Jumper to move the enchanted stones.

The river rose higher and higher. At last an arch formed, leaving the riverbed clear for several feet. "If we can lift it just a little higher, so they can walk under it without ducking—" Dor said eagerly. He moved another handful of stones.

"Perhaps we should refrain from—" Jumper warned.

"Nonsense! It's working beautifully. We don't want the zombies to touch the water at all, because they would get washed out, and they're too stupid to duck properly." Dor scooped some more.

And, abruptly, the river overturned. Instead of arcing forward, it arced backward, forming a loop in the air. It splashed to the ground at the base of the hill, then continued on up and over.

"Oh, no!" Dor cried ruefully. For of course now there was no arch. The river landed beside its original channel, then flowed back into it at the top of the hill and on as before. Instead of fashioning a bridge of water, they had doubled the course of the stream. "We'll have to move it again."

"No," Jumper chittered. "We might create further

difficulties. We can cross it this way." And he showed Dor how there was a narrow channel between the parallel slopes of the river as it spiraled through the air. The water was rising in the west and falling in the east, crossing overhead. It was in fact a variant of the original arch; now the passage across went north-south instead of east-west.

Dor had to agree. He placed a magic marker at the loop, and they went on. What a remarkable feature of the landscape they were leaving for the zombies to find!

Just as they departed, there was a surprised "Oink!" as a seahog was carried through the loop. Dor chuckled.

The landscape beyond the river remained pleasant. It was the nicest region he had seen. He was really enjoying this trek, a complete change of pace from the violence just past, and hoped Jumper was enjoying it too. All too soon they would arrive at the Castle, completing their mission, and after that it would be time to go home. Dor really wasn't eager to return so soon.

The best path curled down into the deeper valley, where the river meandered across to form a handsome lake. Dor marveled at this; in his own day this entire section between the Good Magician's castle and Castle Roogna was deep jungle. How could it have changed so extensively? But he reminded himself yet again that there was no accounting for magic.

Beside the lake was a small mountain, its base the same size as the lake. Perhaps a thousand paces in diameter, were it possible to pace either mountain or lake. Yet the lake looked deep, and the mountain tall; though the water was clear, the depths were shrouded in gloom, while snow capped the peak. So both these features of the landscape were probably magically augmented, being much larger than they seemed.

This was another type of magic Dor didn't understand. What spell kept snow from melting from the tops of the highest mountains? Since the heights were closest to the hot sun, the heat there had to be fierce, yet they acted as if it were cold. What was the purpose in such a spell? Was it the work of some long-gone Magician whose talent was turning hot to cold, permanently? No way to know, alas. Well, he might climb up there and inquire of the features of the landscape—but that would be a lot of work, and he had other things to do. Maybe after he returned to his own time...

People were there, in the water and on the mountain and prancing between. Lovely nude women and delicately shaggy men. "I think we have happened on a colony of nymphs and fauns," Dor remarked. "They should be harmless but unreliable. Best to leave them alone. The problem is our best route passes right between mountain and lake—where the colony is thickest."

"Is it not feasible to march that route?" Jumper chittered.

"Well, nymphs—you know." But of course the spider didn't know, having had no experience with humanity prior to this adventure. "Nymphs, they—" Dor found himself unable to explain, since he was not certain himself. "I guess we'll find out. Maybe it will be all right."

The nymphs spied Dor and cried gleeful welcome. "Gleeful welcome!" They spied Jumper and screamed horror. "Horror!" They did little kick-foot dances and flung their hair about. The goat-footed fauns charged up aggressively.

"Settle down," Dor cried. "I am a man, and this is my friend. We mean you no harm."

"Oh—then it's all right," a nymph exclaimed. "Any friend of a man is a friend of ours." There was a shower of hand-clapping, and impromptu dances of joy that did marvelous things to the nymphly anatomy.

Good enough. "My name is Dor. My friend is Jumper. Would you like to see him jump?"

"Oh, yes!" they cried. So Jumper made a fifteen-foot jump, amazing them. It was not nearly as far as he could go when he tried. Obviously he was being cautious, so they would not know his limitations—just in case. Dor was slowly catching on to adult thinking; it was more devious than juvenile thinking. But he was glad he had thought of the jump exhibit; that made the spider a thing of harmless pleasure, for these people.

"I'm a naiad," one nymph called from the lake. She was lovely, with hair like clean seaweed and breasts that floated enticingly. "Come swim with me!"

"I, uh—" Dor demurred. Nymphs might not be hollow in quite the way woodwives were, but they were not quite the same as real women either.

"I meant Jumper!" she cried, laughing.

"I prefer to skate," Jumper chittered. He stepped carefully onto the water and slid gracefully across it.

The nymphs applauded madly, then dived into the lake and swam after the spider. Once their confidence had been won, it was complete!

"I'm a dryad," another nymph called from a tree. Her hair was leaf-green, her nails bark-brown, but her torso was as exposed and lush as that of the water nymph. "Come swing with me!"

Dor still had not learned how to handle this sort of offer, but again he remembered the hollow woodwife. "I, uh—"

"I meant Jumper!" But the spider was already on the way. If there was one thing he could do better than skating water, it was climbing trees. In a moment the other dyrads were swarming after him. Soon they were squealing with glee, dangling from silken draglines attached to branches, kicking their feet.

Dor walked on toward the mountain, vaguely disgruntled. He was glad his friend was popular; still—

"I'm an oread," a nymph called from the steep side of the mountain. "Come climb with me!"

"Jumper is busy," Dor said.

"Oh," she said, disappointed.

Now a faun approached him. "I see you aren't much for the girls. Will you join us boys?"

"I'm just trying to scout a route through here for an army," Dor replied shortly.

"An army! We have no business with armies!"

"What *is* your business?"

"We dance and play our pipes, chase the nymphs, eat and sleep and laugh. I'm an orefaun, associated with the mountain, but you could join the dryfauns of the trees if you prefer, or the naifauns of the pool. There really isn't much difference between us."

So it seemed. "I don't want to join you," Dor said. "I'm just passing through."

"Come for our party, anyway," the faun urged. "Maybe you'll reconsider after you see how happy we are."

Dor started to demur, then realized that the day was getting late. This would be a better place to spend the night than the wilderness—and he was curious about the life and rationale of these nymphs and fauns. In his own day such creatures were widely scattered across Xanth, and highly specialized: a nymph for every purpose. The fauns had largely disappeared. Why? Perhaps the key was here.

"Very well. Just let me scout the terrain a little farther, then I shall return for your party." Dor had always liked parties, though he hadn't gone to many. People had objected to his talking to the walls and furniture, learning about all the private things that went on under the cover of the formal entertainment. Too bad—because the informal entertainment was generally far more intriguing. There seemed to be something about adult people; their natures changed when they got into small groups, especially when such groups consisted of one male and one female. If what they had to do was good and wholesome, why didn't they do it in full public view? He had always been curious about that.

The fauns danced about him merrily, playing their little flutes, as he walked beyond the lake and mountain. They had horn-like tufts of hair on their heads, and their toenails had grown so heavy as to resemble hooves, but they remained human. In the following centuries the horns and hooves would become real, as the fauns took on their distinct magical identities. He had thought they were real when he first spied the fauns here, but his mind's eye had filled in more detail than was justified.

Dor realized that if he or any other man so chose, he could join them, now, and his own hair and toenails would develop similarly. It made sense; the hooves were much better for running about rocky terrain than ordinary feet were, and the horns were a natural defense, albeit as yet token, that could not be carelessly lost the way other weapons could. And as for dancing—those neat, small, hard feet were much better than Dor's own huge soft flat things. Suddenly he reminded himself of a goblin.

The subspecies of fauns were already distinguishable, as were the species of nymphs. The dryfauns of the forest had greenish hair and bark-brown fur on their legs and lower torsos, and their horns were hooked to enable them to draw down fruit. Their hoof-toes were sharp, almost spiked, so that they could climb sheer trunks, though as yet they had little difficulty walking on land. Perhaps that was the key to their eventual demise as a species, when they became so specialized they could not leave the trees, and something happened to those trees—yes.

The orefauns of the mountains had more powerful legs, their hooves merging like those of goats or deer. Even their hands were assuming a certain hooflike quality, to enable them to scamper up on all fours, and their horns curled back to enable them to butt.

The naifauns of the lake had flattened flipper-hooves and horns pointing straight up like speartips; they speared foolish fish on them when hungry. They had delicate scales on their nether portions instead of fur.

A naifaun saw Dor looking at him. "You should see my cousin the nerefaun," he called, splashing cheerily. "He lives in the sea at the foot of the river, and he has scales like those of a sea serpent, and full flipper feet. He can really swim—but he can hardly walk on land."

Scales and flippers for the sea-faun. Could this specialization eventually lead to the merfolk, the tritons and their counterparts the mermaids, who had lost their legs entirely in favor of a tail? Yet he had already encountered a triton here—no, that was at Good Magician Humfrey's castle, eight hundred years hence. There were no naifauns or nerefauns in Dor's own time because they had become sea and lake tritons, and the naiads and nereads had become mermaids. He was witnessing the first great radiation of the species of nymph and faun, experiencing firsthand the evolution of a major branch of the creatures of Xanth. It was absolutely fascinating!

And subtly horrifying, too—for this was the ongoing dehumanization of Man. There had been much killing in the land of Xanth, but even so, the population had declined over the centuries more than the bloodshed could account for. Because human beings had deserted their kind, becoming such subspecies as these: tritons and mermaids. Eventually, if this continued, there would be no true humans remaining in the Land of Xanth. That was what King Trent was trying to reverse, by establishing contact with Mundania. He wanted to infuse Xanth with new, pure human stock—without suffering another disastrous Wave of conquest. Now Dor appreciated far more clearly the importance of this project. His own parents, Bink and Chameleon, were deeply involved in this effort. "Go to it, parents!" he murmured fervently to himself. "What you are doing is more important than what I am doing."

Meanwhile, he was neglecting what he was doing: the survey of the zombie route. Dor looked about, discovering himself in a realm of increasing brush. The plants seemed harmless, but they grew larger and taller toward the west. Possibly in the heart of their range they would achieve the status of trees. Some had branches sticking up from the top, bare of leaves, with cross branches projecting at right angles. These looked vaguely familiar to Dor, but he could not quite place them. If they represented a threat, what form did it take? They weren't tangle trees, or poison brambles, or needle-cacti. What was there about them that bothered him?

He thought of questioning stray rocks, but didn't want to reveal the nature of his magic in the presence of the fauns. If he became worried enough, he would use his talent; for now he was just looking.

"What are these bushes?" he asked the orefaun, who seemed uncomfortable here on level ground, but had braved it out for the sake of companionship. "Are they dangerous?"

"We never go this far," the orefaun admitted. "We know there are dangers beyond our territory, so we never stray. What is there elsewhere to interest us anyway?"

"Why, the whole world is interesting!" Dor said, surprised.

"Not to us. We like it where we are. We have the best place in Xanth, where monsters don't come and the weather is always nice and there is plenty of food. You should taste our mountain dew!"

"But—but it is so broadening to travel," Dor protested, remembering guiltily how little he had traveled before he entered the tapestry. Yet he knew this adventure had already matured him considerably.

"Who wants to be broadened?"

Dor was taken aback. If these creatures really weren't interested—

"Suppose something happened to this place, so that you had to move? You should at least explore more widely, so you are prepared."

"Why be prepared?" the orefaun asked, perplexed.

Dor realized that the difference between him and these creatures was more than physical. Their whole mutual attitude differed. To question the need for preparedness—why, that was childlike.

Well, he was gaining increasing understanding of the roots of the faunish disappearance in Xanth. Of course the nymphs had similar shortsightedness, but there would always be a market for lovely nude girls, so their survival was more secure. *Anything* that looked like a pretty girl had its market—even hollow mockups like the woodwives. Perhaps, like the harpies, the nymphs would evolve eventually into a single-sex species, mating only with males of outside species.

Dor saw that the orefaun was in distress, so relented and turned about. "I think this is a good route; I'll explore the rest of it tomorrow, with Jumper."

The orefaun was greatly relieved. He danced back toward the mountain, and was soon joined by the less adventurous fauns. "Time for the party!" he cried, doing a caprine skip. The others picked it up as a chant: "Party! Party!"

They made a bonfire between mountain and lake, piling on dry bon-brush and igniting it with a small irritable salamander. The salamanders of Dor's day started fires that burned all substances except the ground itself, but this was a primitive ancestor who made a merely ordinary fire, fortunately. This fire would burn only wood, and could be extinguished.

They put marshmallows—from a mallow bush in the marsh at one end of the lake—on sticks and toasted them in the flames. The lake nymphs and fauns brought out fresh sea cucumbers and genuine crabs for Jumper. Hot chocolate bubbled up from one side of the lake, making an excellent beverage. The tree creatures brought fruits and nuts, and the mountain creatures rolled a huge snowball down to make cold drinks. Dor did sample the mountain dew, and it was effervescent and tasty and heady.

The nymphs and fauns sat in a great circle around the fire, feasting on the assorted delicacies. Dor and Jumper joined them, relaxing and enjoying it. After they had stuffed, the fauns brought out their flutes and piped charmingly intricate melodies while the nymphs danced. The female bodies rippled and bounced phenomenally; Dor had never before seen anything like this!

Soon the fauns responded to the anatomical signals, discarded their flutes, and joined the dance in a most unsubtle manner. Before long it was not a dance at all, but the realization of the ritual the dance had only suggested. These creatures did indeed do openly what the adults of Dor's day did in privacy!

"Is this normal procedure?" Jumper inquired. "Forgive my query; I am largely ignorant of the ways of your species."

"Yes, this is a regular festival celebrating the rites of spring," the orefaun said.

"No festivals for the other seasons?" Dor inquired.

"What other seasons? It is always spring here. Of course, the rites don't result in babies; it has something to do with our immortality. But it's fun to celebrate them anyway. You are welcome to join in."

"Thank you; I regret this is not my species," Jumper demurred.

"I, uh—I'll just wait," Dor said. His body certainly felt the temptation, but he didn't want to commit himself prematurely to this life. The mental picture of the woodwife returned.

"As you wish. No one is forced to do anything, here,

ever. We all do only what we want to do." He watched the proceedings another moment. "Speaking of which —pardon me." The orefaun leaped forward to nab a passing oread. The nymph screamed fetchingly, flung her hair about, and kicked up her cute cloven feet, giving Dor a feeling of *déjà vu* and a glimpse of what clothing normally concealed. Then the faun brought her down and did what evidently delighted them both. Dor made mental notes; if he ever had occasion, he wanted to know how to proceed. He was already certain that never again would he see a nymphly girl kick her feet without thinking of this scene. A new dimension of meaning had been added to the action.

"If they are immortal, and bear no hatchlings," Jumper chittered, "how then do they evolve?"

Dor hadn't thought of that. "Maybe they themselves just keep changing. With magic—"

"Come, join me!" a cute naiad cried, wiggling her delicately scaled hips dextrously.

"I regret—" Jumper began.

"I meant Dor!" she cried, laughing. Dor noted what these laughs and screams did to the nymphs' chest area; was that why they did such exhalations so often? "Take off those silly clothes, and—" She gave a little foot-kick.

"Uh, I—" Dor said, finding himself strongly tempted despite all his private reservations. After all, if the nymph were willing—

But it would be the first step in joining this colony, and he just wasn't sure that was smart. An easy life, filled with fun—yet what was the future in it? Was fun the ultimate destiny of Man? Until he was sure, he had better wait.

"At least you should try it once," she said, as if reading his mind. Probably such mind reading was not difficult; there was only one channel a man's mind would be in, at this stage.

There was an ear-rending roar. A torrent of dark bodies burst upon the party. It was a goblin horde!

"Press gang! Press gang!" the goblin leader cried, making a gap-toothed grin of joyous malice. "Anybody we catch is hereby impressed into the goblin army!" And he grabbed a dryfaun by the arm. The faun was substantially larger than the goblin, but, paralyzed by fear, seemed unable to defend himself.

The nymphs screamed and dived for water, trees, and moutain. So did the fauns. None thought to stand up, close ranks, and oppose the raiders. Dor saw that there were only about eight goblins, compared to a hundred or more fauns and nymphs. What was the problem? Was it that goblins inspired terror by their very appearance?

Dor's hand went for his sword. Goblins did not inspire terror in *him!* "Wait, friend," Jumper chittered. "This is not our affair."

"We can't just sit here and let them take our friends!"

"There is much we do not know about this situation," the spider chittered.

Ill at ease but respectinig Jumper's judgment, Dor suffered himself to be restrained. The goblins quickly ran down five of the healthiest fauns, threw them to the ground, and bound them with vine-ropes. The goblins were capturing, not slaying; they wanted men fit for their army. So Jumper had been correct in his caution, as usual; Dor would have gained nothing by laying about him with his blade. Not anything worth gaining, anyway.

Yet still his mind was nagged: what sort of creatures were these fauns who welcomed strangers yet refused to assist each other in an emergency? If they did not fight for their own—

"That's five," the goblin sergeant said. "One more good one, we need." His darkly roving eye fell on Dor, who stood unmoving. "Kill the bug; take the man."

The goblins closed on the pair. "I think it has just become our affair." Dor said grimly.

"It seems you are correct. Perhaps you should attempt to parlay."

"Parlay!" Dor exclaimed indignantly. "They mean to kill you and impress me into their army!"

"We are more civilized than they, are we not?"

Dor sighed. He faced the goblin sergeant. "Please desist. We are not involved in your war. We do not wish to—"

"Grab him!" the goblin ordered. Evidently these

goblins did not realize that Dor was not merely a larger faun: a creature who could be expected to match five goblins in combat. The seven others dived for Dor.

Jumper bounded over their heads while Dor's sword flashed in its vicious arc. That was one thing this sword was very good at. Two goblins fell, blood oozing and turning black. Then Jumper's silk caught the sergeant, and the spider trussed him up with the efficiency of eight trained legs.

"Look to your leader!" Dor cried, smashing another goblin down.

The remaining four looked. The sergeant was virtually cocooned in silk and helpless. "Get me out of this!" he bawled.

The others rushed to him. They had not been eager to fight Dor anyway, once the ratio dropped from seven to one down to four to one. Now they knew they had a fight on their dirty little hands.

Then, from the sky, shapes dived: harpies. "Fresh meat!" the harpy sergeant screamed. Dor knew that was her rank, because the filthy grease on her wings was striped. "Haul it away!"

The dirty birds clutched the bodies available: five fauns, three wounded goblins, and the cocooned goblin sergeant. Great ugly wings beat fiercely, stirring up dust. "Not the fauns!" Dor bellowed—for one of them was the orefaun who had befriended him. He grabbed for the orefaun's dangling hooves, yanking him down to the ground. Startled at this vigorous resistance, the harpies let go.

Jumper threw up a noose, catching a dryfaun and hauling him down similarly. But the remaining three, together with the four goblins, disappeared into the sky. The other goblins ran away.

Had Jumper been right to chitter restraint? Dor wasn't sure. He didn't care about the goblins, but he was very sorry about the three lost fauns. Could he have saved them if he had attacked before? Or would he merely have gotten himself trussed up and abducted? There was no way to be sure. Certainly Jumper, once he acted, had done so most effectively; he had nullified the leader, instead of mindlessly battling the troops, as Dor had done. Jumper had taken the most sensible course, the one with the least risk. Following this course, they had taken losses, but had not lost the battle.

The nymphs and fauns returned, now that the action was over. They were chastened by the double horror of goblin and harpy raids. Three of their comrades were gone. Obviously their illusion of security had been shattered.

The party was, of course, over. They doused the bonfire and retreated to their various habitats. Dor and Jumper hung from a branch of a large tree; it belonged to no one, since these creatures were not yet at the one-creature-one-tree stage. Night sank gloomily upon them.

In the morning Dor and Jumper were sober—but they had a surprise. The first nymph to spy Jumper screamed and dived into the lake—where she almost drowned, for she was an oread, not a naiad. The fauns clustered around aggressively. Dor had to introduce himself and Jumper, for no one remembered them.

They went through the bit about the jumping again, and quickly befriended the whole community—again. They did not mention the goblin press-gang raid; those lost fauns had been forgotten, literally, and the orefaun Dor had rescued obviously was not aware of his narrow escape. The whole community knew that monsters never came *here*.

For this was part of the secret of eternal youth: the fauns and nymphs could not afford to be burdened by the harsh realities of prior experience. They were forever young, and necessarily innocent. Experience aged people. As it was ageing Dor.

"At least the goblins won't do much successful recruiting here," Dor murmured as they left the colony behind and continued west. "You can't depend on troops who have to be taught again each day."

"The harpies won't have that problem," Jumper chittered.

The harpies had been foraging for fresh meat. They had found it.

"Nevertheless, the effect may wear off after a few days, when individuals are removed from the locale,"

Jumper continued. "Had we remained several days, we would have felt the spell's effect, and remained forever; those who are forcibly removed probably revert slowly to their original states."

"Makes sense," Dor agreed. "Stay a short time, trying it out, having a good time—" He thought of the naiad who had tempted him, and of the other naiads in the water with their floating breasts. "Then get caught by the spell, and not remember what else you have to do." He shuddered, partly from the horror of it, and partly from the appeal of it.

They continued on into the larger bushes, leaving their trail of markers. The fauns and nymphs would not tamper with the markers; they would not remember what they were for. Within a day or so the zombie army should pass this region. Dor judged that they had now marked over half the distance from the Zombie Master's castle to Castle Roogna. The worst was surely over, and by nightfall he and Jumper would be with the King with the good news.

"These plants disturb me," Jumper chittered.

"Me too. But they seem harmless, just strange."

Jumper looked about, as he could do without moving his head or eyes. The direction of his vision was merely a matter of awareness, and Dor had become sensitive to the spider's mannerisms that signaled it. "There seems to be no better channel than this. The ground is level and clear, and there are no hostile creatures. Yet I distrust it."

"The most promising paths are often the most dangerous. We should distrust this one *because* there are no hostile creatures," Dor pointed out.

"Let me survey from another vantage, while you continue as if innocent," Jumper chittered. He jumped over a bush and disappeared.

Dor walked on. He hardly had to pretend innocence! It was a good system they had. The spider was more agile and could not be caught by sudden drops, thanks to his dragline, while Dor had the solidity of his big Mundane body and the power of his sword. He would distract potential enemies while Jumper observed them from concealment. Any who attacked Dor might find themselves looped and hoisted on a line of silk.

The bushes now rose taller than his head and seemed to crowd about, though they did not move. The true walking plants seemed not to have evolved in Xanth yet. Dor checked that carefully, however, since there were other ways to move than walking. Tangle trees, for example, snatching prey that passed; predaceous vines that wrapped around anyone foolish enough to touch them, or plants that simply uprooted themselves periodically to find better locations. But these particular plants were definitely stationary; it was his forward progress into their thickening midst that made them seem to swell and crowd closer. They were all so similar that it would be easy to get lost among them—but since he was leaving magic markers, he would not mislay his way, and could always retreat. And of course Jumper was watching.

What would his venture have been like without Jumper? Dor shuddered to think of it. He was sure the big spider's presence was accidental, not planned or anticipated by Good Magician Humfrey when he arranged this quest. But without that coincidence, could Dor have survived even his first encounter with the goblins? Had he died here in the tapestry, what would have happened to his body back home? Maybe Humfrey had some way to rend the tapestry and reweave it, so that Dor's death would be eliminated and he could return safely—but even so, that would have been a humiliating failure. Far better to survive on his own —and Jumper had enabled him to do that.

So far.

Even more important was the maturity of perspective brought by the big arachnid. Dor was learning constantly from that. The juveniles of any species tended to be happy but careless, like the fauns and nymphs; it was easy to contemplate being locked into such innocence indefinitely. But the longer prospects showed this to be a nightmare. Dor was, as it were, emerging from faun stage to Jumper stage.

He laughed, finding the mixed image funny. He imagined himself starting with little horns and hooves, then growing four more limbs and six more eyes to resemble the spider. Before this adventure he would not have understood such imagery at all!

In the midst of his laugh, something chilling happened, causing him to choke it off. He looked around, but saw nothing. Only the plants, which were now half again as tall as he. What had happened to disturb him so? He hadn't quite caught it.

He shrugged and walked on. After a moment, to demonstrate better his unconcern, and incidentally to make sure his exact location was known to Jumper—just in case!—he began to whistle. He was not a good whistler, but he could carry a fair tune.

And the subtle thing happened again. Dor stopped in his footprints and looked again. Had he seen Jumper from the corner of his eye? No, he would have recognized his friend without even trying. How he wished for several extra eyes now! But to hell with caution; he had seen something, and he wanted to know what.

There was nothing. The tall bushes merely sat there, basically mundane, their leaves rippling periodically in the breeze. At the base they were full, their foliage so dense that their trunks could hardly be seen. At the top they thinned, their leaves sparser and smaller, until at the apex they were bare. Some had the central stem projecting straight up for several feet, with several bare cross branches. A strange design, for a plant, but not a threatening one. Maybe they were sensors for the sun or wind, conveying information to the plant's main body. Many plants liked to know what was going on, for small changes in the weather could spell great changes in vegetable welfare.

Dor gave it up. There was simply nothing here he could detect. He could ask one of the sticks that lay on the ground, of course. But again he balked at that. Something about the naïveté of the fauns and nymphs made him resist that device. The fauns and nymphs depended foolishly on their ignorance, their mountain, trees, and lake—instead of on their own intelligence, alertness, and initiative. If he depended on his magic instead of his powers of observation and reasoning, he would never become the man he should be. He recalled how little King Trent used his transforming power; now that made some sense to him. Magic was always there as a last resort; it was the other qualities of existence that needed to be strengthened. So he held off, avoiding the easy way, determined to solve this one himself.

Maybe what he sought was invisible. In his own day there were said to be invisible giants, though no one had ever seen one. How could they? He chuckled.

Again it happened, as if triggered by his noise. And this time he caught it. The top of one of the plants had moved! Not swaying in the wind; it had moved. It had turned deliberately, rotating on its trunk-axle to orient on him.

Dor considered this. He took several steps forward, whistling, watching—and the antenna swiveled to follow his progress. No doubt about it now. The thing was focusing on him.

Well, plants were also wise to keep track of mobile creatures, for the approach of monster or man could signal instant destruction—especially if it were a salamander in a bad mood, or a man looking for wood to build a house. What better way to keep informed than a rotary antenna! So this was probably harmless. Dor had been concerned because he had seen the movement without an object. He had been thinking in terms of animals or tangle trees, not simple wooden rotation.

He walked on with renewed confidence, still whistling. More of the antenna-plants were evident now; this seemed to be the mature stage of the bush. The little ones at the fringe had no antennae; the medium ones had antennae but couldn't rotate them; the grown ones were fully operative.

Just so long as they did nothing but watch . . . Assuming they could watch without eyes. Probably they could; Dor knew there were other senses than man's, some just as effective. Maybe the plants resonated to sounds, hence reacted to his laughter, which must seem strange indeed to them. Or to the heat of his body. Or the smell of his sweat. How would they react to the zombies? He smiled privately; the zombies might make quite a stir wherever they passed!

The forest—for such it had become—opened into a grassy glade. In the center there was a depression, and there was a mound in it. The mound appeared to be made of wood, yet had no branches or leaves. What was it?

The antenna-trees merely looked; they did not act. That would not protect this forest from threats unless there was something else. Something that could act, once the trees had pinpointed the threat. Could this be an action device?

Dor would ordinarily have left it alone, for it could be folly to mess with things not understood. But he was scouting a path for the zombie army, and he did not want to lead it into some devious trap. Probably this growth was harmless, as it seemed to be immobile. But he had to be sure.

He was not so foolish as to step on it, of course. He cast about for deadwood, found an old dry branch, and used it to poke the object. He could just reach it, this way, standing on the rim of the depression. He would not have been surprised if water poured forth in a fountain, filling the bowl, or if the knob had sunk into an awesome hole. This whole woods could be carnivorous, luring animals to the center, dumping them into its maw—

But nothing happened. His speculations had been foolish. Why should trees go to so much trouble, when it was so much easier simply to grab passing prey, as tanglers did, or to repel intrusions by brambles or forget spells or bad odors? There had been no lure, either; he had come here only because he needed a good route through.

Well, whatever it was did seem to be inert, therefore probably harmless. The zombies could pass safely. Dor turned about and saw Jumper.

"There seems to be no threat," Jumper chittered. "Have you determined the nature of this formation?"

Dor froze. The spider had come up quietly behind him, sneaking up, intent on mischief. Only by chance had Dor turned in time. Now the sinister creature was pretending to be innocuous, until he could get close enough to bite off Dor's head with his gruesome chelicerae.

"Is there something the matter?" Jumper chittered, his ugly huge green front orbs glinting evilly. "You look unwell. May I render assistance?" And the monster took a step toward Dor with his hairy long legs.

Dor whipped out his sword. "Back, traitor!" he cried. "Come not near me!"

The spider stepped artfully back, as if confused, only far enough to remain beyond slash range. "Friend, what is the meaning of this? I seek only to help."

Goaded beyond endurance by the thing's duplicity, Dor lunged. The sword sped forward with a precision that would have been unattainable by his own body. But the hairy arachnid jumped right over his head, out of the way.

Dor whirled. Jumper had landed on the wooden knob. Even in his righteous rage, Dor had some caution; he did not wish to step into that mysterious depression. So he stood at the rim, on guard, watching the enemy spider.

Jumper's attitude had changed. He balanced neatly on six legs, his long front two legs stroking the air softly. Dor recognized this as a fighting stance. "So you attack me without provocation?" the creature demanded, and there was a harsh edge to his chitter. "I should have known better than to trust an alien thing."

The stick Dor had used to poke the knob lay at his feet. He picked it up awkwardly with his left hand, keeping his sword ready with his right. "You were the one who betrayed trust!" he cried, poking at the spider.

It was a tactical mistake. Jumper threw a line around the end of the pole and jerked it to him. Dor was almost hauled into the depression before he let go. He staggered back.

The spider seized his opening. He jumped across the depression, landing beside Dor. He threw another loop, catching Dor's sword arm, drawing him off balance. But Dor reacted with the fighting reflexes of his powerful body. He jerked the arm back. Such was the strength and weight of his body that it was the gross arachnid who was now hauled off balance. No single leg of the spider's could match Dor's arm; the muscle tissue simply wasn't there. Jumper came forward, not falling because it was just about impossible for a thing with eight legs to fall, but lurching toward Dor. Dor reversed his motion and slashed viciously with his sword.

The spider shot straight up, barely avoiding the cut. There was no overhanging branch here, so what went up had to come down. Dor stood below with his point straight up, waiting for the spider to skewer himself on it.

But he had reckoned without the creature's monstrous agility. Jumper landed on the sword—feet first, all eight of them closing about the tip of the blade, supporting him. His weight carried blade and arm down, and Dor collapsed under it. Immediately the spider's sickening strands of web were all about him, entangling him.

Dor closed his left fist and rammed it into the spider's soft abdomen. The flesh gave way disgustingly, and strands of silk stretched and snapped. Then Dor put both hands on the sword and hauled it up, half-carrying the spider with it. He kicked with one foot to dislodge his antagonist—but this was another error. The spider looped that leg, drew his line in tight, and Dor had two hands and the leg tied together. Those spindly spider legs were savagely swift!

Dor fell on his back, fighting to free his limbs. But now the spider was all over him, throwing strand after strand around him, drawing them in tight. Dor heaved mightily, snapping more strands, but his strength was giving out. Soon he was hopelessly bound.

The monster brought his head close to Dor's head. The horrible hairy green chelicerae parted, ready to crush Dor's helpless face into a pulp. The sharp fangs were extended. The two largest green front eyes glared.

Dor screamed and kicked his bound feet and flung his head about as uselessly as Millie ever had. How had he come to this? Yet even in this moment of annihilation he retained some human perspective. "Why did you ever pretend to be my friend?" he demanded.

Jumper folded his jaws closed. "That is an excellent question," he chittered. Then he backed off, adjusted his lines, and dragged Dor over the ground toward a large tree. The antenna at the tree's top rotated to cover him, but could do nothing. The spider jumped to a stout branch, fastened a line, then hauled Dor laboriously into the air to dangle helplessly. Then he descended his own dragline to land beside Dor.

"The answer is, I did not pretend to be your friend," Jumper chittered. "I made a truce with you and treated you fairly, believing that you would honor that truce in the same fashion I did. Then, suddenly, without warning, you attacked me with your sword, and I had to defend myself. You were the one who pretended."

"I did not!" Dor cried, struggling vainly against his bonds. "You sneaked up on me!"

"I suppose it could be interpreted that way. But you attacked me, not I you."

"You jumped right at me, snagging my sword. That was an attack!"

"That was after you took your blade to me, and prodded me with the stick. Then I recognized your hostile nature, and took appropriate action." But the spider paused, considering. "I felt no hostility to you until that moment. Why should a stick provoke me when a sword did not?"

"Don't you understand your own alien nature?" Dor demanded.

"Something incomplete here. When did you become antagonistic toward me?"

"When you tried to sneak up on me and kill me, of course!"

"And when did that happen?"

"What fool game are you trying to play?" Dor demanded. "You know I was looking at the wooden knob."

"The wooden knob," the spider repeated thoughtfully. "My own realization of antipathy came when I landed on that knob. Can that be coincidence?"

"Who cares!" Dor cried. "You sneaked up on me first!"

"Consider: you poked that knob; you touched it, indirectly, and became hostile to me. Then I touched it and became hostile to you. That knob must have something to do with it."

The logic began to penetrate Dor's emotion. He *had*

poked the knob, just before . . . what happened. He knew the spider was his enemy, yet—

"Magic can do many things," Jumper continued. "Can it change friendship to enmity?"

"It can make strangers love each other," Dor said unwillingly. "I suppose it could do the opposite."

"The antenna-plants were tracking our approach. Had we been hostile to this forest, how would it have defended itself?"

"It would have thrown some spell, of course, since the trees aren't active the way tanglers are. Make us fall asleep, or get itchy, or something."

"Or get angry with each other?"

"Yes, that too. Anything is possible—" Dor paused. "Our fight—a spell?"

"The antennae observed us. Had we passed through without stopping, perhaps nothing would have happened. But we remained too long, poking into things —so the forest struck back. Setting us against each other. Reversing our feeling for each other. Would that not be an excellent defense?"

"Reversing emotion! That would mean the stronger the friendship, the worse the—"

"I am extremely angry with you," Jumper chittered.

"I am absolutely furious with you."

"Are we both as angry as it is possible to be? That would indicate a very strong friendship."

"Yes!" Dor cried, and it was as if a band about his heart had burst. "This spell—it could set whole armies against each other!" he exclaimed, seeing it. "The moment anyone jogs the knob, he activates it." The logic had now penetrated to his core; he had no further doubt they were the victims of a malignant spell. His hate for his friend was dissipating. It simply was not reasonable in the circumstance. Jumper's approach had not really been sneaky; the spider normally moved silently, and Dor's attention had been taken by the knob. Dor had assumed Jumper was his enemy for no good reason—except enchantment.

"May I release you now?" Jumper chittered.

"Yes. I realize what happened. It was a temporary spell, losing power with time."

"Reason abates much magic," Jumper agreed. He

swung across, and with a few deft motions freed Dor. "I regret this happened," he chittered.

"So do I! Oh, I'm sorry, Jumper! I should have realized—"

"I was caught too. Emotion overcame reason—almost."

"But tell me—why didn't you bite my head off? I thought you were about to."

"The temptation was great. But one does not ordinarily kill a defenseless enemy unless one is hungry. One stores the meat alive until needed. And I do not like the taste of your type of flesh. So it was counter to logic to slay you, and that bothered me. I prefer to be governed by logic. I try to understand the complete situation, to achieve perspective at all times. To get all eight eyes on it, as we arachnids chitter."

"I didn't try to think things out," Dor admitted ruefully. "I just fought!"

"You are younger than I."

Therefore immature, and thoughtless, prone to errors of ignorance and emotion. How well he knew it! The spider's maturity had saved them again, providing the time and thought they needed to fight free of the spell. "Just how old are you, Jumper?"

"I hatched half a year ago, in the spring."

"Half a year!" Dor exclaimed. "*I* hatched—I mean was born—twelve years ago. I'm way older than you!"

"I suspect our cycles differ," Jumper said diplomatically. "In another quarter year I shall be dead of old age."

Dor was shocked. "But I've hardly had time to know you!"

"It is not how long one lives, but how well one lives that is important," Jumper chittered. "This quest with you has been generally excellent living."

"Except for the goblins and the Mundanes," Dor said, remembering.

"You ventured in quest of the healing elixir at great peril to yourself to enable me to survive the Mundanes' torture," Jumper reminded him. "Perhaps the episode was worthwhile, showing me the extent of your loyalty. Come, let us finish our mission without regret."

Would he had been so nice about having one of his own legs pulled off, to verify the friendship of the spider? Dor doubted it. It seemed he still had some maturing to do.

They dropped to the ground and set their markers to skirt widely around the enchanting wooden knob. This forest defense seemed unnecessarily devious, but of course an obvious trap could more readily be circumvented.

Dor found himself sobered, and not merely by the hostile magic. Jumper—dead in three months!

Chapter 10. Battle

They arrived at Castle Roogna without further significant event, in the afternoon. The King was highly gratified by their tidings. "So you persuaded the Zombie Master! How did you do that?"

"Actually, Millie did it," Dor said, remembering the possible limitations of his own actions. "She is marrying the Zombie Master."

"That must have been some effort you people put forth!"

"It was." Better to omit the details.

"How soon will the zombies arrive?"

"It should be within a day of us, if nothing goes wrong." Then Dor put his hand to his mouth. "But we marked the route so that nothing *can* go wrong!"

"Let's hope so," the King said drily. "We had better establish regular communication. That will be a problem, because the goblin forces control the ground and the harpy forces control the air. I did not summon my troops home because their passage through monster-controlled territory would have been unconscionably hazardous. So I have no military couriers. Let me see." He pondered briefly, while Dor suffered a bad qualm: no troops to defend Castle Roogna! "Too bad there's not a river flowing between us. We'll have to use the ground."

"The dragon-horse!" Dor exclaimed.

"No, I let my dragons go, too, to defend their own homesites, which are more vulnerable than this tall Castle. Let's see what sort of fish we have."

"Fish?" Dor asked blankly. "But they can't—"

The King led the way to the royal fishpond, while Dor's prior qualm grew into a full-fledged funk. No troops, no dragons—and now the King planned to depend on fish?

King Roogna netted a bright goldfish. "Let me see," he said, concentrating.

The fish turned blue. Ice formed on the water. "Oops—I made it into a coldfish," Roogna said. "That's no help." He concentrated again. The fish became a fiery red, and the water boiled with the thrashing of the creature's tail. "No, that's a boldfish. I am having a difficult time!"

Dor merely watched. The King was performing significant magic, his misses more potent than any lesser person's wildest successes.

The King concentrated again. The fish turned brown, its skin wormlike. "Ah! There's my groundfish!" he exclaimed, satisfied. He scribbled a note, wadded it into a ball, and inserted it in the fish's mouth. He spoke to it: "Go check on the zombie army and report back here with the Zombie Master's reply."

The fish nodded, then swam through the net and into the wall of the pond, disappearing. "Now let's see what else offers," the King said. He moved to the Royal Aviary and netted a bird shaped like a ball. Its wings were so stubby it could hardly fly, and its beak and claws projected only marginally. "This round dove really isn't much use in this form." He concentrated.

Suddenly a great ugly strap appeared, constricting the dove's body. "No, no!" the King said, annoyed. "Must Murphy's law foul me up even on minor details? Not a bound dove. I want a ground dove!" And the bird turned the color of the groundfish. "There! Now you wait here until I have a message to send; then you fly through the ground and deliver it."

He returned his attention to Dor. "You are a comparative stranger to me, Magician, yet I have faith in you, and in your friend Jumper. I am extremely short of personnel at the moment. Will you accept a position in my service?"

Dor was taken aback. "Your Majesty, I am only visiting here. Soon, very soon, I must go home."

The King smiled grimly. "I would offer you transportation, as I did before. But I am short of that, too, and the goblins have closed in about the Castle. Your only egress is toward the castle of the Zombie

Master, and even that is uncertain now. I would prefer that you weather the siege here at Castle Roogna, even if you choose not to participate."

"Another siege!" I was just in one!"

"This one will be worse, I assure you. We have greater resources than the Zombie Master did, but the situation is more complicated. I would rather oppose Mundanes than goblins and harpies."

The Dragon King had suggested the same thing. Worse than what they had gone through at the Zombie Master's castle? Dor still could not believe that. He had fought goblins and harpies and found them revolting but not that devastating. And the enemy forces were not actually attacking Castle Roogna; they just happened to be staging their own private war here. Still, it would be pointless to try to travel through the midst of those hordes. "Well, I have a few days yet. Might as well be of what help I can."

"Excellent! I shall put you in charge of the north ramparts. You will have to keep strong rein on the centaurs there, but they'll mind you if they respect you. They must be kept working on the wall as long as possible; every stone laid in place augments our security."

"Oh, I'm not a leader!" Dor protested. "I'm only—"

"My roadrunners kept me informed of your progress, before enemy forces closed in. It is true that you are not yet an experienced leader, but you seem to have good potential. You responded excellently during the Mundane attack on the Zombie Master's castle."

"Your spies saw that? I thought you had no knowledge of what happened there!"

The King laughed. "It is wise for a King to have greater information than he allows others to be aware of. My spies could not approach near the battle itself. But there were reports of a man answering your description making a deal with monsters, and something about green sashes, and of course the message I received from the Dragon King. I inferred that you knew what you were doing. I really do not have first-hand information, however—which is why I was eager to have your report."

But the King had pretty good secondhand information! King Roogna resembled King Trent in certain fundamental ways. Perhaps all kings had an inherent similarity. There was something about them. Perhaps it was a special aspect of maturity.

"One day you will understand, Dor," Roogna said. "It is evident that your land is grooming you for the office, and in this way I can to a certain extent repay you for your services to me. You should make a creditable king, with proper experience."

Dor doubted that, but didn't argue. He didn't follow how doing another service for King Roogna constituted Roogna's repayment to him for a prior service. If this were adult logic, he certainly fell short of it.

The groundfish poked its head out of the ground at their feet. The King reached down to take the wadded paper from its mouth. "Thank you, courier," he said. "You may return to your pond for some refreshment now." He spread out the paper, frowning. "This is from the Zombie Master himself. Your marked path is good, but they are now surrounded by goblins and cannot proceed."

"How far are they?"

"Just beyond the antenna grove."

An image of himself fighting his dearest friend came to him. What a horror! "If any goblins bother the center of that grove—"

"They are too canny for that. They are waiting for the zombies to clear the grove, before taking any action."

"Why do the goblins care about the zombies? It's the harpies they're fighting, isn't it?"

"An excellent point. The zombies should be able to march on unmolested. Unless something is wrong."

"And obviously something is wrong," Dor said. "I'm beginning to get annoyed at Magician Murphy."

"I have been wrestling with this sort of thing since our contest began. Do you suppose I normally require several efforts to adapt magic to my specific purpose? Yet it is a good exercise in discipline."

"Yes," Dor agreed. "After this, I will be much more careful about everything I do, because I know things don't have to go right just by themselves."

The King looked east, though the problem was too

far away to see. "Quite likely the antenna forest is annoyed by the presence of so many troops, so has put the notion into the goblins' minds that zombies are enemies."

"But if the goblins have stayed out of that forest—"

"Their army has. But their advance scouts would naturally poke into everything, exactly as you did. If a scout brought back news of an enemy force—"

"We'll have to rescue them!" Dor cried.

"We really lack the personnel," the King said regretfully. "All we have are the centaurs, who must remain at work on the wall. That is in fact why we need the zombie help. It is uncertain that we have enough force to protect the unfinished Castle, and we dare not deplete our resources further."

"But the zombies are coming to help you! Without them you may lose anyway!"

"Yes. It is a problem whose solution I have not yet fathomed. Murphy's curse is taking hold very powerfully, blocking all my efforts."

"Well, I didn't go to all this trouble only to get the Zombie Master and Millie captured by goblins!" Dor said hotly. "I'll go out myself and bring them in."

"I would prefer that you not risk yourself," Roogna said, frowning. "It is not that I am insensitive to their fate; it is that I am sensitive to the fate of the greater number. We can help them best from Castle Roogna—if we can help them at all."

Dor started a hot retort—then remembered how Jumper had controlled his reactions in the antenna forest, and saved the situation. Logic had to prevail, not emotion! "How can we do this?"

"If it were possible to bring a squadron of harpies to that vicinity—"

"Yes!" Dor cried. "Then they'll fight the goblins, and neither side will have a chance to worry about zombies. But how can we do this? The harpies will hardly honor any request we might make."

"The problem, as I see it, is the lure. We need to attract them to the region, without sacrificing any of our own personnel."

"No problem at all!" Dor said excitedly. "Do you have a catapult?"

"We do. However, harpies will not pursue flying rocks."

"They just might—after I've spelled those rocks. Let me talk to the ammunition."

"There is a unit on the north wall. Where I had thought to place you anyway."

"What, is something going right?" Dor asked, smiling.

"This is a complexly developing situation. Murphy cannot cover every detail of every contingency. His talent, like mine, is being stretched to its utmost. We shall soon know who is ultimately the more powerful Magician."

"Yes, I guess so. And we have several Magicians on our side."

"However, a single bad foul-up could foil all our efforts. In that sense, Murphy can match any number of Magicians."

"I'd better get to that catapult. Do we have the location of the harpy forces?"

"The centaurs are conversant. They have no love for harpies or for goblins, and their senses are keen." The King turned. "I will send a message to the Zombie Master, asking him to move forward as soon as the harpies appear."

Dor hurried to the north wall. Incomplete as it was, it was still far more substantial than the walls of the Zombie Master's castle. It was hard to imagine little goblins successfully storming such a massive rampart, especially when they were actually fighting harpies. Narrow stairs led around and up through the interior of the wall, until they debouched on the level upper ramp.

The centaurs were nervously pacing the rampart. They were neither the scholars of Dor's day nor the warriors of another day; they were comparatively simple workers not well equipped for war. Each carried a bow and quiver of arrows, however; centaurs always had been fine archers.

The crew was supposed to be engaged in construction, but the big stone blocks lay where they had been hauled, unplaced, while the centaurs looked out over the terrain.

"The King has put me in charge of this wall," Dor announced, attracting their attention. "We have three things to do. First, we must complete the construction of this wall as far as we can before the fighting starts. Second, we must defend it when the monsters arrive. And third, we have a special mission. I am going to —to put a spell on the shot for this catapult, and—"

"Who are you?" a centaur demanded. It was the first one Dor had met—the one who had refused to tell him where King Roogna was, and who had incited the other centaurs against Jumper. What a foul break, to have to work with this particular creature and crew!

Foul break? It was a Murphy break! That curse was getting stronger, not weaker, as the end approached. The supposedly good break of having the catapult right where Dor had been assigned anyway —was no good break at all. This was his worst possible location.

But he had to fight that curse. After all, he was a Magician too, and if that meant anything—

"Centaur, I am the Magician Dor," he said coldly. "You will address me with the respect my status requires."

"The bug lover!" the centaur exclaimed. He put his hands on his front hips. He was a large, muscular brute, taller than Dor's body. Dor was sure that his body's facility with the sword would give him a physsical advantage over this creature, but he hardly wanted this to degenerate to a common brawl.

Now that the centaur had called his bluff, defying him, what was Dor to do next? This was no occasion for nicety of expression, and there was no time to win the centaur's confidence or respect slowly. Dor had to get to the heart of the matter in minutes. So—he would have to use his talent. "Come aside with me, centaur," he said. "What I have to say to you is private."

"Aside with you, bug lover?" the creature demanded incredulously. He strode forward and made as if to swing his fist—and Dor's sword pointed at his throat. Dor's body had done it after all, acting before thought. But in this case it was an appropriate response.

The centaur blinked. He had been impressively countered. That gleaming blade could have pierced his arteries before he drew back—and could still do so. He decided to accede to the private talk, at least until he could get his hooves into fighting position.

Dor sheathed his sword abruptly and turned his back, as if completely unconcerned about any action the centaur might take. And of course if the centaur struck now, it would be an act of cowardice in full view of his crew. He followed Dor to a separate place on the wall, where the catapult stood behind a battlement.

Dor turned and looked at the centaur's work harness. "What is his name?" he asked it.

"Cedric Centaur," the harness replied. The centaur jumped, startled but unspeaking.

"What is his real problem?" Dor asked.

"He's impotent," the harness responded.

"Hey, you can't—" Cedric started. But it was too late for him to conceal his secret.

This was a thing Dor did not properly understand —and he needed to, in this case. "What is impotent?"

"He is."

"I mean, what does impotent mean?"

"Impotence."

"What?"

"You should have said 'What is impotence?'" the harness said.

"Never mind!" the centaur exclaimed, agitated. "I'll work the catapult!"

"I'm not trying to tease you," Dor told him. "I'm trying to solve your problem."

"Ha!" the harness said derisively.

"No smart remarks from you!" Dor snapped at it. "Just explain what is impotence."

"This stallion can't stallion. Every time he tries to—'"

"Enough!" Cedric cried. "I told you I'd work the catapult, or any other chore! And I won't call you bug lover any more! What more do you demand?"

Dor was getting a notion of the problem. It was similar to what his body felt when he stopped it from responding to Millie or to an inviting nymph. "I'm not demanding anything. I'm just—"

"Put him with a filly, he's a gelding," the harness quipped. "You never saw anything so—"

Cedric put his hands to the harness and ripped it off by brute strength, his face purple-red.

"That will do," Dor said. "I just want to have harmony among us. I won't tell anyone else about this." He addressed the broken harness. "You may be broken, but you can still talk."

"Oh, I'm hurting!" the harness groaned.

"Now you understand how Cedric feels. It is not nice to make fun of anyone's incapacities." Dor was thinking of the way the bigger boys had made fun of him, back in his own time.

"It sure isn't!" the centaur agreed.

"What is responsible for Cedric's impotence?"

"A spell, of course," the harness said, chastened.

Now the centaur was startled. "A spell?"

"What spell?" Dor asked.

"An impotence spell, dummy!"

"Don't you talk to the Magician like that!" the centaur exclaimed, giving his harness a shake.

"I mean, how does it operate?"

"It reverses the normal urges at the critical moment, so—"

"So the stronger the urge, the stronger the hang-up," Dor said, remembering his experience in the antenna forest. That was a mean sort of spell!

"So when he gets close to his sexy dapplegray filly, he—"

"I'm going to burn this harness!" Cedric cried. But he did not seem wholly displeased. He must have believed his condition was a fault of his own, and the discovery that an external spell caused it was good news.

"How may that spell be abolished?" Dor asked.

"I wouldn't know that," the harness said. "After all, I'm only an item of apparel. I only know what I have observed."

"Then how do you know about this spell?"

"This oaf was asleep when the spell was cast, but *I* wasn't. I never sleep."

"How can you sleep when you're not alive?" Cedric demanded, some of his natural belligerence returning.

"Who cast that spell?" But the harness did not answer him. "Was it my rival Fancyface? I'll boot his tail through his snout!"

"Who cast it?" Dor asked.

"Celeste did it," the harness replied smugly.

"That's my filly!" Cedric cried. "Why would she—" He paused, his unhandsome face working. "Why that little bitch of an equine! No wonder she was so understanding! No wonder she always made such a point of being true to me! She *knew* why I couldn't—"

"I'm sorry I can't discover the cure," Dor said.

"Don't bother about that, Magician!" Cedric said. "Centaurs don't work magic; she had to have gotten the spell from some human witch. All I need to do is go to a shyster warlock and buy a counterspell. But I won't tell Celeste—" He smiled with grim lust. "Oh, no, I won't tell her! I'll just let her lead me on as usual, teasing me, and I'll fake it until—oh, is she going to get a surprise!"

They returned to the crew. "How's the bug lover doing?" one of the other centaurs called, neighing.

Cedric turned to fix the other with a steely stare. "I'm doing just great," he said. "So is the Magician. We're going to help him all we can, and do just exactly what he says, aren't we." It was not a question.

Dor affected not to notice the chagrin of the other centaurs. They had been brought in line, without doubt! "Where is there a harpy flight, within catapult range?" he asked.

A centaur at the parapet cocked his head. "That way," he said, pointing north.

"That way, *sir!*" Cedric corrected him, delivering a swift cuff on the flank. "You address the Magician with proper respect."

"Uh, just call me Dor," Dor said. He had made an issue of respect, but now was disinclined.

"They're coming in from the Gap, Sir Dor," the parapet centaur said.

"Can you drop a shot to the southwest of them?"

"I can drop a shot down the leader's beakface, Dor!" Cedric said. "Right in her craw."

"Well, I really want it to their southwest."

Cedric shrugged. "Colt's play." The centaurs gath-

251

ered about the catapult, cranking it back and fastening its boom and lifting a hefty rock into its sling. They oriented the device toward the northeast and adjusted the elevation.

"Now repeat after me, until you strike ground," Dor said to the stone. "Harpies are birdbrained stinkers!"

"Harpies are birdbrained stinkers!" the rock repeated gleefully.

"Fire," Dor said.

Cedric fired. The arm of the catapult sprang up. The missile arced over the forest, and the rock cried out: "Harpies are birrr—" and was lost to Dor's hearing.

"Now we want to lob the next one southeast of that," Dor said. "Until we have a chain of them leading the harpies to our due east, near the antenna forest."

"I understand, Magician," Cedric said. "Then what?"

"Then they'll encounter the goblin band in that region."

The centaur smiled. "I hope they wipe each other out!"

Dor hoped so too. If there were too few harpies, the goblins would still block the zombies' route; but if there were too many harpies, *they* would block the zombies' route. And the ploy might be too late. Already reports were coming in of tremendous goblin armies advancing from the south, and the harpy flights from the north were swelling voluminously. Castle Roogna was still the focus of the war, thanks to the continuing and dire power of Murphy's curse.

"Magician," a dulcet voice said behind Dor. He turned to find a mature woman standing on the ramparts. "I am neo-Sorceress Vadne, come to assist the defense of this wall. How may I be of service?"

"Neo-Sorceress?" Dor asked with undiplomatic blankness. He remembered Murphy saying something about a Sorceress who was helping the King, but the details had fogged out.

"My talent is judged to be shy of Sorceress level," she said, her mouth quirking.

"What is your talent?" Dor realized he was being

too direct, but he simply had not yet mastered the social graces of adults.

"Topology."

"What?"

"Topology. Shape-changing."

"You can change your shape? Like a werewolf?"

"Not my own shape," she said. "Other shapes."

"Like making rocks into pancakes?"

"No, my talent is limited to animate shapes. And I can't change their natures."

"I don't understand. If you changed a man into a wolf—"

"He would look like a wolf in outline, but would still be a man. No heavy fur, no keen wolf nose. Topology is not true transformation."

Dor thought of King Trent, who could change a man into a wolf—a wolf who could do everything a real wolf could, and who would produce wolf offspring. That was a superior talent, much greater than this mere shape-changing. "I guess you're right. You're not a Sorceress." For some reason he didn't know, there were no female Magicians, only Sorceresses. "Still, it sounds like good magic."

"Thank you," she said distantly.

"We won't know how you can help here until we see what side attacks, if either side does. The goblins will have to scale the wall, so we can push off their ladders as they hook them over, but the harpies will fly in. Can you top—topol—can you perform at a distance?"

"No. Only by touch," she said.

"That's not much help." He pondered, oblivious to her grimace. "Maybe you better stand at the rim and change goblins into the shape of rocks as they come over the top."

"We can use them for catapult shot!" Cedric exclaimed.

"Good idea!" Dor agreed. "Now I'll make the stone of the ramparts talk, to distract enemies, so don't any of you be fooled. The object is to make the enemy creatures attack the wrong things, breaking their weapons or their heads and giving you time to handle them. Of course we hope they won't try to storm this castle, since they really have no reason to, but you know Murphy's curse. If the goblins and harpies leave us alone, we'll leave them alone. Meanwhile, you centaurs get as many blocks placed on the wall as possible; a single one could make the difference."

The centaurs went to work with a will. Stones were emplaced and mortared rapidly. This was a good work crew, when it wanted to be.

In due course, the King summoned Dor and Vadne to a staff meeting. Jumper was there too; he had been given charge of the east-wall defense. Magician Murphy was also present, to Dor's surprise.

"The goblins have sent an envoy," King Roogna said. "I thought all of you should be present for this meeting." As he spoke, a typically gnarled goblin entered. He wore short black pants, a small black shirt, and enormous shoes. He had the usual goblin scowl.

"We require your castle for a camping base," the goblin said, showing his discolored and jagged teeth. "We give you one measly hour to clear out."

"I appreciate your courtesy," King Roogna said. "But this Castle is as yet incomplete. I doubt it would be of much use to you."

"You deaf, or just stupid?" the goblin inquired. "I said clear out."

"I regret we are not disposed to do that. However, there is some nice level ground to the east that you might use—"

"Useless against flying monsters. We need elevation, battlements, shelter—and great supplies of food. We come in one hour. If you are not gone, we shall eat you." The goblin spun awkwardly about on his ponderous feet and departed.

"Now we have the envoy from the harpy forces," the King said, half-concealing a quirky smile. The oldest and croniest of harpy hens flapped in.

"I saw that goblin!" she screeched. "You are consorting with the enemy. Your gizzards will bleed for this!"

"We declined to let the goblins use our premises," King Roogna said.

"I should think so! *We* will use your premises!" she

screeched. "We need roosting space, cells for captives, kitchens for raw meat!"

"I regret we can not make our facilities available to you. We are not choosing sides."

That was for sure, Dor thought. Both sides were repulsive.

"We'll claw you into quivering chunks!" she screeched. "Making deals with goblins! Treason! Treason! Treason!" She flapped out.

"So much for the amenities," King Roogna said. "Are the ramparts ready?"

"As ready as possible," Jumper chittered. "The situation is not ideal."

"Agreed." The King frowned. "The rest of you may not appreciate the full gravity of the situation. Goblins and harpies are very difficult creatures to deal with. They are more numerous than humans, and have massed themselves, while our kind is dispersed all across the Land of Xanth. We can not reasonably expect to withstand siege by their forces without the aid of the zombies, and even then it will be difficult. The Zombie Master has been delayed—" He glanced at Magician Murphy. "But is on the move again." He glanced at Dor. "The question is, will he arrive in time?"

"An excellent question," Murphy said. "Shall we agree that if the Zombie Master fails to arrive before the battle commences—?"

The King glanced at the others questioningly.

Dor visualized the battlements. The goblins would have to scale some thirty feet of wall buttressed by the square corner towers and round midwall towers, after fording the deep moat. He couldn't see how they could be a serious immediate threat. The harpies normally struck by picking people up and carrying them away. The centaurs were too heavy to be handled that way. Why, then, was the King so grave? Even unfinished, Castle Roogna should be proof against these threats. A long siege seemed unlikely, because the besiegers would be killing each other off, and running out of food.

"What happens if the zombies don't arrive before the battle starts?" Dor asked.

"It would be a shame to have damage done to this fine edifice, perhaps loss of human life," Murphy explained. "It is only sensible to abate the curse before the situation gets untoward."

"You mean you can call off the whole goblin-harpy battle, this whole siege, just like that?"

"Not just like that. But I can abate it, yes."

"I find that hard to believe," Dor said. "Those armies are already well on their way. They aren't just going to turn around and go home just because you—"

"The King's talent is shaping magic to his own ends. Mine is shaping circumstance to interfere with others' designs. Alternate faces of similar coins. All we have to determine is whose talent shall prevail. Destruction and bloodshed are no necessary part of it. In fact I deplore and abhor—"

"There has already been bloodshed!" Dor exclaimed angrily. "What kind of macabre game is this?"

"A game of power politics," Murphy responded, unperturbed.

"A game where my friend was tortured by Mundanes, and my life threatened, and the two of us were pitted against each other," Dor said, his anger bursting loose. "And Millie must marry the Zombie Master to—" He cut himself off, chagrined.

"So you have an interest in the maid," Vadne murmured. "And had to give her up."

"That's not the point!" But Dor knew his face was red.

"Shall we be fair?" Murphy inquired meaningfully. "Your problem with the maid is not of my making."

"No, it isn't," Dor admitted grudgingly. "I—I apologize, Magician." Adults were able to apologize with grace. "But the rest—"

"I regret these things as much as you do," Murphy said smoothly. "This contest with the Castle was intended to be a relatively harmless mode of establishing our rights. I would be happy to remove the curse and let the monsters drift as they may. All this requires is the King's acquiescence."

King Roogna was silent.

"If I may inquire," Jumper chittered, Dor's web

translating for all to hear. "What would be the long-range consequence of victory by Magician Murphy?"

"A return to chaos," Vadne replied. "Monsters preying on men with impunity, men knowing no law but sword and sorcery, breakdown of communications, loss of knowledge, vulnerability to Mundane invasions, decrease of the importance of the role of the human species in Xanth."

"Is this desirable?" Jumper persisted.

"It is the natural state," Murphy said. "The fittest will survive."

"The *monsters* will survive!" Dor cried. "There will be seven or eight more Mundane Waves of conquest, each with awful bloodshed. The wilderness will become so dense and horrible that only spelled paths are safe for people to travel. Wiggles will ravage the land. There will be fewer true men in my day than there are in yours—" Oops. He had done it again.

"Magician, exactly where are you from?" Vadne demanded.

"Oh, you might as well know! Murphy knows."

"And did not tell," Murphy said.

"Murphy has honor, once you understand his ways," Vadne said, glancing at the Magician obliquely. "I once sued for his hand, but he preferred chaos to an organized household. So I am without a Magician to marry."

"You sought to marry above your station," Murphy told her.

Vadne showed her teeth in a strange crossbreed of snarl and smile. "By your definition, Magician!" Then she returned to Dor. "But I let my passion override me. Where did you say you were from, Magician?"

Dor suddenly understood her interest in him—and was glad he could prove himself ineligible. It would be as easy to deal with Helen Harpy as with this woman, and for similar reason. Vadne was no soft and sweet maid like Millie; she was a driven woman on the prowl for a marriage that would complete the status she craved. "I am from eight hundred years hence. So is Jumper."

"From the future!" King Roogna exclaimed. He

had stayed out of the dialogue as much as possible, giving free rein to the expression of the others, but this forced his participation. "Exiled by a rival Magician?"

"No, there is no other Magician in my generation. I am on a quest. I—I think I'm going to be King, eventually, as you surmised before. The present King wants me to have experience." Obviously King Roogna had not discussed Dor's situation with anyone else, letting Dor present himself in his own way. More and more, Dor was coming to appreciate the nuances of adult discretion. It was as significant as much in what it did not do as in what it did do. "I'm only twelve years old, and—"

"Ah—you are in a borrowed body."

"Yes. It was the best way for me to visit here, using this Mundane body. Another creature animates my own body, back home, taking care of it during my absence. But I'm not sure that what I do here has any permanence, so I don't want to interfere too much."

"So you know the outcome of the Roogna-Murphy wager," the King said.

"No. I thought I did, but now I see I don't. Castle Roogna is complete in my day—but it stood deserted and forgotten for centuries. Some other King could have completed it. And there have been all those Waves I mentioned, and all the bad things, and the decline of the influence of Man in Xanth. So Murphy could have won."

"Or I could have won, and held off the onset of chaos for a few more decades," Roogna said.

"Yes. From my vantage, eight hundred years away, I just can't tell whether the chaos started in this year or fifty years from now. And there are other things that don't match, like the absence of goblins on the surface in my day, and the relative scarcity of harpies—I just don't know how they all fit in."

"Well, what will be, will be," Roogna said. "I suppose from that vantage of history, what we do here has little significance. I had hoped to set up a dynasty of order, to keep Xanth wholesome for centuries, but that does not seem fated to be. It is a foolish vanity, to believe that a man's influence can extend much beyond his own time, and I shall be well rid of it. Still, I hope to do what good I can within this century, and to leave Castle Roogna as a monument to my hope for a better Xanth." He looked around at the others. "We should make our decision according to our principles."

"Then we should fight to preserve order—for as long as it can be preserved!" Dor said. "For a decade, for a year, or for a month—whatever we can do is good."

Murphy spread his hands. "We shall in due course discover whether even a month is feasible."

"I believe the consensus is clear," King Roogna said. "We shall defend the Castle. And hope the Zombie Master gets here in time."

They returned to their stations. Almost immediately the trouble arrived. From the south the dusky banners of the great goblin army came, marching in a gathering tread that shook the Castle foundations. Dor stood atop the northeast corner tower and looked over the ramparts to spy it in the distance. Drums beat, horns tooted, keeping the cadence. Like a monstrous black carpet the army spread across the field beyond the Castle. Light sparkled from the points of the goblins' small weapons, and a low half-melody carried under the clamor, like muted thunder: the goblins were chanting, *"One two three four, Kill two three four, One two three four, Kill two three four,"* on and on endlessly. There was not much imagination to it, but plenty of feeling, and the effect expanded cumulatively, hammering into the mind.

They had allies, too. Dor spied contingents of gnomes, trolls, elves, dwarves, ghouls, and gremlins, each with its own standard and chant. Slowly a gnarly tapestry formed, a patchwork of contingents, the elves in green, dwarves in brown, gnomes red, trolls black, marching, marching. There seemed to be so many creatures they could bury the Castle under the sheer mass of their bodies, stretching the grisly fabric of their formation across the ramparts. Yet of course they could not; mere numbers could not scale a vertical wall.

Then from the north flew the harpies and their

winged minions, casting a deep shadow across land and Castle, blotting out the sun. There were contingents of ravens and vampires and winged lizards and other creatures Dor didn't recognize, in their mass resembling gross storm clouds darkening the sky in segments, the light permitted to penetrate at the perimeters only to delineate the boundaries. Thus the shadows traversed the ground in large squares, an ominous parallel advance.

The point of convergence, of course, was Castle Roogna. The two armies might indeed obliterate each other—but they would wreak havoc on the Castle in the process—if they ever got inside it. Suppose the battle took a long time? The inhabitants of the Castle could starve, waiting for it to end, even if the walls were never breached. And if the goblins had siege machinery or used the larger trolls to batter the walls, while the harpies and vampires ravaged the upper reaches—

Now Dor was coming to appreciate how unpleasant this siege could get. The Mundanes had made only sporadic assaults against the castle of the Zombie Master, but the goblins and harpies were here in such great numbers that their attack would be unremitting. There would be inevitable attrition of the Castle defenders, until no further defense was possible, and the Castle was overrun. They had to have renewable defenders. That was the key role the Zombie Master played: as long as the battle continued, there would be raw material for new zombies, who would protect the ramparts from intrusion by living creatures.

As yet there was no sign of the zombies. Even if they appeared at this moment, there would not be time for them to shuffle to the Castle before the goblins closed in about it. The Zombie Master was too late. Had Dor's ploy with the talking catapult stones failed? Or been insufficient? He should have had the King check on that with his ground-fish.

Magician Murphy walked by. He seemed to have complete freedom of the premises. "Tut. It really is too bad. Sensible people would spare themselves the awkwardness of the curse."

Cedric Centaur glowered. "Were you not a Magician, I might call you an illegitimate snot-winged dungfly."

Dor kept quiet. The centaur had put it aptly enough. Dor spied a boomerang in the arms rack on the wall of the center brace-tower. "Are you magic?" he asked it.

"Naturally. I always return to the sender's hand."

Magician Murphy shook his head, shrugged, and departed. His curse seemed to operate independently of his presence; he had just been poking around.

"Well," Dor said to the boomerang, "take a look and see if you can spy the zombie army." He hurled the boomerang out over the landscape to the northeast. He was conscious of the anomaly of calling two hundred fifty creatures an army, when the harpies evidently had thousands and the goblins tens of thousands. But the zombies were renewable; they could become an army of thousands, in due course.

The boomerang spun far out, flashing in the dwindling patch of sun remaining before the harpy force, describing a tilting circle. Soon it smacked back into Dor's hand.

"Many goblins," it reported. "No zombies."

Dor sighed. "We'll just have to hold out until they come." But he was pessimistic. Nothing in his experience had prepared him for the magnitude of this confrontation. There were so many monsters! Once the goblins closed about the Castle, how could the zombies ever get through?

First things first. There were harpy forces to deal with. They were looming much faster, like an ugly storm, already about to break over the north wall. "Cease construction. Ready bows," Dor ordered the feverishly laboring centaurs. They obeyed with alacrity. But immediately he saw that there were more flying monsters than there were arrows in all the centaurs' quivers; this would be no good.

"Do not shoot," he told them. "Let me speak first to any arrow that you fire."

A squadron of vampires bore down on them, their huge leathery wings repulsive, their glistening fangs horrifying. "Repeat after me," Dor told the first arrow

Cedric had ready. "Neighbor, you couldn't puncture a rotten tomato!"

The arrow repeated it. Objects really enjoyed simple insults. "Keep saying it," Dor said, and nodded to the centaur to fire. "Over their heads," he told Cedric.

Cedric looked surprised, but didn't argue. He raised his elevation and let the shaft go.

They watched as the arrow flew high. It missed the forward rank of vampires and sailed over their heads. Dor knew the other centaurs thought this was a wasted effort. Why fire an arrow intended to miss?

Suddenly there was a disturbance in the forward ranks. "Oh yeah?" a vampire cried—at least his shriek sounded very much like that—and spun in air to sink his long fangs into his neighbor's wing tip. The victim reacted angrily, sinking his own fangs into the nearest other wing tip available, thus involving a third vampire. The formation was so tight that in a moment the whole configuration was messed up, with vampires fighting each other in an aerial free-for-all, milling about and paying little further attention to the castle or the goblins beyond it.

"That was a neat ploy, Magician," Cedric said. Dor was glad he had taken the trouble to convert the surly creature, instead of fighting him. Jumper had shown him that. If there were any way to make friends with the goblins and harpies—

Could it be done, at this late date? Suppose the goblin females could be convinced to appreciate the best of the males, instead of the worst? And the harpies—if they had males of their own species again? All it would take was some sort of mass enchantment for the goblins, and the generation of at least one original harpy male from the union of a human with a vulture. There was a love spring north of the Gap—

And no way to get to it, now. Anyway, the thought was plausible, but it revolted him. What human and what vulture would volunteer to—? In any event, it would be too late to save the Castle for it took time for any creature to be conceived and birthed and grown. Years to produce a single male harpy, even if everything were in order. They needed something to abate this battle right now—and Dor knew that no matter what he tried, Murphy's curse would foul it up, as it had the effort to parlay with the two sides. Castle Roogna would just have to weather the storm.

Now a horde of goblins charged from the east, surrounding the castle. The goblin army had advanced from the south, but spread out so far to east and west that they had been able to view the wings plainly from the corners of the north wall. At this stage it was closing in like water flowing around a rock in a stream. There was no longer any disciplined marching or measured tread or beat of drums; the army had reverted to its natural horde state. The goblin allies must be attacking the other walls; here in the north there were only pure goblins, and Dor feared they would be the most determined opponents.

The disorganized cloud of vampires was now impinging on the ramparts. Quickly Dor walked the battlement, addressing the projecting stones of the completed portions. "Repeat after me: Take that, fang-face! My arrows are trained on you! Here comes a fire arrow!" Soon he had a medley of such comments from the wall, calculated to faze the vampires as they came close. Dor hoped the vampires were too stupid to realize there were no archers there. This allowed him to concentrate his centaurs on the incomplete section of the wall, which still lacked its battlements.

The centaurs on the east wall threw cherry bombs to disrupt the onslaught. Bang! and a goblin flipped over and collapsed. Bang! and another went. But there were more goblins than cherry bombs available. Then Boom! as a pineapple blasted a crater, hurling bodies outward like straw dolls.

But the goblins did not even pause; they charged through the smoking hole, over the fresh corpses of their comrades, right up to the moat. The moat-monsters rose up to meet them, snatching goblins from the back and gulping them down whole. But still the goblins came, forging into the water.

"I didn't know goblins could swim," Dor remarked, surprised.

"They can't," Vadne said.

The goblins surrounded the moat-monsters, clawing, punching, and biting them. The monsters snapped quickly, gorging themselves. And while each could consume a dozen or so goblins, there were thousands crowding in. The monsters retreated to deeper water, but the goblins splashed after them, clinging like black ants, pinching like nickelpedes. Many were shaken loose as the moat-monsters thrashed, and these sank in the murky depths, while others came on over them.

"What point in that?" Dor asked incredulously. "Aren't they going to try to build bridges or something? They're dying pointlessly!"

"This whole war is pointless," Vadne said. "Goblins aren't builders, so they don't have bridges."

"They don't seem to have ladders, either," Dor remarked. "So they can't scale the wall. This is completely crazy!"

On and on the goblins came, sinking and drowning in droves, until at last the moat itself filled with their bodies. The water overflowed the plain. Now there was a solid mass of flesh across which the horde poured. The moat-monsters had been stifled in that mass; there was no remaining sign of them. The goblins advanced to the base of the wall.

There was no great strategy in their approach; they simply continued scrambling over each other in their effort to mount the vertical rampart. Dor watched with morbid fascination. The goblin-sea tactic had filled in the moat and gotten the survivors across—but that could not carry them straight up the stone wall!

The goblins did not stop. The hordes behind kept shoving forward, refusing to recognize the nature of the barrier. As the first ones got trampled down, the next ones got higher against the wall. Then the third layer formed, and the forth. The wall here was not complete, yet there were some thirty feet from moat to top even at this lowest point; did the foolish creatures think they could surmount that by trampling the bodies of their comrades? It would take thirty layers of crushed goblins!

Amazingly, those layers formed. Each layer required a greater number of bodies, because it sloped farther back across the moat. But the creatures kept coming. Five layers, six, seven, eight, nine, ten—already they were a third of the way up, building an earthwork of their own dead and dying.

Cedric stood beside Dor, looking down at this horror. "I never thought I'd feel sorry for goblins," he said. "We're not killing them, they're killing themselves— just to get up over a wall of a castle they don't need!"

"Maybe that's the difference between men and goblins," Dor said. "And centaurs." But he wondered. The Mundanes, who were after all true men, had stormed the castle of the Zombie Master with as much determination and little reason as this, and the centaur crew had not shown any particular enlightenment prior to Dor's private session with Cedric. When the fever of war got into a society...

Still the goblin tide rose. Now it was halfway up, and still progressing. It was no longer possible to tell where the moat had been; there was only a monstrous ramp of bodies slanting far out from the wall. The goblins charged in and up from their seemingly limitless supply, throwing their little lives away. There did not even seem to be any conscious self-sacrifice in this; it was plain lack of foresight, as they encountered the barrier and were ground down by those still shoving from behind. Those below chomped savagely on the feet of those above, before the increasing press of weight killed them. Maybe the goblin chiefs behind the lines knew what they were doing, but the ordinary troops were just obeying orders. Maybe there was a "charge forward" spell on them, overriding the selfish self-preservation goblins normally evinced.

With horror that mounted as the mass of goblins mounted, Dor watched. Against such a tide, what defense did they have! Arrows and cherry bombs were pointless; they would only facilitate the manufacture of bodies to use as support for the next layer. Now at last Dor understood why the King had been so concerned about this threat. Goblins *were* worse than Mundanes.

Meanwhile the harpy forces were regaining some semblance of order. Dor had prepared a number of arrows, and these had fooled the dull vampires for some time. The speaking battlements had helped considerably. But now the harpies themselves were massing for a charge. They had nearly human intelligence, and would hardly be fooled long by inanimate devices. They seemed to be progressing toward an assault timed for just about the moment the goblins would finally overflow the wall. Probably this was neither coincidence nor Murphy's curse; the dirty birds merely wished to make certain that the goblins did not capture the Castle.

Dor and the centaurs would be jammed to death the same way the moat-monsters had been. The worst of it was, there did not seem to be anything they could do about it. The enemy forces were too numerous, too mindless.

"This is where I come in," Vadne said, though she was tight about the mouth. "I can stop the goblins—I think."

Dor hoped so. He glanced nervously around at what he could see of the other walls. They were higher, and had more explosive armament, so seemed to be in less difficulty. He wondered how Jumper was doing; he could not see the spider from here. Even the arachnid's great facility with silk could hardly stop these myriad goblins.

The first goblin hand hooked over the rim of the battlement, or rather the place where the battlement had not yet been constructed. Vadne was ready. She touched the hand—and the goblin became a ball that rolled down the slope of piled bodies.

Another hand appeared. She balled the second goblin. Then a host of hands came, keeping her moving. The layers were piling up to either side of the low spot, now, so that she had to jump to one side and then to the other to catch them. Soon she would be overwhelmed. She could not hold the wall alone; no one could.

"Let the harpies come in," Dor cried to the archers, who had been selectively shooting the leaders of any potential charge, delaying that aspect somewhat.

As the arrows stopped, the harpies and vampires swarmed in. The vampires were not bright, but they had caught on that they were being manipulated, and now were bloodthirsty. But the most obvious enemy was the goblin horde. The flying creatures fell upon the goblins, literally, and plunged fangs and claws into them. The goblins fought back viciously, jabbing fists into snouts and stubby fingers into eyes, and wringing necks. They seemed to have lost what weapons they had, in the course of the scramble upward, or maybe they just preferred to meet their enemies on the most basic level of animosity.

It was a respite of sorts for the Castle defenders—but now the bodies piled up even faster, higher and higher, mounding as tall as the rampart. Soon the goblins would be able to roll down into the castle, and Vadne's magic would be largely ineffective. No sense getting buried in balls!

"Can you make them smaller—like grains of sand?" Dor yelled over the noise of battle.

"No. Their mass is the same, whatever shape I give them. I can't stop the mounding."

Too bad. King Trent could have stopped it, by changing them into gnats, so small they would never mound up over the wall. Or he would have changed a centaur into a salamander, and used it to set the bodies on fire, reducing them quickly to ashes. Vadne really was less than a Magician. Not that Dor was doing any better; he had helped hold them off for a while, but could not stop them now.

Then he had an inspiration. "Make them into blocks!" he cried.

She nodded. She got near the gap in the battlement, while Dor protected her flank with his sword. Suddenly the goblin blocks began appearing. These were much smaller than the big stone blocks used in the construction of the Castle, but larger than ordinary bricks. The centaurs shoved them into position on the wall, shaping it crudely higher. The goblin blocks were now holding back the tide of goblins!

"Now there's what I call a good goblin," Cedric exclaimed. "A blockhead!"

But even good blockheads weren't enough. They tended to wiggle and sag, though Vadne made some with interlocking edges. They were not as dense as stone, or as hard, and squished down somewhat as the weight of other blocks went on top. As Vadne had suggested: a goblin in the shape of a block was still a goblin, not much good for anything.

Again Dor scavenged his brain for an answer. How could Castle Roogna be defended against this horrible mass of attackers? Even the corpses were enough to bury it!

A ground dove poked its head out of the floor. Dor took the message from its beak, while continuing to slash about with his sword, protecting Vadne's back. HOW GOES IT? the paper inquired.

"Repeat after me, continuously until the King hears," Dor told the paper. He could not afford to take his attention off the goblins and harpies long enough to write a note. "We can hold out only five minutes more. Situation desperate." He put the repeating paper back in the dove's beak and watched it swim, or rather fly, down out of sight through the stone. He didn't like making such a bleak report, but had to be realistic. He and Vadne and the centaurs had done everything they could, but it was not enough. If this wall fell, the castle would fall. The attack was more than ever like a savage storm, with the tide of goblins on the surface and the clouds of harpies in the air, and now there was no way they could halt the sheer avalanche of creatures. Could even the zombies have abated this menace?

Yes, they could have, Dor decided. Because the Zombie Master would change the piled-up bodies to zombies, who would then hurl the live goblins and many of the dead ones back away from the ramparts. If only the Zombie Master were here!

In moments the King himself was at the wall. "Oh my goodness!" Roogna exclaimed. "I had no idea it was this bad! The two wings of the goblin horde must have converged here on the far side of their thrust, and doubled the pileup. On the other walls it is only halfway up. You should have summoned me before."

"We were too busy fighting goblins," Dor said. Then he shoved the King, moving him out of the way as a harpy divebombed him. She missed, cursing.

"Yes, this is definitely the region of greatest crisis," the King said, as several goblin balls rolled across the wall and dropped off inside the Castle courtyard. He bent to peer at a goblin block, and it peered back, balefully cubic. "The highest tide, the lowest wall. You have done well."

"Not well enough," Dor said, skewering another diving harpy. "We are about to go down under their charge." As if that was not obvious!

"I have some emergency enchantments in the arsenal," Roogna said. "They are hazardous to health, so I have not wished to employ them, but I fear the occasion has arisen." He ducked a vampire.

"Get them!" Dor cried, growing desperate at this delay. Why hadn't the King told him there was more magic available? "Your Majesty!"

"Oh, I brought them with me, just in case." The King brought out a vial of clear fluid. "This is concentrated digestive juice of stomach of dragon. It must be dispensed upwind of the target, downwind of the user. If any drifts—" He shook his head dolefully. "Murphy's curse could cost us one King. Seek cover, please."

"Your Majesty!" Vadne protested. "You can't risk yourself!"

"Of course I can," the King reproved her. "This is my battle, for which all the rest of you are risking yourselves. If we lose it, I am lost anyway." He wet a finger and held it to the wind. "Good; it is blowing west. I can clear the wall. But don't get near until it clears." He went to the northeast corner.

"But the curse will make the wind change!" Dor protested.

"The curse is stretched to its limit," the King said. "This magic will not take long, and I don't think the wind can shift in time."

The goblins were now scrambling over the wall, being met by screaming harpies. Dor and Vadne and the centaurs drew back to the inner surface of the wall, and crowded toward the eastern end, upwind of the proposed release.

The King opened his vial. Yellowish smoke puffed out, was caught by the wind, and strewn across the rim of the wall. It sank down upon swarming goblins —and they melted into black goo. They did not even scream; they just sank into the nether mass. They dissolved off the wall, flowed across the stone, coursed in rivulets through the crannies, and dripped out of sight. Harpies snatched at dissolving goblins, got caught by the juice, and melted into juice themselves. A putrid stench rose from the fluid: the odor of hot vomit.

The wind gusted sidewise, carrying a wisp of magic smoke back across the wall. "The curse!" Dor cried in horror. The closest centaurs danced back, trying desperately to avoid it, but with the evil humor of the curse it eddied after them. One got his handsome tail melted away. "Fan it from you!" Dor cried. "We need fans!"

Vadne touched the nearest goblin. It became a huge fan. Dor grabbed it from her hands and used it to set up a counterdraft. Vadne made another, and another, and the centaurs took these. Together they set up a forced draft. The yellow smoke reared up as if trying to get around, horrible in its mindless determination.

"Where are you going?" Dor cried at it.

"I'm drifting east another six feet, then north over the wall," it replied. "The best pickings are there."

They scrambled out of its projected path. The smoke followed its course, then was gone.

"Ah, Murphy," Vadne said. "It took Magician's magic to foil you, but we foiled you."

Dor agreed weakly. King Roogna, narrowly missed by the smoke, stepped away from the parapet. "It tried to go wrong, but could not. Quite."

Dor peered over the wall. There, below, was a bubbling, frothing ocean of glop, subsiding as the effect penetrated to the bodies underneath. A sinking tide, it ebbed along the rampart and sucked down into the moat, liquefying everything organic. Before long, there was nothing on the north side except the black sea.

"More of that on the other walls will abate the whole goblin army!" Dor remarked to the King, his knees feeling weak and his stomach weaker.

"Several problems," King Roogna said. "First, the wind is wrong for the other sides; it would do as much damage to us as to the enemy. Second, it is not effective against the airborne harpy forces, since it tends to sink and they are flying above it. Third, this vial is all I had. I deemed it too dangerous to store in greater quantity."

"Those are pretty serious problems," Dor admitted. "What other magic is in your arsenal?"

"Nothing readily adaptable, I regret. There is a pied-piper flute I fashioned experimentally from a flute tree: it plays itself when blown, and creatures will follow it indefinitely. But we don't need to lead the goblins or harpies here; we want to drive them away. There is also a magic ring: anything passing through it disappears forever. But it is only two inches in diameter, so only small objects can be passed. And there is a major forget spell."

Dor considered. "Could you reverse the flute, so that it drives creatures away?"

"I might, if the curse didn't foul it up. But it would drive us away, too."

"Um. There is that. Could Vadne stretch out the ring to make it larger?"

The King searched in a pocket. "One way to find out." He brought out a golden ring and passed it to Vadne.

"I really am not skilled with inanimate things," she said. But she took it and concentrated. For a moment nothing happened; then the ring expanded. It stretched out larger and larger, but at the same time the gold that composed it was thinning. At last it was a hoop some two feet in diameter, fashioned of fine gold wire. "That's the best I can do," she said. "If I try to stretch it any farther, it will break." She looked washed out; this had evidently been a real effort.

"That should help," Dor said. He picked up the body of a goblin and shoved it through the hoop. It failed to emerge from the other side. "Yes, I think we have something useful, here." He returned it to the King, whose fingers disappeared as he took it. But they reappeared when the King changed grips, so it seemed the hoop was not dangerous to handle.

"And the forget spell," Dor continued. "Could it make the goblins and harpies forget what they are fighting about?"

"Oh, yes. It is extremely powerful. But if we detonated it here at the Castle, we would all forget why we are here, even who we are. Thus Magician Murphy would have his victory, for there would be no completion of the Castle. And the goblins and harpies might continue to fight anyway; creatures of that ilk hardly need reason to quarrel. They do it instinctively."

"But Magician Murphy himself would forget too!"

"No doubt. But the victory would still be his. He is not vying for power for himself; he is trying to prevent it from accruing to me."

Dor looked out at the barren north view, and at the battle still raging elsewhere around the Castle. A pied-piper flute, a magic ring-hoop, and a forget spell. A lot of excellent and potent magic—that by the anomaly of the situation could not seem to be used to reverse the course of this predicament.

"Murphy, I'm going to find a way," he swore under his breath. "This battle is not over yet." Or so he hoped.

Chapter 11. Disaster

"**Z**ombies ahoy!" a centaur cried, pointing east.

There they were, at last: the zombies standing at the edge of the forest, beyond the milling goblins. The dragon-stomach smoke had obliterated the monstrous mound of goblins at the north wall, but that effect was abating now, and they were surging back from the east and west wings. Either the newly encroaching goblins would be dissolved also, in which case the region wasn't safe for zombies either, or they wouldn't, in which case the zombies couldn't pass there. So how could the Zombie Master get through?

"The Zombie Master must get to the Castle, where he can set up his magical laboratory and work undistracted," Dor said. "Now that we have him in sight, there just has to be a way."

"Yes, I believe at this stage it would tip the balance," King Roogna agreed. "But the problem of transport still seems insuperable. It is difficult enough keeping the monsters outside the Castle; anything beyond the ramparts becomes prohibitive."

"If we believe that, so must they," Dor said. "Maybe we could surprise them. Cedric—would you join me in a dangerous mission?"

"Yes," the centaur said immediately.

The King glanced at him, mildy surprised at the change in attitude. Evidently Dor had done better with the centaurs than Roogna had expected.

"I want to take the King's flute and lure away the creatures from the vicinity of the zombies, to someplace where we can safely detonate the forget spell. That will stop the goblins from coming back here in time to interfere with the Zombie Master. Could you hold the magic hoop in such a way as to make any airborne attackers pass through it, while outrunning groundborne attacks?"

"I am a centaur!" Cedric said. Answer enough.

"Now really," the King said. "This is a highly risky venture!"

"So is doing nothing," Dor said. "The goblins are still mounding up at the other walls; before the day is out they will be coming over the top, and you have no more dragon juice to melt them down. We've got to have the zombies!"

Magician Murphy had come up again. "You are courting disaster," he said. "I respect your courage, Dor—but I must urge you not to go out so foolishly into the goblin horde."

"Listen, snotwing—" Cedric started.

Dor cut him off. "If you really cared, Magician, you would abate the curse. Is your real objection that you fear this ploy can succeed?"

The enemy Magician was silent.

"You'll need someone to lead the zombies in," Vadne said.

"Well, I thought maybe Jumper—"

"The big spider? You'd better have him with you, protecting your flank," she said. "I will guide the zombies in."

"That is very generous of you," Dor said, gratified. "You can transform any creature that gets through the zombie lines. The Zombie Master himself is the one who must be protected; get as close to him as you can and—"

"I shall. Let's get this mission going before it is too late."

The King and Magician Murphy both shook their heads with resignation, seeming strangely similar. But Roogna fetched the flute and the forget spell. They organized at the main gate. Dor mounted Cedric, Jumper joined him and bound him securely in place with silk, and Vadne mounted another centaur. The remaining centaurs of the north wall disposed themselves along the east wall, bows ready. Then the small party charged out into the melee of goblins and harpies.

There was a withering fire from the wall, as the

centaurs shot fire arrows and the goblins, trolls, gnomes, and ghouls withered. It cleared a temporary path through the thickest throng. Cherry bombs and pineapples were still bombarding the allied army. This didn't seem to faze the goblins or their cohorts, but it made Dor extremely nervous. Suppose a pineapple were to land in his vicinity? He would be smithereened! And, considering Murphy's curse—

"Change course!" he screamed.

Startled, Cedric jounced to the side, through a contingent of elves. There was an explosion ahead of them. Shrapnel whizzed by Dor's nose, and the concussion hurt his ears. Eleven bodies sailed outward. Cedric veered to avoid the heavily smoking crater.

"Hey!" a centaur bellowed from the wall. "Stay on course! I almost catapulted a pineapple on you!"

Cedric got back on course with alacrity. "Centaurs have sharp eyes and quick reflexes," he remarked. "Otherwise something could have gone wrong."

Murphy's curse had tried, though, almost causing Dor to interfere with the centaur's careful marksmanship. Dor realized that he would do best to stick to his own department.

He put the flute to his lips, thankful that Jumper was there to help him, so that he had his hands and attention free. He blew experimentally into the mouthpiece. The flute played an eerie, lilting, enticing melody, which floated out through the clamor of battle and brought a sudden hush. Then dwarves and gremlins, vampires and harpies, and numberless goblins swarmed after the centaurs, compelled alike by that magic music.

The winged monsters closed in faster, diving in toward Dor. Cedric twisted his human torso in that supple way centaurs had, facing back while still galloping forward. He swung the hoop through the air in an arc, intercepting the dirty birds as they came—and as each passed through the hoop, she vanished. Dor wondered where they went, but he was too busy playing the flute—if his labored blowing could be called playing—and keeping his body low so as not to get snagged by the hoop himself. He could not keep his attention on all the details!

With two of his legs, Jumper held a spear with which he prodded any goblins or similar ilk that got too close. No ilk could match the galloping pace of the centaur, but since they were forging through the whole goblin allied army, many closed in from the sides. Dor saw Vadne converting those goblins that she touched to pancake disks, and her centaur was fending off the aerial creatures with his fists.

Quickly they reached the zombie contingent. "Follow the woman in!" Dor cried. "I'll lead the monsters away! Block off your ears until I'm beyond your hearing!" Yes, that would be a fine Murphy foul-up, to lure the goblins away only to lure the Zombie Master and Millie into the same forget-spell trap! But a problem anticipated was a problem largely prevented.

Then he was off, playing the magic flute again. No matter how grossly he puffed into it, the music emerged clear and sweet and haunting. And the creatures followed.

"Where to?" Cedric inquired as they galloped.

Dor had an inspiration. "To the Gap!" he cried. "North!"

The centaur put on some speed. The air whistled by them. Experimentally Dor held the flute into the wind, and sure enough: it played. That saved him some breath. The goblins fell behind, and the elves and dwarves, but the trolls were keeping up. Cedric accelerated again, and now even the vampires lost headway. But Dor kept playing, and the creatures kept following. As they had to.

At centaur speed, the Gap was not long in drawing nigh. They had to wait for the land and air hordes to catch up.

"Now I want to get them close to the brink, then detonate the forget spell," Dor said, dropping the flute to his side for the moment. "With luck, the harpies will fly on across the Gap and get lost, and the goblins will be unable to follow them, so won't be able to fight any more."

"Commendable compassion," Jumper chittered. "But in order to gather a large number here, to obtain maximum effect from the spell, you must remain to play the flute for some time. How will *we* escape?"

"Oops! I hadn't thought of that! We're trapped by the Gap!" Dor looked down into the awesome reaches of the chasm, and felt heightsick. When would he stop being a careless child? Or was Murphy's curse catching them after all? Dor would have to sacrifice himself, to make the goblins and harpies forget?

"I can solve it." Jumper chittered. "Ballooning over the—"

"No!" Dor cried. "There is a whole hideous host of things that can and will go wrong with that. Last time we tried it—"

"Then I can drop us down over the edge, into the chasm, where the goblins cannot follow," Jumper suggested. "We can use the magic ring to protect us from descending harpies."

Dor didn't like the notion of descending into the Gap either, but the harpies and goblins and ilk were arriving in vast numbers, casting about for the missing flute music, and he had to make a quick decision. "All right. Cedric, you gallop out of here; you're too heavy to lower on spider silk."

"That's for sure!" Cedric said. "But where should I go? I don't think I can make it back to the Castle. There are one or two zillion minor monsters charging from there to here, and I'd have to buck the whole tide."

"Go to Celeste," Dor suggested. "Your job is honorably finished, here, and she'll be glad to see you."

"First to the warlock!" Cedric exclaimed, grinning. He made a kind of salute, then galloped off west.

Jumper reattached the dragline to Dor, then scrambled over the cliff edge. This easy walking on a near-vertical face still amazed Dor. However, it was decidely handy at the moment.

Dor resumed playing the flute, for the goblins were beginning to lose interest. That brought them forward with a rush. They closed on him so rapidly that they wedged against each other, blocking themselves off from him. But they were struggling so hard that Dor knew the jam would break at any moment. Yet he kept playing, waiting for Jumper's signal of readiness.

Finally his nerve broke. "Are you ready?" he called. And the goblins, loosed momentarily from their relentless press forward, eased up—and the jam did break. Dor fumbled for his sword, knowing he could never fight off the inimical mass, yet—

But what was he thinking of? It was the magic ring he should use. Cedric had left it with him. He picked it up and held it before him. The first goblin dived right at him. Dor almost dropped the hoop, fearing the creature would smash into him—but as it passed through the ring, it vanished. Right before his face, as if it had struck an invisible wall and been shunted aside. Potent magic!

"Ready!" Jumper chittered from below. Just in time, for three more goblins were charging, and Dor wasn't certain he could get them all neatly through the hoop. More likely they would snag on the rim, and their weight would have carried him back over the cliff. "Jump!"

Dor trusted his friend. He jumped. Backward off the cliff. He sailed out into the abyss, escaping the grasp of the surging goblins, swinging down and sidewise, for Jumper had providently rigged the lines so that Dor would not whomp directly into the wall. The spider always thought of these things before Dor did, anticipating what could go wrong and abating it first. Thus Murphy's curse had little power over him. That was why Jumper had taken so much time just now, despite knowing that Dor was in a desperate strait at the brink of the canyon; he had been making sure that no mistake of his would betray Dor.

And there it was, of course: the answer to the curse. Maturity. Only a careless or thoughtless person could be trapped by the curse, giving it the openings to snare him.

Now the vampires and harpies swarmed down, though the majority of them were fighting with the goblins above. "Snatch! snatch!" they screamed. A perfect characterization.

Dor found himself swinging back. He held the hoop before him, sweeping through the ugly flock—and where the ring passed, no harpies remained. But they clutched at him from the sides—

Then Jumper hauled him in against the wall, so that he could set his back to its protective solidity and hold the hoop before him. Dor saw now that the brink of the chasm was not even; the spider had skillfully utilized projections to anchor the framework of lines, so that Dor had room to swing clear of the wall. A remarkable feat of engineering that no other type of creature could have accomplished in so brief a time.

"Give me the ring!" Jumper chittered. "You play the flute!"

Right. They had to call as many creatures to this spot as possible. Dor yielded the hoop and put the flute to his lips. Jumper maneuvered deftly, using the hoop to protect them both.

Now the harpies dived in with single-minded intent, compelled by the music. They swooped through the hoop; they splatted into the wall around it, knocking themselves out and falling twistily down into the chasm, dirty feathers flying free. The vampires were no better off.

Then the goblins and trolls started dropping down from the ledge above, also summoned by the flute.

Dor broke off. "We're slaughtering them! That wasn't my intent! It's time to set off the forget spell!"

"We would be trapped by it too," Jumper reminded him. "Speak to it."

"Speak to it? Oh." Dor held out the glassy ball. "Spell, how are you detonated?"

"I detonate when a voice commands me to," the ball replied.

"Any voice?"

"That's what I said."

Dor had his answer. He set the sphere in a niche in the cliff. "Count to one thousand, then order yourself to detonate," he told it.

"Say, that's clever!" the spell said. "One, two, three-four-five—"

"Slowly!" Dor said sharply. "One number per second."

"Awww—" But the spell resumed more slowly. "Seven, eight—what a spoilsport you are!—nine, ten, a big fat hen!"

"What?" a nearby harpy screeched, taking it personally. She dived in, but Jumper snagged her with the hoop. Another potential foul-up defused.

"And don't say anything to insult the harpies," Dor told the spell.

"Ah, shucks. Eleven, twelve—"

Jumper scurried away to the side, fastened the other end of a new line he had attached to Dor, and hauled him across. This was not as fast as running on level land, but it was expedient.

They moved steadily westward, away from the spell sphere. Dor continued playing the flute intermittently, to keep the goblins massing at the brink without allowing too many to fall over. He heard the spell's counting fading in the distance, and that lent urgency to his escape. The problem was now one of management; he and Jumper had to get far enough away to be out of the forget range, without luring the goblins and harpies beyond range too. Inevitably a good many monsters would escape, but maybe the ones fazed by the forget detonation would lend sufficient confusion to the array to inhibit the others from returning to the Castle. There seemed to be no clearcut strategy; he just had to fudge through as best he could, hoping he could profit enough to give Castle Roogna the edge. It had worked well with the Mundane siege of the Zombie Master's castle, after all.

How much nicer if there were simple answers to all life's problems! But the closer Dor approached adulthood, the less satisfying such answers became. Life itself was complex, therefore life's answers were complex. But it took a mature mind to appreciate the convolutions of that complexity.

"One hundred five, one hundred six, pick up a hundred sticks!" the spell was chanting. "One hundred seven, one hundred eight, lay all hundred straight!" Now *there* was a simple mind!

Dor wondered again how wide a radius the detonation would have. Would the chasm channel it? Then the brunt would come along here, instead of out where the goblins were. Maybe he and Jumper should climb over the rim before the spell went off, and lie low there, hoping to be shielded from the direct effect. But they couldn't come up too close to the goblins, who were milling about near the brink. The harpies were still dive-bombing him, forcing Jumper to jump back with the hoop. Fortunately, the bulk of their attention was taken by the goblins, their primary enemy; Dor and Jumper were merely incidental targets, attacked because they were there. Except when Dor played the flute, as he continued to do intermittently.

"Three hundred forty-seven, three hundred forty-eight, now don't be late," the spell was saying in the fading distance. As long as he could hear it, he had to assume he was within its forget radius.

"Can we go faster?" Dor asked nervously. He had thought they were traveling well, but the numbers had jumped with seeming suddenness from the neighborhood of one hundred to the neighborhood of three hundred. Unless the spell was cheating, skipping numbers—no, the inanimate did not have the wit to cheat. Dor had just been preoccupied with his own efforts and gloomy thoughts.

"Not safely, friend," Jumper chittered.

"Let me take back the hoop," Dor suggested to the spider. "Then you can string your lines faster."

Jumper agreed, and passed back the hoop.

Another harpy made a screaming dive. Dor scooped her into the hoop, and she was gone without recall or recoil. What happened to the creatures who passed through it? Harpies could fly, goblins could climb; why couldn't either get out? Was it an inferno on the other side, killing them instantly? He didn't like that.

Jumper was ahead, setting the anchor for the next swing. Dor had a private moment. He poked a finger into the center of the hoop, from the far side, watching it disappear from his side. He saw his finger in cross section, as if severed with a sharp sword: the skin, the little blood vessels, the tendons, the bone. But there was no pain; his finger felt cool, not cold; no inferno there, and no freezing weather either. He withdrew it, and found it whole, to his relief. He poked it from the near side, and got the same effect, except that this time he could not see the cross section. It seemed that either side of the ring led to wherever it led. A different world?

Jumper tugged, and Dor swung across, feeling guilty for his surreptitious experimentation. He could have lost a finger that way. Well, maybe not; he had seen the King's fingers disappear and reappear unharmed.

"Let's check and see if the goblins are clear," Dor said. He had not played the flute for a while.

The spider scurried up the wall to peek over with two or three eyes, keeping the rest of his body low. "They are there in masses," he chittered. "I believe they are pacing the harpies—who are pacing us."

"Oh, no! Murphy strikes again! We can't get clear of the Gap, if they follow us!"

"We should be clear of the forget radius now," Jumper chittered consolingly.

"Then so are the goblins and harpies! That's no good!" Dor heard himself getting hysterical.

"Our effort should have distracted a great number of the warring creatures," Jumper pointed out reasonably. "Our purpose was to distract them so that the Zombie Master could penetrate to Castle Roogna. If he succeeded, we have succeeded."

"I suppose so," Dor agreed, calming. "So it doesn't really matter if the harpies and goblins don't get forget-spelled. Still, how are we ever going to get out of here? It is too late to turn off the spell."

"Perseverance should pay. If we continue until night—" Jumper cocked his body, lifting his two front legs so as to hear better. "What is that?"

Dor tried to fathom what direction the spider was orienting, and could not. Damn those ubiquitous eyes! "What's what?"

Then he heard it. "Nine hundred eighty-three, nine hundred eighty-four, close to the hundredth door; nine hundred eighty-five—"

A harpy was carrying the spell toward them—and it was about to detonate! "Oh, Murphy!" Dor wailed. "You really nabbed us now!"

"What's the big secret about this talking ball?" the harpy screeched.

"Nine hundred ninety-two, buckle the bag's shoe," the spell said.

"Stop counting!" Dor yelled at the spell.

"Countdown can't be stopped once initiated," the spell replied smugly.

"Quick," Jumper chittered. "I will fasten the draglines so we can return. We must escape through the magic hoop."

"Oh, no!" Dor cried.

"It should be safe; I saw you testing it."

"Nine hundred ninety-seven, nine hundred ninety-eight," the spell continued inexorably. "Now don't be late!"

Jumper scrambled through the hoop. Dor hesitated, appalled. *Could* they return? But if he remained here—

"One thousand!" the spell cried gleefully. "Now at last I can say it!"

Dor dived through the hoop. The last thing he heard was "Deto—"

He arrived in darkness. It was pleasant, neutral. His body seemed to be suspended without feeling. There was a timelessness about him, a perpetual security. All he had to do was sleep.

You are not like the others, a thought said at him.

"Of course not," Dor thought back. Whatever he was suspended in did not permit physical talking, because there was no motion. "I am from another time. So is my friend Jumper the spider. Who are you?"

I am the Brain Coral, keeper of the source of magic.

"The Brain Coral! I know you! You're supposed to be animating my body!"

When?

"Eight hundred years from now. Don't you remember?"

I am not in a position to know about that, being as yet a creature of my own time.

"Well, in my time you—uh, it gets complicated. But I think Jumper and I had better get out of here as soon as the forget spell dissipates."

You detonated a forget spell?

"Yes, a major one, inside the Gap. To make the goblins and harpies and cohorts and ilk stop fighting. They—"

Forget spells are permanent, until counterspelled.

"I suppose so, for the ones affected. But—"

You have just rendered the Gap itself forgotten.

"The Gap? But it's not alive! The spell only affects living things, things that remember."

Therefore all living things will forget the Gap.

Stunned, Dor realized it was true. He had caused the Gap to be forgotten by all but those people whose forgetting would be paradoxical. Such as those living adjacent to it, who would otherwise fall in and die. Their deaths would be inexplicable to their friends and relatives, leading to endless complications that would quickly neutralize the spell. Paradox was a powerful natural counterspell! But any people who had no immediate need-to-know would simply not remember the Gap. This was true in his own day—and now he knew how it had come about. He had done it, with his bumbling.

Yet if what he did here had no permanence, how could . . . ? He couldn't take time to ponder that now. "We have to get back to Castle Roogna. Or at least, we can't stay here. There would be paradox when we caught up to our own time."

So it would seem. I shall release you from my preservative fluid. The primary radiation of the spell should not affect you; the secondary may. You will not forget your personal identities and mission, but you may forget the Gap once you leave its vicinity.

"I'm pretty much immune to that anyway," Dor said. "I'm one of the near-Gap residents. Just so long as I don't forget the rest."

One question, before I release you. Through what aperture have you and all these other creatures entered my realm? I had thought the last large ring was destroyed fifty years ago.

"Oh, we have a two-inch ring that we expanded to two-foot diameter. We can change it back when we're done with it."

That will be appreciated. Perhaps we shall meet again—in eight hundred years, the Coral thought at him.

Then Dor popped out of the hoop and dangled by his dragline. Jumper followed.

"I had not anticipated immobility," the spider chittered ruefully.

"That's all right. We can't all think of everything, all the time."

Jumper was not affronted. "True."

The harpies were visible in the distance, but they paid no further attention to Dor and Jumper. They were milling about in air, trying to remember what they were doing there. Which was exactly what Dor had wanted to happen. The goblins, however, were in sadder state. They too seemed to be milling about—but they had forgotten that sharp dropoffs were hazardous to health, and were falling into the chasm at a great rate. Dor's action had decimated the goblin horde.

"It can not be helped," Jumper chittered, recognizing his disgust. "We can not anticipate or control all ramifications of any given course."

"Yeah, I guess," Dor agreed, still bothered by the slaughter he had wrought. Would he get hardened to this sort of carnage as he matured? He hoped not.

They climbed to the brim and stood on land again. The goblins ignored them, not remembering them. The forget detonation had evidently been devastating near its origin, wiping out all memories of everything.

Dor spied a glassy fragment lying on the ground. He went to pick it up. It was a shatter from the forget-spell globe. "You really did it, didn't you!" he said to it.

"That was some blast!" the fragment agreed happily. "Or was it? I forget!"

Dor dropped it and went on. "I hope Cedric got clear in time. That spell was more powerful than I expected."

"He surely did."

They hurried back toward the Castle, ignoring the wandering hordes.

The battle was not over at Castle Roogna, but it was evident that the tide had turned. As the distance from the forget-spell ground zero lengthened, the effects diminished, until here at the Castle there was little confusion—except that there were only about a third as many goblins and harpies as before, and the ramparts were manned by zombies. The Zombie Master had gotten through!

The defenders spied them, and laid down a barrage of cherry bombs to clear a path to the Castle. Even so, it was necessary to employ sword and hoop to get through, for the goblins and harpies resented strangers getting into their battle. So Dor was forced to slay again. War was hell, he thought.

King Roogna himself welcomed them at the gate. "Marvelous!" he cried. "You piped half the monsters off the field and made them forget. Vadne led the Zombie Master in while the goblins were distracted by the flute, and he has been generating new zombies from the battlefield casualties ever since. The only problem is fetching them in."

"Then there's work for me to do," Dor said shortly. He found he didn't really want to accept congratulations for doing a job of mass murder.

The King, the soul of graciousness, made no objection. "Your dedication does you credit."

Jumper helped, of course. Covered by centaur archers on the ramparts, they went out, located the best bodies, looped them with silk, and dashed back under cover. Then they hauled the corpses in on the lines. They were really old hands at this. When they had a dozen or so, they ferried them in to the Zombie Master's laboratory.

Millie was there, wan and disheveled, but she looked up with a smile when Dor entered. "Oh, you're safe, Dor! I was so worried!"

"Worry for your fiancé," he said shortly. "He's doing the work."

"He certainly is," Vadne said. She was moving the bodies into position for him by converting them to great balls that were easily rolled, then returning them to their regular shapes. As a result, he was evidently manufacturing zombies at triple the rate he had at his own castle. Time was consumed mainly in the processing, not the actual conversion. "He's making an army to defend this Castle!"

"Dor's doing a lot too!" Millie said stoutly.

Flattered despite himself, Dor realized that Millie still had feeling for him, and still might— But he had to suppress that. It was not only that his time in this world was limited, and that if he interfered with this particular aspect of history and it stayed put, he would paradoxically negate his whole original mission. It was that Millie was now betrothed to another man, and

Dor had no right to—to do what he wished he could.

"We're all doing what we can, for the good of the Land of Xanth," he said, somewhat insecurely, considering his thought. How much better it would be for him, if he could find some girl more nearly his own age and status, and—

"I wish I had full Magician-caliber talent like yours," Vadne said to the Zombie Master as she shape-changed another corpse. Dor saw that she was able to handle living things, and once-living things, and inanimate things like the magic ring: a fair breadth of talent, really.

"You do have it," the Zombie Master said, surprised.

"No, I am only a neo-Sorceress."

"I would term your topological talent as Magician-caliber magic," he said, rendering the corpse into a zombie.

She almost glowed at the compliment, which carried even more impact because it was evident that he had made it matter-of-factly, unconscious of its effect. She looked at the Zombie Master with a new appraisal. What potency in a compliment, Dor thought, and filed the information in the back of his mind for future reference.

Dor went out to fetch more bodies. Jumper helped, as always. They kept working until daylight waned, and slowly the goblin and harpy forces dwindled while the zombie forces increased. Harpy zombies were now waging the defense in the air, greatly easing that situation.

Yet this left Dor unsatisfied. He had entered the tapestry for one mission, the acquisition of the elixir to restore a zombie to full life. But by the time he had that, he had been enmeshed in another mission, the conversion of the Zombie Master to King Roogna's cause. Now he had accomplished that also—and was casting about for yet another quest. What was it?

Ah, he had it now. This foolish war between the goblins and harpies—was it possible to do something about it, instead of preserving Castle Roogna by wiping out both sides? Why not simply abate the problems that had caused the war?

He had gone over this before, in his mind, and had no answer. But then time had been too much of a factor. Now the Castle was prevailing, now there was time, and he knew more about the magic available. The magic hoop, for example, leading into the Brain Coral's somber storage lake—

"That's it!" he exclaimed.

Jumper cocked four or five eyes at him. "There is something I missed?"

"Anchor me, so I can't fall in. I have to go through the hoop to talk with the Brain Coral."

The spider did not argue or question. He fastened a stout dragline to Dor. Dor propped the magic hoop against a wall and poked his head through.

"Brain Coral!" he thought, again finding it impossible to breathe or speak in the preservative fluid. This stuff was not mere water; it had stasis magic. "This is Dor of eight hundred years from now, again."

What is your concern? the Coral inquired patiently.

"Have you a male harpy in storage?"

Yes. An immature one, exiled three hundred years ago by a rival for the harpy throne.

"A royal male?" Dor thought, startled.

By harpy law a royal person cannot be executed like a commoner. So he was put safely away, and the access ring destroyed thereafter.

"Will you release him now? It would make a big difference to our present situation."

I will release him. Bear in mind you owe me a favor.

"Yes. I will talk to you again in eight hundred years." Dor removed his head from the Coral's realm. His head had been in stasis, but the rest of his body was responsive.

In a moment a bird-shape popped out of the hoop. "Greetings, Prince," Dor said formally.

The figure spread his wings, orienting on him. "And what ilk be ye, man-thing?"

"I am Magician Dor. I have freed you from storage."

The harpy glanced an imperial glance at him. "Show your power."

Dor picked up a fallen harpy feather. "What is the

age of the Prince?" he inquired. "Exclusive of storage time."

"The Prince is twelve years old," the feather answered.

"Why, that's my age!" Dor exclaimed.

"You'll sure be a giant when you get your full growth!" the feather said.

The Prince cut in. "Very well. I accept your status, and will deal with ye. I am Prince Harold. What is it ye crave of me?"

"You are the only male harpy alive today," Dor said. "You must go forth and claim your crown, to preserve your species. I charge you with two things only: do not cohabit with any but your own kind, and give to me the counterspell to the curse your people put on the goblins."

The Prince drew himself up with hauteur. "One favor ye did me, yet ye presume to impose on me for two favors! I need no stricture of cohabitation for when I come of age—not when I have the entire world of harpies to build my harem from. As to this spell, I know naught of it."

"It happened after your exile. You can discover its nature from your subjects."

"I shall do so," the harpy said. "An I discover it, I shall provide the counter as your recompense."

Dor conducted the Prince to King Roogna, who did a polite double take as he observed the harpy's gender. "Rare magic indeed!" he murmured.

"We must release Prince Harold Harpy to his kind without mishap," Dor told the King. The harpies will have no need to fight, once they have him."

"I see," the King said. He glanced obliquely at Magician Murphy, standing beside him. "We shall declare an absolute cease-fire until he is free. I shall walk the ramparts myself, to be sure that nothing goes wrong."

"You may manage to free the harpy," Murphy said grimly. "But my curse will have its impact elsewhere. You have not prevailed." But he looked tired; his talent was evidently under severe strain. No single Magician, however gifted, could stand forever against the power of three. Dor was almost sorry for him.

"But we're getting there," Roogna said. He escorted the Prince to the wall, cautioning the centaurs not to fire at the harpy. Prince Harold spread his pinions and launched into the sky.

There was a screech of sheerest amazement from the nearest female. Then the harpies swarmed to the Prince. For an awful moment Dor feared they had mistaken him, and would tear him to pieces; but they had instantly recognized his nature. They lost all interest in the goblin war. In moments the entire swarm had flapped away, leaving the goblins nothing to fight except a few tired vampires.

Then a lone female harpy winged back from the flock. A centaur whistled. "Helen!" Dor cried, recognizing her.

"By order of Prince Harold," Helen said. "The counterspell." She deposited a pebble in his hand. She winked. "Too bad you didn't take your opportunity when you had it, handsome man; you will never have another. I used the ring you gave me to wish for the finest possible match, and now I am to be first concubine to the Prince." She tapped her ringed claw.

Things evidently happened fast among the harpies; it had been only a few minutes since the Prince mounted the sky. "Good for you," Dor said.

"I knew I could do it," the ring replied, thinking Dor had addressed it. "I can do anything!"

She glanced down at it. "Oh, so you're talking again!"

"It will be silent hereafter," Dor said. "Thank you for the counterspell."

"It's the least I could do for you," she said, inhaling. The centaurs goggled.

Then Heavenly Helen spread her pretty wings and was away, with all males on the parapet staring after her, and even a few of the healthier zombies were admiring her form. There were covert glances at Dor, as people wondered what he had done to attract the attention of so remarkable a creature.

Dor was satisfied. Helen had, in true harpy fashion, snatched her opportunity. And who could tell: maybe the wish ring really had had something to do with it.

Dor turned his attention to the pebble spell. "How are you invoked?" he asked it.

"I am not invoked; I am revoked," it replied. "I am not a counterspell, I am the original spell. When I am revoked, the enchantment abates."

"How are you revoked, then?"

"You just heat me to fire temperature, and my magic pours out invisibly until it is all gone."

Dor handed the pebble to the King. "That should abate the goblin complaint. With no further reason to fight, the goblins should go home. Then Murphy's curse can't make the battle continue here."

"You are phenomenal, Magician!" King Roogna said. "You have used your mind instead of your body, in a truly regal manner." He hurried away with the pebble spell.

The King cooked the goblin spell according to the directive, but no change in the goblin horde was apparent. Yet he was not dismayed. "The original spell was subtle," he explained. "It caused the goblin females to be negatively selective. The damage has been done to the goblins over the course of many generations. It will take many more generations to reverse. The females are not here on the battlefield, so the males do not even know of the change yet. So we do not see its effect immediately, or benefit from it ourselves, but still the job is worth doing. We are not trying merely to preserve Castle Roogna; we are building a better Land of Xanth." He waved a hand cheerfully. "Evening is upon us; we must go to our repast and sleep, while the zombies keep watch. I believe victory is at last coming into sight."

It did look that way. Magician Murphy looked glum indeed. Dor, suddenly tired, ate perfunctorily, fell on the bed provided in the completed section of the Castle, and slept soundly. In the morning he woke to discover the Zombie Master on an adjacent bed, and Magician Murphy on another. Everyone was tired, and there was as yet very little space within the Castle.

The goblins had largely dispersed in the night, leaving their copious dead in the field. The zombies remained on guard. The centaurs had resumed their building labors, no longer needed for the defense of the Castle. Now it did seem likely that Castle Roogna would be completed on schedule.

A buffet breakfast was being served in the dining hall, amid the clods of earth, stray pieces of zombies, and discarded weapons. King Roogna was there, and Magician Murphy, and Vadne and Jumper and Dor. Murphy had little appetite; he seemed almost as gaunt as the Zombie Master.

"Frankly I think we have it in hand," the King said. "Will you not relinquish with grace, Murphy?"

"There remains yet one aspect of the curse," Murphy said. "Should it fail, then I am done, and will retire. But I must hold on until it manifests."

"Fair enough," Roogna said. "I hung on when it seemed your curse had prevailed. Indeed, had not young Dor arrived with his friend—"

"Surely nothing I did really affected the outcome," Dor said uneasily. For there, ultimately, could be Murphy's victory.

"You still feel that what you do is invalid?" the King inquired. "We can readily have the verification of that. I have a magic mirror somewhere—"

"No, I—" But the King in his gratitude was already on his way to locate the mirror.

"Perhaps it *is* time we verified this," Murphy said. "Your involvement, Dor, has become so pervasive and intricate that it becomes difficult to see how it can be undone. I may have been mistaken in my conjecture. Was my curse opposing you also?"

"I believe it was," Dor said. "Things kept going wrong—"

"Then you must have validity, for otherwise my curse would not care. In fact, if your efforts lacked validity, my curse might even have promoted them, so that they played a larger part in the false success. If the King depended on you instead of on his own—"

"But how can I change my own—" Dor glanced at Vadne, then shrugged. He could not remember whether she knew about him now or did not. What did it matter, so long as Millie remained innocent? "My own past?"

"I do not know," Murphy said. "I had thought that would be a paradox, therefore invalid. Yet there are aspects of magic no man can fathom. I may have made a grievous error, and thereby cost myself the victory. Is the Gap forgotten in your day?"

"Yes."

They mulled that over for a while, chewing on waffles from the royal waffle tree. Then Murphy said: "It could be that spots of history can be rechanneled, so long as the end result is the same. If King Roogna is fated to win, it may not matter how he does it, or what agencies assist. So your own involvement may be valid, yet changes nothing. You are merely filling a role that some other party filled in your absence."

"Could be," Dor agreed. He glanced about. The others seemed interested in the discussion, except for Vadne, who was withdrawn. Something about that bothered him, but he couldn't place it.

"At any rate, we shall soon know. My power has been stretched to its limit," Murphy continued. "If I do not achieve the victory this day, I shall be helpless. I do not know exactly what form my curse will take, but it is in operation now, and I think will prove devastating. The issue remains in doubt."

The King returned with his mirror. "Let me see—how shall I phrase this?" he said to himself. "Mirror queries have to rhyme. That was built into them by the Magician who made this type of glass. Ah." He set it on the floor. "Mirror, mirror, on the floor—can we trust ourselves to Dor?"

"Corny," Murphy muttered.

The forepart of a handsome centaur appeared in the mirror. "That signifies affirmative," Roogna said. "The hind part is the negative."

"But many centaurs are far handsomer in the hind part," Dor pointed out.

"Why not simply ask it which side will prevail?" Murphy suggested wryly.

"I doubt that will work," the King said. "Because if its answer affects our actions, that would be paradox. And since we have been dealing with very strong magic, it could be beyond the mirror's limited power of resolution."

"Oh, let's discover the answer for ourselves," Murphy said. "We have fought it through this far, we might as well finish it properly."

"Agreed," Roogna said.

They ate more waffles, pouring on maple syrup from a rare maple tree. Unlike other magic beverage trees, the maple issued its syrup only a drop at a time, and it was dilute, so that a lot of the water had to be boiled off to make it thick enough for use. This made the syrup a special delicacy. In fact, maple trees no longer existed in Xanth in Dor's day. Maybe they had been overtapped, and thus this most magical species had ironically gone the way of most mundane trees.

The Zombie Master came in. Vadne perked up. "Come sit by me," she invited.

But he was not being sociable. "Where is Millie the maid, my fiancée?"

The others exchanged perplexed glances. "I assumed she was with you," Dor said.

"No. I worked late last night, and it would not be meet for such as she to keep my company unchaperoned. I sent her to bed."

"You didn't do that at your own castle," Dor pointed out.

"We were not then engaged. After the betrothal, we kept company only in company."

Dor thought of asking about the journey from the zombie castle to Castle Roogna, which had had at least one night on the road. But he refrained; it seemed the Zombie Master had conservative notions about propriety, and honored them rigidly.

"She has not been to breakfast," the King said. "She must be sleeping late."

"I called at her door, but she did not answer," the Zombie Master said.

"Maybe she's sick," Dor suggested, and immediately regretted his directness, for the Zombie Master jumped as if stung.

The King interceded smoothly. "Vadne, check Millie's room."

The neo-Sorceress departed. Soon she was back. "Her room is empty."

Now the Zombie Master was really upset. "What has happened to her?"

"Do not be concerned," Vadne said consolingly. "Perhaps she became weary of Castle life and returned to her stockade. I will be happy to assist you during her absence."

But he would not be consoled. "She is my fiancée! I must find her!"

"Here, let me query the mirror," the King said. "What's a rhyme for Maid?"

"Shade," Murphy said.

"Thank you, Magician," the King said. He propped the mirror in a niche in the wall where it was in shadow. "Mirror, mirror, in the shade, tell us what happened to—"

Dor's chair thunked on the floor as he craned forward to see the picture about to form. The mirror slipped from its perch and fell. It cracked in two, and was useless.

The Zombie Master stared at it. "Murphy's curse!" he exclaimed. "Why should it prevent us from locating the maid?" He turned angrily on Murphy.

Magician Murphy spread his hands. "I do not know, sir. I assure you I have no onus against your fiancée. She strikes me as a most appealing young woman."

"She strikes everyone that way," Vadne said. "Her talent is—"

"Do not denigrate her to me!" the Zombie Master shouted. "It was only in gratitude to her that I agreed to soil my hands with politics! If anything happens to her—"

He broke off, and there was a pregnant silence. Suddenly the nature of the final curse was coming clear to them all. Without Millie, the Zombie Master had no reason to support the King, and Castle Roogna would then lose its major defensive force. Anything could happen to further interrupt its construction—and would. Murphy would win.

Yet the harpies and goblins were gone, Dor thought. Did anything remain that could really threaten the Castle? And he realized with horror that one thing did: the zombies themselves. They now controlled Castle Roogna. If they turned against the King—

"It seems your curse has struck with extreme precision," King Roogna said, evidently recognizing the implication. The issue was indeed in doubt! "We must find Millie quickly, and I fear that will not be easy."

"It was my chair that jolted the mirror," Dor said, stricken. "It's my fault!"

"Do not blame yourself," Murphy said. "The curse strikes in the readiest manner, much as water seeks the lowest channel. You have simply been used."

"Well, then, I'll find her!" Dor cried. "I'm a Magician, same as you are." He looked about. "Wall, where is she?"

"Don't ask me," the wall said. "She hasn't been here in the dining hall since last night."

Dor marched out into the hall, the others trailing after him. "Floor, when was she last here?"

"Last night after supper," the floor said. Neither wall nor floor elected to be difficult about details; they knew whom Dor meant, and recognized his mood, and gave him no trouble.

Dor traced Millie's whereabouts randomly, pacing the halls. A problem became apparent: Millie, like the others, had moved about considerably during the evening, and the walls, floors and limited furnishings were not able to distinguish all the comings and goings. It was a trail that crossed and recrossed itself, so that the point of exit could not be determined. Millie had been here at the time the Zombie Master sent her to bed—and not thereafter. She had not arrived at her own room. Where had she gone?

"The front gate—see whether she left the Castle," the King suggested.

Dor doubted Millie would depart like that—not voluntarily. But he queried the front gate. She had not exited there. He checked the ramparts. She had not gone there. In fact she had gone nowhere. It was as if she had vanished from the middle of the hall.

"Could somebody have conjured her out?" Dor wondered aloud.

"Conjuring is not a common talent," King Roogna said. "I know of no conjurers today who could accomplish this."

"The magic hoop!" Jumper chittered.

Oh, no! They fetched the hoop, still at its two-foot diameter. "Did Millie the maid pass through you last night?" Dor demanded of it.

"She did not," the hoop said acerbically. "No one

has been through me since you stuck your fool head through and brought out the harpy Prince. When are you going to have me changed back to my normal size? I'm uncomfortable, stretched out like this."

"Later," Dor told it, experiencing relief. Then his relief reversed. If Millie had gone through there, at least she would be alive and safe and possibly recoverable. As it was, the mystery remained, growing more critical every moment.

"Query the flute," Jumper suggested. "If someone played it and lured her somewhere—"

Dor queried the pied-piper flute. It, too, denied any involvement. "Could it be lying?" Vadne asked.

"No," Dor answered shortly.

They crossed the Castle again, but gained nothing on their original information: Millie had left the Zombie Master in the evening, going toward her room—and never gotten there. Nothing untoward had been seen by anyone or anything.

Then Jumper had another notion. "If she is the victim of malodorous entertainment—"

"What?" Dor asked.

"Foul play," the web said, rechecking its translation. "Can't expect me to get the idiom right every time."

Dor smiled momentarily. "Continue."

Jumper chittered again. ". . . victim of smelly games, then some other person is most likely responsible. We must ascertain the whereabouts of each other living person at the time of her disappearance."

"You have an uncommonly apt perception," King Roogna told the spider. "You approach things from new directions."

"It comes from having eyes in the back of one's head," Jumper said matter-of-factly.

They checked for the others. The centaurs had remained on the ramparts, backing up the zombies. Dor and Jumper and King Roogna had slept. The Zombie Master had worked till the wee hours, then gone to the male room and thence to his sleeping cot. Magician Murphy had taken an innocent tour of the premises, also stopped at the male room, and slept. Neo-Sorceress Vadne had assisted the Zombie Master, but gone to the female room shortly before

Millie was dismissed. She had returned to work late with the Zombie Master, then gone to her own room to sleep. Nothing there.

"What occurs in the female room?" Jumper inquired.

"Uh, females have functions too," Dor said.

"Excretion. I comprehend. Did Millie go there?"

"Often. Young females have great affinity for such places."

"Did she emerge on the final occasion?"

The men stared. "We never checked there!" Dor cried.

"Now don't you men go snooping into a place like that!" Vadne protested. "It's indecent!"

"We will merely ask straightforward questions," the King assured her. "No voyeurism."

Vadne looked unsatisfied, but did not protest further. They repaired to the female room, where Dor inquired somewhat diffidently of the door: "Did Millie the maid enter here late last night?"

"She did. But I won't tell you what her business was," the door replied primly.

"Did she depart thereafter?"

"Come to think of it, she never did," the door said, surprised. "That must have been some business!"

Dor looked up to find one of Jumper's green eyes bearing on him. They had located Millie! Almost.

They entered. The female room was clean, with several basins and potties and a big drainage sump for disposal of wastes. In one corner was a dumbwaiter for shipment of laundry and sundry items upstairs. Nothing else.

"She's not here," Dor said, disappointed.

"Then this is her point of departure," the King said. "Question every artifact here, if you have to, until we discover the exact mode of her demise. I mean, departure," he amended quickly, conscious of the presence of the somber Zombie Master.

Dor questioned. Millie had come in, approached a basin, looked at her pretty but tired face in a mundane mirror—and Vadne had entered the room. Vadne had doused the Magic Lantern. In the darkness Millie had screamed with surprise and dismay, and there had been a swish as of hair flinging about, and a tattoo on the floor as of feet kicking. That was all.

Vadne had departed the room alone. The light had remained doused until morning—when there was no sign of Millie.

Vadne was edging toward the door. Jumper threw a noose and snared her, preventing her escape. "So you were the one!" the Zombie Master cried. His gaunt face was twisted with incredulous rage, his eyes gleaming whitely from their sockets.

"I only did it for you," she said, bluffing it out. "She didn't love you anyway; she loved Dor. And she's just a garden-variety maid, not a Magician-caliber talent. You need a—"

"She is my betrothed!" the Zombie Master cried, his aspect wild. Dor echoed the man's passion within himself. The Zombie Master did love her—as Dor did. "What did you do with her, wretch?"

"I put her where you will never find her!" Vadne flared.

"This is murder," King Roogna said grimly.

"No it isn't!" Vadne cried. "I didn't kill her. I just—changed her."

Dor saw the strategy in that. The Zombie Master could have reanimated her dead body as a zombie; as it was, he could do nothing.

Jumper peered down the drainage sump with his largest eye. "Is it possible?" he inquired.

"We'll rip out the whole sump to find her!" the King cried.

"And if you do," Vadne said, "what will you do then? Without me you can't change her back to her stupid sex-appeal form."

"Neo-Sorceress," King Roogna said grimly. "We are mindful of your considerable assistance in the recent campaign. We do not relish showing you disfavor."

"Oh, pooh!" she said. "I only helped you because Murphy wouldn't have me, and I wanted to marry a Magician."

"You have chosen unwisely. If you do not change the maid back, we shall have to execute you."

She was taken aback, but remained defiant. "Then

you'll never get her changed, because talents never repeat."

"But they do overlap," Roogna said.

"In the course of decades or centuries! The only way you can save her is to deal on my terms."

"What are your terms?" the King asked, his eyes narrow.

"Let Dor marry Millie. She likes him better anyway, the stupid slut. I'll take the Zombie Master."

"Never!" the Zombie Master cried, his hands clenching.

Vadne faced him. "Why force on her a marriage with a man she doesn't love?" she demanded.

That shook him. "In time she would—"

"How much time? Twenty years, when she's no longer so sweet and young? Two hundred? I love you *now!*"

The Zombie Master looked at Dor. His face was tight with emotional pain, but his voice was steady. "Sir, there is some truth in what she says. I was always aware that Millie—if you had—" He choked off, then forced himself to continue. "I would prefer to see Millie married to you, than locked in some hideous transformation. If you—"

Dor realized that Millie was being offered to him again. All he had to do was take her, and she would be restored and Castle Roogna would be safe. He could by his simple acquiescence nullify the last desperation aspect of Murphy's curse.

He was tempted. But he realized that this transformation was the fate that had awaited her throughout. If he took Millie now, he could offer her . . . nothing. He was soon to return to his own time. Vadne evidently didn't believe that, but it was true. If he eschewed Millie, she would remain enchanted, a ghost for eight hundred years. A dread but fated destiny.

If he interfered now, he really would change history. There was no question of that, for this was personal, his immediate knowledge. He would fashion a paradox, the forbidden type of magic—and by the devious logic of the situation, Murphy would win. The curse had at last forced Dor to nullify himself by changing too much.

Yet if he turned down Vadne's terms, King Roogna would lose anyway, as the Zombie Master turned against him. Either way, Magician Murphy prevailed.

What was he, Dor, to do? Since either choice meant disaster, he might as well do what he believed to be right, however much it hurt.

"No," Dor said, knowing he was forcing Millie to undergo the full throes of ghosthood. Eight centuries long—and what reward awaited her there? Nursemaid to a little boy! Association with a zombie! "She goes to her betrothed—or to no one."

"But I am her betrothed!" the Zombie Master cried. "I love her—and because I love her, I yield her to you! I would do anything rather than permit her to suffer!"

"True love," King Roogna said. "It becomes you, sir."

"I'm sorry," Dor said. He understood now that his love for Millie was less, because he chose to let her suffer. He was knowingly inflicting terrible grief upon them all. Yet the alternative was the sacrifice of what they had all fought to save, deviously but certainly. He had no choice. "What's right is right, and what's wrong is wrong. I—" He spread his hands, unable to formulate his thought.

The Zombie Master gazed somberly at him. "I believe I understand." Then, surprisingly, he offered his hand.

Dor accepted it. Suddenly he felt like a man.

"If you will not restore her," the King said angrily to Vadne, "you shall be passed through the hoop."

"You're bluffing," Vadne said. "You won't throw away your Kingdom just to get at me."

But the King was not bluffing. He gave her one more chance, then had the hoop brought.

"I'll change it back to its original size," she threatened. "Then you won't be able to use it."

"You are very likely to go through it anyway," the King said, and there was something in his expression that cowed her. She stepped through the hoop and was gone.

The King turned to the Zombie Master. "It is a matter of principle," he explained. "I cannot allow any subject to commit such a crime with impunity. We shall ransack this Castle to locate Millie in whatever form she may be, and shall search out every avenue of magic that might restore her. Perhaps periodically we can recall Vadne from storage to see if she is ready to restore the maid. In time—"

"Time . . ." the Zombie Master repeated brokenly. They all knew the project could take a lifetime.

"Meanwhile, I apologize to you most abjectly for what has occurred, and will facilitate your return to your castle in whatever manner I can. I hope some year we will meet again in better circumstances."

"No, we shall not meet again."

Dor did not like the sound of that, but kept quiet.

"I understand," King Roogna said. "Again, I apologize. I would not have asked you to bring your zombies here, had I known what form the curse would take. I am sorry to see them go."

"They are not going," the Zombie Master said.

Dor felt gathering dread. What was the Zombie Master about to do, in his betrayal and grief? He could destroy everything, and there was no way to stop him except by killing him. Dor held his arms rigid, refusing to touch his sword.

"But nothing holds you here now," King Roogna said.

"I did not buy Millie with my aid, I did not bargain for her hand!" the Zombie Master cried. "I came here because I realized it would please her, and I would not wish to displease her even in death by changing that. My zombies will remain here as long as they are needed, to see Castle Roogna through this crisis and any others that arise. They are yours for eternity, if you want them."

Dor's mouth dropped open.

"Oh, I want them!" the King agreed. "I will set aside a fine graveyard for them, to rest in in comfort between crises. I will name them the honored guardians of Castle Roogna. Yet—"

"Enough," the Zombie Master said, and turned to Dor. But he did not speak. He gave Dor one enigmatic glance, then walked slowly out of the room.

"Then I have lost," Murphy said. "My curse

worked, but has been overwhelmed by the Zombie Master's loyalty. I cannot overcome the zombies." He, too, walked away.

That left Dor, Jumper, and the King. "This is a sad victory," Roogna said.

Dor could only agree. "We'll stay to help you clean up the premises, Your Majesty. Then Jumper and I must return to our own land."

They made their desolate way to the dining room, but no one cared to finish breakfast. They went to work on the cleanup chore, burying unzombied bodies outside, removing refuse from inside, putting away fallen books in the library. The main palace had not yet been built, but the library stood as it would be eight hundred years hence, apart from details of decor. One large tome had somehow strayed to the dumbwaiter; Dor held the volume for a moment, struck by a nagging emotion, then filed it on the shelf in the library.

In the afternoon they found the Zombie Master hanging from a rafter. He had committed suicide. Somehow Dor had known—or should have known—that it could come to this. The man's love had been too sudden, his loss too unfair. The Zombie Master had known Millie would die, known what he would do. This was what he had meant when he told the King they would not meet again.

Yet when they cut him down, the most amazing and macabre aspect of this disaster manifested: the Zombie Master was not precisely dead. He had somehow converted himself into a zombie.

The zombie shuffled aimlessly out of the Castle, and was seen no more. Yet Dor was sure it was suffering —and would suffer eternally, for zombies never died. What awful punishment the Zombie Master had wreaked upon himself in his bereavement!

"In a way, it is fitting," King Roogna murmured. "He has become one of his own."

The lesser personnel of the Castle, whom the King had sent away for the crisis, were now returning. The maids and the cooks, the steeds and dragons. Activity resumed, yet to Dor the halls seemed empty. What a victory they had won! A victory of grief and regret and hopelessness.

Finally Dor and Jumper prepared to depart, knowing the spell that placed them here in the tapestry world would soon bring them home. They wanted to be away from Castle Roogna when it happened. "Rule well, King Roogna," Dor said as he shook the monarch's hand for the last time.

"I shall do my best, Magician Dor," Roogna replied. "I wish you every success and happiness in your own land, and I know that when your time comes to rule—"

Dor made a depreciating gesture. He had learned a lot, here—more than he cared to. He didn't want to think about being King.

"I have a present for you," Jumper said, presenting the King with a box. "It is the puzzle-tapestry the Zombie Master gave to me. I am not able to take it with me. I ask you to assemble it at your leisure and hang it from the wall of whatever room you deem fit. It should provide you with many hours of pleasure."

"It shall have a place of honor, always," the King said, accepting it.

Then Dor thought of something. "I, too, have an important object I can't take with me. But I can recover it, after eight hundred years, if you will be so kind as to spell it into the tapestry."

"No problem at all," King Roogna said. Dor gave him the vial of zombie-restorative elixir. "I shall cause it to respond to the words 'Savior of Xanth.'"

"Uh, thanks," Dor said, embarrassed.

He went up to the ramparts to bid farewell to the remaining centaurs. Cedric was not there, of course, having returned home. But Egor Ogre was present, and Dor shook his huge bony hand, cautiously.

That was it. Dor was no more adept at partings than at greetings. They walked away from the Castle, across the deserted, blasted battlefield—and into a vicious patch of saw grass at the edge. Jumper, more alert than Dor, drew him back from the swipe of the nearest saw just barely in time.

They were back in the jungle. The visible, tangible

wilderness, where there was little subtlety about evil. Somehow it seemed like home.

Yet as they sloughed methodically through the forest, avoiding traps, skirting perils, and nullifying hazards in dull routine fashion, Dor found himself disturbed by more than human-related grief. He mulled it over, and finally had it.

"It is you, Jumper," he said. "We are about to return home. But there I am a boy, and you are a tiny spider. We'll never see each other again! And—" He felt the boyish tears emerging. "Oh, Jumper, you're my best friend, you've been by my side through the greatest and awfulest adventure of my life, and —and—"

"I thank you for your concern," the spider chittered. "But we need not separate completely. My home is by the tapestry. There are many fat lazy bugs trying to eat into the fabric, and now I have special reason to keep them from it. Look for me there, and you will surely find me."

"But—but in three months I'll only be an older boy—and you'll be dead!"

"It is my natural span," Jumper assured him. "I will live as much in that time as you do in the next thirty years. I will tell my offspring about you. I am thankful that chance has given me this opportunity to learn about your frame of reference. I would never otherwise have realized that the giant species have intelligence and feelings too. It has been a great and satisfying education for me."

"And for me!" Dor exclaimed. Then, spontaneously, he offered his hand.

The spider solemnly lifted a forefoot and shook Dor's hand.

Chapter 12. Return

One moment Dor was swinging on spider silk across a minor chasm; the next he was standing on the floor of the Castle Roogna drawing room before the tapestry.

"Is that you, Dor?" a familiar voice inquired.

Dor looked around and spied a tiny, humanoid figure. "Of course it's me, Grundy," he told the golem. "Who else would it be?"

"The Brain Coral, of course. That's who it's been for the past two weeks."

Of course. Quickly Dor readjusted. He was no longer a great-thewed Mundane; he was a small, spindly twelve-year-old boy. His own body. Well, it would grow in due course.

He focused on the tapestry, looking for Jumper. The spider should be where they had been when the spell reverted, in the wilderness—ah, there was a speck. Dor leaned forward and spied the tiny creature, so small he could crush it with the tip of his littlest finger. Not that he ever would do a thing like that! It raised a hairlike foreleg in a wave.

"It says you look strange in your real form," Grundy said. "It says—"

"I need no translation!" Dor snapped. Suddenly his eyes were blinded by tears, whether of joy or grief he was uncertain. "I'll—I'll see you again, Jumper. Soon. Within a few days—a few months of your time—I mean—oh, Jumper!"

"Who cares about a dumb bug?" Grundy asked.

Dor clenched his fist, for an instant tempted to smash the golem into the pulp from which he had been derived. But he controlled himself. How could

Grundy know what Jumper meant to Dor? Grundy was of the old order, unenlightened.

There was nothing Dor could do. The spider had his own life to lead, and Dor had his. Their friendship was independent of size or time. But oh, he felt a choke in his heart!

Was this another aspect of becoming a man? Was it worth it?

Yet Dor had friends here, too. He must not allow his experience of the tapestry world to alienate him from his own world. He turned away from the tapestry. "Hello, Grundy. How are things in the real world?"

"Don't ask!" the golem exclaimed. "You know the Brain Coral, who took over your body? Thing was like a child—I mean even childier than you, at times —poking into everything, making *faux passes*—"

"What?"

"Cultural errors. Like belching into your soup. That thing really kept me hopping!"

"Sounds like fun," Dor said, smiling. Already he was getting used to this little body. It lacked the strength of the Mundane giant, but it wasn't a bad body. "Listen, I have to talk to that Coral. I owe it a favor."

"No you don't. You owe it a punch in the mouth, if anything. If it has a mouth. All's even—it got the fun of using your body, while you went into tapestry land for a nice vacation."

Some vacation! "I owe it from eight hundred years ago."

"Oh. Well, sure, tell the gnome."

"Who? Oh, the Good Magician Humfrey. I will. Right now I have to go see Jonathan the zombie."

"Oh, yeah. You got the stuff?"

"I got it. I think."

"This will be something! The first restored zombie to go with the first restored ghost! For centuries, she untouchable and he not worth touching. Grisly romance!"

Dor might have snapped something nasty at the golem, but recent experience had lent him discretion. So he changed the subject. "Maybe I'd better check first with King Roog—King Trent. He's the one who put me up to this."

Grundy shrugged. "Just so I don't have to exchange another word with the Coral."

"That's next. Dor couldn't help teasing the golem a little.

"Look, you know what that creature was doing with your body and Irene?"

"Who?" Dor was distracted, thinking about his upcoming interview with the Brain Coral. What kind of favor would he have to repay, after eight hundred years?

"Princess Irene, daughter of the King. Remember her?"

"Well, it has been eight centuries, in a manner of—" Dor did a double take. *"What* did my body do with Irene?"

"Coral was real curious about the distinction between male and female anatomy. Coral's asexual, or bisexual, or something, see, and—"

"Enough! Do you realize I'm about to see her father?"

"Why do you think I mentioned the matter? I tried to cover for you, but King Trent's pretty savvy and Irene's a snitch. So I'm not sure—"

"When did I—I mean, my body—?"

"Yesterday."

"Then there may still be time. She doesn't speak to her father for days at a time."

"In a case like this she might make an exception."

"She might indeed!" Dor agreed worriedly.

"Ah, what does it matter? The King knows she's a brat."

"It is my own reputation I am thinking of." Dor had been accorded the respect due a grown man, in the tapestry world, and the feeling was now important to him. But it was more than that. Other people had feelings too. He thought of how Vadne had glowed when the Zombie Master complimented her talent—and how Murphy's curse had perverted that into her doom and his. And Millie's. Feelings were important—even those of brats.

Dor addressed the floor. "Where is Irene?"

308

"Hasn't been here for days."

He moved into the hall, questioning as he went. Soon he located her—in her own apartment in the palace. "You go elsewhere," he told Grundy. "I have to handle this myself."

"Aw," the golem complained. "Your fights with Irene are so much fun." But he obediently departed. Dor inhaled deeply, the act reminding him fleetingly of Heavenly Helen Harpy, squared his shoulders, then knocked politely. Quickly she opened the door.

Irene was only eleven, but with his new perspective Dor saw that she was an extremely pretty child, about to blossom into a fair young woman. The lines of her face were good, and though she had not yet developed the feminine contours, the framework was present for an excellent enhancement. Give her two years, maybe three, and she might rival Millie the maid. With a different talent, of course.

"Well?" she said, with the sharpness of nervousness.

"May I come in?"

"You sure did yesterday. Want to play house again?"

"No." Dor entered and closed the door quietly behind him as she retreated. How to proceed? Obviously she had strong reactions and was wary of him without actually being frightened. She had potted plants all around the room, and one was a miniature tangler: she had no need to fear anyone! She hadn't told her father yet; he had, in the course of locating her, determined that she had not been near the library in the past day.

Irene was a palace brat whose talent fell well short of Magician caliber. No one would ever call her Sorceress. She had a sharp tongue and some obnoxious mannerisms. Yet, Dor reminded himself again, she was a person. He had always held her in a certain contempt because her talent was substantially beneath his own—but so was Millie's. Magic was important, certainly, and in some situations critical—but in other situations it hardly mattered. The Zombie Master had recognized that.

Now Dor felt ashamed, not for what his body might have done yesterday, but for what he, Dor, had done a month ago, and a year ago. Stepping on the feelings of another person. It did not matter that he had not done it maliciously; as a full Magician, in line to inherit the crown of Xanth, he should have recognized the natural resentment and frustration of those who lacked his opportunities. Like Irene, daughter of two of the three top talents in the older generation, doomed to the status of a nonentity because she had only ordinary magic. And was female. How would he feel in such a circumstance? How had his father Bink felt, as a child of no apparent magic?

"Irene, I—I guess I've come to apologize." He remembered how freely King Roogna had apologized to the Zombie Master, though the problem had only deviously been the fault of the King. Royalty had no need to be above humility! "I had no right to do what I did, and I'm sorry. It won't happen again."

She looked at him quizzically. "You're talking about yesterday?"

"I'm talking about my whole life!" he flared. "I—I have strong magic, yes. But I was born with it; it's an accident of fate, no personal credit to me. You have magic yourself, good magic, better than average. I make dead things talk; you make live things grow. There are situations in which your talent is far more useful than mine. I . . . looked down on you, and that was wrong. I can't blame you for reacting negatively; I would do the same. In fact you fought back with more spunk than I ever did. You're a person, Irene. A child, as I am, but still a human being who deserves respect. Yesterday—" He stalled, for he had no clear idea what the Coral had done. He should have gotten the specifics from Grundy. He spread his hands. "I'm sorry, and I apologize, and—"

She raised a finger in a little mannerism she had, silencing him. "You're taking back yesterday?"

Dor couldn't help thinking of his own yesterday, piping goblins and harpies after him with the magic flute, swinging on spider silk inside the Gap, detonating the forget spell that still polluted the Gap, hauling corpses from battlefield to laboratory to make zombies —unparalleled adventure, now forever past. Yesterday was eight hundred years ago. "I can't take back yesterday. It's part of my life, now. But—"

"Listen, you think I'm some naïve twit who doesn't know what's what?"

"No, Irene. I was the naïve one. I—"

"You claim you didn't know what you were doing?"

Dor sighed. How true that statement was! "I really can't make excuses. I'll take my medicine. You have a right to be angry. If you want to tell your father—"

"Father, hell!" she snapped. "I'll take care of this myself! I'll give back exactly what you gave me!"

Dor was not reassured. "As you wish. It is your right."

"Close your eyes and stand still."

She was going to hit him. Dor knew it. But it seemed he had it coming. He had let the Brain Coral use his body; he was responsible. He closed his eyes and stood still, forcing his hands to hang loose at his sides, undefensively. Maybe this was the best way to settle it.

He heard her step close, almost felt the movement of her body. She was raising her arm. He hoped she wouldn't hit him low. Better on the chest or face, though it marked him.

It was on the mouth. But strangely soft. In fact—
In fact, she was kissing him!

Totally surprised, Dor found himself putting his arms around her, partly for balance, mostly because that was what one was supposed to do when kissed by a girl. He felt her body yield to him, her hair shifting with the motion. She smelled and tasted and felt pleasant.

Then she drew back a little within his embrace and looked at him. "What do you think of that?" she asked.

"If you intended that to be punishment, it didn't work," he said. "You're sort of nice to kiss."

"So are you," she said. "You surprised me yesterday. I thought you were going to hit me or yank off my panties or something, and I was all set to scream, and it was all awkward and bumpy, noses colliding and stuff. So I practiced last night on my big doll. Was it better this time?"

A kiss? That was what they had done yesterday? Dor's knees felt weak! Trust Grundy the golem to blow it up into something gossipy! "There's no comparison!"

"Should I take off my clothes now?"

Dor froze, chagrined. "Uh—"

She laughed. "I thought that would faze you! If I wouldn't do it yesterday, what makes you think I'd do it today?"

"Nothing," Dor said, relaxing with a shuddering breath. He had seen naked nymphs galore, in the tapestry, but this was real. "Nothing at all. Nothing absolutely at all."

"You want to know what yesterday was?" she demanded. "It was the first time you really got interested in me, for anything. The first time *anybody* got interested in me who didn't want a plant grown fast, instead of calling me a palace brat who should have been a sorceress but could only grow stupid green stuff. Do you have any idea what it's like having two Magician-caliber parents and being a big disappointment to them because not only are you a girl, you have lousy talent?"

"You have good talent!" Dor protested. "And there's nothing wrong with being a girl!"

"Oh sure, sure," she countered. "You never had no talent. You never were not male. You never had people being polite to your face because of who your father was and what your mother might do to them, while they cut you down behind your back and called you skunk cabbage and garden-variety talent and weed girl and—"

"I never called you that!" Dor cried.

"Not in so many words. But you thought it, didn't you?"

Dor blushed, unable to deny it. "I . . . won't think it again," he promised lamely.

"And on top of that," she continued grimly, "you know your own parents only stand up for you because they have to, but privately they think just the same as all other people do—"

"Not the King," Dor protested. "He's not that type—"

"Shut up!" she flared, her eyes filling with angry tears. Dor did, and she composed herself. Girls of any age were good at quick composures. "So then yesterday you were different. You kept asking questions, and you paid real attention, just as if you didn't have a sexpot like Millie the ghost in your cheesy house to sneak peeks at and get the whole story, and you didn't say a word about magic, or make anything talk, or anything. It was just you and me. All you wanted to know was what it was like being a girl. It was as if something else were speaking, something awful smart and ignorant, wanting to learn from me. First I thought you were poking fun at me, teasing me—but you never smiled. Then you wanted to kiss me, and I thought, *Now he's going to bite my lip or pinch me and fall over laughing*, but you didn't laugh. So I kissed you, and it was awful, I bruised my nose, what the hell, I thought at least you'd know how but you didn't, and you just said, 'Thank you, Princess,' and left, and I lay on my bed a long time trying to figure out where the joke was, what you were telling the boys—"

"I didn't—" Dor protested.

"I know. I snooped. Some. You didn't say anything, and neither did the golem. So it seemed you really were interested in me, and—" She smiled, and she looked brilliantly sweet when she did that. "And it was the greatest experience of my whole life! You're a real Magician, and—"

"No, that has nothing to do with—"

"So I practiced kissing, just in case. Then you came in just now apologizing, as if it were something dirty. So I thought you hadn't meant it, had just been slumming, and—"

"No!" Dor cried in sudden anguish. "That wasn't it at all!"

"I know that now. Can't blame me for wondering, though." She smiled again. "Listen, Dor, I know tomorrow it'll be just like before, and I'll be a snotty palace brat to you, but—would you kiss me again?"

Dor felt deeply complimented. "Gladly, Irene." He bent to kiss her again. He was young yet, and so was she, but it was a foretaste of what they might experience when they both grew up.

"Maybe again, sometime?" she inquired wistfully. "I sort of like being a girl, now."

"Sometime," he agreed. "But we've got to fight some, too, or the others will tease us. We're still too young—" But not very much too young, he thought. He could see the road ahead rather clearly now, after his tapestry experience.

"I know." They broke, and there seemed to be nothing more to say, so Dor went to the door and opened it. He paused to look back at her, remembering what she had said about her parents being disappointed in her. She was sitting on her bed, bathed in a forlorn joy.

"Not the King," he repeated quietly. "I believe that."

Irene smiled. "No, not the King."

"And not me."

"Same thing," she said.

He stepped out and closed the door, knowing he wasn't through with her. Not today or tomorrow, or for some time to come. Not through at all.

Grundy was waiting for him. "Any black eyes? Broken teeth? Throttle marks? It was awful quiet in there."

"She's a nice girl," Dor said, walking toward the library. "Funny I never noticed that before."

"Brother!" the golem expostulated. "First he notices Millie the ghost, then Irene the brat. What's he coming to?"

Maturity, Dor thought. He was growing up, and new horizons were opening, and he was glad.

They arrived at the library. "Come in," King Trent called before Dor could knock.

Dor entered and took the seat indicated. "Remember how you sent me on a quest, Your Majesty? I have returned."

The King held up one hand, palm out. Dor thought of Jumper's mode of greeting. "Let me not deceive you, Dor. Humfrey advised me, and I could not resist watching the tapestry. I have a fair notion what you have been doing."

"You mean the tapestry showed *me*—what I was doing while I was doing it?"

"Certainly, once I knew which character to watch. You and that spider—you're lucky you didn't kill yourself in the Gap! But there was no way for me to revoke the spell before its natural span expired. I sweated to think of what I would have to say to your father, if—"

Dor laughed compulsively. "And I was worried about Irene's father!"

King Trent smiled. "Dor, I really don't like to snoop around the palace, but the Queen does. She quickly noticed the change in you, saw that you never used your talent, and found out about the Brain Coral. Her picture hangs in Irene's room; the Queen merely substituted her own illusion image for the picture and had what they call in Mundania a ringside seat. She watched everything yesterday—and today. And advised me, just now."

Dor shrugged. "I stand by what I did. Both days."

"I know you do, Dor. You're coming onto manhood nicely. Do not assume the Queen is your enemy. She wants her daughter to follow her, and knows what is required though she may resent it strongly. I am aware how ticklish the situation in the bedroom was. You handled it with the finesse I would expect in a leader."

"That wasn't finesse! I meant every word!"

"Finesse and meaning are not mutually incompatible."

"Irene's not bad at all, once you get to know her! She—" Dor stopped, embarrassed. "What am I doing, telling you this? You're her father!"

The King clapped a friendly hand on Dor's shoulder. "You have pleased me, Magician. Now through your adventure, I know the secret of the flute and the hoop in the Royal arsenal; they could be extremely useful on occasion. I shall not keep you from the completion of your quest. You must wrap it up, for there will be assignments for you in today's world, as you learn to govern Xanth." He walked to a low bookshelf and brought out a rolled rug. "We saved this for your convenience." It was the magic carpet.

"Uh, thanks, Your Majesty. I do have some traveling to do."

Dor mounted the rug. "Brain Coral," he told it, and it took off.

As the carpet ascended the sky and the landscape of modern Xanth opened out like a tapestry, Dor felt abrupt nostalgia for the tapestry world he had left. It was not that that world was superior to his own; its magic was generally cruder, its politics more violent. It was his experience of manhood and friendship, especially with Jumper. He knew he would never be able to recover the personal magic of that experience. Yet, as his session with Irene had shown, there was unexpected magic in this world too. All he had to do was appreciate it.

Down into the underworld, through the cavern passages. Goblins still reigned here, he knew, though they had almost disappeared on the surface of Xanth. What had happened to them? They had not all been slaughtered at the battle of Castle Roogna, and the forget spell would not have wiped them out. Had there been some later goblin calamity?

Then he was at the subterranean lake. Modern transport was certainly an improvement over ancient; this had hardly taken any time at all.

No Goblin calamity, the Brain Coral thought to him. *The harpy curse on the goblin populace was nullified on the surface, but lingered in the depths. Therefore the goblins above became, generation by generation, more intelligent, handsome, and noble, until they were no longer recognizable as monsters. The only true goblins today are those of the caverns.*

"Then I wiped out their species!" Dor exclaimed. "In a way I never anticipated!"

Their species, as you knew it, was a horrendous distortion, a burden to themselves as much as to others. They cared so little for themselves they were glad to die in goblin-sea tactics when storming a castle. You did well in releasing them from their curse, and in restoring the male of the species to the harpies.

"About that," Dor said. "You gave up Prince Harold Harpy as a favor to me, and now I have come to return the favor, as I said I would."

No need, Magician. When you came two weeks ago, I did not make the connection. After all, you wore a different body when I first met you, eight centuries ago. But in the past two weeks I worked it out. You returned that favor eight hundred years ago.

"No, I came back here to my own time. So—"

You brought victory to King Roogna. Therefore his rival Magician Murphy retired from politics, preferring to wait until some better situation arose. He came to me.

"Murphy was exiled?" Dor asked, startled.

It was voluntary. King Roogna would have liked to have his company, but Murphy was restless. He is in my storage now. Perhaps one century I will release him, when Xanth has need of his talent. Now, in exchange for the harpy Prince, I have Murphy and Vadne, who may one day make a fine pair. You owe me nothing.

"I, uh, guess so, if you see it that way," Dor said. "Still—"

If ever you choose to travel from your body again, keep me in mind, the Coral thought. *I learned a great deal about life, though I do not yet properly comprehend the sexual nature of Man.*

"No one does," Dor said, smiling.

I do not experience emotion. But in your body I did. I liked the little Princess.

"She is likable," Dor agreed. "Uh, look—I promised to have the access hoop shrunk back to ring size, but—"

Forgiven. Farewell, Magician.

"Farewell, Coral." The rug took off and zoomed back through the cavernly passages. When it emerged into the sky it hesitated, until Dor remembered that he had not told it where to go next. "Good Magician Humfrey's castle."

Dor was reminded again that Humfrey's castle stood where the Zombie Master's castle had once been. The two were of different designs; probably the site had been razed more than once, and rebuilt.

Humfrey was as usual poring over a massive tome, paying no attention to what went on around him—

supposedly. "What, you again?" he demanded irritably. "Listen, gnome—" Grundy began.

The Good Magician smiled—a rare thing for him. "Why listen, when I can read? Observe." And he gestured them to look at the book, over his shoulder.

"But I'm not a killer!" Dor protested vehemently. I'm only a twelve-year-old—" He caught himself, but didn't know how to correct his slip.

"A twelve-year veteran of warfare!" she exclaimed. "Surely you have killed before!"

It was grossly misplaced, but her sympathy gratified him strongly. His tired body reacted; his left arm reached out to enclose her hips in its embrace, as she stood beside him. He squeezed her against his side. Oh, her posterior was resilient!

"Why, Dor!" she said, surprised and pleased. "You like me!"

Dor forced himself to drop his arm. What business did he have, touching her? Especially in the vicinity of her cushiony posterior! "More than I can say."

"I like you too, Dor." She sat down in his lap, her derrière twice as soft and bouncy as before. Again his body reacted, enfolding her in an arm. Dor had never before experienced such sensation. Suddenly he was aware that his body knew what to do, if only he let it. That she was willing. That it could be an experience like none he had imagined in his young life. He was twelve; his body was older. *It could do it.*

"Oh, Dor," she murmured, bending her head to kiss him on the mouth. Her lips were so sweet he—

The flea chomped him hard on the left ear. Dor bashed at it—and boxed his ear. The pain was brief but intense.

He stood up, dumping Millie roughly to her feet. "I have to get some rest," he said.

She made no further sound, but only stood there, eyes downcast. He knew he had hurt her terribly. She had committed the cardinal maidenly sin of being forward, and been rebuked. But what could he do? *He did not exist in her world.* He would soon depart, leaving her alone for eight hundred years, and when they rejoined he would be twelve years old again. He had no right!

But oh, what might have been, were he more of a man.

Dor found himself blushing. "That's—you mean that book records everything, even my private feelings?" Yet obviously it did.

"We were not about to let a future King of Xanth go unmonitored," Humfrey remarked. "Especially when our own history was involved. Not that we could do anything about it, once the tapestry spell was cast. Still, as vicarious experience—"

"Was it valid?" Dor asked. "I mean, did I really change history?"

"That is a question that may never be answered to absolute satisfaction. I would say you did, and you did not."

"A typically gnomish answer," Grundy said.

"One must consider the framework of Xanth history," the Good Magician continued. "A series of Waves of Mundane conquest, with the population decimated again and again. If every person lived and reproduced without a break, any interruption in that process would eliminate many of todays residents. All the descendants of that person. But if a subsequent Wave wiped them out anyway—" He shrugged. "There could be considerable change, all nullified a generation or two later. In which case there would be no paradox relating to our own time. I would say that the original Castle Roogna engagement was real, and that you changed that reality. You rewrote the script. But you changed only the details of that particular episode, not the overall course of history. Does it matter?"

"I guess not," Dor said.

"About that page I was reading," Humfrey said. "It seems you have been concerned about manhood. Did it occur to you that you might be more of a man in the declining of the maid's offer than in the acceptance of it?"

"No," Dor admitted.

"There is somewhat more to manhood than sex."

As if on cue, the gorgon entered the room, in a splendidly sexy dress but still without a face. "That's male propaganda," she said from the vacuum. "There is certainly more to womanhood than sex, but a man is a simpler organism."

"Oooo, what you said!" Grundy exclaimed, rubbing his tiny forefingers together in a condemning gesture.

"I said organism," she said. "You authenticate my case."

"Get out of here, both of you," Humfrey snapped. "The Magician and I are trying to hold a meaningful dialogue."

"Thought you'd never ask," Grundy said. He hopped to the gorgon's shoulder, peering into the nothingness framed by her snake-ringlets. A snakelet hissed at him. "Same to you, slinky," he snapped at it, and the snake retreated. He peered down into the awesome crevice of her bodice. "Come on, honey; let's go down to the kitchen for a snack."

When they were alone, Humfrey flipped a few pages of the history tome idly. "I was surprised to learn that the Zombie Master's castle was on this very site," he remarked. "Were he alive today, I would gladly share this castle with him. He was a remarkably fine Magician, and a fine man, too."

"Yes," Dor agreed. "He was the real key to King Roogna's success. He deserved so much better than the tragedy he suffered." He felt another surge of remorse.

Humfrey sighed. "What has been, has been."

"Uh, have you given the gorgon your Answer yet?"

"Not yet. Her year is not yet complete."

"You are the most mercenary creature I know!" Dor said admiringly. "Every time I think I've seen the ultimate, you come up with a worse wrinkle. *Are* you going to marry her?"

"What do you think?"

Dor visualized the gorgon's body with historical perspective. "She's a knockout. If she wants you, you're sunk. She doesn't need a face to turn a man to stone. In a manner of speaking."

The Good Magician nodded. "You have learned a

new manner of speaking! The key concept is 'she wants.' Do you really think she does?"

"Why else did she come here?" Dor demanded, perplexed.

"Her original motive was based largely on ignorance. How do you think she might feel once she knows me well?"

"Uh—" Dor searched for something diplomatic to say. The Good Magician had his points, but was no easy man to approach, or to get along with.

"Therefore the kindest thing to do is to give her sufficient opportunity to know me—well enough," the Magician concluded.

"The year!" Dor exclaimed. "That wait for her Answer! Not for you—for her! So she can change her mind, if—"

"Precisely." Humfrey looked sad. "It has been a most enticing dream, however, even for an old gnome."

Dor nodded, realizing that the Good Magician had not been proof against the attractions of the gorgon any more than the lonely Zombie Master had been proof against Millie. The two Magicians were similar in their fashion—and a similar tragedy loomed.

"Now we must conclude your case," Humfrey said briskly, refusing to dwell further on the inevitable. "You owe me no further service, of course; the history book has provided it all, and I consider the investment well worthwhile. I have now fathomed many long-standing riddles, such as the origin of the forget spell on the Gap. So I may send you on your way, your account quit."

"Thank you," Dor said. "I have brought back your magic carpet."

"Oh, yes. But I shall not leave you stranded. I believe I have a conjuration spell stashed away somewhere; have the gorgon locate it for you as you leave. It will take you home in a flash."

"Thank you." It was a relief not to have to contemplate another trek through the jungle. "Now I must go give the restorative elixir to Jonathan."

The Good Magician frowned at him. "You have had an especially difficult decision there, Dor. I believe you have acted correctly. When you become King, the discipline of emotion and action you have learned in the course of this quest will serve you in excellent stead. It may be more of an asset to you than your magic talent. King Trent's hiatus in Mundania matured him similarly. It seems there are qualities that cannot be inculcated well in a secure, familiar environment. You are already more of a man than most people ever get to be."

"Uh, thanks," Dor mumbled. He had yet to master the art of graciously receiving compliments. But the Magician had already returned to reading his tome.

Dor moved toward the door. Just as he left the room, Humfrey remarked without looking up: "You rather remind me of your father."

Suddenly Dor felt very good.

Grundy and the gorgon were sharing a scream soda in the kitchen; Dor heard the noise from several rooms away. They were using straws; hers poked into her nothing face, where the soda disappeared. She had a face, all right; it just could not be seen. Dor wondered what it would be like to kiss her. In the dark she would seem entirely normal. Except for those little snakes.

"I need the conjuration spell," Dor said. "The one that flashes."

The screams faded as she left the soda. "I know exactly where it is. I have every spell classified and properly filed. First time there's been order in this castle in a century." She reached for an upper shelf, her figure elongating enticingly. What a woman she would be, if only she had a visible face! But no, that would be ruinous; her face petrified men, literally.

"There," she said, bringing down an object that looked like a closed tube. It had a lens on one end, and a switch on the side. "You just push the switch forward, there, when you're ready."

"I'm ready now. I want to go to the tapestry room in Castle Roogna. Are you coming, Grundy?"

"One moment." The golem sucked in the last scream from the soda—no more than a whimper, actually—and crossed the room.

"Do you really want to marry the Good Magician

—now that you know him?" Dor asked the gorgon curiously.

"What would he do for socks and spells, without me?" she retorted. "This castle needs a woman."

"Uh, yes. All castles do. But—"

"What kind of a man would give a pretty girl board and room for a year, never touching her, just to think it over, knowing she probably would change her mind in that period?"

"A good man. A patient one. A serious one." Then Dor nodded, understanding the thrust of her question. "One worth marrying."

"I thought I wanted him, when I came here. Now I am sure of it. Under all that grouch is a remarkably fine Magician, and a fine man, too."

Almost exactly the words Humfrey had used to describe the Zombie Master! But it seemed that tragedy was about to bypass the gnome, after all. Parallels went only so far. "I wish you every happiness."

"Would you believe there are three happiness spells on that shelf?" She winked. "And a potency spell too —but he won't need that, I suspect."

Dor eyed her once again with the memory of his erstwhile Mundane barbarian body. "Right," he agreed.

"Actually, all he needs for happiness is a good cheap historical adventure tome, like that one he's reading now, about ancient Xanth. I'm going to read it too, as soon as he finishes. I understand it has lots of sex and sorcery and a really stupid barbarian hero—"

Hastily, Dor pushed the switch. The spell flashed— and he stood before the tapestry. "Savior of Xanth," he said, feeling foolish, and his vial of restorative elixir popped out from whatever invisible place it had lain for eight hundred years. He had to catch it before it could shatter on the floor, but he lacked the muscle and reflexes his Mundane body had had, and missed. The vial plummeted—

And jerked short on an invisible thread, and swung there, undamaged. A silken dragline had been attached to it. "Not this time, Murphy!" Dor cried as he nabbed it. He looked for his friend Jumper, who had surely rescued him again in this fashion, but did not see him.

Now, with the object of his quest in hand, he wondered: how could an object be spelled into a tapestry-within-a-tapestry—how could it emerge from the main tapestry? Or were the two tapestries the same? They had to be, because—yet they couldn't be, because— He seemed to be skirting paradox here, but couldn't quite grasp it. Anyway, he had the elixir. Best not to question too deeply; he might not like the answer.

Yet he lingered, watching the tapestry. He saw Castle Roogna, with its returning personnel cleaning out the last of the debris of battle and doing preparatory work for the zombie graveyard beyond the moat—the graveyard those zombies still resided in today. They had protected the Castle well, all these centuries, but now it was in no danger, so they lay quietly out of sight. Except for Jonathan, the strange exception. It seemed there were personality differences among zombies, just as there were in people. "One in every crowd," he murmured.

His eye focused on the spot he had vacated. He and Jumper had been trying to get as close to the place they had entered the Fourth Wave world as possible. They had cut into the jungle—and the jungle had tried to cut into them, when they encountered that saw grass—navigated the Gap with the use of silk lines for descent and ascent—fortunately the Gap dragon had been elsewhere at the time, perhaps suffering from the forget spell—and forged into northern Xanth. As they drew near the spot, their presence seemed to activate the spell, and it had reverted.

There, near that place, was the Mundane giant. He had no huge spider now as companion. He had wandered to a stockaded hut, begging a place to stay the night. He faced the mistress of the hut, an attractive young woman. As Dor watched, the tiny figures animated.

"What are they saying?" Dor asked Grundy.

"I thought you said you needed no translation!"

"Grundy—"

The golem hastily translated: "I am a barbarian, recently disenchanted. I was transformed, or driven, into the body of a flea, while an alien shade governed my body."

"The flea!" Dor exclaimed. "The one that hid in my hair and kept biting me! That was the Mundane!"

"Shut up while I'm translating," Grundy said. "This lip reading is hard." He resumed: "That creature did its best to destroy me, yanking me across the Gap on a rope, throwing me among zombies, thrusting me single-handed against an army of monsters—"

"Now that's a distortion!" Dor cried indignantly.

"And that awful giant spider!" the translation continued. "I lived in daily fear it would discover my flea body and—" The barbarian shuddered. "Now at last I have fought free. But I am tired and hungry. May I stay the night?"

The woman looked him over. "For a story like that you can stay three nights! Know any more?"

"Many more," the barbarian said humbly.

"Nobody who can lie like that can be all bad."

"Right," he agreed abjectly.

She smiled. "I am a widow. My husband was roasted by a dragon. I need a man to run the farm— a strong, patient man, not too bright, willing to settle for . . ." She spread her hands and half-turned, inhaling.

The barbarian noted her inhalation. It was a good one, the kind barbarians normally paid attention to. He smiled. "Well, I'm not too patient."

"That's close enough," the woman said.

Dor turned away, satisfied. His erstwhile Mundane body would be as happy as he deserved to be.

Something about this scenelet reminded Dor of Cedric the centaur. How was he making out with Celeste, the naughty filly? But Dor restrained himself from peeking; it really was not his business, any more.

Something caught his eye. He focused on the corner of the tapestry. There was tiny Jumper, waving. There was another little spider beside him. "You've found a friend!" Dor exclaimed.

"That's no friend, that's his mate," Grundy said. "She wants to know where he was, those five years he was gone. So when the popping-out of the elixir vial alerted him to your presence, he brought her out here to meet you."

"Tell her it's true, all true," Dor said. Then: "Five *years?*"

"Two weeks, your time. It only seemed like two weeks to him, too. But back at his home—"

"Ah, I understand." Dor exchanged amenities with the skeptical Mrs. Jumper, bade his friend farewell again, promised to return next day-month or so, and strode from the room feeling better.

"You move with a new assurance," Grundy remarked. He seemed sad. "You won't be needing me much longer."

"Penalty of growing up," Dor said. "One year I'll get married, and you can bodyguard my son, exactly as you have me."

"Gee," the golem said, flattered.

They departed the Castle, going to Dor's cheese cottage. He felt increasing apprehension and nostalgia as he approached his home. His parents should still be away on their Mundane mission; only Millie would be there. Millie the maid, Millie the ghost, Millie the nurse. What had the Brain Coral animating his body said to her? What should he say to her now? Did she have any notion what he had been doing the past two weeks?

Dor steeled himself and went inside. He didn't knock; it was his own cottage, after all. He was just the lad Millie took care of; she did not know—must never know—that he had been the Magician who looked like a Mundane warrior, way back when.

"Say," Grundy inquired as they passed through the familiar-unfamiliar house toward the kitchen. "What name did you use, in the tapestry?"

"My own name, of course. My name and talent—"

Oh, no! The most certain identifiers of any person in the Land of Xanth were name and talent. He had thoughtlessly given himself away!

"Is that you, Dor?" Millie called musically from the kitchen. Too late to escape!

"Uh, yes." No help for it but to see if she recognized him. Oh, those twelve-year-old-boy mistakes!

"Uh, just talking to a wall." He snapped his fingers at the nearest wall. "Say something, wall!"

"Something," the wall said obligingly.

She came to the kitchen doorway, and she was stunningly beautiful, twelve years older than she had been so recently, but almost regal in her abrupt maturity. Now she had poise, elegance, stature. She had aged, as it were overnight, more than a decade, while Dor had lost a similar amount. A gulf had opened between them, a gulf of age and time, huge as the Gap.

He loved her yet.

"Why, you haven't talked to the walls in two weeks," Millie said. Dor knew this had to be true: the Coral had animated his body, but had lacked his special magical talent.

"Is something wrong?" Millie asked. "Why are you staring at me?"

Dor forced his fixed eyes down. "I—" What could he say? "I—seem to remember you from somewhere."

She laughed with the echo of the sweetness and innocence he had known and loved in the tapestry maid. "From this morning, Dor, when I served you breakfast!"

But now he would not be put off. The thing he most feared was recognition; he had to face it now. "Millie—when you were young—before you were a ghost—did you have friends?"

She laughed again, and this time he noticed the fullness and rondure of her body as it laughed with her. "Of course I had friends!"

"Who were they? You never told me." His heart was beating hard.

She frowned. "You're serious, aren't you? But I can't tell you. There was a forget spell detonated in the vicinity, and as a ghost I was near it a long time. I don't remember my friends."

The forget spell! It had made her forget . . . him. Yet he tried, perversely, driven by an urge he refused to define. "How—did you die?"

"Someone enchanted me. Turned me into a book—"

A book! The book he had found in the dumbwaiter leading from the female room. Vadne must have transformed her into it, then hoisted that tome to the upper floor, and no one had caught on. A stupid mistake, courtesy of Murphy's curse. He himself had placed it on the shelf in the library—where it had remained eight hundred years, unmolested.

"I couldn't even remember what my body was, or where," Millie continued. "Or maybe a spell was on that too. So much was vague, especially at first—and then I was a ghost, and it was easier not to think about it. Ghosts don't have very solid minds." She paused, studying Dor. "But sometimes there are flashes. Your father reminded me of someone—someone I think I loved—but I can't quite remember. Anyway, he's eight hundred years dead, now, and there is Jonathan. I've known Jonathan for centuries, and he's awful nice. When I was alone and lonely and confused, especially after King Roogna died and the Castle fell into oblivion—he had a long and good reign, but it had to end sometime—Jonathan came and helped me to hold on. He didn't seem to mind that I was only a ghost. If only—"

So she had loved Dor—and forgotten, in the ambience of the forget spell. His name and talent—no giveaway after all. Nothing in his birth and youth in this world had alerted her, since she had never known the origin of that bygone hero, and she could hardly be expected to make the connection.

Only Jonathan had been her comfort across the centuries. She had not forgotten Jonathan, because he had always been there. A ghost and a restless zombie, bolstering each other when the rest of the world had forgotten them. Why torture her by restoring her memory of prior heartache? Dor knew what he had to do.

"Millie, I have obtained the elixir to restore Jonathan to life." He held up the vial.

She stared at him, unbelieving. "Dor—now I remember something. Your father—he reminded me of you. Not in appearance, but in—"

"I wasn't born yet!" Dor said harshly, repenting his recent urge to have her remember exactly this. "You've got it backward. I remind you of my father—because I am growing up."

"Yes, yes of course," she agreed uncertainly. "Only somehow—your talent of—I remember talking to pearls in a big nest, or something—"

"Take the elixir," he said, presenting it to her. "Call Jonathan." *Oh, Jonathan,* he thought in momentary agony. *Do you know you fill the shoes of her lover, and of her betrothed? Be good to her, for the sake of what was never allowed to be!*

Millie was too distracted to take the vial. "I—still, there is something. A big barbarian named—"

"Jonathan!" Dor bellowed as well as his present body permitted. "Come here!"

The door opened, for Jonathan was always near Millie. The loyalty of centuries! He shuffled into the kitchen, dripping the usual clods of dirt and mold. No matter how much fell, a zombie always had more; it was part of the enchantment. His body was skeletal, his eyes rotten sockets, and the nauseating odor of putrefaction was about him.

"Yet I know now that was only passing fascination," Millie continued. "The barbarian left me, while Jonathan stayed."

Dor tore open the corked vial. "Take this!" he cried, hurling the precious drops onto the zombie.

Immediately the body began to heal. Flesh was magically restored, tissues filled out, skin formed and cleared. The figure unhunched, became fuller, taller.

"And so my true love is Jonathan," Millie concluded. Then she looked up, realizing what transformation was taking place, and her hair flung out as of old. "Jonathan!" she screamed.

Rapidly the last of the zombie attributes disappeared. The figure shaped into a gaunt but healthy living man.

"The Zombie Master!" Dor exclaimed, recognizing him at last. "I never knew your given name!"

Then he stepped back out of the way, letting true love assume its rightful place. Jonathan and Millie came together, she with a little skip-kicking of feet, and Dor knew his quest was done.

J.R.R. TOLKIEN'S
Epic Fantasy Classic
The Lord of the Rings

One Ring to rule them all,
One Ring to find them,
One Ring to bring them all,
And in the darkness bind them.....

Twisting the skills he learned from the Elven-smiths, the Dark Lord created a Ring of awesome, malevolent power, a Ring to control all the other Rings of Power, bending them to the will of whoever controlled the One. And then, the One Ring was lost.

Available at your bookstore or use this coupon.

—THE HOBBIT, J.R.R. Tolkien 27257 2.50
The enchanting prelude to **The Lord of the Rings**, in which the One Ring is found by the unlikliest character of all.

—THE FELLOWSHIP OF THE RING, J.R.R. Tolkien 27258 2.50
Part One of **The Lord of the Rings**: the quest to destroy the evil Ring is begun, as the Dark Lord prepares to make war upon Middlearth.

—THE TWO TOWERS, J.R.R. Tolkien 27259 2.50
Part Two: the armies gather for the battle which will decide the destiny of Middlearth, while the Ring Bearer moves ever closer to the fulfillment of his quest.

—THE RETURN OF THE KING, J.R.R. Tolkien 27260 2.50
Part Three: the concluding volume tells of the opposing strategies of the wizard Gandalf and the Dark Lord as they vie for victory in the War of the Ring, and of the fate of the Ring Bearer. Also includes appendices and index.

—J.R.R. TOLKIEN FOUR VOLUME BOXED SET 27493 10.00

BB BALLANTINE MAIL SALES
Dept. NE, 201 E. 50th St., New York, N.Y. 10022

Please send me the BALLANTINE or DEL REY BOOKS I have checked above. I am enclosing $.......... (add 35¢ per copy to cover postage and handling). Send check or money order — no cash or C.O.D.'s please. Prices and numbers are subject to change without notice.

Name_____

Address_____

City_____ State_____ Zip Code_____

Allow at least 4 weeks for delivery.

NE-6